Winter Book Two

Keven Newsome

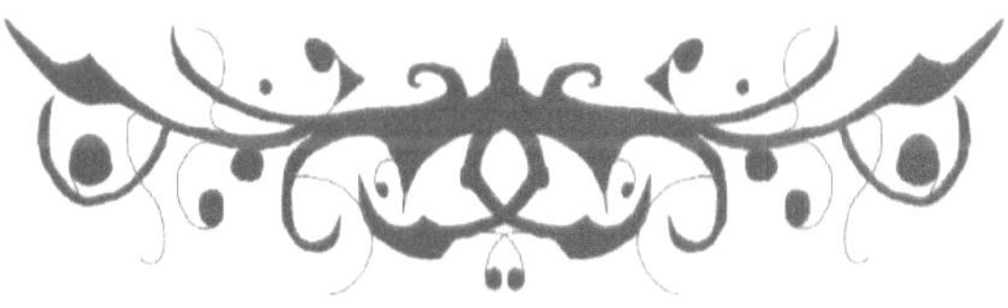

*Prophetess*

---

*Keven Newsome*

2nd Edition

ISBN: 978-0-9989596-2-7



KevenNewsome.com

PRESS EPIC



This is a work of fiction. All the characters, events, and locations portrayed in the book are either products of the author's imagination or are used fictitiously.

*Who is your story really about, Winter?*

*Who are you meant to protect?*

*The answer could change the world...*

*or end it.*

*To Aron.*
*For leading me into a greater adventure.*

# 0

*Twelve Years Ago*

"One," Gains whispered. Inhale. Exhale. The muzzle of his Glock glinted six inches from his face. A bead of sweat dropped into his eye. He blinked it away, watching the wall opposite him as bullets from the intersecting corridor pelted the surface.

"Two." Inhale. Exhale. The drone of the alarm blaring from every school speaker compressed his eardrums, almost as much as the concussion of the offending gun. He turned his head to the right and made eye contact with his partner, Agent Stevens. Gains flicked two fingers. His gray-haired partner nodded.

"Three." Gains took two giant steps into the center of the hall, turned and extended his gun back to the corner where he had been standing.

Inch. He moved a little, revealing more of the hall beyond.

Inch. Gunfire. A bullet struck the fully exposed wall next to him…only feet away.

Inch. A little more.

Gunfire. Another bullet.

Inch. The alarm. The sweat.

Inch.

Gunfire.

A man in a silver and black mask crouched near the exit. Gains sighted him down.

Gunfire.

The wall exploded inches from Gains's face. He flinched. Squeezed. The shot went wild.

On his knees, Stevens thrust his gun around the corner. He sent several blind shots down the corridor, as Gains tried to line the masked man up again. The man slid around into an adjacent hall before Gains could discharge another round.

He ground his teeth. "Let's go."

Gun still extended, he rushed down the hall. He leaned his back to the wall opposite the connecting hall, just out of line of sight. Stevens did the same on the opposite side, repeating the same thing they had just done. Training. Stick to the training. Gains began inching around, watching his sights for the man in the mask.

Before he could maneuver far enough to see the end of the corridor, something rolled into view. Something round and black.

Gains's heart clenched. "Down!"

He dove away, scrambling back the way he had come. His partner hustled at his side.

Fire and thunder consumed the hall around the corner where they had been. Mortar and debris flew through the air. The lights flickered overhead and ceiling tile fell. The shockwave compressed his head for only a moment before relenting back to the drone of the bell tone and the pattering of debris.

Gains looked back at the cloud of dust, no longer able to see the joining corridor.

Something slammed. A door.

"Come on!" Gains shouted. "He's getting away."

With gun at the ready, Gains plunged through the debris and

dust. Stevens followed close behind and two steps to the side. The debris cleared midway down the hall, and they sprinted to the end where steel double doors waited. Gains leaned against the wall near one door. Stevens on the other side. They paused. Gains tilted his head closer to the door. Listening.

Scuffling and shouts echoed through the door. Gunshot.

Gains leaned against the push bar and swung out his gun as the door opened. Bullets spattered the building and the door. Gains dropped to his knees. The man in the mask fled, firing blindly behind him. Gains steeled himself and lined him up, ignoring the random gunfire. And squeezed.

The man collapsed.

Gains leaped up, Glock stretched out, and ran toward the fallen monster.

An arm moved.

Thunder.

Gains jumped to the ground and rolled, keeping his eyes on the target. The man stood to run again. Gains rose to one knee. Easy kill.

"Markus!"

He pushed away his partner's voice and took a deep breath. His finger twitched against the trigger.

"Markus!"

The urgency in his partner's voice made him turn his head as his gun remained stationary. Stevens knelt next to a man lying face down.

"Bevaldi," said Stevens.

Gains swore and turned back to the man in the mask. Gone.

"He's still alive, Markus."

Gains went to his partner's side. Bevaldi's back was saturated with blood. "Stay with him," Gains said.

Sirens wailed in the distance. Lots of sirens.

"Where are you going?" asked Stevens.

"To finish this." Gains lifted the Glock to his shoulder and ran forward.

The land sloped to a small ravine with a flowing stream snaking across the bottom. Gains bent his knees for balance and slid down the loose scree. Tight shrubs guarded the water below, and Gains carefully crawled through them. Blood on the ground marked the masked man's trail.

On the other side of the shrubs, he glanced in both directions, leading with his Glock. Clear. The stream was a mere trickle, but the impressions of boots were easily recognizable.

He pointed his Glock in the direction of the blood trail and walked. Quickly. Gains panned his gun over the brush and strained his ears for the smallest sound beyond that of his own rolled footsteps and the gurgling water.

A crackle in the bushes. Gains swung the gun around and held his breath. A moment later, a bird chirped and flew away. He brought the gun back around and continued. After a hundred yards or so, broken branches, skid marks in the dirt, and drops of muddy blood indicated the man's exit from the ravine. Gains followed through the underbrush, muscles coiled and senses engaged.

On the other side, boot prints ended where asphalt began. Gains swore again. His phone vibrated and he snatched it from his belt.

"What?"

"You need to come back." Agent Stevens's voice was grave.

"Coming." Gains returned the phone to his belt and looked again at the road. He hated losing. He wanted to roar and toss his gun in frustration. Instead, he holstered it and turned back to the ravine.

When Gains reached the school again, men in SWAT uniforms with M4s secured the area. A pair of paramedics worked over Bevaldi. Gains shook his head. The idiot. He should have listened.

Agent Stevens stood near the exit door with another man.

Gains went to them. "He's in a car. Have the roadblocks been set up like I instructed?"

The other man answered. "Yes. Every road in a mile radius of the school and every major thoroughfare in a five-mile radius."

"Gains, this is Detective McKenzie," said Stevens.

Gains nodded. "You're too late."

"Markus," said Agent Stevens. "So were we." The older man's countenance fell with more wrinkles than normal.

Gains felt a gnawing in his stomach. He looked one more time at Bevaldi lying beneath the frantic work of paramedics, and sighed. He turned back to his partner. Stevens shook his head and then motioned toward the building.

"There's more, Markus. Inside."

"But…"

"Bevaldi was wrong. We were late."

Gains suppressed his boiling frustration and allowed Stevens to lead him back into the building.

Inside, he noticed the details of the hall for the first time. White and brown—like any other school, with latex ceiling panels and laminate square floors. Colorful bulletin boards hung beside each door, displaying the students' latest achievements. An elementary school.

The gnawing grew.

Beyond the explosion debris and where the chase had begun, bloody footprints and smears painted the floor like wayward strokes of a brush. Agent Stevens and Detective McKenzie followed these, leading Agent Gains around another corner and through an adjacent hall. As they walked, the bloody footprints darkened and become more defined, less hurried.

Even without seeing the end of the trail, Gains knew where the footprints led. A door near the end of that hall was flanked by at least half a dozen SWAT and several other men, whom Gains took to be more detectives. The detectives watched them approach. One of them spoke, but Gains didn't listen…something about waiting for CSU. Gains pushed past them all.

Five bodies lay strewn throughout the room. One was an adult…the teacher. Shot in the back and lying in a puddle of blood.

The other four bodies were in their own dark pools of blood. Tiny hands and faces, pale and lifeless. Gains clenched his teeth and fists…shaking all over, unable to control the boiling within any longer.

Seconds. If only they had come seconds earlier. That's all it would have taken. Seconds lost. Seconds hesitated. And they had been too late.

A touch on the shoulder. Gains flinched, turning the hatred of his glare onto his partner.

"There's a survivor," Stevens said. His old face void of its usual hardness.

Gains allowed the edge to fade away. "Where?"

Detective McKenzie stepped forward. "She's at the principal's office. I'll take you."

He led Gains and Stevens toward the central area of the school. A set of double glass doors indicated the main entrance. Outside, police cars flashed their bright lights, beyond which Gains could see a crowd of students huddled in a parking lot.

Near the entrance were the glass windows of the school's reception area. Several police officers stood beside the door. Beyond the reception area was an office near the back. The office door had a glass panel, through which Gains could see a man and a woman seated next to a little girl.

"The principal and the superintendent," said Detective McKenzie.

Gains nodded.

The girl had a soft face, sallow and smeared red with dried blood. Her dirty blonde hair matted crimson, and her clothes were saturated to the point of almost being black. She stared at the floor with wide eyes, her lips clenched tight. Her entire body trembled as if the temperature were below freezing.

All of Gains' anger melted away, leaving a pulsing sense of despair in its wake. "Is she hurt?"

"That's what is so odd," said McKenzie. "She's not injured at all. Paramedics checked her from head to toe."

"Why is she still in here?"

"With the school secured, we thought it best to keep her isolated, so as not to risk the other children seeing her."

Gains glanced out the nearest window to the children gathered outside. Some screamed and cried. Some just stared around in shock. A few played chase. The teachers all looked like frightened deer.

He turned back. "How old is she?"

"Seven."

"Where are her parents?" asked Stevens.

"Dead," said McKenzie. "A call from a neighbor came in just before you called. Said she saw both cars still at home and went to go check on them, to see if they were sick. When there was no answer she peeked in a window and saw them on the floor. Looks like they were shot earlier this morning. Murdered just like the class. MO is the same and we're pretty sure it was the same killer. Ballistics will verify it later this week."

Stevens and Gains exchanged nervous looks.

"We think," McKenzie continued, "that the gunman was looking for her." He nodded his head in the direction of the little girl.

Gains pressed his lips together and nodded to his partner.

McKenzie tilted his head. "Do you know something I don't?"

"I'm sorry. But that information is classified."

"Is this about that nut-job Bevaldi?" asked McKenzie.

Gains glared at him. "Next of kin?"

"We're working on that. It may take some time though. In the meantime, I'm afraid I'll have to bring in social services."

"That won't be necessary. She'll be coming with us." Gains twisted the doorknob and stepped into the room.

The girl jerked her head up, fear-stricken. She darted her eyes to the principal and then back to him.

Gains eased closer and knelt. A backpack sat open near the girl's feet. A few books and papers peeked out. Gains reached in and withdrew a colored sheet of a farmhouse. The sun blue, and the sky purple. The farmhouse was a mixture of orange and green. A yellow cow stood nearby. Yet it was obvious that the color choices were deliberate and calculated, the strokes measured and even—a child with a surrealistic eye for art. A second sheet was of a butterfly, purple and black. The coloring perfectly delicate. Realistic.

"Did you color this?" asked Gains softly.

The girl did not respond.

"It's very pretty," he said. "You're very talented."

Her body trembled.

"I know you're scared, but you're safe now. I'll make sure of it, okay?"

The girl nodded, just a slight bob of her head. She lifted her face and looked Gains in the eyes, penetrating deeper into Gains's heart than a first grader should be able to do.

"I'm with the FBI. Do you know what that is?"

She shook her head almost imperceptibly.

"I'm like a special policeman…we help people like you who are really scared. We'll take care of you and keep away the bad men. Would you like that?"

She nodded again.

"Soon I'm going to take you with me. We're going to take you away from the school for a little while…someplace safe. I'm even going to send one of my friends to get some of your favorite things from home. Would that be all right?"

Her trembling lips parted and, in a whisper that was barely audible, she said, "Mommy and daddy say I'm not supposed to go with strangers."

Gains smiled. "Your mommy and daddy are very smart. I bet they told you all about policemen too."

She nodded.

"And I'm a very special policeman, here to protect you. But I tell you what, how about I tell you my name and talk with you. Then we won't be strangers anymore. Then I'll be a policeman and your friend. Is that better?" He pulled out his badge and opened it. "Would you like to hold this?"

She nodded and took the badge from his hand.

"My name is Agent Gains. What's yours?"

A small smile pulled at the corners of her mouth. She leaned forward and whispered, "Sandy."

*"When I passed by you and saw you squirming in your blood, I said to you while you were in your blood, 'Live!' Yes, I said to you while you were in your blood, 'Live!'"*
Ezekiel 16:6 (NAS)

# 1

*Present Day*

Behind the Dodge Dakota, the trailer jolted and rattled over the uneven pavement.

"Could you not do that? I have breakable stuff back there," said Winter Maessen. She flashed her baby blue eyes at her dad, glaring beneath the strands of jet-black hair that swung forward. "I'd like everything to make it to school in one piece."

"Sorry. Didn't see the bump."

Steve Maessen slowed his truck as they neared the cul-de-sac at the end of the street.

"That one." Winter pointed to the correct house.

Steve pulled up along the curb and stopped. "All right. Here we are. We've still got a long way before reaching Cherithville, so we can't stay too long."

"I know, Dad. Just an hour, okay?"

She opened the door and stood on the pavement, staring at the front of Kaci's house. She had only been here once before, after Xaphan had taken her and had her beaten. Maybe one day she could actually visit for a happy reason.

A flicker of heat coursed through her body at the thought of what waited inside. She relaxed and let the sensation pass.

"Are you okay?" asked her dad. He closed his door, the sound filling the neighborhood far too easily.

"It's happening more often." She eased her door closed. "The rumbling, feeling like my skin is about to split. I don't know what it means."

"You'll figure it out when God's ready for you to. It may take years."

"I hate waiting, and I hate having to figure things out even more."

Steve laughed. "Of course you do. That's why God makes you do it."

She rolled her eyes and moved around the truck to the sidewalk. The rubber soles of her black shoes were all but noiseless, but her cargo pants made a swishing sound to rival the wind. Why was she trying to be so quiet? They were expected. Except for Kaci. She didn't know they were coming.

Winter stayed focused on the front door, trying not to think too much on Kaci. She didn't want the rumbling to start again. Not now. Not here.

She paused in front of the door, staring at the morbid reflection in the oval glass. Her hair was longer now than last year, but not by much. Winter wondered if maybe she should have left out a few piercings and self-consciously ran a finger over the five small hoops in her left ear. Only one hoop was in her eyebrow now. She'd let the other two grow closed over the summer.

"Is something wrong?"

Winter glanced over her shoulder. "No. Everything's fine." She took a deep breath and lifted her hand to the door.

But the door opened before she could knock. Kaci's mom stood there with a small smile. "I heard you talking."

"Hi, Beverly," said Winter.

"I'm so glad you came. I know you've been wanting to all summer, but well…you'll see. Come in." Beverly backed away and opened the door wide.

"Beverly," Steve said and shook her hand.

"There's coffee in the kitchen. Chris is at the church, he'll be home in a little bit. He wants to see you two before you leave." She closed the door and followed them to the kitchen.

"I'll take some of that coffee," Steve said.

Beverly went to a cabinet and retrieved a cup for him.

Winter looked around. "Where is she?"

Beverly sat at the dining room table. "In her room. Where she's been all summer."

Winter nodded and began the short trip down the hall to Kaci's room. The door was closed and she thought briefly of knocking. Then, gritting her teeth, she grabbed the doorknob and just walked in.

Kaci sat on her daybed staring out of the window.

For the merest second Winter saw her friend's broken body as it had been when she found her, almost lifeless, in the tower on that terrible night three months ago. A knot pushed up in her throat and she choked it back.

Kaci turned a little when Winter entered, revealing dark circles under her eyes and sunken cheeks. Her other injuries had miraculously healed in the hospital last May, when Winter had broken into the surgery room and prayed over Kaci.

As Kaci turned more into the light, Winter winced. Small white lines covered Kaci's face like chicken scratch. One eyelid had a scar across it. Spanning her throat was a slightly larger scar that deformed the skin like an embedded worm.

At the sound of Winter's involuntary intake of air, Kaci shook her disheveled hair to hide her face. "Why did you come?" she croaked.

Winter straightened and closed the door as she entered. "You haven't spoken to me all summer, what did you expect me to do?"

"I didn't want you to see me like this."

"And why not? I'm your friend."

"Still?"

"Are you insane?" Winter sat down beside Kaci. Kaci looked away. "Of course I'm still your friend. Why on earth would you think otherwise?" She reached out to touch Kaci's exposed arm. There were white scars covering its surface and, in the middle of her forearm, the scars created a pentagram. Winter frowned. "You can't avoid me. You should know better. I'm famously stubborn."

Winter thought she saw a smile flash across Kaci's face. She leaned in. "I listed you as my roommate for the fall."

"You shouldn't have done that," Kaci said. "I'm not going back."

"You have to. You preregistered."

"I can't go like this." Kaci turned to face her, slinging her hair away from her marked face. "I'll be humiliated—treated like a freak!"

"When has being treated differently ever bothered you? Last year you encouraged it. You said people liked who I was because of my differences. And you made me stay at school when I wanted to go home. Remember that?"

"For different reasons. You weren't a hideous monster."

"Plenty of people would disagree with you on that. Looks don't mean anything. Nobody cares what you look like. It's what's inside that counts. You may be broken on the outside, but I'm the one broken on the inside. I'm far more a monster than you'll ever be. Those people that hurt you? That used to be me. Think about it."

"You've changed…I've changed. Things will never be the same. I can never go back."

Winter pursed her lips. "This is not who you really are. I mean, the way you're acting and the way you're talking. It's not you. You don't have to change who you are, because if you do it means they won."

"They won, Winter. Not us. Don't you realize what they did to me?" Kaci's eyes flashed with anger and pain.

For a brief moment, Winter thought she could see something of those memories in her own mind. A rumble formed in her eyes. Heat surged through her body. She blinked and pushed it all away. The phantom image disappeared. "Yes. Yes I do. I'm the one who found you. I'm the one who pulled you out of that tower. I'm the one who broke into the surgery room to pray over you. I know exactly what they did. And I'm still here. I'm still your friend, and all of your other friends feel exactly the same way. They've been trying to call, same as I have. How dare you demean your friends by suggesting we're so shallow that we care about a few insignificant scars? So drop the stupid act and let's get to the real problem. You're not mad at us at all. I know what's wrong with you…so just say it already."

Kaci looked away, crying. "Why did God let this happen to me? I did everything for him, everything he asked. So why me? I wanted to get married. I wanted a family. God took that away."

Winter rubbed Kaci's shoulder. "No, he didn't. Do you think God is the only one pulling strings on this planet? Everyone's trying to pull their own strings and the strings of everyone around them. Then you have sickos like Xaphan who come along just to tie knots in everything. God's the only one who can unravel the mess. So your dream isn't gone. You've just got to let God rewire the strings."

"But I'm ugly, and they…they did things to me. No man will want me now."

"Would you rather meet someone who loves you for your looks or for who you really are?"

Kaci's shoulders slumped.

"And your virginity is not something that can be taken away. It's more than just a physical condition. It is something you choose to give, and any man who thinks otherwise is not worth having."

"Easy for you to say."

Winter raised an eyebrow. "Do you think? I've made my mistakes, thank you."

Kaci looked at her questioningly. "Sorry."

"I'm not. Yes I made mistakes, but through those mistakes I can be here to help you now. And I'll tell you this—hiding behind your pain will only increase it. The only way to overcome this is to face it head-on. I've been there. I used my pain to push people away. And it nearly destroyed me."

Kaci looked away.

"It's a lot to face at one time. I know it sucks. But I'll help you through it. We'll be living together and I'll be there all the time. There's nobody else on this planet who understands you and what you're going through like I do. So you can sit here and rot in your own self-pity, or you can come with me and learn to live again."

"I'm not sure I can."

"The old Kaci wouldn't have said that. The old Kaci would remember that all things can be done through Christ."

Kaci turned back to Winter. "Have you always been like this?"

"What?" Winter definitely recognized a grin playing at the corners of Kaci's mouth.

"Sitting there in your black clothes with your black hair and more earrings than ear, lecturing me like a preacher on steroids. I don't remember you being so…profound. Did I miss something last year?"

"Um…no," said Winter. "I guess that's new. It happened some last year. I guess…well, things like that are happening more lately. I don't really do it on purpose. It's like all these thoughts just get poured into my head, and if I don't open my mouth to relieve the pressure, I'll pop like a zit."

"Eww."

"Sorry. Pop like a…"

"A balloon?"

"No. Not graphic enough."

Kaci chuckled.

"See? There you go. A little humor for you. Maybe I should be graphically gross instead of motivational." Winter smiled.

"We're not in junior high." Kaci shook her head.

"Poop."

Kaci laughed and shoved Winter in the shoulder. "Stop it!"

"Hey, whatever works."

Kaci leaned back. "So why are you moving in early?"

"Summer's an RA in Carmichael, remember? She needs help getting her floor ready, so she got permission from the Dean of Students for me to come a day early and help."

"Oh, I see."

"Upperclassmen can move in tomorrow. Freshmen in two days. But classes don't start until next week. Will you come back? Just give it one semester, that's all I ask."

Kaci turned back to the window. "I'll think about it."

"That's better than what I got when I came in. So I'll take that as progress."

"What about him?"

"Who?"

Kaci's lips firmed and she seemed to stare harder out the window.

Winter ground her teeth and the rumbling began again. This time she didn't try to suppress it. "I'm going to find him. And when I do…he won't get away."

# 2

*Four Years Ago*

The ticking of the clock dominated the bulk of conversation. Winter, fifteen years old, slouched in a leather armchair, alternating between staring at a dark wooden floor and the teal and brown rug in the center of the room. She flicked her eyes up to see if the others were still watching her. Her unwashed greasy hair fell on her face, so that the other two could not see her eyes through the black strands.

Her dad, in an identical chair to her left, sat upright and watched her with a mixture of concern and disgust. The disgust was not lost on Winter. Steve drummed his fingers on the arm of his chair.

The room's third occupant did not sit behind the polished cherry desk at the back of the room. Rather, he sat in another armchair, making a sort of triangular circle. He was younger than her dad, with blondish hair and a neatly trimmed goatee. He leaned forward and peered at Winter. Unlike her dad, this man's face showed nothing but genuine concern. This was not lost on Winter either. His name was Daniel Lucas, and he was the youth pastor at a church just a few miles from where Winter and Steve lived.

Winter turned away from them, ignoring the last question, and scanned the books filling the bookshelves that lined the study. Most of the titles were out of range of the dim light coming from the iron floor lamp nestled between two shelves. The ticking clock sat on one shelf.

"Winter," said Daniel. "We've been here over fifteen minutes, and you haven't said a word. Let's try something different. Tell me about your mom."

Winter rolled her eyes and shifted her body even farther away from the others, but the leather chair did not relent much.

"We're just concerned and we're only trying to help. I realize you were close to your mom and it's been difficult for you. I understand where you're coming from."

"No you don't," she said.

"No, I do. My mom died when I was in high school, too. And my wife died when Ryan was in fifth grade. We both know what it's like."

Winter clenched her teeth.

"What helped us, me when I was your age and both of us when my wife died, was talking. We had friends, family, people who loved us, who we were able to sit and talk to. It took lots of time to heal, but we did. Keeping it in will only make it worse."

"My mom is dead, what else is there to talk about?" She refused to look at him.

"Talk about her, talk about how you feel, talk about whatever you want. Just talk."

"Winter," her dad said.

"It's all your fault anyway, Dad. You should have told him that while you two were pretending I wasn't in the room."

"There's no need to pass blame," Daniel said.

"I'm not passing blame. Blame is already implied. He assumed the blame when he left us."

Steve huffed. She mustered the deepest hate she could and threw it at him with her eyes. He opened his mouth to say something in reply, but Daniel stopped him. Steve looked away and crossed his arms.

"No," Daniel said, "let her talk."

"Don't try to shrink me." Winter shifted the hate to Daniel.

He didn't flinch. "I'm not, but obviously there's more to this than just your mom dying. Perhaps if we could resolve all these other issues it could help."

"There's nothing wrong with me."

"I didn't say there was. Do you think there's something wrong with you?"

"Isn't it obvious?"

"No it's not," said Daniel. "You seem pretty normal to me. Tell me about it. Maybe I can help."

"I don't need your help. Why am I even here?"

Steve turned back to her. "We're here because you haven't been yourself since your mom started getting sick. Everything's changed about you. And after she died you haven't talked to your friends or me or even come out of your room."

"How about we completely screw up your life and see how you deal?"

Steve's face turned crimson.

"Isn't that overstating it a bit?" Daniel asked.

"How would you know? Has he told you what he did? What I'm reminded of every day?"

"You have no idea what you're talking about!" Steve shouted.

Daniel held up a hand, before Winter could let out the string of profanities clawing her throat. "Let's start over," he said. "Winter, your mother's just died. You were forced to move to a new home and live with your father, who you don't really get along with. Things have changed, we're not pretending they haven't. But your dad's concerned…"

She snorted. "Is that what he told you? That's he's concerned?"

"Well, he is. He's concerned about the changes you've made."

"The only thing he's concerned about is his pocketbook and how much I could cost him."

Steve leaned toward her, his face twisted and red. "What's wrong with you? Why do you keep…"

Daniel touched a hand to Steve's shoulder. "Perhaps we should discuss the relationship between the two of you first."

"We can't discuss something that doesn't exist," said Winter.

"Then perhaps," Daniel said, "we should find a way to build one."

"What's the point?"

"The point is you need a support system. You need someone you can talk to and rely on."

"Do you honestly think I'll get that from him?"

Steve clenched his eyes and turned his face.

"Look at him! He won't even respond! He won't even deny what I've said!"

"Maybe," Daniel said to Steve, "you could leave us alone for a few minutes?"

"Absolutely," Steve said. Relief spread over his face, and he quickly got up and walked through the office door.

When he had gone, Daniel looked back at Winter. "So what's your problem with him?"

"I thought we covered that already."

He leaned forward and clasped his hands together. "No, you said what you wanted him to hear. Now he's gone. Now I want the real truth. I want the real Winter to talk."

Winter's chin started to quiver and she looked away. "He doesn't want me. He never has."

"He took you in, he takes care of you."

"Out of obligation only."

"He's your father."

"He left us. He left me and my mom because he didn't want to be with us."

Daniel frowned. "I'm sure there's more to it than that."

"Then why did he hardly ever come to see me? Why did he not try harder when my mom was still alive? He hates me and he's stuck with me. I've only got to put up with it for a few more years. Then…I'm gone."

Daniel sat back and eyed her. "Is there any way you can find some common ground with him? Learn to get along?"

"No."

"Maybe you'll change your mind if you try."

"Nothing could change my mind. The sooner I can leave the better."

"So, what will you do then? You must live with him and depend on him. It's the law."

"But I don't have to love him, and I don't have to be around him. I'll just keep to myself as long as he leaves me alone."

Daniel furrowed his brow. "And this arrangement is satisfactory to you?"

"No. I want to be with my mom."

"But she died."

Winter pursed her lips.

Daniel tapped two fingers together in front of his face. "Do you want to die?"

"What do you think?"

He tapped his fingers some more. "I think you are a very intelligent young woman. I think that you don't care much about the life you have, but you do care about life. I think you'll exhaust every way of changing your life before you'll consider ending it. Am I right?"

Winter shrugged. "Maybe."

"What would you say if I told you that I knew of a way you could change your life?"

She rolled her eyes. "You mean church? No thank you. My mom

was into that and she tried to get me to go a long time ago."

"No, not church…something more than church."

Winter cocked her head sideways. "Dress it up in whatever words you want, it still boils down to church. So, no thank you."

"I see there's no fooling you." He tapped his fingers again.

Winter narrowed her eyes. What kind of game was he playing?

"Well, there's not much more for us to discuss today, I'm afraid. Will you come back?"

Winter tilted her head to the other side in thought. "Why? I don't have a problem. The problem is my dad, remember? Maybe he should come back."

"Perhaps. But will you come with him?"

"No."

Daniel frowned. There was a knock at the door. "Excuse me, Winter." He stood and cracked open the door. After speaking quietly for a moment, he opened it wide.

A boy about Winter's height walked in, wearing baggy jeans and a T-shirt. He rubbed a hand through his dark hair and smiled at her, dimples forming on his cheeks.

Daniel turned to her. "Winter, I'd like you to meet my son, Ryan. He's a Junior at Trenton Hills. Have you two met before?"

Ryan shook his head. "It's a big school, Dad." He took a step closer to her and extended his hand. "Nice to meet you, Winter. I've heard a lot about you. I lost my mom too, so I know how you feel."

Winter crossed her arms and glowered at his hand. She shoved past him and fled from the room.

# 3

*Present Day*

As Steve turned onto Hoole Boulevard from the Interstate Highway, Winter could not help but think of the first time he had brought her to Tishbe University. The weather was a complete opposite from the year before, though her dad's choice of music was still the same—Randy Travis.

The sun shone in bright green and yellow waves through the leafy netting of the trees lining the road. The wind sighed through the branches and Winter could almost feel it touch her skin within the seclusion of the truck. Perhaps it was just the AC.

Though the coolness on her skin was definitely artificial, the smell was not. It was the smell of late summer and of an early autumn. The smell of eating watermelon though the leaves fell in swarms from the trees. These trees were not yet turning colors, but they were considering it, almost glowing in anticipation at the edges of each leaf.

Winter watched hopefully for the sight of a student bent beneath a backpack, late for a class, trudging along the sidewalk. But there were none. And when they passed by the Raven, only a few patrons sat among the umbrellaed tables, enjoying delicious deli sandwiches—far from the long lines that usually snaked away from the counter and the dozens who sat in the grass or along the sidewalk because there were no more tables available.

No traffic. No guard waiting for them at the gate. No people crawling across the Meadow like a kicked anthill.

There was no life here. Yet. Strange.

Winter consulted her campus map and directed Steve through the streets of Tishbe until they came to Winter's new dorm. The road passed between identical parking lots. At the ends of each lot were identical dorms. They sat a little apart so the road could pass between, yet they curved back upon themselves. The one on the right was Boon Hall, and the one on the left was Devine Hall.

"Here, Dad. Devine Hall. That's the one."

Steve turned as instructed. "This looks much nicer than the last one."

"I should tell Summer we're here." She fished her cell phone out of the pocket of her black cargo pants, scrolled through her phone book, and began pressing buttons.

Steve parked beneath the awning and looked at Winter. "Now what?"

Winter grabbed the door handle. "I'll be right back."

She passed through the double glass doors that led to the lobby and stopped just within. A tiled walkway divided the carpeted floor of the large room…easily twice the size of the lobby in Carmichael. The walkway led to the main interior doors which led to the dorm rooms.

Winter checked the short desk built into the far right wall to see if a lobby attendant was on duty. Nobody. She did a quick scan over the study tables, chairs, and couches strewn about in small groups. A glassed-in section on one side of the lobby housed a row of washing machines and dryers.

Still nobody. Winter let her lungs deflate in a long, frustrated sigh.

She walked down the center walk to the dorm entrance, acutely aware of how loudly her shoes squeaked. The lights on the electronic lock were all dark. Winter pushed on one of the doors and it swung open.

"A lot of good that does," she said. "I still don't know where my room is."

She slammed the door and walked quickly back to the front doors. As she exited, her dad raised his eyebrows at her and she shrugged. Then a flash of lime green caught her eye and she looked to the road.

A Volkswagen Beetle turned toward them. Winter smiled.

Summer pulled in behind the trailer attached to Steve's truck. She leaped out of the car, leaving her door open and the engine running. Summer ran over and flung her arms around Winter. Winter sighed and hugged her back. She smelled like roses.

"I missed you!"

"Ditto," Winter said.

Summer pulled away, bouncing on her heels and grinning. She wore an orange T-shirt and a pair of low-rise blue jeans.

"You cut your hair," said Winter.

Summer grabbed the ends of her blonde hair where they hung in soft waves just above her shoulders. "Do you like it? I decided it was time for a bit of a change."

"It looks great. You don't look so…" Winter bit her bottom lip.

"So what?"

"So…blonde." Winter laughed.

Summer furrowed her brow. "I'm not sure I appreciate that."

"Sorry. I guess this would be a bad time to say you put on some weight?"

Summer crossed her arms. "Are you saying I've gotten fat?"

Winter laughed again. "No. But you don't look anorexic anymore."

"I've actually missed that." Summer smiled.

"Missed what?"

"Your mouth."

Winter laughed and shoved Summer in the shoulder. "Hey!"

"Too bad we live so far apart," Summer said. "I'd like to have seen you this summer."

"Again, ditto. Listen, my dad can't stay for long. He has to get back this evening."

"Oh, right. Well, here's the deal. I've got your room number and everything, but you can't officially check in and get your card key activated until tomorrow."

"Then how am I supposed to get into the room?"

"My RA key works in all the girls' dorms. I'll get us in so we can move your stuff, but you'll have to crash with me tonight. The interior lock system stays active. Since I'm the only one with a key, we have to stay together, and…well, my room's not a mess. Hope that's okay." Summer watched her nervously.

Winter smiled with one side of her mouth. "It'll be fine."

"Good. First thing in the morning, we'll come over here, get you checked in, and get your card."

Winter narrowed her eyes. "You know…There's something different about you."

"What do you mean?"

Steve shut his door and rounded the front of his truck.

"Hi, Mr. Maessen!" Summer said.

"Hi, Summer. You really don't have to call me that, you know. Steve will do."

Summer flushed. "Mr. Steve."

"Close enough."

"I can move in today," Winter said to him, "but I can't check in till tomorrow. I'll be staying with Summer tonight."

"You still helping her?" he asked.

"She's going to help me get everything ready for the freshmen," Summer said.

Steve nodded. "So where do we go?"

"Room 510," Summer said.

Winter groaned. "Fifth floor?"

"There are elevators just inside there." She pointed past the lobby to the unlocked double dorm doors.

Steve clapped his hands together. "Well, let's get started!"

It took them less than an hour to haul Winter's things to her new room. She didn't bother to unpack anything, leaving everything stacked in boxes and thrown on top of the drab bed.

With the last of her things brought up, Winter took a last look at her new room. It looked like a slab of concrete strewn with random tan building blocks. She'd tend to it later. Winter shouldered her backpack with the few things she needed for the night, turned out the light, and closed the door.

Downstairs, Summer gave Steve a quick goodbye and headed to her car to wait for Winter.

Steve took a deep breath and gave Winter a tight hug. "Don't go getting delusions of grandeur."

Winter smirked as they separated. "You know me."

"That's what I'm afraid of." He furrowed his brow. "Be careful."

"I will do nothing more than what God asks of me."

"That's not a promise to be careful."

"The Bible doesn't say anything about following God being safe."

"I suppose you're right." The furrow lessened and he reached out to embrace her again.

"Dad…" she moaned.

"I can still want you to be safe. Call me often."

She squeezed him. "I will."

"I love you."

"I love you too, Dad."

Winter waited beneath the awning as she watched her dad drive away. She kept her jaw tight and her muscles clenched in an effort to bottle up an urge to cry.

A loud buzzy chirp erupted from Summer's car. Winter shook her head and went to get in.

# 4

"Do you have plans for dinner?" Winter asked as she buckled her seatbelt.

Summer put the car into gear. "Well, everything's closed on campus. How about the Raven?"

"I've never eaten there before."

Summer grinned. "There's got to be a first time for everything!"

Summer guided her green Bug through the deserted college streets and back to the front of campus. She parked in the half-full parking lot of the Raven and the two girls got out.

An old-fashioned bell hanging from a coiled strip of metal rang as the door opened. Winter paused on the threshold and peered at it. She hadn't seen a bell like that since…

"What's wrong?" Summer asked from just behind.

"Nothing. The bell just reminded me of someone…um…" She shook the memories away. "…somewhere. Sorry." She rushed to the counter before Summer could ask another question.

A vast array of collegiate paraphernalia plastered every wall. The only space that wasn't a billboard for Tishbe University was the menu. Winter scanned the various sandwiches listed and chose a simple turkey.

Half the tables were occupied. They took their drinks to a high bistro table in the corner and waited for their sandwiches. Summer shuffled her straw in her drink and wouldn't look Winter in the eyes.

"Spill it," Winter said. "What's on your mind?"

Summer cut her eyes to Winter. "I haven't seen you all summer."

"Yeah. We've covered that, I think."

"Do you even remember what happened at the hospital?"

Winter took her turn at shuffling her straw. "Maybe."

"Then tell me what it was. You really freaked us out with wind blowing everywhere, lights exploding, doors bursting open, eyes glowing…"

Winter looked up.

"Does that always happen now when you get upset?"

"Sure. I always check if my eyes are glowing when I get mad."

"Really?"

Winter shot her a scowl. "Seriously, Summer? No."

Summer half grinned. "So what did happen?"

Winter shrugged. "I'm not sure. There's this rumbling that happens sometimes. And I feel like my skin is stretching. Maybe my eyes glow too, I don't know."

"What does it mean?"

Winter gazed at the exposed iron joists and slipped through her thoughts. "I'm not sure. It's been happening more often, and I can't seem to control when it happens. It's linked to my emotional state, somehow. But it's more than that. It's like…"

"Yeah?"

Winter leaned closer to Summer. "You know when you're sick and you've taken all this medication that makes you loopy? And you do things and say things, but somewhere in your muddy mind you feel like it's someone else talking, like you aren't in control anymore?"

"Yeah, I suppose."

"It's like that. It's like someone else has stepped in. I'm just along for the ride. I can't control it, I can't make it start. Sometimes I can suppress it. But when it happens, it's always the same. I'm not…me anymore."

Summer lowered her voice. "If you're not you, then who are you?"

Winter shook her head. "Whatever you think of me, whatever you think of this prophecy thing I have…it's not me, I'm not doing it."

"So when you say you're not yourself…"

"Almost there, Summer. You can do it."

"Are you saying God is taking over?"

Winter shrugged. "It's the best explanation I can think of."

The food arrived, placed gently before them by a perky blonde waitress. Winter sat back and waited for her to leave before reaching for the sandwich.

Summer eyed her.

"How was your summer?" Winter took a giant bite. "Meet any new boys?"

Summer shook her head. "No. I've decided to stay single for a while."

"Really?"

"You sound surprised."

"Well, considering last year…"

"After you slammed me for it, I decided you were right. I needed to change."

"Oh. Yeah. Um…" Winter shoved more sandwich in her mouth.

"I spent most of the summer doing some volunteer work with my church's youth group, as a chaperone."

"Wow. That's awesome. What kind of work did you do?"

Summer shrugged. "Outreach to at-risk teens. You know, runaways and druggies."

Winter stopped chewing. "People like me."

"Wait, I didn't mean..."

"I know what you meant, don't worry about it."

Summer bit her bottom lip for a moment and then took another bite. "What about you? What did you do over the summer?"

"Nothing much to report. Did a lot of nothing. A little reading and some shopping. Hung out with this one friend of mine from high school. Tried to figure out what to do about Xaphan. Nothing but dead ends. Didn't have any new visions or premonitions. I saw Kaci this morning."

Summer's face brightened. "How was she?"

"Much better, actually. But I'm not sure she's coming back to school."

Summer frowned. "I hope she does. I don't think things would be the same without her."

"Maybe." Winter shrugged. "Then again, it may be best for her to take some time off. I don't know. I mean, I'll miss her, but I want what's best for her. You know? Anyway, housing knows about the situation, and she's listed as my roommate if she shows up. Otherwise, I get a private room."

"That's good, I guess. But it still won't be the same without her."

Winter looked her in the eyes with a calm sternness. "I don't think it's going to be the same regardless. Nothing happened over the summer. But I've got this growing feeling that the storm's just about to start."

"And are you going to get involved again?"

"Of course."

Summer frowned and continued to eat in silence. Winter was grateful for the break in conversation.

When she finished, she wiped her mouth with a napkin and took a long sip from her drink. "What's on the agenda for tonight?"

"Well," said Summer. "I've got a big box full of T-shirts in my trunk. We've got to fold and roll them with rubber bands, and stick on size labels."

Winter groaned.

"It shouldn't take too long."

Winter slid out of her chair. "Well, no need wasting time. Let's go get started."

The next morning, Summer brought Winter back to Devine Hall. Winter was the first to arrive for check-in. While Winter took care of the room deposit and her new ID, Summer made use of her RA status to drift behind the desk and peruse the rooming list. Winter watched from the corner of her eye for any reaction or sign from Summer that Kaci had arrived. But Summer's face remained unreadable.

Winter grabbed her new ID and the obligatory T-shirt and found Summer waiting near the locked doors leading to the dormitory rooms. "Well?" Winter swiped her new card to see if it worked. The LED light turned green and the magnetic lock at the top of the door released. They went through.

Summer pressed the elevator call button. "There's nothing on any of the lists saying that Kaci's coming. Actually, the room list says you have a private room."

Winter sighed. "That's what it's supposed to say, unless she changes her mind. I guess we won't know until she shows up."

"If she shows up."

The elevator doors opened and they stepped on. Winter pressed the button for the fifth floor. "Best not to hope for it then. That way we aren't disappointed."

Winter led Summer back to her room. She slid the card into the lock on the door. It clicked and the light turned green. She opened the door and found the room exactly as she had left it.

Exactly. Boxes stacked everywhere. Nothing unpacked. And no

Kaci.

The corners of Winter's eyes throbbed and tingled. "I'll be just one moment." Winter ran in and found her suitcase. She dug through it until she retrieved her phone charger. Then she grabbed her laptop backpack and shoved a change of clothes inside. She had to get out before Summer noticed…

Summer stood in the doorway looking confused.

Winter shouldered the backpack and walked to her, stomach churning and throat aching.

"Let's get back to your room, I guess."

"You don't want to unpack?" Summer asked. "I thought I was going to help you unpack."

"Not today. I don't feel like it."

Summer blinked.

Winter tightened her jaw. "Is it okay? You don't mind if I stay one more night, do you? I just…I just think I need to be with a friend tonight." She tried to keep her voice level and calm.

"Yeah, sure. You can help me make welcome notes to put in all the rooms on my floor."

Winter rolled her eyes to keep up the facade. "Thanks."

# 5

*Four Years Ago*

The doorbell rang. Winter peeked through the curtains and saw Claire and Phillip waiting on the doorstep. She sighed and pushed her hair behind her ear. It felt stringy. She should shower. She was starting to smell herself.

She opened the door and turned, allowing Claire and Phillip in. They stumbled past her, giggling, with their arms snug against each other's waists. Winter glanced over her shoulder and heaved another sigh of impatience.

"Where are your shoes?" Claire asked. She turned to kiss Phillip.

"I don't think I want to go," Winter said with a croak.

"You have to! I've been working for this all summer!"

"I don't want anything else to do with your witchcraft." She plopped onto the couch, sinking deep into the cushions.

Claire stopped laughing. "My witchcraft? We were doing this together, remember?"

"Yeah. Were."

Claire narrowed her eyes and stood in front of Winter. "Just because that one spell failed, it doesn't mean you can give up. You can accomplish so much if you just try."

Phillip left the room and ambled into the kitchen. The clatter of cups and the icemaker floated into the living room.

Winter sat up, the leather squeaking against itself. "It was supposed to be just for that one thing. Just to save my mom and help you. I never agreed to become a witch like you."

Claire's chin jutted out. "It's Wiccan."

"Whatever. All it does is remind me of what happened. I don't want to go."

Phillip returned with a glass of soda, half empty already.

"So you're not even going to come to my induction ceremony?" Claire sat beside her.

"No," said Winter. She glared at Phillip, then turned to Claire. "Why are you doing it, anyway?"

"Because these people understand me…like you. They'd understand you too if you gave them a chance."

"You mean, you're not just doing this for the power?"

"It's not like that. Come with me and you'll see. There's more to it than just spells and stuff. It's a support system, a circle of friends."

Winter studied Claire's face, trying to find some excuse to refuse. She sighed. "Okay. I'll go with you tonight. But that doesn't mean I'm going to join your little group."

Claire smiled. "I'm not asking you to. I just want my new friends to meet my best friend."

Phillip turned off the highway onto a gravel road. A moment later, Winter could see nothing but passing trees.

Winter leaned forward and shouted over the drone of the crunching gravel. "Where are we?"

Claire turned in the front seat to face her. "Someplace out of the way. We can't exactly be public. Most people don't understand this sort of thing."

"Have you been here before?"

"Once. A couple of weeks ago."

Winter sat back and watched the scrolling road between the silhouettes of Phillip and Claire. After a few minutes, they came to a wide spot where several cars were parked.

Claire led them along a narrow path lined by candles. A few figures glided ahead of them in the shadows. A chill ran down Winter's spine. The path ended at a small glade with a circle of willow trees. Tiki torches surrounded the circle of trees and one torch stood in the middle.

A group of hooded figures holding candles waited at the entrance to the circle. Claire walked up to them and they pulled back their hoods, revealing a man and woman close to her dad's age and a girl close to Winter's age.

"Welcome, Claire," said the woman.

"Hey, everybody. I want you to meet my friends Phillip and Winter."

They all smiled at Phillip. But when they looked at Winter, the smiles faded away. The girl's eyes rounded and she grabbed the woman's arm.

"It's okay, Shannon."

"What's wrong with her?"

"Shh…"

"What's going on?" asked Winter.

The woman looked at Claire. "She can't be here."

Claire stepped back. "Why not? What's wrong?"

"She needs to leave."

"You said I could bring friends. She's my friend."

Winter touched Claire on the shoulder.

"Don't worry, Winter," Claire said.

The woman took a threatening step forward and pointed back toward the vehicles. "She cannot be here. Take her away."

Winter clenched her teeth and turned to run. The chills trickled down her back and into her arms and legs. She wanted to scream.

"Winter, wait!"

Winter slammed into Phillip's car and wrenched open the door. Claire grabbed her arm.

"Stop, Winter."

Winter spun on her. "I thought you said these people were your friends!"

"They are…"

"I thought you said they would understand me!"

"They do…would. I don't know what's going on, but I'll find out."

Winter shook her head. "I knew I shouldn't have come. I knew better than to get involved in your witch stuff. Just take me home, okay?"

"I can't do that. I'm being inducted with the rest of the novices. I have to stay."

"Then make Phillip take me home."

"No. I want him here too."

Winter screamed. Her grating voice bounced from the trees. "What's wrong with you? I thought you were my friend!"

"I am. But I want him here. I want both of you here. I just…I don't know what's wrong. Please, give me a chance to find out."

"Fine. I'll wait."

Claire ran back into the forest. Winter sat on the edge of the seat with her feet still on the ground. She rested her head in her open hands and tried to shove down the anger that had boiled into her empty heart. She preferred the void.

The minutes ticked by. Winter heard some shouts coming from the trees. Then running footsteps. She looked up.

Claire came back out with Phillip behind her. Her lips were

squeezed tight. "I'm sorry. You have to go."

Winter stood. "Are you serious?"

Phillip moved around the car and got into the driver's seat.

"Only novices and the members of the coven."

"But you said you could invite friends! Tell me what's going on. What's wrong with me?"

"Don't worry about it. Just go, okay?"

"So our friendship comes down to this? You're betraying me for new friends? Just like you did Alison?"

"She was never a good friend anyway."

Winter felt her jaw slacken. She sat back down and grabbed the door handle.

"Winter, I didn't mean that. I'm sorry."

"No, I think I understand now."

"Stop it! I didn't mean it like that. It just came out."

"Well, Alison's still my friend. She's always been good to me. Maybe I should just go tell her the truth."

"You don't want to do that," Claire said.

"And why not? She's my friend! She deserves to know the truth. She deserves to know what you and Phillip really did to her."

Phillip snorted.

"Us?" Claire said. "You were involved too. Don't forget that. If you tell Alison, she'll hate you too."

Winter clenched her fists.

"Winter, there's no need to get so upset. Just forget all of this. Forget I brought you here. I shouldn't have done it…I wasn't supposed to."

"Whatever."

"Don't be so quick to judge me. You don't know the whole story. I'll explain later, okay? Just go calm down, please."

Winter grunted.

Claire grabbed Winter's door. "I'll see you at school next week." She shut the door and Phillip drove away.

# 6

*Present Day*

When light peeked in through the unclad window, Winter awoke. She stretched to ease the catch in her back. The floor may have been carpeted, but it felt like concrete. She checked the clock. It was only six—check-in wasn't until eight. As she sat up, Winter wiped away the crust at the corners of her eyes and decided a shower would put her back to rights. She grabbed her backpack containing her change of clothes and stood.

Summer lay splayed beneath her disheveled blanket. One foot hung off the side of the bed. She snored like a clown honking its nose.

Winter smiled. She was going to miss that. But maybe there would be more chances for her to crash here. Especially if she was going to have a room to herself.

After a warm shower she grabbed her Bible and wandered the familiar route to the lobby of Carmichael. Though silent now, Winter knew what kind of madhouse it would become in just a couple of hours. From beneath the awning, she could just see the top of the

Olamel bell tower looming over the nearest building. It was only a little way away. She set her sights upon it and walked.

She entered the chapel garden from the entrance opposite the Meadow, using one of the shortcuts she had discovered last year. As she passed the first building, the base of the bell tower emerged before her like the Bastille of Paris.

She stopped and stared. Everything was so quiet. So…peaceful. The last time she was here…Winter shoved the spasm in her chest down and dredged up enough numbness to take its place. She wandered to her old study spot and stared at the chapel and tower for a long time. The emotions within her clashed and stirred, hollowing out her chest and igniting a fire of anger all at the same time. Winter wiped the tears from her eyes with the knuckles of her clenched fists. The Bible study could wait. She just didn't have it in her right now.

Winter left the garden and walked into the Meadow. She stopped halfway to the Ancient and stared at the giant tree. A pang coursed through her heart, as the memories from last year filled her mind. Good memories…now tainted. This one tree stood there unchanged. Unaffected. Uncaring. It wasn't fair.

Winter ducked her head down and hurried past the boughs. Then she took the longer path back to Carmichael.

The parking lot was half full and a line was beginning to form within the lobby. The early risers had arrived – new students hoping to shed their parents before lunch. Probably locals, Winter thought.

Summer was easy to find. The smile on her face and bounce in her step was like a beacon from across the room. Winter waved at her, but she didn't seem to notice. Summer went back to her clipboard and looked up to speak to another student. Winter eased to her side and peered at the room list in Summer's hand.

"Having fun?"

"Oh, hi!" Summer flashed a grin at Winter and went back to the room list. "You'll be in room 204," she told the child across from her.

Winter did a double take. *Did we really look that young last year?*

Summer turned to her. "Got your cell?"

"Yeah."

Summer looked her up and down, and frowned. "I was hoping you'd dress a little more…"

"More what?"

"Normal."

Winter grinned. "Not a chance."

"You might scare some of the freshmen."

"Good. They should be scared."

Summer shook her head and rolled her eyes. "If you want, you can start helping with unloading and I'll text you if I need anything."

"You seem tense," Winter said. "And a little…extra perky."

Summer gave her a bright smile. "Sorry. Just a lot more paperwork than I was expecting. I had coffee."

Winter laughed. "Coffee? That's hardcore. I'll leave you alone then." Winter slapped her on the shoulder and walked away.

As she entered the first floor, she spotted a girl dragging a suitcase with a half dozen other items hanging from straps across her shoulders.

"Hey, need a hand?" Winter asked.

The girl paused and brushed the stray strands of brown hair from her face. "Yeah."

"What room?"

"112."

Winter took the suitcase and headed to the room. "How much more do you have?"

"Not much."

"My name's Winter. I'll follow you back to your car and help."

"Thanks. I'm Sandy. I'm so nervous about this. I've never been away from my parents for more than a few days." Sandy pushed open the room door and shuffled in. She leaned over the bed and dropped everything.

"Don't worry about it," Winter said. "It'll be fine."

"How do you know?"

Winter smiled and stood the suitcase up in the middle of the bare floor. "Because I thought the same thing last year."

Sandy took a deep breath and sat. Her face was as white as the naked mattress.

"Do you need to rest a minute?" Winter asked.

"No, I'm fine. I'm just…"

"What?"

"It's silly."

Winter shook her head. "I promise. It's not."

"I'm just…scared."

Winter took a step closer. "God wouldn't have brought you here if he didn't have a plan."

Sandy smiled. "I know. Doesn't make it any easier though."

"No. I guess it doesn't. God's plans aren't always easy. But easy isn't the point."

Sandy tilted her head and wrinkled her brow.

"What's wrong?" Winter asked.

"You don't seem the type to be so…I don't know…insightful."

Winter chuckled. "I'm full of surprises."

Sandy laughed. "Yeah, well. I'm sure I am too. This is a big step for me, coming here. It took a lot of convincing for my parents to let me."

"Really? Why?"

"Long story." Sandy bit her lip.

"Didn't they come to help you move in?"

Sandy looked at the floor. "They were…busy. Long story."

"Okay, I get it." Winter went to the door. "I've got a long story too, and I sure don't want to tell it to many people. No more questions, I promise."

Sandy smiled. "Thanks."

"Come on, let's go get the rest of your stuff."

Winter spent the next two hours meeting, comforting, and helping as many new girls as she could. She was surprised at the level of insecurity and immaturity of most, and wondered if she and Summer had been the same. Surely not. Most of the time Winter talked with the parents. Only a few gave her any hesitation over the way she dressed. In a way, Winter was disappointed. Maybe she should have put on her black make-up.

Back in the lobby, Winter sought out Summer yet again for her next assignment. When their eyes met, Summer nodded to the redhead standing in front of her.

"Hi, I'm Winter," she said when she came within a couple feet.

The redhead turned and considered her with something akin to fear, that quickly turned to suspicion, and dropped her eyes to the floor. Finally. A decent reaction.

"I'm Ayden."

"Can I help you unload?"

Ayden looked up and met Winter with her eyes.

The room twisted and spiraled in a blur of colors. It faded and became someplace else.

She was *someone* else.

She was in a kitchen. The counters and chairs were larger than normal. Somehow, Winter was little…maybe younger. A man sat at the table drinking coffee. He wore dark blue pants and a checkered shirt.

"What is it, sweetie?" he asked.

"I don't want to go to school today," a child's voice cried from Winter's mouth.

"But it's your first day in second grade. You're a big girl now."

The scene morphed and mixed.

The same man…older. The same room…remodeled.

"You're going to college. You're a woman now."

Flash. "You're a big girl…"

Flash. "…a woman now…"

The room twisted again and the colors rushed away and became the colors and structure of the Carmichael lobby.

"Winter, are you okay?" Summer put a hand on her shoulder.

Ayden watched her with narrow eyes.

"Uh, yeah." She raised a hand to her forehead. *What just happened?* For the first time she noticed the man standing just to the side of Ayden, talking with someone behind the counter. He was the man in the vision.

"Maybe you should take a break. Get a soda or something." Summer guided her to a chair. Ayden and her dad left in the company of another helper.

"What happened?"

Summer frowned. "Let me get you something."

"No, I'm fine, really. What happened?"

"You kinda went all stiff-like. And you started muttering. Come on." Summer grabbed Winter by the arm. "We're taking a break."

They bought sodas from the machine in the lobby and went outside.

Summer started down the sidewalk. "What's going on…did you have another vision like last year?"

Winter took a sip. "Well…kind of."

"What do you mean?" They paused at a crosswalk to allow an SUV pulling a trailer to pass.

"Last year, I saw things from my own perspective. Like I was watching what was happening. If I focused on one person, I could see things about them that I needed to see. This time it was different…I was her. It was like I was living her memories or something."

"But it was still a vision, right?"

They turned down a sidewalk that led to the Meadow.

"Yeah, I suppose." Winter took a quick sip. "I don't know. Maybe it was just a different kind of vision. The others were of things that hadn't happened yet. This, I think, was of the past."

They came to the edge of the Meadow and sat on the first bench they found. The breeze from earlier still rustled the leaves with lazy abandon, but clouds dulled the sun.

"What did you see?" Summer asked.

"Nothing important. It was a random memory, maybe, sparked by moving in. I was Ayden talking to her dad on the first day of school."

"So does that mean something? Is it important?" Summer asked.

"I don't know."

Winter took a long drink to finish the soda.

"Well, it must mean something."

"I know. I'll figure it out, I'm sure. But make sure you remember where she's staying. And maybe keep an eye on her." Winter tossed her empty can at a nearby trash bin and missed. She grunted and stood to retrieve it. "We should go back, you know. They probably need you."

Summer sighed. "But it's so peaceful here. And quiet."

"Yeah…everything Carmichael isn't right now. But you're an RA. Get used to it."

Summer slowly stood and they made their way back to the dorm.

"Okay, we can do this," Summer said when they stepped back into the chaotic lobby.

"I'm okay, really," said Winter.

Summer gave her a stressed look as if to say, *I'm not talking to you.*

Winter smiled. "I'll be upstairs, text me."

Summer nodded and went back to the desk.

After lunch, Winter walked back to Devine Hall alone to unpack. She threaded her way through the crowded lobby, full of students, parents, luggage, and boxes. So far she didn't recognize anyone she knew from last year. The constant drone of voices, rolling luggage, and scraping furniture grated in Winter's ears. She wished someone would hurry up and plug in a radio so blaring music could cover it all up.

Winter stood in front of her door and looked at the electronic lock. She had tried all day not to think of Kaci or to get her hopes up about Kaci's return. But in the back of her mind the doubt and anticipation grew like fungus in the dark. She tried to ignore it, but it refused to budge. Now she stood before her door on the fifth floor of Devine Hall, skin chilled and heart pounding. Not finding Kaci inside might drag her over the edge.

Winter considered going back to the front desk and asking if Kaci had checked in. But what if she found out she had been assigned a new roommate? What if there was a stranger in her room right now? Would finding out at the desk be better or worse than finding out here?

Winter bit her lip and pulled out her ID. She could feel the expectant looks from everyone passing by or standing around in the crowded hall. Everyone was watching to see what the freak was doing. One girl started walking toward her as if she had something to say.

Winter slid her ID into the lock. It clicked. The light turned green. She turned the handle and stepped in before the girl made it to her. Thank God for small motivations.

The room was exactly as she had left it. The energy and strength drained out of her in a cold wave as the adrenaline flow crimped shut. Her knees wobbled.

*No. I'm not going to cry again.* She tensed her body to hold back the emotional surge that took the place of the adrenaline. *I refuse to cry again.*

Winter turned the light out and fled to her bed, crashing down and letting her body tremble.

# 7

*Four Years Ago*

Winter pushed through the crowded hall of Trenton Hills shortly after homeroom on the first day of school. She checked the slip of paper with her locker assignment and scanned the row of lockers for the right number. She found it near the end of the hall and groaned. Winter retrieved her padlock from her backpack and threaded it through the latch.

Someone touched her on the shoulder and she jumped.

"It's just me," Claire said. "What's wrong?"

"Nothing."

"Listen, I wanted to talk to you about the other day. I'm sorry, okay? I guess I just wasn't thinking when I invited you. It's not your fault."

"They said something was wrong with me."

"Oh, it's not that. It's just…you're not one of them, that's all."

Winter narrowed her eyes, certain Claire was lying.

"I talked with them and they're cool with you, really. It was just bad timing and everything. Madam Morial wants to meet you properly, at her shop some time."

"I'm not sure about that. I really don't want any more of the magic stuff. I'm done with it."

"It's not like that. She just wants to meet you, that's all."

"Forget it."

Claire looked at the ground.

Winter sighed. "I'm sorry. I'll think about it, is that better?"

"Yeah," said Claire.

"I don't know what's happening to me. I just want to shout at everyone lately." She spun the new lock to test the combination.

Claire placed a reassuring hand on her shoulder. "It's understandable. Just know that I'm here if you need to talk."

"Why does everyone keep saying that?" She pounded her fist against the locker. "What is wrong with this stupid lock?"

"Calm down, Winter."

"Don't tell me..." She looked over Claire's shoulder and spotted Ryan watching her from across the hall. "I'm sorry. I just...I can't do this right now."

"Can't do what?" Claire asked.

"I don't know. I just can't...I can't be happy I guess." She turned and walked away without giving Claire time to respond.

Winter rushed down the hall, trying to skirt by Ryan without having to look at him.

"Hey, Winter. Wait up."

Winter rolled her eyes and walked faster. But a moment later Ryan was beside her.

"Go away," she said.

"What did I do?"

"You're bothering me."

"Okay then. Maybe I'll just be quiet."

"Great."

Winter turned at the hall junction. Ryan turned with her.

"Do you want something?" she asked. "Don't you have a class to be getting to?"

"Well, I just wanted to say hi. So I thought I'd wait until you were ready. And yes, I do have a class to go to. I'm a little afraid you're going to make me late."

"God, you're annoying."

"That's not fair. I'm not exactly God. And how do you know he's annoying?"

Winter stopped and faced him with planted feet. "Seriously, can't you take a hint? Leave me alone. I'm not in the mood to put up with you."

Ryan frowned. "Yeah, sure. Listen, I just wanted to check on you, that's all. You know, to see how you're doing."

"I'm happy. Can't you tell?" She flashed him a tight-lipped fake smile.

"Wait." Ryan tilted his head and pointed a finger at her. "Was that a joke? It was! You made a joke." He laughed.

Winter closed her eyes with an effort to not smile back for real. She took a deep breath and softened. "Look…I appreciate your concern. I just need some space, okay?"

"Fair enough," Ryan said. "But if I see you, can I say hi?"

"Will you always be this annoying?"

"Not if you just say hi."

Winter hesitated, wondering what Ryan was up to. "Yeah, sure. Whatever."

Ryan grinned. "Great! Then let's start over. Hi." He waved his hand a little bit.

Winter couldn't help the chuckle that escaped. "Um. Hi."

Ryan clapped his hands together. "Okay…so that's it. Same time tomorrow?"

"Just hi?"

He nodded. "Just hi."

"Are you trying to hit on me?"

Ryan's face fell into feigned insult. "Well, that would be

completely inappropriate, don't you think?"

"Sure."

"To be honest, we have similar stories, you know? Not many people around here understand what I've been through."

"Yeah, well, don't expect a new best friend or anything."

"Nope. Not expecting anything. Just want to say hi."

"Just hi?"

"Haven't we already covered this?" Ryan shook his head and walked away.

Winter stood there for a moment, shocked and confused. The warning bell sounded and she rushed away to her class.

*Present Day*

Winter stared at herself in her make-up mirror, trying to decide how much would be too much. The standard "punched eye" look already covered her face. Winter reached for the lipstick and hesitated over the black. That might be too much. She didn't want to scare Summer…again. Winter passed over the black and picked up the purple.

As she leaned forward, her attention wandered to the empty bed in the reflection. She paused and set the makeup down. Winter turned around a looked at her half-decorated room. It wasn't right. It wasn't supposed to be like this. A deep numbing went through her chest.

"This is stupid," she said out loud. "I'm just fine on my own. Always have been."

Her phone chirped with a text message. From Summer: *I'm here.*

Winter stood and shoved her phone into the deep pockets of her cargo pants. She took one more look at herself in the mirror and tugged her baggy shirt straight. Then she went to the parking lot to meet Summer.

As she climbed in the passenger side, Summer raised her eyebrows at Winter.

"Shut up," Winter said. "I didn't feel like dressing up."

Summer smiled. "Old habits, huh?"

"We can't all be a model like you. Some of us would rather be impaled."

Summer grimaced and flicked back her perfectly styled hair. "Whatever." She pulled into a parking spot in the front of the CLC building.

"Have you talked with Davis yet?" Winter asked as they walked to the main entrance.

"We talked over the summer, but not since we came back to school. He'll probably be here."

They took the stairs to the gathering room below where the annual welcome back party was in full swing. It was already teeming with upperclassmen hugging and laughing together. The freshmen clung wide-eyed against the walls.

As soon as they entered the room, the praise band took the stage and the two girls had to quickly find their seats. After a few songs, the ceremonial greeting and annual recitation of CLC activities, Winter jumped up to get a drink from the refreshment table. Summer padded behind her like a puppy.

Davis appeared at their side. "Hey." He waved a cup of soda in his hand and grinned at Summer.

Summer bounced on her heels a little. "Hey!" She took a step and hugged him.

"Whoa," he said. "That's new."

"Sorry, it's just good to see another friend. It's been awhile."

"But I called you last week."

"Not the same." Summer touched his arm and then fled to the snack table.

Davis stared after her.

Winter raised her eyebrow, a smile tugging the corner of her mouth.

Davis turned to Winter with a grunt. "Have you seen Kaci?"

"No," Winter said. "She hasn't come yet."

Davis frowned.

"I'm not sure she will," said Winter.

Davis nodded. "I was afraid of that. What's her excuse?"

Winter sighed and shook her head. "She's afraid everyone will see her differently. She's a little messed up right now. It's going to take her a long time to get through this. I just wish she would get it through her thick head that she needs us to help."

"Stubbornly independent, as always," said Davis.

Winter looked away. Her own stubborn past flickered through her thoughts. "I know."

Summer came back with a plate full of snacks, watching them with wide eyes and stuffing her mouth.

Winter chuckled. "Chew a little. It helps. I can't get free tuition if you die this year, so don't bother killing yourself."

Summer's face paled and her jaw slacked. Slowly she started chewing again.

Davis smiled at Summer and turned back to Winter. "Give Kaci some time. Even if she doesn't come back this semester or this year or ever, she'll come *back*. Kaci's a fighter."

"Kaci?" said a voice slightly behind Winter. Peter Strong stepped around and joined them. "How is she?"

Winter folded her arms and took a step back, throwing her gaze to the floor.

"Not too good, I'm afraid," Davis said adjusting his glasses. "She hasn't come back."

"I'm sorry to hear that," said Peter.

"How are you?" asked Davis.

"Better. I'm still a little stiff sometimes. Nothing I can't work through."

"Did you have to do rehab?" asked Summer.

"Some. The doctors said I shouldn't have recovered as quickly as I did." He shrugged. "Maybe some of what happened to Kaci spilled over on me. I walked myself out of the hospital, but they still couldn't admit a miracle happened. What about you, Winter? How are you?"

Winter looked up. For a moment, she felt herself sinking into his bright blue eyes…eyes that were the same as hers. It took an effort to notice his dimpled chin…his high cheekbones…his freckles…

She tore her ogling away and gazed back at the ground, forcing a grimace on her face. "I'm fine."

"I don't believe that," Peter said. "Did I do something?"

"No…um. Just a bad day. Don't take it personal."

Davis snorted. "Don't push it. It's her defense mechanism."

Winter wanted to glare at him but refused to look up and give him the satisfaction.

"Winter," said Peter. "I know it's been tough on you, as well as me and Kaci. I understand the push-away reaction, right now. But we can help each other, I think. We should talk sometime. Will you do that?"

She didn't move.

"Look at me." He tapped the underside of her chin.

His touch was firm but gentle. The tips of his fingers were perfectly smooth. She lifted her face to him and tried to project as much anger as she could…but those eyes. Once again she found herself sinking deeper and deeper. *What was wrong with her?* The room became blue…her whole world engulfed by the singular color of his eyes. It spun and swirled…

And she was in a car, approaching an intersection. The light turned yellow and she applied the brakes. Nothing happened. She pressed harder. Still nothing. Ahead, a semi-truck barreled toward the intersection from the other side. She slammed the brake pedal…nearly stood on it, putting all her weight and will into stopping the car. Still, the vehicle plunged through the red light. Momentarily, she looked to her right and saw the bumper of the truck as it crushed through the car.

Then she was back. Staring at Peter's blue eyes. He had dropped his hand. Summer was standing closer, white as a sheet and clutching her arm.

"Are you okay?" Peter asked. His face wore an expression of shock and…revulsion?

"Don't look at me like that," Winter snapped.

Peter held up his hands. "I just want to make sure you're okay."

Winter glared at each of them in turn. The effort made her feel flushed and weak. The room seemed to still spin. Others in the room were turning to look.

"Winter?" Davis asked.

"Come on." Summer grabbed Winter's arm.

Winter tried to apologize before Summer dragged her away, but no words came. Winter stumbled at Summer's side all the way to the car. The world continued to spin until she sat and closed her eyes.

"What's going on?" Summer asked.

"I don't know," Winter said.

"Something's happening, you know it."

Winter sighed. "I know."

"Well?"

"Well, what?"

Summer leaned closer. "What are you going to do about it?"

Winter's jaw fell a little. She stared at Summer, not knowing quite how to respond. "I…I can't just control it like that. You know that, Summer."

Summer shook her head. "That's not what I'm talking about."

"Then enlighten me, please, since you seem to have suddenly sprouted great wisdom."

Summer narrowed her eyes. "Has anything happened since last spring?"

"You mean visions and stuff?"

Summer nodded.

"Not until now."

"Now that you're back."

"Yeah."

Summer paused and looked forward. She turned the key in the ignition and the green Bug purred to life. "It's happening again. Something…something is happening. You're back. The visions have started. And that means something else is going to happen this year."

"Maybe."

"Maybe?" Summer put the car in gear. "You should know better than that. These things happen to you for a reason, remember? The difference this time is that you actually know a little about what it means."

"I know where it comes from, but I certainly don't know what any of this new stuff means."

"Doesn't matter. You know enough to start figuring it out. Maybe this time you can figure it out before anyone gets hurt."

Summer's words were like a punch to the gut.

# 9

She sat alone in the Union the next morning, hoping Davis or Summer would show up to join her. Waking up to an otherwise empty room, Winter realized just how much she missed having Summer for a roommate. There was too much silence there…a silence that pressed Winter like the weight of being underwater. As she ate she tried to amuse herself with the anxious stares from this year's freshmen or the polite avoidance from the returning students, but she could find no joy in it.

She pulled out her Bible and read through Psalm 52 while crunching on a piece of bacon. Her dad had directed her to this passage over the summer and she nearly had it memorized now. It helped her to remember her commitment to find Xaphan. *How am I going to do that?* But Summer was right. Something was happening and this time she needed to be ready. More than ready…she needed to be ahead.

At a quarter till eight, she gathered her things and chunked her trash on the way out the door for her first class. The Meadow was just as she remembered, heaving with crowded bodies like boiling water. The Ancient stood silently watching the daily ritual. Winter took a deep breath and plunged into the human river on the sidewalk below.

The religion building felt like an oasis of quiet as she entered. It took her only a few minutes to find the room for her New Testament class. Peter Strong waved at her from the far side of the room. Winter half-smiled, a little embarrassed at how she had acted last night. But otherwise glad to finally see a familiar and friendly face that day. She took a seat beside him and pulled out her notebook.

Peter leaned over. "I didn't expect to see you here."

Winter flopped the spiral notebook on the desk. "Why not?"

"Well, usually only religion majors take this class."

"So that would mean…"

Peter blinked at her. "Are you a religion major?"

Winter grinned with one side of her mouth. "I bet your brain feels better now that the hard question is over."

Peter laughed. "Yeah, well…maybe it does."

"What about you? Shouldn't you be done with this class by now?"

"I put it off for two years, and alas…" he sighed "…I must repeat my junior year."

"Really?"

"Well, I didn't exactly finish any classes last year. Not so quick yourself, are you?" He grinned. "At least the school was gracious enough to give me tuition credit from last year. But I'm still a year behind. There's nothing to be done for that. On the other hand, it is nice that you're actually being civil to me…sort of."

Winter exhaled and rolled her eyes. "Yeah…sorry about last night. I have, um, moments sometimes. I'm working on it. I'm not exactly a butterfly or anything. Just be happy I actually go out in public."

Peter nodded. "Hey, I get it. No problem. We all have our baggage. I'll just remember to poke you with a stick next time to see if you're going to bite or not."

Winter glared at him.

He laughed. "Maybe I should get a longer stick."

At that point, Dr. Lubbock walked in, pulling his fedora off his mostly bald head and setting the hat beside his leather briefcase. For the next hour, the class reviewed the syllabus and discussed some of the finer points of New Testament canonization.

When Dr. Lubbock dismissed the class, Winter shoved her things back into her backpack and tried to escape quickly. With less than ten minutes between classes, she had a long trek across the Meadow to the English building for World Lit.

"Hey Winter! Wait up!" Peter called as Winter stepped out of the religion building. Peter caught up and fell into pace beside her. "Where you headed?"

"World Lit."

"No wonder you're practically running." Peter settled his backpack onto both shoulders. "What else are you taking?"

"I've got Intro to Psychology after lunch."

"With Rand?"

"Yeah, I think."

Peter nodded. "Shouldn't be too hard. But be careful. I hear she acts like a robot."

Winter smiled. "Is there something I can help you with?"

He seemed to falter. "Uh…no. Just thought I'd walk you to class. Is that all right?"

Winter huffed. "Why?"

Peter shrugged. "So, have you heard from Kaci?"

"No. Don't you have a class now?"

"Yeah, physics."

"Isn't that at the other end of the Meadow?"

Peter glanced over his shoulder and slowed. "Right. See you later."

Winter rolled her eyes.

Winter wandered back to Devine to crash after her long first day. She opened her dorm door and froze.

Kaci stood unpacking a box sitting atop the newly claimed bed. She wore her light brown hair pulled back in a ponytail, with a flower-shaped pendant hanging from her neck. A thick layer of make-up covered her face, making her look almost porcelain, and she wore a long-sleeved turtleneck despite the heat outside.

"Hi," said Kaci.

Winter eased into the room and closed the door. "Hi." She crossed to her bed and sat. "I'm glad you came. It wasn't any fun sleeping here by myself."

"I had a long talk with my parents. They convinced me that this would be for the best. And that…that this is where I needed to be."

"I can't believe the school let you come late."

"Well, they've been very gracious," Kaci said.

"Yeah. They gave Peter tuition credit from last year."

Kaci set the empty box on the floor and picked up another. "How is he?"

"He's great, actually, but he's got to repeat last year." She dumped her backpack on the floor and went to Kaci's side. "Can I help?"

"Sure."

"He's asked about you."

Kaci looked away. "He was my freshman group leader. We hung out a lot that year."

"Do you mind if I call Summer and Davis? They'll want to see you."

Kaci paused with her hands inside of the box.

"You can't hide in here. I mean, you've got to go to class tomorrow."

"Fine, I guess."

Winter smiled. "I'm glad you're back." She turned and gave Kaci a tight hug.

After a moment, Kaci hugged her back. "Me too."

# 10

*Four Years Ago*

Winter stood with her arms crossed in the lunch line, waiting for her rations. After reciting her lunch number to the attendant, she scanned the room for a place to sit. She was relieved to find Stacy sitting alone. No sign of Alison, Claire, or Phillip. Maybe their classes were on a different lunch schedule.

"Hey." Winter sat opposite Stacy.

Stacy glanced up and then went back to her hamburger.

"Did you have a good summer?" Winter lifted her carton of milk.

"I suppose," Stacy said without looking up.

Winter grabbed a French fry and paused with it halfway to her mouth. "Is everything okay?"

"I don't wanna talk about it."

Winter took a quick bite of her burger. "Not you, too? Why is it everyone hates me?"

Stacy sighed. "I don't hate you, Winter. Stop it. It's personal, okay? I'll tell you later."

"Fine. Whatever."

Alison plopped down beside Winter and turned to look at her expectantly.

"What?" Winter asked.

Alison bit her lip. Stacy's eyes darted from one to the other.

"What?" Winter asked again. "Am I missing something here? Spill it."

"I need to know the truth," Alison said. "I know you know."

"The truth about what?"

"Claire and Phillip."

Winter swallowed hard. "I think you know just as much as I do."

"That's a lie, something else happened. I know it. Tell her, Stacy."

Stacy pursed her lips. "I told her I'd tell her later."

"You mean something happened to you?" Winter asked. "What's going on? Why is it everyone wants to keep secrets from me?"

Alison glared at Stacy and Stacy shook her head.

"I don't care," said Alison to Stacy. "She needs to know. And she probably knows how it happened."

"But I don't want to start anything, Ali. Just drop it, okay?"

Alison ignored her and faced Winter again. "This summer, Stacy and Claire got into a fight over something. The next day, Stacy's mom got so sick she had to go to the Emergency Room. Claire called and asked how Stacy's mom was doing, *before* anyone knew that she was sick. She was gloating about it."

Winter took another hard swallow. "So? What makes you think I know anything about that?"

"You and Claire were best friends last year. How did she know when no one else did? Do you think she had something to do with it? Do you think she did a spell or something? Tell us the truth, Winter. It doesn't matter how good a friend Claire is to you, if she's been hurting people she'll hurt you too."

"Why would she hurt people? Claire wouldn't do something like that. And what makes you think it was a spell?"

"I know you two were messing around with that stuff," said

Alison. "And I bet you still are. Am I right?"

Winter frowned.

"I am, aren't I? So it's possible Claire did do a spell."

Winter huffed and looked at Stacy, now resting her forehead on the heel of one hand. "What was the fight about?"

Stacy closed her eyes and took a deep breath. "Church," she said.

"Church?"

Stacy looked up. "Yeah. I've been going to church. And I made the mistake of asking her to go with me one Sunday."

"You called her and not me?"

"Of course. You've made it quite clear to everyone that you're not interested. So I didn't bother you." Stacy shook her head. "Sorry. But Claire acted like I was stabbing her in the back, or something. I don't know what got into her."

Claire and Phillip walked into the cafeteria. All three girls turned to watch them. Claire gave them a sardonic smile.

"I've got to go," Winter said as she picked up her tray and took her half-eaten food to the trash. She heard a laugh and turned to see Claire sitting pressed up against Phillip. Winter ground her teeth and shoved her tray into the rack. Then she stormed to the table where Phillip and Claire sat.

Claire laughed again as she looked up. "Hey, Winter. Sit down."

Winter crossed her arms and glared. "How could you?"

"Whoa…what's going on?" asked Claire. Phillip looked up with a scowl.

Winter glanced over her shoulder. Alison and Stacy were watching and whispering. She turned back. "Stacy's mom, Claire? Really?"

"Hey, I didn't do anything to Stacy's mom."

"You made her sick over some stupid fight about church."

"I don't want to have anything to do with that God stuff. But I did *not* do anything."

"I don't believe you. How else would you have known? You're

crossing a line, Claire."

"Phillip's mom is a nurse…I got a text. Besides, there are rules about that sort of thing. I took an oath the other night. I may hate that stupid religion, but I'm not about to harm someone maliciously. What kind of person do you think I am?"

"I don't know anymore. What kind are you?" Winter looked around and found most of the cafeteria looking at them, including several teachers. She hadn't realized they were shouting. She took a calming breath.

Claire glanced around and then lowered her voice. "It's not like that, Winter. I wish you could believe me. I know you need someone to blame for your mom and everything…"

Winter screamed. She grabbed Claire's cafeteria tray and flung it across the room. Static filled her head and she pressed her hands to her ears. Her heart pounded. Her muscles trembled. She rushed to the nearest door, glaring at and slamming her shoulder into any student who dared to not get out of her way.

# 11

*Present Day*

Screams woke Winter in the middle of the night…the same screams that had filled her visions at the end of last year and now haunted her dreams. Winter's heart drummed in her chest when the screams reached her ears, alive and real. She groped for her lamp and snapped it on.

Kaci sat upright in her bed and flinched away from the light. She pressed her hands against her eyes and a sob escaped her mouth. "I'm sorry." Kaci's voice trembled.

Winter swung her feet to the floor. "Can I get you something?"

Kaci shook her head and fell back to her pillow.

Winter stared at Kaci's back. Her pulse calmed, replaced by a hopeless void. What if this never stopped? She sighed and eased back to her pillow. She could still hear Kaci whimpering, but there was nothing she could do. No words or consolation could fix this. Not even a summer at home with her parents had helped Kaci. This was Kaci's life now. It was Winter's life too. And Winter knew that the nights together were going to be very long.

Winter tried to relax again and find sleep. But her mind raced with the what-ifs. A million what-ifs. Any of them could have saved Kaci this pain. Eventually, she passed out from exhaustion.

The following morning, Kaci stayed close to Winter throughout their walk to the Union. She didn't talk and she didn't look up from the ground often. When it came time to separate for classes after breakfast, Kaci grabbed Winter's arm, holding her back at the foot of the Union steps.

"You'll be fine." Winter squeezed Kaci's hand.

Kaci's lips moved as if she wanted to say something, but nothing came out.

"If anything happens, just text me. I'll keep my phone where I can see it, okay?"

Kaci nodded and slowly lowered her hand to her side.

"We'll meet back here for lunch. Got it?"

Kaci nodded again.

Winter turned and left her behind, forcing herself not to look back. She hurried to the religion department for History of the Bible and Intro to Theology.

After the second class, Winter watched for Kaci while walking through the Meadow to the Union, but there was no sign of her. Winter waited for ten minutes on the steps before deciding to go on in to get her food. Moments after she sat down to eat, her phone vibrated with a text from Kaci: *Went back 2 room. Sorry.*

Winter ate quickly and rushed back to Devine. Kaci sat on her bed watching TV. She looked up when Winter walked in.

"Sorry," Kaci said. "When I got out of class…there were just too many people in the Meadow."

"Don't worry about it." Winter crossed to her desk chair and sat down. "We'll try again tomorrow. It shouldn't be as crazy."

"I'm trying."

"I know you are." Winter stood.

"Where you going?"

"I've got Self-Defense next. I just rushed over here to check on you."

"You didn't have to do that."

Winter smiled. "Yeah, I did."

Winter jogged to the Health and Fitness building, arriving just as the class was starting. She had agreed on taking Self-Defense at the urging of her dad. It turned out to be a beginner's karate class for girls. The teacher had them change into white pajama-like uniforms, and Winter reluctantly put aside her baggy clothes. She tried to keep up with the stretches and exercises, but after ten minutes she was already out of breath. The teacher watched her with a bemused smile. Winter tried to project as much loathing toward the teacher as she could.

The next day was not much better. After the first class, Kaci texted and asked if Winter would walk with her to the next class.

"Sorry," she told Peter as they exited the Religion building.

"It's fine. Go. She needs you. Maybe you can convince her that some of us could help too."

"I'm working on it." Winter bolted away to the other side of the Meadow, where Kaci stood at the top of the stairs of another building.

They walked in silence and Winter had to run back across the Meadow to her own class. This time she was late, slipping in at the back of the room beneath the stern look of the professor.

Thursday was more of the same, but easier because Kaci's classes were closer to Winter's. She took Kaci back to Devine after lunch and ran back to the Health and Fitness building.

*At least I'll be in shape soon.*

The weeks went by with gradual improvement. Kaci's good days grew more frequent, but Winter still never knew what would set Kaci off and send her fleeing back to the room to hide.

Near mid-October, Winter hobbled back to Devine after Kaci didn't show for their normal rendezvous.

"What's wrong?" Kaci asked when Winter stumbled in.

"That stupid karate class." Winter clenched her teeth to hold in her frustration with Kaci. "I want a hot shower and then I want to just crash for a while."

Kaci laughed in a stiff way that cut off abruptly. Winter wondered if it was just a show. Would she ever laugh again like she used to?

The hot shower soothed Winter's muscles and her stress. For half an hour she put Kaci out of her mind and soaked in the relaxing steam. Afterwards, she pulled on the most comfortable lounge-around clothes she could find and crashed on her bed.

A few minutes ticked by. Kaci grew still and Winter could feel her stare.

"Did you mean it?" Kaci asked.

"Mean what?"

Long silence. Winter rolled her head to the side and opened her eyes.

Kaci turned away. "That you'll find him. You said at my house that you were going to find him."

"Yes," Winter said.

"How?"

"I'm not sure."

"When?"

"I don't know that either."

Kaci stood and laid her hand on the doorknob. "Don't tell me, okay? Not until it's over."

"I won't."

Kaci nodded and left the room.

All desire to nap dashed away. Winter's adrenaline kicked in. Guilt gnawed at her like termites. What if? She had to get out of there too.

She shoved her shoes back on and left, hoping a walk would clear her head. Minutes later, she found herself standing before the bell tower again. She only watched it for a moment before impulse moved her toward the doors. She expected maybe some nudge or some flicker of premonition. But nothing came.

The busted door from last spring had been replaced and painted to match the others. She couldn't even tell which door it had been. She reached out and opened the nearest one. Only after she pushed it open did she wonder if it had been locked or not, or if somehow it had unlocked for her. Just one nudge. That's all she wanted.

Inside she paused and turned back to the door...the very door she had once tried to flee through. Winter looked at her feet to the spot where once she had crumpled to the ground. She allowed her gaze to trace a path up the aisle and to the cross hanging in front of the rows of pipes at the back of the chapel. A hint of prismed light played across portions of the walls.

Winter started walking and let her hand touch the tops of each pew. No dust. The building smelled like fresh paint and carpet cleaner. Last spring had been erased as much as possible. The chapel purified again. What was the point? It was hollow anyway.

Standing before the podium, Winter turned to look at the balcony staircase and to the old wooden door at the top.

The tower.

Her heart fluttered and she chewed the inside of her lip, wondering if she dared to return. Yes. She had to. Winter drifted up the stairs and stopped before the tower door.

The door had been chained and padlocked. Winter stared at the lock, not really thinking much about how to open it. She took the padlock in hand and tugged it against the chain. It popped open as if she had turned a key. Finally…a small nudge. The hope of it trickled into her hollow chest.

On the other side, the old wooden stairs curved up into the black. But they didn't breathe. They didn't watch her or speak to her. They were just plain stairs. She stepped and heard the familiar creak. But it was just a creak…nothing more.

Winter climbed, allowing her mind to numb against the

memories pressing in on her conscience. She climbed slowly, taking heavy breaths that had more to do with emotional weight than fatigue.

Finally she came to a door. *The* door. It stood ajar. Winter reached out and brushed the knob with her fingers. Just a knob. Warm and ordinary. She took it firmly in hand and pushed.

Winter took only a couple steps in and she sank to the floor. She couldn't take it anymore. *What if?* She took a slow breath and let her heart settle into a numb cocoon. Tears trickled down her cheeks and dripped into her lap. She leaned her head forward, hair swinging as a curtain around her face, and let them drip.

When the last had fallen, she brushed her hair behind her ears and looked to the spot on the floor where the blood had been.

Where Xaphan had stood.

Where she had almost died.

And where Kaci had been…

She looked away, blinking back more tears. "God…why? Why do you give me a friend like Kaci, and then let this happen? It's not fair. I just want…" A knot formed in her throat and she clenched her eyes. "I just want something normal for once."

"Normal's overrated," said Davis.

Winter jerked her head up in time to see him step through the door. She ground the heel of her hand into her eyes. Davis sat beside her.

"Didn't you hear?" Winter said. "Normal's the new unique." She looked at her hands and wrung them together. "What are you doing here?"

"I saw you come in. Thought I'd follow."

Winter nodded.

"So this is it?"

"Yeah. I thought maybe if I came back…"

"That maybe God would tell you something?"

Winter looked at him. "I don't know what to do. I promised I'd find him, but I…I just don't know how."

Davis looked around the room a moment. "Well, maybe you're not supposed to."

"But I promised."

"Maybe. But did you do that because God told you to?"

Winter stared at the wooden floor between her knees.

"Maybe God has something else for you to do right now. Maybe what you're supposed to do isn't what you think."

"Yeah, maybe." Winter wrenched her hands together.

Davis stood. "In any case, it's not going to do you any good to sit here and dwell on what happened." He held a hand out to her. "Come with me. I want you to check out something with me."

Winter stood with the help of his outstretched hand. Davis led her further up the stairs until they ended beneath a hatch. He pushed the hatch up and went out.

Winter emerged behind him and her eyes widened. From the top of the tower she could see the entire campus…every tree and flowerbed. Every minuscule person walking below. She lifted her eyes up and saw Cherithville further away. Turning in a circle, she traced the horizon all the way around. Miles of hills and trees stretched toward hazy obscurity in every direction.

Winter rubbed her eyes. "This is amazing. Have you been up here before?"

Davis laughed. "Yeah right. But I've always wanted to. Thanks for the excuse."

Winter shook her head and grinned. She followed Davis to the side wall.

Davis pressed on the ledge before resting his weight against it. "I'm sure if you look long enough, you'll see what you're supposed to do." He peered toward the Meadow.

Winter moved to stand beside him and followed his gaze. Kaci sat alone beneath the Ancient.

"You want something normal in your life? You're not the only one." Davis turned to her. "Maybe don't think so much about the prophet stuff. Maybe just wait on God. If he hasn't shown you what to do, then don't worry about it. It seems to me that the most important thing for you to do right now..." He cut his eyes back to Kaci. "…is helping someone else feel normal for a change. Being a prophet can wait."

Winter put an arm around Davis. She squeezed him into a side-hug. "Thank you. But it's prophetess."

Davis laughed. "I'm not saying that."

Winter shoved him, laughing too. "Yes you will." Before he could retaliate, she turned and bolted for the hatch.

"Where are you going?"

"To take your advice. Don't let it go to your head."

Winter never stopped to wait on Davis. She went straight down all the stairs and out of the chapel. Kaci still sat beneath the Ancient, reading a book. She glanced up as Winter came closer and a small smile lit behind her eyes. Winter sat with her shoulder touching Kaci's.

"What are you doing?" Kaci asked.

"Getting away from Davis."

Davis waved at them from the other side of the Meadow as he walked toward the Union.

"Um, why?"

"He's too smart for his own good. It bothers me." Winter waved back.

Kaci laughed. "Then why are you waving at him?"

"Because I don't want to hurt his feelings."

"Are you flirting with him?"

Winter froze and yanked her hand down. She turned to face Kaci. "What? No. Of course not. Besides, Summer likes him."

"She what?"

"But she won't tell anyone yet. And I think Davis likes her back, but he's pretending not to."

"How do you know?"

Winter shrugged and wiggled her fingers in Kaci's face. "I had a vision…Ooooo…"

Kaci slapped her hands away, laughing again.

"Listen, you want to help me do something?" Winter asked.

"Like what?"

"Get the two of them to start dating."

"How are we going to do that?"

Winter grinned. "I think we need to do a group outing. Maybe put them in a position so they'll figure it out."

Kaci frowned. "I don't know. What do you have in mind?"

"Oh, nothing big." Winter laid her arm around Kaci and squeezed. "Just something, you know…normal."

# 12

*Four Years Ago*

Alison met Winter at the locker, her blonde roots showing beneath her dyed black hair. "Hi." Alison slumped against the aluminum doors and twirled a finger through her hair.

"Hey." Winter emptied her backpack, shoving every textbook she had into the locker.

"Can you believe them?"

"What?"

Alison nodded to one side. Winter turned to see what she was talking about. The crowded hall parted for a moment and Winter spotted Claire and Phillip leaning against the wall a little ways down, pawing at each other and giggling.

Winter sighed. "Maybe you should just get over it."

Alison glared at her. "Get over it? Something's wrong here and I want to know what's going on. Don't you?"

"Just drop it, Ali." Winter slung her empty backpack over her right shoulder. "Come on. We're going to be late for the bus."

Alison stiffened. "Wait. Here they come."

Claire and Phillip walked by, hand in hand. Claire waved at them as she passed.

Alison fumed. "If you're not going to tell me, I'll find out for myself." She took off following Claire.

"Ali…" Winter huffed and ran after her.

Claire was already outside. Alison hit the double doors at a run. Winter had to jog to keep up. A group of departing students clogged the exit and Winter waited for them to move. Eventually she made it to the tall awning. Lines of bright yellow school buses stretched in both directions. She looked around for Alison, but couldn't see her in the crowd of students.

"Tell me what you did!" Alison shouted.

Winter turned to the voice just in time to see Alison grab Claire by the shoulder.

Claire spun on her. "What are you talking about? I didn't do anything."

Winter stayed several feet away, but close enough to hear. She crossed her arms and waited.

"I know you did something! Don't lie to me!" Alison backed away a step.

"Ali, calm down." Claire looked at Winter and Winter looked away.

Phillip snickered.

"Stay out of this, Phillip!" Alison started to cry.

"Let's just talk about this, okay?" Claire reached a hand out to Alison, but Alison shoved it away.

"Why can't you just tell me the truth? We've been friends since third grade, I deserve the truth!"

"There's nothing to tell," Claire said. "I really don't know what you're talking about."

Alison slapped her across the face. "I know what you are! You're a witch! How could you betray me like that? And the worst part about it is you won't even admit to what you did!"

Claire stepped forward and leaned into Alison's crimson face. "I didn't do anything!" She looked at Winter. "Tell her!"

Winter shook her head and walked away. Most of the buses had started their engines. A few were beginning to move. Winter searched the line for the spot where her bus could normally be found. The brake lights were on and it was inching forward. She'd have to stop the driver. She hefted the backpack more firmly on her shoulder and started to jog.

Shouting behind her, but she ignored it.

The roar of a bus engine.

A scream.

Tire squeal.

Something jolted in Winter's stomach and she turned around.

Alison lay in the middle of the road, a bus's front wheels straddling her. Claire and Phillip were gone. A crowd gathered and teachers rushed to Alison's aid. Winter ran back and pushed through the crowd.

Alison pushed herself up, shaking and gasping for air. With one arm she kept herself balanced. With the other she shoved away all the teachers.

"Leave me here!"

Winter reached out to Alison, but Alison slapped her hand away too.

Winter turned and scanned the crowd for Claire. She saw Claire glancing at the scene from between two buses briefly before she disappeared. Winter shoved through the crowd and took off running. She rounded the front of the next bus and paused at the aisle between the line of buses. She looked both ways, and then rushed forward to the next line. There she found Claire walking fast toward her bus. Phillip wasn't with her anymore. Winter ran after her.

"How could you!" She shoved Claire in the back.

Claire stumbled forward. She caught her balance and turned to face Winter. "What's wrong with you? I didn't do anything!"

"You pushed her in front of that bus!"

"No! She tripped!"

"You tried to kill her!"

"I did NOT!"

"Liar!"

Claire crossed her arms. "Is that what you saw? Did you see me push her?"

"No…I…"

"You just assumed I would try to kill someone who was my friend? Are you crazy?"

"But you're lying to her, so why wouldn't you lie to me? How do I know you didn't push her? How do I know you're telling the truth? How am I supposed to trust you now?"

"You don't trust anyone anymore! You need help!"

Winter leaned forward and shouted. "There's nothing wrong with me!"

"Look at you! You used to be my friend, why do you hate me so much?"

Winter ground her teeth. "I don't hate you, I just don't like the way you've been acting. You're a different person. I'm not sure you're my friend anymore. And Alison used to be your friend too. You've thrown all that away!"

"It's not my fault she blames me."

"Yes it is! You're out of control! First the thing with Phillip, then Stacy's mom, and now this?"

Claire shook her head. "You can't blame me for Phillip. Those spells didn't work last year, remember? We didn't know what we were doing. As for Stacy and Alison, I didn't do anything. Got it? It's Alison that's the problem. She's turning you against me by making you think all these things are my fault. But they're not, Winter. You should know that. When I tried to leave for my bus, Alison grabbed me. I pushed her away and ran off. She must have tripped while chasing me. That's what happened. Please. Believe me."

The buses started their engines again. Winter and Claire stared at each other without moving. Finally, Claire broke eye contact and ran away toward her bus.

# 13

*Present Day*

The dull sound of flesh striking flesh resounded in the old rundown house. Agent Gains's face flew sideways and he spat blood. His head rolled back to the front and he looked up with swollen eyes. The Federal Agent had been stripped of most of his clothing and was bound tightly with duct tape to an old dining chair. His breath came in ragged gasps. Another strike…more blood.

"Stop," said a cold, calculating voice.

The man who dealt the blows stopped in mid-strike. His sinewy muscles flexed beneath his old flannel shirt. Shark-like eyes, black as pitch and glinting with demented pleasure, gazed out from underneath a worn red ball cap.

The man who had issued the command to stop rose from his place in the shadows and stepped into the illumination of the safety light just outside the window. He wore a dark brown suit and his brown hair brushed his shoulders. His very presence radiated cold and evil. The man with the red hat slunk out of his way.

"Now, let's start over, shall we?" said Xaphan. He stepped closer to Agent Gains.

Gains glared at Xaphan.

"I already know where she is," Xaphan said. "I spent all last year preparing for her arrival. But what I don't know is *who* she is. The FBI changed her name and you're the primary handler. So tell me…who is she?"

"You'll never find her." Gains blinked back sweat and blood.

The man with the red hat stepped forward and backhanded him across the face.

Gains looked up and smiled, revealing bloodied teeth. He released a slow, hollow laugh. "There's nothing you can do to me to make me tell."

Xaphan nodded at the other, who snatched a gun from his back waistline and shot Gains in the thigh. The thunder seemed to press against the walls, threatening to tear the decrepit house apart.

Gains screamed as the blood gushed from his leg. He breathed heavily through his nose and clenched his teeth defiantly. "My name is Markus Gains. My rank is Senior Special Agent. My serial number is…"

Xaphan smiled and held up a hand to silence him. He reached into a pocket and pulled out a piece of paper. "Perhaps this will persuade you." He walked closer to the window and read. "141 Chestnut Avenue."

"NO!" Gains shouted.

"Plainsville, New York."

"NOOO!"

"This is where your family lives, isn't it? Perhaps I should pay them a little visit."

"Leave them alone!"

"Then tell me what I want to know. Your family is not worth the name of one little girl."

Gains snarled and bared his teeth, his eyes narrowed and his breaths settled into a calculating rhythm.

"Your wife's name is Deidra and your daughter's name is…Jessie. Oh, I bet we could have some real fun with…"

Gains hissed. "All right! I'll tell you, just leave them out of this."

Xaphan walked closer and knelt in front of the federal agent. They were eye to eye, inches from each other. "See? Every man has his price. Now talk."

Winter sat up and sucked in air as if she had been under water.

Kaci stared at her, alarm crossing her face. "What's wrong?"

Winter looked at her, sweat beading on her forehead. "A dream."

"I don't want to know." Kaci turned back to the quiet TV.

It took her a few days, but Kaci had finally relaxed enough to wear T-shirts, shorts, and no make-up while hanging out in the room. Winter's eyes traced the scar across Kaci's neck in the dim TV light.

"What time is it?" Winter asked.

"About three AM."

Winter swung her feet out of bed and reached for her cell. "I've got to make a phone call. I think something's happening."

"I said I don't want to know."

"Fine." Winter went into the hall. She scrolled through the phone book until she found Agent Gains's number. She pushed send and waited, but the call went straight to voicemail.

Winter paced the hall not knowing what to do. What if the dream had already happened? Was she too late? Her visions the year before were usually about things that had not happened yet. If that was the case now, then she could still save him. But if he wasn't answering his phone…

Agent Erickson. He could help.

Her fingers flew over the number pad. It wasn't until she pushed send that she realized she didn't know Erickson's number.

*"Erickson,"* he answered.

"Agent Erickson! It's Winter!"

*"Winter? How did you…"*

"Where's Agent Gains?"

Erickson hesitated. *"He's taking a couple weeks off at home."*

Winter's mind raced. "He's in trouble. Can you get in touch with him?"

*"Trouble? What kind of trouble? How do you know?"*

"I just do! He didn't answer his cell just now when I called. I think Xaphan has him."

Silence on the end of the line. *"He didn't answer?"*

A door cracked next to her. "Can you keep it down?"

"Sorry." Winter walked toward the stairwell. "No. He didn't answer."

*"I'm sure he's fine. I'll contact him and call you back."*

Winter sat in the stairwell and waited. What if Xaphan really did have him? What could she do about it? Would it be a repeat of what happened to Kaci? She looked at her phone impatiently. Only three minutes had passed. She took the stairs down to wander to the lobby. What was taking so long? Maybe Erickson was able to reach him. Maybe they were discussing how crazy she is. This was silly…it was just a stupid dream.

Wasn't it?

Winter grunted in frustration.

The phone rang. She fumbled with it and almost dropped it before answering.

"Hello?"

*"Winter, I'm coming to get you."* Winter could hear a siren wailing in the background.

"What? Why?"

*"I'll explain when I get there. Meet me outside your dorm."*

Her stomach tingled and she held her breath a moment. This was it…it was happening again. Could she handle it this time? "Okay…"

*"And dress comfortably. Wear black if you can."*

"I always wear black," she said softly.

*"Right. I'll be there in ten minutes."* The phone clicked and was silent. Winter turned and ran back to the room.

"What's wrong?" Kaci asked when she burst through the door.

A roulette wheel rolled through Winter's head as she tried to figure out what the cryptic phone call could mean. She was right…Xaphan had him.

"Winter?"

"Um…" She looked at Kaci and then down at her feet. "I thought you didn't want to know?"

"With the way you burst in here. I thought maybe…But you're right. Don't tell me."

Winter grabbed a black tee-shirt, black jeans, and her boots, and started changing.

"Are you leaving?" Kaci asked.

"Yeah. I have to. Sorry. Something came up. I've got to…go help someone."

Kaci frowned and looked back at the TV. "Maybe I can get some laundry done while you're gone."

Winter shoved her boots on and left, intending to tie them in the car. At the door she turned back to Kaci, but Kaci seemed to be making an effort at ignoring her. Biting her lip, she left and went back to the lobby.

Winter stood in front of Devine Hall with her arms crossed. The clear sky seemed to morph from the bright orange city lights in the west to the dark blue rural areas in the east. The air blew gently, a warm breeze with the smell of fall. She watched one stray wisp of cloud glide in front of the stars before she heard the siren. Shifting her weight to the other leg, she unfurled her arms and tried to smooth the front of her shirt that draped her petite frame. Shifting back, she crossed her arms again.

The siren grew louder, harmonizing with itself in dissonant

echoes from the walls of the various buildings. After a moment, the lights appeared around the corner of the nearest building. With the emerging lights came the roar of an overworked engine.

The speed of the black sedan frightened Winter, and she took a couple quick steps back. The car swung onto the road to Devine and the siren cut off abruptly. The car squealed to a stop.

Agent Erickson's head appeared over the roof, and he hesitated, face bathed in the alternating red and blue. Then he sprinted around the front of the car.

"Come on, let's go." Winter stepped to the passenger door.

Erickson grabbed her arm. "Wait."

"We don't have time!" Winter jerked away.

"We're not going anywhere until you tell me what you know."

Winter planted her feet. "You come screaming onto campus like someone's dying, and for all we know someone might be, and now you want to talk about it? Do you really want to do this now? We need to go!"

"What do you know? Tell me. Why did you call me?"

Winter crossed her arms and huffed. "I had a dream, okay? Xaphan has Agent Gains, or will soon. I don't know. He's going to kill him. His family may be in trouble too. And my dreams are usually right."

"I know."

Winter narrowed her eyes. "You know? What do you mean…"

"Can you find him?"

Winter studied Erickson's face. What was going on? "I thought you said you called him."

Erickson shook his head. "I didn't say that."

"Then what are you not telling me? Why were you in such a hurry to get here and now you don't want to leave?"

A flicker of movement caught the corner of Winter's eye. Winter turned back to the lobby and saw Kaci step out of the elevator with a basket of laundry.

Kaci wore a long-sleeved turtleneck again. Her hair fell like a curtain across most of her face, allowing only a small window to see her facial features. As she crossed the lobby to the laundry room, she glanced up and met Winter's eyes. Then she looked back into her basket and quickened her pace.

The despair in Kaci's eyes tore at Winter's heart. Winter fought the urge to rush in and wrap her arms around Kaci.

"Get in the car. We'll finish talking there. It's probably best we get out of sight." Erickson jerked his head around, peering into the shadows.

"No! What's going on? I told you what I know, now it's your turn. Did you talk to Gains or not? And what do you know about me?"

Erickson ground his teeth and then took a deep breath, stealing a glance at the people in the lobby. "No, I didn't. I don't know where he is. He didn't answer his cell."

"You don't know?"

He sighed. "I don't know. You were right…I think he has him. And that makes you my only lead. Can you find him or not?"

Winter bit her lip. She hated being right. "How can he do that? I mean…Gains is FBI. He can't just take someone from the FBI, can he?" The tremor in her voice surprised her. She pulled her arms tighter to her chest and shifted her feet away from the car.

Erickson shook his head. "I've spent over ten years working with Markus, and chasing this monster. And Xaphan has never ceased to take us by surprise. I've no doubt that by now he could do anything he wanted."

Winter took a step back. Over ten years? Her mind spun like tumblers in a lock.

*Click.* Ten years.

*Click.* Xaphan had said the same thing last year. *It's been over ten years getting to this point, and no child like you is going to stand in my way, understand?*

*Click.* The head resident of Carmichael after telling them about the Federal court order last year. *It's not a private university. It hasn't been for ten years.*

But it wouldn't unlock. She still needed a key.

"It's all connected." She looked at Erickson. "It's all connected, isn't it? Why's it all connected? Why ten years? What's going on? What's the key? You know, don't you?"

Agent Erickson ran a hand through his hair. "I can't answer those questions. How in the world...Never mind. We've got to go find Gains."

"Why do you want me to come? Why do you need me?" Her stomach churned and her voice squeaked. *What's wrong with me?*

"You're the only one who can help. And we should go now."

"I…I don't know. Don't you have people to do this?"

"Please," said Erickson. "Protocol says that he has to be available for contact at all times. But being out of contact for so short a time is not reason enough for investigation. Another day…maybe. But not after only an hour."

"You mean nobody's looking for him yet?"

"No. I've reported it, but they won't do anything so soon. We're the only ones that know what happened. You're the only lead I have. Once we find him, then I'll have grounds to call backup."

"I don't know. I think I've changed my mind." She looked back to the lobby to buy time to think. Ten years. What was the connection? What was the key?

She took a step toward the lobby window and peered in. A few people were hanging out watching the TV. But they seemed to be ignoring the strobing lights outside. One person even scanned the windows without focusing or even seeming to notice the car. *A loud siren and flashing lights and no one comes to investigate?* Winter's train of thought momentarily derailed in confusion. *Do they even see us?*

Kaci set her basket on the floor and sat with her back to the window. Winter thought of the fear and hopelessness on the faces of Kaci's parents when the doctor told them she might not live. She remembered the brokenness of Kaci's spirit. She wanted to be at Kaci's side right now, but she needed to keep her promise. She needed to find Xaphan…and she definitely couldn't allow what happened to Kaci to happen to someone else. This was the reason God had made her a prophetess…the reason for her gift. Only she could find Xaphan and only she could stop him.

Winter clamped her jaw and let the internal heat buildup again. *Not again, not Gains's family.* She turned, fists clenched at her sides.

Erickson's eyes widened and he took half a step back.

"All right. I'll go. But under one condition."

"What?"

"I want information. I want to know what everyone's been doing for ten years. I want to know what Xaphan is after."

Erickson frowned, then nodded. "I'll see what I can do." He opened the passenger door for her.

She jumped in while simultaneously fishing her cell from her pocket.

"What are you doing?" Erickson asked when he got behind the wheel.

"Letting someone know where I'm going." She sent Summer a text that read: *Gone 2 find xaph. Will call ltr. Tell Kac I'll b bck soon.*

# 14

"Okay, what do you want me to do?"

Agent Erickson floored the accelerator and the car barreled out of campus. "I don't know…whatever it is you do."

Winter grunted. "When did he leave to go home?"

Erickson looked at her briefly then back at the road. "This afternoon."

"Then he couldn't be far. He's probably still in Cherithville."

"I agree. And we know Xaphan hasn't gone far either. When we find Gains we'll find Xaphan."

Winter felt another surge of adrenaline at the thought of capturing Xaphan. "Do you have a map? I may be able to pinpoint the location."

"Yes, back at the office. We're almost there."

Erickson doused the lights and pulled into the parking lot of a nondescript apartment complex that housed the FBI's field office. He brought them to a jerky halt right in front of the building. When he jumped out, he drew his gun.

Winter climbed out of the car slowly. "What's wrong? Didn't you come from here?"

"Of course I did." He began moving toward the entrance.

"Then why the gun?"

He looked at her, his lips pressed firmly together. "I don't want to take chances. Come on, we need to hurry. Stay close to me."

She followed him to the door. Erickson took out his key and turned it in the locks.

"Wait here."

He opened the door and swung the gun in. Winter watched as he pivoted from corner to corner, checking for intruders. He disappeared down the hall and she stepped across the threshold. A moment later, he came back with his gun holstered. He reached past her and locked the door.

Winter walked through the living room, scanning for answers. What could she do that the FBI hadn't already done? She looked to Agent Erickson for help, but he just watched her.

"Are you doing it?" he asked.

"Doing what?"

"It."

Winter rolled her eyes. "You said something about a map."

"Right. Over here." He walked to the table.

Winter followed. Papers lay scattered all over the table. Winter scanned them for something recognizable.

"What are these?" She reached down and picked up a folder.

Erickson stepped quickly to her side and snatched it out of her hand. She only saw one word on the tab: Butterfly.

"What does 'Butterfly' mean?"

Erickson stared at her a moment. "Classified."

Winter's hands went to her hips. "Do you want me to help or not?"

"It's classified."

"It's about him, isn't it?"

He frowned at her, then nodded.

Winter narrowed her eyes. "You promised me information."

"But not that information." He gathered the papers together and shoved them into a briefcase.

"A map?"

Erickson tossed the briefcase on top of a filing cabinet and then opened the second drawer. He pulled out a folded map and brought it to the table, spreading it on the surface.

Winter scanned the color-coded street map and sighed. "I don't think this is going to help."

"What would help?"

"I don't know. I saw the entry of a house, that's all."

"Can you describe it any?"

"Yeah."

"I've got an idea." Erickson pulled out his cell and pushed in a number. "Kent, it's Erickson. Listen I need some help." He looked at her a moment. "We need to find a location, can you access infrastructure and housing demographics? Great…hold on, let me put you on speaker." He pushed a button and set the phone on the table. "Can you hear me?"

"Loud and clear. What's going on?"

"Trying to locate a suspect. We have some info on the location, that's all. We hope you can cross reference some of the details and help us narrow it down."

"I'll do my best."

"Kent, I have with me Winter Maessen. She was civilian help in Operation Olamel last spring. She's here assisting us again tonight and has the information."

"Ah, yes. I remember. The Goth girl, right?"

"That's right," said Winter. She folded her arms.

"Okay," said Kent. "So what do we know?"

"Start with Cherithville," said Erickson.

"Got it."

Erickson looked at her. "Your turn. What do you remember?"

"Um. It was an old house."

"How old? I need details to narrow it down."

Winter closed her eyes and tried to form the scene in her mind again. It came easily…one of the perks of having a photographic memory when it came to things prophecy-related. "Okay. The window is mostly boarded up. Everything seems to be made of wood."

Clicking could be heard through the speakerphone. "Okay, we're looking for a still-standing condemned house, probably pre-1950's. We'll overlay that to the map." Silence for a moment. "Several locations in the Cherithville area. Two entire neighborhoods and sixteen individual houses."

"The neighborhoods," said Erickson. "He wouldn't want neighbors."

"You mean, entire neighborhoods can be condemned?" asked Winter.

"Sometimes."

"So which one is it?"

"What else do you have?" Kent asked.

Winter closed her eyes. "There's light coming in from the boarded window. A street light."

"Either of those old neighborhoods still on an active power grid?" asked Erickson.

"Hold on…yes. Only one."

"That's it," said Erickson. "Where is it?"

Kent recited an address and Erickson wrote it down. He snatched up his phone from the table. "Come on."

Winter followed him back to the car. As soon as they were out of the parking lot he turned the strobe lights back on, but not the siren.

"It's not far. With any luck we'll be there in less than ten minutes. I'll turn the lights off when we get near so we can creep in as close as possible."

Winter nodded.

"Whatever it is you do, whatever this prophet thing is…I hope you're ready."

Winter closed her eyes and tried to relax. She opened up her thoughts and emotions to God. Tingling flooded her body. Rumbling filled her ears. And her flesh stretched tight. "I'm ready."

# 15

*Four Years Ago*

"Turn right here," the teacher said.

Winter tapped the blinker and slowed to turn.

"Not so fast."

Winter took her foot off the accelerator and pressed the brake just a little too much. The car lurched and the tires squeaked.

Alison snickered from the backseat.

Winter glared at her in the rearview mirror. "Shut up."

"You're doing just fine," said the teacher. "You just need a little more practice. Now, pull into this parking lot up here and let's give Alison a turn."

"Why do I even need to do this?" Alison asked. "I already have my license."

The teacher turned and looked at her. "You may have your license, but you're still required to pass Driver's Ed. And that means you drive when I say you drive."

"Whatever," said Alison. "It's stupid."

"Here." The teacher directed Winter to a specific parking space.

Winter managed to stop the car with no jerk at all this time. She took off her seatbelt and swapped places with Alison.

The teacher took out a clipboard and began flipping through the papers without looking up. "Why don't you take us back to the school?"

Alison rolled her eyes at Winter in the mirror. "Fine."

Winter stared out the window as the suburban streets of Trenton Hills passed by. Every time Alison spoke to her, the gnawing inside Winter's chest grew. Winter knew something was on Alison's mind, but Alison wouldn't talk about it. She just pretended everything was fine. She even pretended the incident in front of the bus had never happened. Winter looked back to the rear-view mirror and Alison's eyes darted away. The gnawing chewed a little bit more.

They arrived just before lunch and the Driver's Ed teacher dismissed them to the cafeteria a few minutes early. Alison and Winter crossed the outside space between buildings. Winter tried to walk fast enough to avoid talking. But Alison kept up, chewing her lip with unspilt words.

They reached the entrance and plodded through the empty corridor toward the ruckus of the nearby cafeteria.

Alison touched Winter's arm. "I want you to teach me."

The gnawing inside of Winter lurched. "Is that a joke? You already know how to drive."

"Witchcraft."

Winter stopped just short of the cafeteria doors and stared at Alison. She shook her head and then shoved through the doors.

"It's not what you think." Alison caught back up and joined the lunch line right behind Winter.

Winter turned in the line to face her. "And what is it you think I think?"

Alison leaned forward and lowered her voice. "That I want to hurt Claire and Phillip. That's not it at all."

"What is it then?" Winter grabbed a tray of food.

"I just want to know the truth. If she can do it, so can I. Claire did something…a spell, maybe. I just want to know what she did. I want to know how it happened."

"How is witchcraft supposed to help you find out?"

"I don't know. I just thought maybe it could help."

"It won't help." Winter recited her lunch number at the register. She left Ali behind and headed for their usual table. It was empty. Most of the cafeteria was so far.

Alison sat down across from her, eyes narrow. "Are you not telling me something?"

Winter shook her head. She couldn't take it anymore. The gnawing wouldn't stop. It was eating her alive.

Alison's eyes widened. "You know. You know and you haven't told me? What did she do?"

"Ali…"

Alison leaned forward and whispered through clenched teeth. "What did she do?"

Winter sighed and looked at her plate. "It was a test spell…a way to see if the spellbook we had actually worked."

"What kind of spell?"

"I told her not to, but she insisted. It didn't work, anyway. None of the spells did. It was just some stupid book Claire found at a bookstore. It wasn't real, so don't worry about it."

Alison leaned forward again. "What kind?"

Winter looked around, but nobody was watching. Alison continued to glare at her. There was no escape. And she couldn't stand the gnawing any longer. She had to tell. "It was a love spell."

Alison looked down. Her face turned dark red and she twisted her jaw to one side. "And you didn't stop her?"

"Ali…"

"You owe me." She looked up, jaw firmly set.

The gnawing stopped and solidified into a cold rock.

Alison slammed her fork to the table. "Did you actually think I would never find out?"

"Ali, I told you the spell didn't work. We did other spells much more important that didn't work. Phillip was cheating on you already, long before we did the spell. You know that. So this had nothing to do with the spell. It would have been only a matter of time until the same thing happened with or without the spell."

"I don't care. How could she even think a spell like that would be okay? She had her eye on Phillip, even then. That's all she wanted."

Winter shook her head. "It was a mistake. She picked the spell because it was easiest."

"Then why did she start dating Phillip so quickly? Spell or no spell, she stabbed me in the back, and I hate her!"

"I don't think it was like that. She never wanted to hurt you."

"She tried to kill me last week. Or did you forget? She pushed me in front of a bus."

Winter shook her head. "Claire said that was an accident. She said you tripped."

"And you actually believe her? It was not an accident." Alison stared at Winter until Winter looked away. "You have to teach me."

Winter took a deep breath. "Is this what you really want?"

"Are you going to teach me or not?"

"I don't really know much. It won't do you any good. Claire's the one who had the book and read about how to do everything. And the stupid book was a fake anyway. Nothing in it worked."

"I don't care. You know more than me, and Claire's told you some of what she's been doing this summer. I want to know everything you know…fake spells, where Claire's been going to learn the real stuff, the people she's learning from. Everything. You owe me."

Winter sighed and nodded. "Fine. I'll tell you."

# 16

*Present Day*

Winter stood on top of the hill with her head bowed in prayer. Below her was an abandoned street, dark with only a single safety light casting a small radiant pool. Several old shotgun houses stood on each side of the street…one or two angling strangely, partially off their foundations. Some of the roofs sagged in the middle. The street was blocked off with a barricade, the pavement cracked and uneven from years of environmental neglect.

"Let's go." Erickson stepped to her side.

"No," she said quickly, without looking up. "You wait here for backup. I need to do this alone."

"I don't think so."

Winter looked at him from under her tilted brow. "How many times have you actually seen him? Doesn't he disappear anytime you get close? In the past year I've seen him five times."

"I don't think…"

Winter held up a hand to silence him. "For whatever reason, I can get past his defenses where you can't. I'm the only one who can get close enough. And if you want to save Agent Gains, that's exactly what has to be done."

Erickson put his hands on his hips. "I don't care. You're not going down there by yourself."

Winter turned and glared at him.

"You need some kind of weapon. At least a baton…just in case. I'll be right back." The soft crunch of his shoes echoed as he stepped back.

Winter looked down at the forsaken community below, and took a deep breath. The rumbling filled her ears and saturated her limbs. She relaxed, allowing the sensation to fill her completely. "God is my weapon."

She lowered her head and started down the hill…slowly at first, but gaining speed with each passing stride. Soon she ran as fast as the wind and as silent as the darkness itself.

At the bottom of the hill she passed several houses without hesitation. The rumbling transcended the premonition from the previous year, leading her like a magnet to the steps of a half-broken house just like all the others, about a quarter of the way down the abandoned street.

A gunshot from within. She slowed and took the sagging steps carefully.

Winter eased to the door and listened. Voices argued inside. She recognized the words from her dream, playing precisely like she had heard them before. Gains had just been shot in the leg. Xaphan was reading the address.

"NOOO!" Gains shouted.

"This is where your family lives, isn't? Perhaps I should pay them a little visit."

"Leave them alone!"

"Then tell me what I want to know. Your family is not worth the name of one little girl."

Silence. Winter leaned closer to the door, straining to hear.

"Your wife's name is Deidra and your daughter's name is…Jessie. Oh, I bet we could have some real fun with…"

Gains hissed. "All right! I'll tell you, just leave them out of this."

Footsteps inside. "See? Every man has his price. Now talk."

Winter trembled as the rumbling morphed into an intense furnace. She planted her feet and shoved open the door with one hand. It swung with a loud creak. The sound echoed through the room like an irreverent moan. Time seemed to slow and the loud wooden groan lasted for minutes. Finally, the door hit the opposite wall with a hollow thud.

Xaphan spun to face her. The dim light filtered through the slatted window, highlighting his shocked expression. A figure stood in the shadows…the man with the red hat, she assumed. Agent Gains sat as she remembered…strapped in a chair and stripped of most of his clothes. His face was swollen and bloody. Blood gushed from his leg. She took a confident step forward.

"Winter!" Xaphan seethed.

"Let him go!" Winter took another defiant step into the room, muscles trembling against her instinct to run.

"You're too late. Again." Xaphan reached to the man in the shadows and came back with a gun. He pointed it at Gains and fired. The concussion numbed Winter's ears.

"NO!" she shouted and took another step. Xaphan swung his arm to her and fired again.

A hammer against her chest. The air in her lungs fled from her body as if it had been siphoned from her mouth. She fell back onto the porch, slamming her head against the old wood. Her body pressed into the boards as if filled with concrete. She clawed and slapped at the floor, her mouth open…desperate for life-giving oxygen. A thousand bricks had been piled on her chest, crushing all chances of survival. Stars speckled her vision. A tunnel stretched out before her. Gains's cries faded into obscured echoes. She flopped a hand to her chest trying to ease the pain, but it didn't help.

Something gave way. The crushing pressure disappeared. She gasped, sweet air filling her lungs and restoring her sight. The back of her head throbbed, reminding her that she was still alive. She looked down at her chest. Nothing. No blood.

An engine roared to life nearby. Xaphan…

Winter propped herself up and forced her legs beneath her. Strength returned, and she gritted her teeth through the pain and stood.

Gravel crunched nearby. She hurried down the steps and into the street. A black sports car fishtailed from the side of the house, stopping to face her. Winter planted both feet and clenched her fists.

Sirens blared in the distance. Backup was coming.

The black car revved its engine. The bright headlights flooded her body like whitewash. Winter set her jaw and waited. They would not pass…could not pass. The rumbling filled her again. Power pushed beneath her skin and out of her eyes like a liquid fire. A phantom wind rustled her hair and she smiled.

Several police vehicles topped the hill behind the car, speeding toward the deserted houses and bathing everything in red and blue. If she could only keep Xaphan here a little longer…She spread her feet for a better stance. She tried to stare past the headlights, and could just see the silhouettes of the driver and the passenger.

The engine revved again.

Erickson appeared, running toward them from behind the car. He knelt and extended his gun. "Winter! Get out of the way!"

It revved a third time, and suddenly the tires squealed and the car lurched toward her.

She clenched her teeth and squeezed her fists. They would not pass…they *could* not pass. The wind swirled around her stronger than ever.

Something flashed in her mind as the headlights raced toward her. She saw another car…another set of headlights. The car was mangled at the foot of an old tree. Flames leapt from the car windows. And there was a scream…a scream that called her name. A scream from someone dead. "WINTER! HELP ME!"

Winter took a frightened shuddering breath. Her body rattled with a pain she had not felt for years.

The black sports car barreled down upon her, and again she flashed to the memory of the other car. Her muscles seized from the searing pain. The rumbling disappeared. The wind fell silent. The black car was nearly upon her.

Winter leapt aside and the black sports car sped into the night. She lay on the ground gasping, desperately trying to shake the hellish memory away. She looked up and saw that the police cars were nearly there. Erickson ran past in the car's wake.

Then she remembered Agent Gains.

Winter stood and ran back to the house. She rushed through the open door, sliding on her knees in front of Gains. Blood saturated his stomach and oozed onto the floor below. He lifted his pale face and met her eyes, with a weak flicker of astonishment.

"How…"

She reached for the duct tape around one of his wrists and started picking at it to find the seam. "Your partner made me wear a vest. Save your strength. An ambulance is coming."

"It's too late for me," he whispered.

"No, just hang on."

"You have to keep her safe. She's the key…she's special. Promise me you'll keep her safe. He doesn't know who she is, you have to ke...ke...ke…" His body shuddered.

"Keep her safe. Got it."

"He's not alone. Others."

"Others?"

"S…Skotos. Dark magic. They could be anywhere. Don't trust anyone."

"I don't understand."

"Keep her safe. Don't let any of them find her. Promise me."

"I promise. Where is she?"

"Tish…Tish…Tish..."

"Tishbe. Okay. Who is she? Who am I looking for?"

His eyes rolled into the back of his head and his body sagged against his bonds.

Winter stood and shook him by the shoulders. "Stay with me! What's her name? AGENT GAINS! What's her name?"

His lips moved in a barely audible whisper. "Sandy…"

# 17

Winter shook him again. "Agent Gains! Agent Gains!"

Pounding feet. A vice grip on her shoulder. Winter flew backward and landed on her back.

Agent Erickson knelt in her place, barking words into a radio. He pulled out a knife and sawed at the tape.

Other men charged in. One carried a white rectangular bag. They laid Gains on the floor and two men began CPR. A third applied wires to Gains' chest.

Agent Erickson turned to her. "Wait outside."

"But…"

"Outside!"

Winter turned and crawled to her feet. More men rushed in, and she moved to let them pass. Then she ran onto the porch. A dozen unmarked cars flashed blinding blue lights into her eyes. Winter looked around for a shadow to hide in, but found no refuge. She walked beyond the flashing cars and waited. Her chin quivered and she felt prickling at the corners of her eyes. She turned to jog further away into the darkness.

"Winter, wait," said Erickson from behind.

She paused and looked back at him.

"Keep walking." He came alongside her.

"Is he…?"

Erickson sighed and nodded. "We need to get you out of here. I can contain the men who are here, all FBI. But once the locals show up, I don't want to deal with the questions of why you're here."

Winter nodded. "I can call someone."

"Did he say anything to you?"

"Xaphan?"

"No. Gains."

Winter's stomach lurched. "Why do you want to know?"

"Because he was my partner and it might be important."

"If he was your partner, do you think he kept secrets from you?"

Erickson stopped and grabbed her shoulder. "Answer me. Did he say anything?"

"Let me go." Winter shrugged away.

"Tell me!"

Winter took a step back. "What's wrong with you? Your partner just died, and this is all you care about? And would it even matter if he did? Whatever he might have said, you should already know."

Erickson stepped toward her. "He did say something, I can see it in your eyes. I need to know what it was."

"No!"

"WHAT DID HE SAY?"

Winter planted her feet and curled her hands into fists. "He said not to trust anyone."

Erickson stopped. "You think…Winter, you can trust me."

"Can I? How am I supposed to know? You know who these people are we're fighting…You know what they're capable of. How do I know you're not one of them?"

Erickson narrowed his eyes and pursed his lips. "You don't."

"Then I'm sorry. I can't trust you."

"But what he said…"

"If it's that important, then you already know. And if you don't know…then Gains didn't trust you either."

Erickson stared at her for several tense seconds. "I might could help you."

Winter crossed her arms. "No you couldn't. Your job won't allow it."

"Try me."

"What does Butterfly mean?"

Erickson looked at the ground. "I wish I could tell you. But I can't."

"You promised me information. You promised me you'd tell me what Xaphan is after. Did you lie?"

Erickson hesitated. "No."

"Then tell me. If I can trust you, tell me what I want to know."

"We have a witness." Erickson stepped closer. "We've been keeping this witness protected for a long time. That's what he wants."

"Why?"

"I don't know."

"You're lying to me."

Erickson shook his head. "I'm not. We really don't know why he wants…the witness."

"Is that the best you can do? Who is the witness?"

"I can't tell you."

"What is Butterfly?"

"I can't tell you."

Winter stuck out her jaw and tapped her foot. "If you can't tell me anything else, then I guess I shouldn't trust you."

Erickson nodded. "I understand. That's probably for the best."

More sirens sounded in the distance. Winter cocked her eyebrow and tilted her head toward them.

"The locals, and an ambulance most likely," said Erickson. "You need to go. You should be able to reach the highway pretty easy if you go that direction." He pointed down the road in the same direction that Xaphan fled.

Winter peered into the darkness.

"Winter, I want you to remember that you really can trust me. If you get into trouble, call. Don't do anything stupid. We're on the same team. I just wish I could prove that to you."

Winter shook her head, not knowing what to say.

"Go." Erickson pointed into the darkness.

Winter turned and ran. She had to cut across a couple of ditches to get to the highway. From there she watched the ambulance and several local police cars speed by, aiming for the turnoff another mile down the road. She pulled out her cell and stuck it to her ear.

*"Hello?"*

"Kaci. I need you to do me a favor."

*"What's going on?"*

Winter hesitated. "Um…I'm fine. Don't worry. I just need a ride."

*"Yeah…sure. Is anyone with you?"*

"No. I'm by myself now."

*"Okay. Where are you?"*

Winter gave her directions and hung up. She wandered down the road in the direction Kaci would be arriving from. It took another fifteen minutes before Kaci showed up. They sat in silence most of the ride back. Winter kept her arms crossed and stared out the window, trying not to think about what had just happened.

"That was a strange place to be stranded," Kaci said as they came within just a couple miles of the school.

"What time is it?"

"A little after four in the morning."

"Sorry." Everything, from the moment Agent Erickson had picked her up until the moment Kaci came for her, had only taken a little over an hour.

"No it's okay. I wasn't asleep anyway."

As they entered campus, Winter took a deep breath. "Something happened tonight. I need to talk with you. Agent Gains…"

"I don't want to know."

Winter turned from the window to look at her. "Why? He helped save your life."

"I'd rather stay out of things."

Winter shifted in the seat to swing her whole body around. "You mean, you don't care?"

"Please leave me alone, Winter."

"You can't do this. You can't ignore what's going on around you. And you promised to help me."

"Not anymore. Things have changed…I don't want to be involved."

"He's dead!"

Kaci looked at her and then back to the road, squeezing her lips. She pulled into the dorm parking lot and stopped.

"He saved your life and now he's dead…and you don't even care." Winter slung off her seatbelt, and grabbed the door handle. "But you know what hurts more than that? I need you. I need to talk because I was there when it happened. I don't care if you get involved or not. I just need you to listen to me."

Kaci's head drooped until her chin rested on her chest. "Winter, I…I can't…"

Winter shoved open the door. "Yeah…whatever." She slammed the door and headed back to her room.

She didn't bother to change. She just kicked off her shoes and collapsed.

Winter awoke sometime near lunch. Kaci was gone, probably to class. Winter showered and changed, and then walked to the cafeteria to get a take-out box. But as she crossed the Meadow, she couldn't contain the previous night's images any longer. She sagged onto a bench beneath the Ancient, her appetite displaced by pent-up aching. There was no release, no help. Erickson was right. This time she really was on her own.

Agent Gains was dead. Markus Gains. He had a family…a wife and daughter…loved ones who would never speak to him again, never hold his hand or stroke his cheek. Was he a good father? A good husband?

Tears dripped down her face.

Could she have stopped it? What would have happened if she had followed Erickson's instructions? *I should have waited.*

She stood to walk, but sagged back down, replaying the what-ifs in her mind. There was something about seeing the life drain out of a person's eyes…

"Winter?"

She glanced up. Peter was coming toward her. She looked away, hiding her face behind a curtain of hair. She pushed the ache in her chest back down and tried to dredge up the heart of stone she used to call upon so easily.

"Are you okay?" Peter grabbed her shoulder and tugged.

She turned and instinctively fell against his chest. As she wept, he rubbed her gently and just let her cry.

Maybe she didn't have to be alone after all. When Winter found her voice she told him everything.

Everything.

*Four Years Ago*

Alison picked up Winter in her mom's compact car.

"Do you know where this place is?" Alison asked.

Winter shrugged. "Sort of. I haven't really been there myself."

"But you're sure this is the place Claire goes to?"

Winter nodded. "She has…lessons…I think."

"Then we'll find it, I'm sure."

Winter directed Alison downtown to a side street that looked little more than an alley. "I think it's here."

About halfway down, an old wooden sign hung from the building. Faded letters read "The Moon and Willow" above an engraved picture of a willow tree inside the arms of a crescent moon.

Parking was limited to the sides of the street, and most of it was full. Alison found an open spot and jumped out. Winter hesitated on the passenger seat staring at the sign of The Moon and Willow.

*This is a mistake. Why did I let Alison talk me into this?*

Alison slapped the window of her door. "Come on! Let's go!"

Winter skulked out of the car, still not sure how Alison had talked her into coming here when Claire had begged all summer.

Grime clung to the edges of the cramped sidewalk and trash littered the street around a remnant of thriving stores. In addition to The Moon and Willow, there was an antique store, a children's consignment store, a fitness center that seemed to take up at least three of the old storefronts. And across the street was another small bookstore. The sign read "Beacon Books" and had a picture of a lighthouse with a cross attached to the front. Several crosses stood in the window.

Winter looked at The Moon and Willow and back to Beacon Books. It felt as if she had wandered into a mystic battle much older than herself. The two stood at odds with each other, almost as if an invisible wall rose between them in the middle of the street.

The air swirled, stirring bits of trash.

"Come ON!" Alison was already standing at the door. Winter hurried forward.

An old-fashioned spring bell rang as the door opened. The store looked older on the inside than it did on the outside. The floors were faded wood, and most of the shelves along the walls were wood as well. An old stained counter was on the right. Several wooden gondolas stood in neat horizontal rows. Soft light came from a few floor lamps, a couple of wall sconces, and several flickering candles on the check-out counter. It made her sleepy.

The strangest thing about the store was the gossamer fabric that billowed over the ceiling and draped the tops of the walls. The whole place reeked of sandalwood incense.

A moment after they entered, a middle-aged lady emerged from a back door that was covered with a beaded curtain. She wore a long dress of earthen colors, and her long reddish-gray hair flowed over her shoulders nearly to her waist. On her nose sat a very small rectangular pair of glasses, and around her neck a very pretty crystal half-moon pendant.

Winter furrowed her brow. Somehow, she thought she'd seen

this woman before.

"What can I help you with, girls?" The woman's eyes trained on Winter and didn't look away.

Then it clicked. Claire's induction ceremony.

Alison placed her hands on the counter and leaned forward. "I want to learn."

The lady looked her over with tight lips. "My name is Jean Morial. I am High Priestess and Elder here. How much are you wanting to learn? I don't often sell my wares to girls without experience."

Alison looked at Winter. "She's done spells before. She's going to help me."

Jean turned to Winter again. Her eyes narrowed. "You have? Did it go well? I suspect it did not."

Winter looked at the floor. "Not really."

Jean crossed her arms. "Two girls like you shouldn't dabble without a teacher, and I'm much too busy to take on any more novices."

"Please?" Alison said, bouncing on her heels. "We're friends with Claire. And I *need* to learn."

"Need? What's so important?"

Alison bit her lip. "I need help on my grades."

Winter looked at her, then quickly away. The movement made her head spin.

Jean watched carefully. She seemed amused and tolerant of Alison. But her scrutiny of Winter felt more…delicate.

"Well, if you're friends with Claire…*An ye harm none*, I suppose. I'll let you buy some basics. But should you have any questions, you must come ask me. Do you understand?"

Alison nodded. "Yes."

"And I'm only going to give you the most basic book of incantations, all white magic of course. That's very important. Whatever you do will return to you three-fold."

"Of course."

"I think a nice amulet is in order as well. That should give you a feel for things. If you want to learn more, you can always come back."

Alison clapped her hands and bounced again.

"I'll wait outside." Winter put a hand to her head and stepped toward the door.

"What's wrong?" asked Alison.

"I need some fresh air."

"I tend to burn the incense a little thick. Go get you some air, child." Jean stared after her.

Winter walked out, triggering the spring bell again. She stuck her hands in her pockets and shuffled back toward Alison's car. After passing the windows of The Moon and Willow, she leaned against the old brick wall.

Her head throbbed. The incense had been like breathing campfire smoke. She gazed across the street to Beacon Books.

She saw movement behind the door. It opened, and Stacy emerged with two others…a girl she didn't know but recognized from school. And Ryan. Winter shuffled her feet and looked away.

"Winter?" Stacy called.

Winter glanced back and tried to smile. Stacy rushed across the street.

"What are you doing here?"

Winter looked up at the sign of The Moon and Willow. "Alison."

Stacy frowned and nodded. "Her, too?"

Winter mimicked the frown and nod. "What about you? Shopping at that Bible store now?"

Stacy blushed and looked at the ground. "Winter…I, uh. Things have changed, Winter."

"What do you mean, changed?"

"Winter, I got saved over the summer."

"You mean you're a Christian now?"

Stacy nodded.

"How could you believe that nonsense? It's stupid!"

"Winter, it's not like that. You don't understand."

"And I suppose those are your new Christian friends over there?"

Stacy nodded. "Yeah, they go to my church."

"So you're officially replacing us? You can't be a Christian and be our friend too? Is that it?"

"Stop it! I'm still your friend, otherwise I wouldn't have come over here and left them. Do you even hear how silly you sound?"

"Well, you stopped sitting with us at lunch."

"My class got switched to a different lunch period."

Winter jutted out her chin and tapped her foot. "Who is she?"

Stacy sighed. "Her name is Madalyn. You've probably seen her at school. And that's Ryan. His dad's the youth minister."

"I know." Winter stared at Ryan. He waved at her and she looked away.

"You've met him?"

"Yeah. We've talked a few times."

"He's a really nice guy, isn't he? Even you can't say something bad about him."

"Yeah, whatever."

"Oh, here they come."

Winter looked up and saw Ryan and Madalyn crossing the street.

"Hi, Winter," Ryan said as he stepped up beside her.

Winter narrowed her eyes.

"Winter and Alison are shopping here." Stacy nodded to the Wiccan store.

Winter shook her head. "Alison is."

Ryan grinned. "Hmm…It's a free country I guess."

"Yeah," said Winter.

Ryan took a step closer to her. "Listen. Is there anything we can pray for you about?"

The question felt like a punch to her stomach. Suddenly Winter wanted to throw up. Pray? What could something as useless as prayer do for her? She looked away and tried to choke back the tears that stung the corners of her eyes. Her mom had started talking like that just before she died. She had prayed about everything.

"It's a simple question," Ryan said.

"Just leave me alone." She looked back at him, but couldn't muster up the glare she wanted.

Ryan nodded. "We'll go. But remember this, will you? There are people in this city praying for you. They pray for you by name."

Winter turned her head, letting her hair swing forward to hide the tears she could no longer hold back.

A moment later, she could hear them walking away.

The door to The Moon and Willow opened with a jingle and she looked up. Alison came out beaming with excitement. "Winter! Look at all this! I got you an amulet too!"

When Winter checked the street. Stacy, Ryan, and Madalyn were already on the other side getting into a car.

# 19

*Present Day*

Winter sat next to Peter in a booth at the Raven, waiting for Summer and Davis to arrive. She took a sip from her soda and then picked up another fried cheese stick. Peter had not asked many questions…she was grateful for that. But now he sat in complete silence, barely touching the food. What was he thinking? Did he think she was a freak? Wait…why does she care what he thinks?

When she saw Summer and Davis walking in, she nearly jumped out of her seat with relief.

Summer slid into the seat across from Winter. Her eyes flitted from Winter to Peter.

"Summer, do you want anything?" Davis asked.

She looked up at him and smiled. "Will you bring me a drink?"

"No problem." Davis left and went to the counter.

Summer looked back to Winter and furrowed her brow. "Are you okay? You sounded pretty upset on the phone."

"Yeah, I'm fine."

Summer's eyes darted back to Peter.

"It's okay," said Winter. "He knows."

Summer slumped back into the seat. Davis slid in beside Summer and passed her a soda, and Summer smiled and sat up straight.

"Listen. I've got something to talk to you about." Winter leaned forward.

"What's going on?" asked Davis.

Winter sighed and closed her eyes. She began with her dream and the call to Agent Erickson. Winter made sure to include the connection she made about the ten years, the witness Erickson spoke of, Butterfly, the fight with Kaci, and finally her confession to Peter.

Summer and Davis stared at her wide-eyed when she finished.

"Wow," Summer said.

Peter rested his elbows on the table and clasped his hands. "I know, right?"

"There's something else that we really have to discuss now," Winter said. "Just before Gains died, he told me two things. He said I need to find someone named Sandy, that she's the key to all of this, and made me promise to protect her. And he said that Xaphan's not the only one after her."

"There's someone else?" asked Davis.

Winter shrugged. "Some secret group of dark Wiccans. I don't know. But he said they could be anywhere and not to trust anyone."

Summer looked around at the other people in the Union.

"What about us?" asked Peter.

"I trust you," said Winter. "No doubt."

Peter nodded. "What else do you know about them?"

"Nothing."

"Well, that doesn't help." Davis grabbed one of the cheese sticks and took a bite. "What about this person you're supposed to protect? Is that the witness?"

"I think so. That's why I think Erickson may be okay. But I also know that not very many people knew Gains was taking some time off. I don't want to take chances."

Davis nodded. "Okay. So how do we find this person? Who is it?"

"Sandy. He told me that neither Xaphan nor Skotos knows her name. So we're ahead of them."

"Why do we need to protect her?" Peter asked.

Winter narrowed her eyes at the word *we*. "Gains said she was the key…that means she's important."

"The key to what?" asked Davis.

"I don't know." Winter took a long drink from her soda. "Maybe the key to what's been going on around here or what Xaphan's been up to. If she's the witness, then maybe she knows something that can send Xaphan to prison. I don't know. But Xaphan is looking for her. It's why he killed Gains...maybe even to stop Gains from telling me about her. He wants her for some reason. Really bad."

Peter clenched his jaw. "Well, we can't let him find her."

Summer swallowed. "Where is she?"

"Gains said she was here, but he didn't say if she was a student or a teacher. I don't even know how old she is."

"Hmm…" Davis tapped his cheek and then picked up another cheese stick.

Winter patted the table. "I think she's a student, maybe even a freshman this year, because Xaphan said he spent last year *preparing* for her."

"Maybe he was trying to get her last year, but you kept getting in the way," Summer said.

Peter nodded. "That's certainly possible. So to be safe we should consider all freshmen and sophomores. For that matter, she could be anyone in any year."

"What about the attacks the year before?" asked Davis. "Maybe he was after her then too."

"Right," said Peter. "That'll include all freshmen, sophomores, and juniors for sure. If we can figure out what triggered Xaphan to show up here in the first place, maybe it'll help narrow it down."

Summer smiled. "This should be a lot of fun."

Winter slammed a fist on the table and glared at Summer, choking back a curse word.

"Calm down, Winter," said Summer.

"Calm down? You weren't there. Gains died! And you weren't there when we pulled Kaci out of the tower! If we don't find Sandy…Do you think this is a game? He shot me last night! Would you like to see the bruise?"

Summer's face paled. "No. I…I'm sorry." Her shoulders slumped and she stared at the table.

Peter laid a hand on Winter's shoulder. "Do you remember anything else?"

Winter closed her eyes and took a deep breath. "Only that Xaphan thinks the FBI changed her name. He said Gains was her handler."

"So…is Sandy the new name or the old name?" Davis looked from Winter to Peter and back again.

Winter felt a knot form in the pit of her stomach. She sagged and let all the air in her lungs escape in a sigh. "This is impossible."

Peter straightened beside her. "It doesn't matter. Sandy's the name we have…so it's the name we look for."

Summer and Davis nodded.

Davis leaned in. "If Gains was her handler, that means Erickson may be the new handler. You said you think he can be trusted. Maybe we should try. We might can get more information from him, if you haven't completely offended him."

Winter shook her head. "No. I tried. He seems to be more tight-lipped than Gains. But there's the code word I saw on the folder. Butterfly. Erickson refused to tell me about it, too, even after Gains had died."

"Do you think Butterfly has anything to do with Sandy?" Davis grabbed the last cheese stick. He offered it to Summer, but she waved him off.

"Maybe. I don't know." Winter ran a hand through her hair.

"I don't remember there being any Sandys in our dorm last year," said Summer.

"Me either."

"But I can get a list from the dean of students."

"Really? Can you get a list of the entire student body?"

"I think so. And as far as freshmen…I have a list of all incoming freshmen girls right here." Summer unzipped her pink backpack and started digging in it. She came back with a multi-page list and laid it on the table.

Davis leaned over it. "Is that all freshmen or just the ones in Carmichael?"

"All. Their housing assignments are listed beside their names. Most are staying in Carmichael, but a few have gotten permission to stay in other dorms with upperclassmen friends or are staying off campus."

Davis cleared the table and Summer slid the list to the middle. She twisted it sideways. All four of them leaned in over it. Peter's shoulder pressed against Winter's.

Winter pointed to a name. "There's a Sandy."

Davis pointed to another. "Here's a Sandra. Could it be Sandra?"

"Maybe. Look there's another one. Are these all just first names?" Winter asked.

"Preferred names I think," said Summer.

"So it could be a first or middle name on this list," said Peter.

Summer nodded. "Yeah."

"If they changed her name, then looking for Sandy on this list does us no good." Winter looked up and twisted her mouth.

Peter met her eyes. "Maybe Sandy is the new name, though. Maybe this is the right track."

"What if Sandy is her new name, but now that someone's after her she's going by her new middle name, which we don't know?" asked Davis.

Peter pointed at him. "Or maybe Sandy is her old middle name which she didn't use, but they let her keep it as her new first name and gave her a new middle name, and now that someone's after her she's no longer using her old middle new first name and is now using her new middle name."

"Stop it, you two." Winter crossed her arms and fell back into her seat.

Summer's gaze shifted from Peter to Davis and back again. "Wait. I'm confused."

Winter huffed. "This is completely impossible…especially if she isn't using the name Sandy anymore, real or fake, middle or first."

Davis chuckled. "A little pessimistic? Maybe she actually does go by Sandy. Then it won't be impossible at all."

"Exactly. So, we can start with this list." Peter jabbed his finger on the room assignments. "And we start with that name."

Winter shook her head. "I don't think so. I've got to do this by myself. Thanks for the help, but that's as far as all of you are getting involved."

"There's no way you can do this by yourself," said Peter.

"Of course not. We're helping," said Summer.

Winter pointed at Summer. "If you had gone with me instead of Kaci, it could have been you in that tower."

Summer's face tightened.

Winter turned. "Peter, he almost killed you. And last night he didn't hesitate to shoot me."

"It doesn't matter," said Peter. "You can't do this alone."

"Summer?"

Summer relaxed. "I'm with you."

"Me too," said Davis. "We can't let what happened to Kaci happen to Sandy."

"All of you are idiots." Winter smiled. "All right, so what do we have on the list?"

Summer scanned the list of freshmen. "They're all in Carmichael.

One Sandy, two Sandras, and…what about Cassandra?"

Winter nodded. "She could be nick-named Sandy. But you said this was a list of preferred names. If she prefers Cassandra, then she wouldn't go by Sandy would she?"

"Well, I know the list is preferred first or middle names, but I don't know if these are complete names or if the girls were allowed to give shortened nicknames."

"Okay," said Winter, "one Sandy, two Sandras, and one Cassandra. Make a note of them and I'll go with you to check them out tonight."

Summer tilted her head. "What do we say?"

"I don't know…maybe just ask if they need anything and how they're adjusting."

"What about us?" asked Peter.

"Summer, how soon can you get a list of the student body?"

"It won't take long. I just have to go over there. I'm pretty sure the Student Directory is public, though. So, any of us could probably get it."

Peter's hand shot up. "I'll do it. Or at least I'll try."

"Great," said Winter. "You and Davis look it over and mark anyone that may be Sandy. Find out where they live, and maybe we can make a plan to see them all. When we run out of Sandys, we'll start with the rest of the freshman girls and go from there."

Davis sighed. "This is going to take forever."

Peter raised both hands toward him, palms up. "But not impossible, right?"

"Maybe God will help us find her quickly," said Winter.

"Or at least before Xaphan." Peter turned to her. "How will we know when we've found the right Sandy?"

Winter shrugged. "Maybe I'll get a premonition or something."

Summer grabbed the papers and stuffed them into her backpack. "And what do we do when we find her?"

Winter sighed. "I have no idea."

# 20

Winter huffed, irritated that she'd wasted an entire afternoon with Summer, visiting possible Sandys on the list without a hint of which might be the right one. All of them dead-ends.

Summer stopped in front of room 112. "This is the last one in Carmichael."

Winter narrowed her eyes. "Wait. I've been here before. I think I've met this one already." She reached out and rapped on the door. A moment later a girl answered that she recognized. "Hi…Sandy?"

"That's right. I remember you. You helped me move in." Sandy smiled.

Winter nodded. "That's right."

Summer looked at Winter and grinned.

"What's up?" asked Sandy.

"I just wanted to drop by and ask how things are going. You know…to see if you needed anything."

Sandy's brow wrinkled and the corner of her mouth lifted. "Um…everything's fine, I guess. I've got everything I need."

"Are you sure? Classes going okay? Anyone acting strange

lately?"

Sandy took a step back, frowning. "Um…well, you're being a little strange. Is something wrong?"

Winter shook her head. "No. It's just…we want to make sure everything's okay. How about midterms? Do you need help studying?"

"No. I think I can manage. Thanks."

Summer touched Winter's shoulder and stepped forward. "Well, if you need anything, I'm one of the RAs here. Just come find me, okay? My name is Summer. I'm on the third floor."

"Sure, okay." Sandy backed away and closed the door quickly.

"Well, that was awkward," said Summer. "Brilliant job, by the way."

"Shut up." Winter took off toward the lobby.

"But you knew this one. You met her on move-in day. That's something new. Did you feel anything?"

Winter huffed. "Nothing."

Summer shook her head. "What do we do next?"

Winter found an unoccupied couch and slouched down. "Let me think."

Summer sat beside her on the edge of the cushion and watched her.

Winter shook her head. "We'll just have to broaden our search."

"That may take a while."

"Yeah. But it's the best option we have right now. Either she's not a freshman or she doesn't go by the name Sandy."

"Or she lives off campus."

Winter glared at her. "One step at a time."

"Sorry."

"This is impossible."

Summer shrugged. "Maybe we'll do better with the student body list. That should cover all our options, right?"

"Yeah. Maybe. At least we've eliminated the freshmen."

Summer tilted her head. "Are you really eliminating them? Or are you just not getting anything? It seems to me there's a difference. For all we know, we may have already found the right one."

Winter rolled her eyes. "Thanks. That helps a lot. Really."

"Sorry."

"No. It's okay. I just wish I had a way to be sure." Winter grabbed a fistful of cushion and squeezed.

"Well, I'm going to put a mark by Sandy room 112. She's probably the biggest lead we've gotten, simply because you've met already."

"Yeah, I guess."

Summer smiled. "I'll keep an eye on her, okay?"

"Sure. Fine."

That weekend, Winter, Summer, Peter, and Davis met again in the Union to go over the list of possible Sandys in the entire student body.

Peter placed the list of names in the middle of the table. "There are ninety-six of them."

Winter leaned over. "How did you figure that out?"

"I printed out the entire student directory. Davis took half and I took half. We each highlighted every single possible Sandy. Then I went through it and compiled this list."

Winter set her elbows on the table and cradled her forehead in her hands. "This isn't going to work. There are too many. I think I have to see them all myself…"

"Why? Are you getting premonitions telling you it's the wrong person?" Davis asked.

Winter glared at him. "I'm getting nothing."

Davis twisted his mouth. "What do you mean, nothing?"

"It means nothing! I'm getting zero, understand? No premonition, no vision. Nothing!"

"But we can't do this otherwise."

"Don't you think I know that? It's hard enough having this stupid gift in the first place, much less when it won't even work! Now everyone's blaming me for failing? I don't feel like taking that right now." She leaned forward and pointed a finger at Davis. "So why don't you just shut your—"

"Winter…" Peter placed a hand on her shoulder.

Winter sat back and closed her eyes. She folded her arms and took a deep breath. "Sorry."

Davis shrugged. "Forget about it. With you I'm used to it. But if you're getting nothing, then you haven't found the right one."

Winter nodded. "So we need to keep looking."

"Then we need to find a way to get the addresses for all of these names," said Peter.

"How are we going to do that?" asked Summer.

Peter leaned forward. "If we get the right person on faculty to help, then they could get the housing information. Most of that information is in a single database anyway. The right person can access the database."

"I'm not sure all faculty and staff have that kind of access," said Davis. "But can we even trust any of the ones who do?"

"What about Streffield?" asked Summer. "He kind of helped us out last spring."

Winter shook her head. "I don't think he'd do this. It sounds a little crazy for me. There's just too much to explain and I doubt he'd believe it all."

"You could try," said Summer. "Maybe you could get Agent Erickson to access the records. He can go to Streffield and get what you need."

Davis grunted. "He probably doesn't even have to do that. He's probably got plenty of hackers at his disposal."

Winter shook her head again. "Gains told me not to trust anyone and that includes him. I don't want to chance it yet."

"And Streffield? Do you trust him?" asked Summer.

"I trust him, yes. But even the idea is worse. He was targeted last year and may be again. If he gets involved we might lead Xaphan straight to Sandy."

Peter frowned. "So what we need is someone completely outside the loop that Xaphan probably isn't watching."

"And who can be trusted," said Davis.

"And who won't freak out about your prophecy," said Summer.

"And who has enough authority at the school to get us the Housing info," said Peter.

Winter slowly sat up straight and widened her eyes. "I know! Why didn't I think of him before? It's perfect."

"Who?" asked Peter.

"Dr. Cook, the Dean of the Religion Department. He'll be able to access the student database and he won't freak out about me." Winter pursed her lips and nodded. "Yes. He's the one. We can trust him."

Peter nodded. "Perfect."

Davis stood. "Well, that's settled. Are we done then?"

"I suppose so," Winter said. "Why?"

"Are we still going to celebrate the end of midterms at the lake with Kaci tonight?"

"Oh yeah. What time is it?" Winter checked the time on her phone. She stood. "I need to get back. I'll see all of you tonight."

# 21

*Four Years Ago*

Winter closed the door to Alison's car and adjusted her eye mask.

"Let's go, Winter!" Alison straightened her black pointed hat and tugged down on her short black dress, then beckoned Winter toward her.

"I think your costume may be a little much," said Winter as she stepped up next to Alison.

Alison laughed and twirled, waving her fake wand in the air. The porch light flashed on her pendant. "I just want to play the part!"

Loud music boomed from the house. A few people stood on the porch talking, and shadowed bodies passed the curtained windows.

As they opened the door several people shouted, "Happy Halloween!" Alison smiled as the host of the party weaved toward them, a senior named Donny.

"Glad you could make it!" Donny shouted over the music. He looked Alison from head to toe with a gleam in his eye. "You make a very hot witch!"

Alison giggled and took Donny's arm.

Donny turned to Winter. "Wings, scary mask, and dressed all in black. What are you supposed to be?"

"A dark angel."

"Well, you can be my guardian angel anytime!" Donny stuck out his other elbow toward her. Winter rolled her eyes with disgust and pushed past him.

Alison followed her to the refreshment table, leaving Donny behind. "You need to loosen up a little."

"What if I don't feel like it?"

"Why do you have to be in such a bad mood all the time? This is a party, try to have some fun!" Alison opened a cooler at the end of the table and pulled out a beer. She handed it to Winter. "Here. This will help."

Winter took it and looked it over.

"Drink it! And when you're done with that one, get another."

Winter took a deep breath and grabbed the pull tab. Alison grabbed a can for herself and popped it open.

"Now, drink."

The odor coming out of the can smelled like moldy wheat bread. Winter took a small sip. It tasted exactly like it smelled, leaving a bitter aftertaste in her mouth.

Alison laughed. "They get better the more you drink them."

Winter held her breath and took several more deep swallows. Alison was grinning at her when she stopped.

"Feel better yet?"

Winter smiled. She could feel the alcohol sloshing in her empty stomach. Something about it tingled her skin and made her feel a little more relaxed. "Yeah. Maybe."

"Good! Then we can have some fun!"

Alison grabbed her by the hand and pulled her into the party.

Winter let herself go. She laughed and drank until her head buzzed and the room spun. Lights became brighter…sounds more intense. Everything blurred together like looking through cellophane.

She danced. She made out with some guy.

Eventually, her food-deprived stomach turned on her and she rushed to the bathroom. As she hit the floor and placed her face into the mouth of the toilet, someone came up behind her and grabbed her hair. She retched for several minutes, while the mystery person rubbed her back.

Finally, she was able to take a steady breath. "Who is that?" she croaked.

"It's Ryan."

Winter tried to laugh. "Ryan, the Christian boy?" Her tongue felt thick. She wanted to say more, but the words disappeared from her brain.

"That's right."

"What are you doing here?"

"Keeping you from giving your hair a new dye job."

Winter sat back on her calves and turned to look at him. She sniffed. "Well, thanks. But I think I could have managed to hurl without you."

Ryan crossed his arms and leaned against the bathroom counter. "I'm sure you could have."

"You don't seem the party type, Christian boy." What else did she want to say? Winter lifted a hand to her head. "Do you do a lot of drinking?"

Ryan shrugged. "No, I don't drink. Never saw the sense in it really." He pointed to his temple. "I like to think straight. I just come to the parties to take people home and to make sure no one does anything too regretful."

"Well, that sounds about right." Winter tried to stand, but teetered.

Ryan caught her and helped her to a wall. "Was it fun?"

"Was what fun?" Her face burned. A sinking numbness settled into her stomach.

"Sticking your face in a toilet and puking your guts out."

"What do you think?"

Ryan came to her side and put an arm around her. "I think it looks like an amazing time."

Winter leaned against him, and closed her eyes against the spinning room. "You should try it sometime."

"Well, if it isn't fun, then why did you do it?"

"I didn't exactly plan it."

"But you did drink, right?"

Winter took a frustrated breath. "Yeah, so?"

"Well, what did you expect to happen?"

Winter pushed away from him. She stumbled backward into a wall. "Save me the sermon, will you?"

"Fine."

Winter turned back. "What time is it?"

Ryan checked his watch. "Almost midnight."

"Where's Alison?"

Ryan pointed across the room. "She's over there, giving mouth to mouth to a senior."

"Ha, ha. Funny."

Ryan smirked. "Well, weren't you doing the same thing a little while ago?"

Winter shrugged. "Yeah, maybe."

"And did you know him?"

Winter shrugged again. "That wasn't the point."

Ryan frowned. "Then what was the point? You get drunk, make out with a stranger, and hug the toilet. What's the point in any of it?"

"I said no sermons! Go away."

Ryan shook his head. "I'll be around if you need me again."

"I won't. I'm getting Alison. I'm ready to go."

Ryan grabbed her arm. "Wait a minute. You don't want to go home with her."

Winter shrugged him off. "Why not?"

"Because she's more sloshed than you are. I'll take you home if you're ready to go."

"I don't need your help."

"Sure you do. You want to make it home alive, right?" Winter stumbled into a wall and Ryan put his arm around her again. "Come on, let's go."

Winter sighed and let him lead her out.

# 22

*Present Day*

Kaci parked in the designated gravel area. The lake stretched out before them, a perfect reflection of the evening sky. On the far shore the dark orange sun plummeted toward the trees.

Winter unbuckled her seatbelt. "Wow. This place is amazing."

"I know. We used to come here all the time as freshmen. What made you think of it?"

Winter turned to her. "Peter suggested it."

Kaci nodded. "Sounds right. He's the one that brought me for the first time…with the freshman small group."

Winter panned the shoreline. Several families sat at picnic tables. A couple of men stood on the pier, fishing.

"What do you want to do?"

Kaci smiled. A real smile. "Let's go sit on the end of the pier and watch the sunset."

Winter nodded. "Perfect."

Kaci led the way down the slope to the unrailed pier that jutted out into the water and then teed at the end. She kicked off her shoes and sat near the end of one of the arms, facing the setting sun, and played with the flower pendant around her neck.

Winter sat beside her and let her heavy boots dangle a good two feet above the water. She thought about saying something, but one look at Kaci made her stop. Kaci stared toward the horizon, a look of peace draped over her face. Winter took a deep breath and turned back to the setting sun, which colored the sky like glazed terracotta. Behind them, sluggish ripples splashed against the shore. Children laughed and screamed. The breeze caressed her cheek, sharing with her the sweet aroma of fresh water and pine.

"When I was little," Kaci said, "my dad would take me fishing all the time. And it didn't matter how much I scared the fish with my noise or how many times we came back empty-handed, he always said he was proud of me. He always smiled and said he loved me."

Winter turned to her.

"I haven't been fishing in a long time." A tear rolled down Kaci's smiling face.

"Maybe you should ask him to take you again."

Kaci shook her head. "No. I hate fishing."

"Well, I'm sure he's still proud of you. And I know he loves you very much."

Kaci's smile widened. But the tears flowed more freely. "I know."

Winter grabbed her hand. "And the same goes for me."

Kaci nodded and wiped her face with her other hand. "He taught me to pray on those trips. It was his way of getting us alone so he could teach me more about God." She laughed and looked down at her knees. "I haven't prayed in a long time."

Winter moved her hand to Kaci's back and scooted closer. "It's okay. I'm sure God understands."

"Have you ever been mad at God? I mean…screaming mad? I said some things to God this summer that I'm ashamed of. Do you think he understands that?"

Winter nodded. "I was angry at God for a very long time, since before my mom died. I blamed him for everything. But you know what I've figured out now?"

Kaci looked at her and sniffed. "What?"

"That he was never mad at me. My pain broke his heart. And through it all he stayed one step behind me, waiting for me to turn around. So, yes. I think he understands."

Kaci looked back at the horizon. "Sunsets always make me feel small, like I'll never be good enough for this amazing painting in the sky. And I know it's a gift…just for me, meant to make me feel important and loved. But it's so far away that I can never take it. It just disappears instead. And that makes me feel alone."

"Maybe you should stop thinking of it as a gift."

"What is it then?"

"A preview."

Kaci turned back to her. She chewed her bottom lip. "Is anything ever going to be like it was?"

Winter shook her head. "Not much. But it doesn't have to be bad. It's a new beginning." She pulled Kaci tight. "I'm afraid you're more on my path now. But the good news is I've been down that path already. The fact that I'm here now with you, should give you some hope. They don't come more screwed up than me."

Kaci laughed. "What do I do next?"

Footsteps on the pier made them both turn. Summer and Davis walked toward them.

Winter turned back to Kaci. "What do you do next? Just be Kaci."

Kaci smiled and nodded.

Summer slipped her shoes off next to Kaci's and plopped down beside Winter. "Hey. Cool sunset."

Davis sat next to Summer. "Where's Peter?"

Winter shrugged. "He hasn't shown up yet."

"He said he had to go to the store first," said Kaci.

"You talked with him?" asked Winter.

"Yeah. He called me before we left."

Summer scooted to the edge. "I wonder if I can touch the water." She stretched out her foot.

Davis grabbed her shoulders and shook her. Summer screamed and scrambled for Davis as she lost her balance and slid over the side. She latched onto his arm and pulled him over the edge. At the last minute, Davis twisted and grabbed the edge of the pier with both hands.

Summer splooshed into the lake.

Winter stretched out to grab Davis's hands. Kaci stood and rushed over to help him back onto the pier.

"Davis, I'm going to kill you!" said Summer.

"Nobody told me we were swimming." Peter walked toward them, carrying two plastic shopping bags.

Winter looked back to Summer. Summer had reached the ladder and was climbing up.

"Um, I think I've got a towel in my car." Davis took off running back to the parking lot.

Kaci resumed her seat. Peter sat down beside her.

"What's in the bags?" Winter asked.

Peter reached in and took out two quarts of ice cream and a box of plastic spoons. He grinned. "I thought everyone might like a snack."

"Where is he?" Summer splashed down in the middle of the pier.

"He actually went to find you a towel," said Winter.

"Maybe we should go to a picnic table," said Peter.

Kaci shook her head and swung her feet back to the middle of the pier. "No, let's stay here. Just make a circle."

Winter and Peter turned to join Kaci and Summer. Peter set out the two quarts…chocolate chip cookie dough and rocky road. He opened the box of spoons and passed them out.

Davis returned and draped a towel over Summer's shoulders.

"Why shouldn't I push you in now?" Summer asked.

"I brought you a blanket too. I'm sorry. I didn't mean for that to happen. I was just trying to scare you." His face turned darker than the sunset.

Summer smiled. "It's okay. I was thinking of jumping in anyway, though I'd have preferred to have done it on my own. Sit down." She patted the pier next to her.

Peter passed him a spoon and then scooped himself a large bite. Summer shoved Davis, laughing.

Kaci leaned toward Winter. "Thank you," she whispered.

"For what?"

Peter made a joke that Winter didn't hear. Summer and Davis laughed.

"For making me come. I needed this."

Winter nodded. "Me too."

# 23

Monday afternoon Winter went to the religion department. "I'd like to see Dr. Cook," she said to the secretary.

"Have a seat. I'll let him know." The secretary stood and went to the open door behind her. She leaned against the frame, whispering. Then returned to her desk, smiling at Winter.

Dr. Cook emerged from the back office. "Hello, Winter. Good to see you again. Come on in."

Winter slithered in and sat as quickly as she could. Dr. Cook leaned back in his chair and grinned at her.

"How are your classes?" he asked.

"Um, fine, I guess."

"What about here in the department? Professors and students treating you all right?"

Winter nodded. "Sometimes I don't even think they notice me."

Dr. Cook laughed. "That's good…I think!"

Winter smiled and settled further back into the chair. "I thought about changing my hair to fire-engine red, just to shake things up."

Dr. Cook laughed again. "I think you'd look good as a red-head.

You should try it someday."

"Really? You mean you won't kick me out?"

"It's just hair."

"Can I shave my head?"

"Well, not exactly something encouraged in the Bible, unless you're mourning or defiled."

Winter smiled. "What does the Bible say about dying your hair?"

Dr. Cook shrugged. "Nothing."

"Good."

Dr. Cook leaned forward. "You didn't really come here to chat about the finer points of Biblical salon care, did you?"

Winter looked down at her fidgeting fingers. "What do you know about the gift of prophecy?"

Dr. Cook studied her a moment. "Old Testament prophets did more than just tell the future. They gave words of wisdom, performed miracles, led armies, anointed kings, and defied kings. They were despised, feared, and respected by men. But above all, they were convinced in the sovereignty of God and his supreme control and justice over everything."

Winter twisted her mouth and stared out of the window.

"We teach a class on this, I think it's offered next spring if you're interested."

"What about the New Testament?" Winter asked.

"Well, we see the same kinds of things, but the emphasis of the writers is a little different. Certainly each of the Apostles demonstrated the characteristics of the Old Testament prophets, if not always in the future telling category. The Apostle John wrote the book of Revelation, a collection of three apocalyptic visions…the last actual prophecies recorded."

"And modern times?"

Dr. Cook narrowed his eyes, searching hers. "It is generally accepted that the gift of prophecy disappeared with the last Revelation of John. We really have no need of it now. There are some

Christian denominations, sects, cults, and other religions who still think prophecy is a viable resource. In fact, the Mormons base their doctrine on it, as well as Muslims. But it's not something I put much stock in. On the other hand, I believe some form of prophecy happens from the pulpit in every church every Sunday. Although, this is a far cry from what the Old Testament meant as prophecy." He paused and took a deep breath.

"What would it mean if the gift suddenly showed up today? I mean…the Old Testament kind."

"Why are you asking me this?"

"Please, just answer?"

Dr. Cook sighed. "The book of Revelation says there will be a surge of end-time prophets. The book of Acts says, 'In the last days your sons and daughters will prophesy. Your young men will see visions, and your old men…"

"Will dream dreams."

Dr. Cook nodded. "That's right. I suppose if true Old Testament prophecy showed up today, it would mean something extraordinary was about to happen."

"Like?"

Dr. Cook stared at her until she looked him in the eyes. He didn't flinch, and even though she wanted to she didn't either.

"Why are you here?" he asked.

Why was she here? Why had God chosen her to have this gift, to protect someone impossibly hidden, and to…to what? Save the world?

"Winter? Why did you come to see me?"

"Oh. Uh…"

Dr. Cook stood and came around the desk. He pulled the second chair in front of his desk to the side and sat facing her. He leaned forward on his elbows. "You can trust me. What's on your mind?"

Winter pursed her lips and shoved herself and the chair back a little with her foot so she could face him more directly. "I need your help."

"What's going on, Winter?

She sighed. "All that you said about prophets? I can do that. I've got that gift. I have visions and dreams, and I've made stuff…do things. I've even heard God speak."

"So you're saying you have the gift of prophecy?" He sat back in the chair.

Winter suddenly felt naked. She crossed her arms and legs. "Yeah."

"Can you prove it?"

"Well, it's not exactly something I can turn on and off."

"I'm sorry, of course. It's just a little hard to believe. I mean, I'm no cessationist, but it's wise to be cautious with these sorts of claims."

"I have friends who have seen it. They can back me up. Ask Peter or Kaci. You know them, don't you? They'll tell you."

Dr. Cook shook his head. "No, no. That won't be necessary right now. Why don't you tell me a little about what's happened to you."

For the next thirty minutes Winter told Dr. Cook how she became a Christian and how she first heard God speak.

At first Dr. Cook sat back holding his chin with his index finger and thumb. One eyebrow stayed partially raised with a skeptical glare analyzing every word Winter spoke.

She explained what happened with Jennifer Hollingsworth and Peter, and how she was able to use visions to get clues to finding Xaphan. She made sure to detail every weird thing that had happened to her, the déjà vu and premonitions, the dreams, making doors unlock, and the arrows in the bell tower.

Dr. Cook leaned forward and fired questions at her about Xaphan, most of which she couldn't answer. But he nodded all the same and urged her to continue. His eyes twinkled now. Maybe he believed her after all.

Winter ended by recapping what happened in the bell tower and about healing Kaci. Dr. Cook closed his eyes. He folded his arms and tapped one finger against his chin. Finally, he opened his eyes and spoke.

"In the Bible, prophets were called when something extraordinary was about to happen, and every prophet had to face an adversary. Samuel had to contend with Saul; Elijah with Jezebel; and John the Baptist with King Herod. But these stories were never about the prophets, nor were they about the adversaries. The stories were about that one person whom the adversary struggled to control and the prophet struggled to protect. The destinies of that one person could be beyond comprehension, and the success or failure of the prophet could change the world as a result. Samuel anointed King David – the greatest King Israel has ever known; with Elijah's help, King Ahab saved Israel from annihilation; and John the Baptist, though killed at the hands of the Adversary, paved the way for Jesus Christ—God made flesh.

"Something extraordinary is about to happen. The Bible teaches that Old Testament prophets won't return until the end times…and here you are. A prophetess. The end must be near, and somehow you are connected. Prophets bring messages and have missions…prophets protect someone or something important to God. What is your message? What is your mission? Who is your story really about, Winter? Who are you meant to protect? The answer could change the world…or end it. What do you plan to do about it?"

*The end of the world?* Winter smiled. She waited for Dr. Cook to laugh and lean back, confessing to the joke. But he didn't. He sat and stared. When he narrowed his eyes and raised an eyebrow, urging her to give an answer, Winter's pulse leaped. Her smile shrank to an awkward line.

She blinked as rapidly as her heart fluttered. "Wait…what?"

"You do have a plan, right?"

"End of the world? Are you crazy? I can't do anything about that."

"No, of course not. And the end may not even be near. You may just be a part of the sequence that leads up to the return of Christ. Either way, it's the person or people group you've been divinely assigned to protect and prophesy to, that you should be concerned with."

"I know who it is," said Winter.

Dr. Cook leaned forward on his knees again.

"That's why I need your help. That's why I came, actually. A couple weeks ago I helped to try and rescue an FBI Agent that Xaphan had captured. Before he died, he told me who Xaphan was after and told me to find her. All he said was the name Sandy. She's the one."

"Sandy who?"

"I don't know."

"Where is she?"

"Here…somewhere. That's all I know."

"Then she could be anybody."

"Right," said Winter. "That's the problem. We don't know how to look."

"And how can I help?"

"We need you to get the housing information for our list of possible Sandys."

Dr. Cook sat up. "Do you have the list?"

Winter pulled out a folded piece of paper and handed it to him. "There's ninety-six of them."

"That's a long list. What's your plan?"

"To visit them all, and maybe my prophecy thing will kick in and let me know when we've found the right one."

"Sounds reasonable. It worked for Samuel. That's basically how he found David." He nodded. "Okay."

"Okay?"

"Okay, I'll help."

Winter sagged with relief.

Dr. Cook smiled. "There's one other thing I think you should know."

Winter sat back up.

"The American Foundation for the Rights of Citizens has set up a campus student chapter."

"They can't do that!"

Dr. Cook sighed. "Oh yes, they can. Being a public university, there's not much we can do to stop it under the Constitution. They went through all the proper legal and school channels to get there. It's led by students and privately funded, so it's all legit."

Winter huffed and crossed her arms.

"Based on what you've told me, our friend Xaphan may be a driving force behind them, and I think they may be making another go at what they tried to do last year."

"But we stopped them."

"Temporarily. If they take their time and do it right, they'll probably succeed this time. It may take years, but unfortunately it's probably inevitable. We'd do better to push to have the university revert back to being private than to try to fight what's coming."

Winter opened her mouth, but Dr. Cook interrupted.

"I don't want you to worry about that. In fact, I've already taken steps. I've contacted the Christian Action Foundation, and they'll be coming in to help. If Xaphan can have his legal group, so can we."

"But maybe I can help."

"No, you let me handle this kind of stuff. You just concentrate on finding Sandy. It sounds to me like that's the most important thing anyway." He shrugged. "In the end, it may be the only thing."

# 24

*Four Years Ago*

Winter and Alison sat in Alison's living room in their pajamas, watching a movie, slippered feet propped up on the coffee table. Ali's grandmother sat in the recliner sleeping.

"Gram, wake up," Alison said.

Her grandmother stirred.

"Go to bed, Gram."

"What time is it?" asked her grandmother.

"Almost midnight. You missed the whole movie."

Gram yawned. "Okay. Well, goodnight girls." She rose and ambled down the hall.

Alison watched her Gram's slow progress until the bedroom door closed. Then she stood. "Great. I've got something fun for us to do now that she's gone."

"What is it?" asked Winter.

"Let's go to the kitchen. It's further away from Gram and Gramps's room. I don't want them to hear us."

Winter stood beside her. "Okay."

"I'll be right back." Alison padded down the hall in near complete silence. She returned with a large paper bag and something rolled under her arm. "Come on."

Winter followed Alison into the kitchen. Alison set the bag on the floor and retrieved a flashlight from a drawer. She turned out the light and sat down by the bag. Winter followed suit.

Alison pulled out two candles from the bag and lit them. Then she doused the flashlight. She reached back into the bag and removed a wooden board. The stained grains spread through it like veins. Carefully stenciled in black paint was the entire alphabet, numbers one through zero, the words yes and no, the word goodbye, and several symbols decorating it in the corners.

"A Ouija board? Are you sure about this?" asked Winter.

"Yeah, why not? It'll be fun. Hold this." Alison handed Winter the Ouija board and laid out a small circular carpet woven with the design of a pentagram. She placed the candles to either side.

Winter watched silently.

"Okay, you sit on this side."

Winter did as instructed and sat on the edge of the carpet. Alison sat across from her and their knees touched over the center. Alison took the board from Winter and placed it sideways on their knees so that they could both read the letters. Leaning back to reach the paper bag, Alison dug around in it until she retrieved a heart-shaped piece of wood with small metal casters on the bottom.

"Now what?" Winter asked.

Alison placed the indicator in the middle of the board. "Put your index and middle fingers from both hands gently on it." Alison did it as she instructed and Winter followed. "Now, let's move it in a circle and warm it up."

After moving in several circles, the girls brought the indicator to rest in the middle.

"Just clear your mind and take deep breaths. The spirits can sense the presence of the board." Alison took a deep breath and exhaled slow. "Are there any spirits here to talk with us?"

Winter closed her eyes and tried to relax, but her stomach felt like it was crawling with worms.

After a few silent minutes, the indicator moved.

"What are you doing?" Winter asked as she opened her eyes.

Alison stared at the board. "I'm not doing anything."

"I don't like this."

"It's okay. It's perfectly safe. Madam Morial and I had a lesson on using it a few days ago."

Winter bit her lip, and watched the indicator. Its movement was smooth and slow, but very deliberate. It moved to the corner to Winter's left where the word "Yes" was painted.

"Yes? What's that mean?"

"It answered my first question. There's a spirit here," said Alison.

"What do we do now?

"We talk to it." Alison took another deep breath. "Are you male?"

This time the indicator moved much faster to Alison's side and pointed to "No."

"Stop it," Winter said. "You're moving it."

"No I'm not!"

"Prove it."

Alison looked at the board. "Can you give us a sign that you're really here?"

Nothing happened.

"How did you die?"

The indicator moved to the letters, spelling out a word.

C-A-N-C-E-R.

Chills danced across Winter's skin. "This isn't funny, Ali."

Alison sighed. "Please, just keep going will you, Winter?" She sat up a little straighter and looked back to the indicator. "Will I get Phillip back?"

NO.

"Did Claire cast a spell on me?"

NO.

"Did Claire cast a spell on Phillip?"

YES.

"Is that why he broke up with me?"

The muscles in Winter's arms and legs began to tremble. "Ali, don't do this."

NO.

Alison huffed. "Then why?"

"Alison…"

Y-O-U-D-I-D. The shadows from the candlelight frolicked on the wall behind Alison as if mocking her.

Winter shook her head. "Phillip didn't break up with you, remember? You did it."

Alison ground her teeth and closed her eyes. "You go."

"I don't want to."

"Just ask it something."

A little fear flickered in Winter at the fire flashing in Alison's eyes. She sighed. "Okay…Is there a Heaven?"

YES.

"Is there a God?"

YES.

"How do you know?"

S-E-E-N-H-I-M.

"I still think you're doing this," Winter said.

Alison shook her head and glared at Winter. "When am I going to die?" Ali jerked her eyes back to the board.

"Ali!" Winter said. The shadows behind Ali paused their mimicry and swelled to cover the walls.

"WHEN?"

The indicator moved. S-O-O-N.

"How?"

S-C-R-E-A-M-I-N-G.

Gooseflesh crawled down Winter's spine and arms. All the warmth in the room fled away. The candlelight flickered and the shadows danced faster than ever. "That's enough, Ali. You've had your fun. Let's put it away."

"I'm not done yet. What's your name?" Alison asked.

M-A-R-I-E.

"That's not funny! Stop it, Ali!" Cold fingers clawed at Winter's arms. The shadows seem to reach out to the board. Whispers…like laughter. Winter trembled at the growing cold.

Alison leaned forward, her face absorbing the shadows and her eyes glinting with joy. "Are you Winter's mom?"

"STOP IT! Why are you doing this?" Winter could see her breath ghosting out of her mouth.

YES.

Something touched Winter's back. She screamed, heart plummeting into icy water. Her head buzzed with the shadowy whispers…whispers that morphed into the tone and softness of her mom's voice.

Winter grabbed the indicator and board, squeezing the smooth wood between her clammy fingers, and hurled them across the room. They flew through the air, slicing through the cold, burning through the shadows, beating against the whispers, and clattered upon the wall.

The tension in the air shattered like glass. The candles settled into peaceful flames and the shadows became nothing but shadows. Sweat broke out over Winter's skin at the sudden spike in heat. All she could hear was the throbbing of her own heartbeat.

Winter glared at Alison.

"I'm sorry," Alison whispered.

Winter ground her teeth. "If you ever do that again, I'll literally kill you."

Alison looked down to the pentagram carpet.

"Take me home. Now."

# 25

*Present Day*

Winter wandered lost in thought through the Meadow toward the Ancient, consumed in picking out a topic for her research paper due at finals. There wasn't a single one that excited her. She tugged her stocking cap down against the cold breeze.

She heard raised voices and looked up. Two girls argued near a bench beneath the Ancient. The first was Sophie from her freshman small group last year. It was Sophie who had started the uproar that got her, Summer, and Kaci kicked out of the CLC last Christmas. They suspected Sophie had been part of the conspiracy. She never seemed to like Winter anyway.

The second girl Winter recognized as Ayden, the redhead she had a vision about during check-in when she made eye contact.

Winter slowed as she approached and tried to make out what they were saying. Sophie shut up when she saw Winter coming, crossing her arms and stomping away toward the Union.

Ayden watched Sophie a moment and then turned to Winter. "What do you want?"

Winter shook her head. "Nothing. Is everything okay?"

"Why should you care?"

Winter didn't know what to say. A dozen smart-alecky comebacks bit at the back of Winter's teeth. She refused to let them out. "Well, for one, I know Sophie, and I know she's probably up to no good. And excuse me for wanting to help out a freshman."

"I certainly don't need one hypocrite to save me from another."

"Hypocrite? Are you insane? You don't even know me. What's your problem anyway?" Forget it. Let the comebacks loose.

"My problem is everyone thinking they can convert me. I thought this was a Christian school. And while I'm arguing with an atheist, lo and behold a Satanist comes to my rescue!"

"I couldn't care less about saving you. Do whatever you want. Send me a postcard from Hell. For your information I am a Christian, thanks for asking and thanks for being so judgmental, although I'm not surprised."

"You don't look like a Christian."

"And you don't look like you have any intelligence. I bet that's blonde hair hiding underneath that store-bought red."

Ayden ground her teeth and narrowed her eyes. "Why am I even wasting my time with you, freak? I have homework to do."

"Then leave. And the next time you're in trouble, I'll just walk on by."

"You think I was in trouble? I handled it just fine by myself. Honestly, why do you even get up in the morning?"

"Why don't you just shut up and give that hole in your face a chance to heal." Winter stormed away before Ayden could respond, the paper in her hand crunched in her fist.

Winter went to find Summer, intending to ask her opinion about the research topic. But as she walked, her blood continued to boil. She couldn't get her mind off Ayden. Summer waited for her in the lobby of Carmichael. Winter slammed the list onto the table, sat down in a huff, and crossed her arms.

Summer widened her eyes. "What's wrong?"

"Just some stupid freshman."

"Who?"

"Ayden. Do you know her? She called me a Satanist, and I was trying to help her!"

Summer rolled her eyes and shook her head. "Ayden's…a little like you. She's on my floor."

"What's that supposed to mean?"

"She can have an attitude sometimes."

"I don't have an…" Winter took a deep breath. "Sorry."

Summer giggled. "Well, at least you're getting a little better. So what was going on with Ayden?"

"I don't know. She and Sophie were arguing by the Ancient. When I walked up, Sophie left and Ayden turned on me."

"Look over there," Summer said and nodded to the entrance.

Winter turned as Ayden walked in. Ayden looked at her and then to Summer. Her shoulders dropped.

Summer waved her over. "I hear you've met my friend Winter…well, here she is again. I think you two crossed paths during check-in, too. We were roommates last year."

Winter tried to smile, but it felt like barring her teeth.

Ayden sighed. "Yeah, I remember. Freaked me out a little. Listen, I'm sorry for earlier." She sat down. "I tend to lose control sometimes."

"I understand completely," said Winter. "I'm sorry too."

"So what was going on?" Summer asked.

"Sophie wanted me to join some AFRC student chapter. I told her no and that I didn't want to get involved. She proceeded to argue with me, and I proceeded to rip her a new one. That's when Winter showed up…so I shared some of that love with her."

"Thanks," said Winter. "And for the record, I don't think you're blonde."

Ayden smiled. "And I suppose I don't think you're a Satanist, even though you look like one."

"I didn't know we have an AFRC student chapter now," said Summer.

Winter nodded. "Yeah. Dr. Cook told me a little about it."

Ayden stood. "Listen, I'd love to join your little party here, but I've got homework to do."

"Wait," said Winter. "You said outside that Sophie was an atheist, right?"

"Well, that makes sense with the AFRC," said Summer.

"But why did she want you to join, Ayden?" said Winter. "Are you an atheist too?"

Ayden shook her head. "I'm agnostic."

Winter raised an eyebrow. "Really?"

"Before you get any fancy Christian ideas, I don't want any of it. Okay? I don't need saving."

"Oh it's not that," said Winter.

"Then what is it?"

"Agnostic means you have no opinion, right?"

Ayden nodded. "That's right."

"I was just wondering when you thought you might make up your mind."

Ayden narrowed her eyes. "I'm not a bad person, so drop it. You believe what you want, and I'll believe what I want. Got it?"

Winter stared at her a moment, trying to force the brief vision she had at the beginning of the semester to repeat. Why hadn't it happened again? She shook her head. "Fine."

Ayden rolled her eyes and walked away.

Winter turned back to the crumpled list and smoothed it out on the table.

"Ayden's okay once you get to know her," said Summer.

"Yeah, sure. Whatever. I need your help."

Summer leaned over the list. "What is this?"

"Help me pick out a topic for my research paper."

"You haven't started yet? There are only three weeks left."

"Shut up. I know."

With research papers due and finals looming, the next couple of weeks flew by without Winter having the chance to give much thought to the list of possible Sandys.

"Maybe we should just give up and wait for the right Sandy to find us," said Summer as they walked toward the Union.

"No," said Winter. "I don't think it's going to work like that. This is my responsibility. I have to find her myself. She's not going to come to me. And I have to find her before Xaphan does."

"But we've only seen four."

"So? The right Sandy may be the next one. Look, I know it's been busy. But after finals we should be able to get to most of them during the break." Winter climbed the Union steps and went in.

"Looks like they beat us here," said Summer.

Winter followed Summer's gaze to the couch where Kaci and Peter sat laughing. A little flame of jealousy sprung up. She tamped it down and adjusted the shoulder strap of her backpack.

"Come on. Time to study." Winter led Summer to join the others. Winter sat beside Kaci and opened her backpack. Summer took a seat in the chair just to the right.

Peter leaned forward. "Where do you want to start, Winter?"

Kaci's head pivoted between Winter and Peter.

Winter felt the stirring again. She bit her lip, not sure what to do about it. "Um. Kaci, let's trade places, okay? That way you can be next to Summer, since you two will be working on Chemistry. And Peter and I can work on New Testament together."

Kaci looked at Peter and nodded. "Sure.".

A pang of guilt twinged in Winter's gut as Kaci grabbed her books and stood. Winter bit her lip and scooted over to take her place next to Peter.

"Do you have your study guide?" Peter asked.

Winter nodded and pulled it from her backpack. She stole a glance at Summer and Kaci, who were already comparing notes.

"Do you want me to call it out to you?"

Winter turned back. "Um, yeah. Sure."

Peter scanned the study guide. When he looked up, his gaze focused beyond Winter. A glimmer passed through his eyes. He went back to the study guide and opened his mouth to begin.

"No, wait," Winter said.

"What's wrong?"

"I, uh..." The flicker ignited again and the guilt surged like a crashing wave. A small premonition told her she should probably leave. "I forgot something. I've got to go back to my room real quick. Sorry."

Peter's mouth twisted. "Okay...well, I guess I'll be right here then."

Kaci leaned toward him. "You can call out our questions."

Peter smiled.

Winter sighed and stood. "I'll be back in a few minutes." She slipped into her black trench coat and rushed away. The others were laughing behind her as if they didn't even notice she had left.

As Winter came to the edge of the study area, she saw Sophie leaving the counter of the Grill, to-go bag in hand. The base of Winter's skull tingled.

Sophie walked out the door. Winter hurried after her. At the top of the steps, Winter found Sophie crossing the Meadow. Winter followed, not bothering to hide. She casually walked several paces behind Sophie. Sophie glanced over her shoulder once and quickened her pace. Winter didn't make a show of trying to keep up, so long as Sophie stayed within sight.

Beneath the Ancient, Sophie turned on her. "What do you want?"

Winter stopped. "Nothing. I…"

"Stop following me."

"What makes you think I'm following you?"

"What else would you be doing?"

Winter crossed her arms and glared. "It's not what you think."

"It doesn't matter. Stop it. Stop everything."

"Everything?" Winter's stomach fluttered.

Sophie looked around. "They know what you're doing."

"They?"

Sophie's face paled and her gaze darted around the Meadow.

Winter looked around too. A man walked nearby, coat collar high against his face. Her eyes connected with his. Was he watching? A girl sat on the steps of Ingram Hall. She turned her head away the moment Winter spotted her. Winter looked the other way. A man sat on a bench. Their eyes locked. He pulled a newspaper up.

"What's going on?" Winter turned back to Sophie.

But Sophie was gone.

Winter ran back to the Union, lungs aching in the frigid air. She could feel eyes watching her from every direction. She didn't stop until she was back in front of Kaci, Peter, and Summer. The flicker deep within spared a brief moment to notice just how close Peter sat next to Kaci now.

Peter looked up at her, his laughter dying away. "What's wrong?"

Summer and Kaci looked at her, waiting.

Winter glanced around. Was that man in the booth watching too? Or that old guy in the corner? "Um…I think we're being watched."

Kaci's face went white.

Peter stood. "Watched?" He looked around. "By who?"

"They know," said Winter. "Sophie said they know what we're doing."

"Who's they?"

Kaci bit her lip and stared at the floor.

"Isn't it obvious?" Winter stepped closer and leaned in to whisper. "Skotos."

"Here?" asked Peter.

Winter nodded.

"Maybe we should go back to Devine or Carmichael," said Summer.

"I agree," said Kaci.

Winter chanced another look around the Union. But she saw nothing suspicious this time. Could it have been her imagination? Was she just being paranoid? "Yeah. Let's go just in case."

# 27

The branches clawed at her arms, ripping minuscule cuts into her flesh. She pushed through and continued to pound her feet against the ground. Her muscles ached, and with each step her shin seemed to jam into her kneecap. Every agonizing stride made her heart pound more fierce, made sweat seep through her pores.

She could feel hunting eyes on her back.

Rain fell in torrents, ghosting sideways in the open spaces and cascading into her face from the tree branches. Her hair clung like a wet towel to her cheeks and her clothes felt glued to her skin.

"Where are you going?" asked the girl next to her. Winter turned her head without breaking pace.

The girl's face was blurred and distorted…a shadow of reality. Winter caught her breath. *Was this real?*

"I don't know!" she said. That's what she was supposed to say. The premonition unfolded before her like a map, but the destination was not included. Her voice sounded hollow and distant, smothered by the clatter of the rain.

Lightning flashed, thunder rolled.

"I'm scared!" Summer said. Winter turned to her and could see her face clearly. Another person ran beside Summer…a man. The shadowy face seemed somewhat familiar, but was just nondescript enough to be unrecognizable. *Who is that?*

Thunder rolled again, but this time without lightning. A tree branch just in front of them exploded.

"He's coming!" shouted the distorted girl's face.

"We need to hide!" said the shadowy man. The voice definitely sounded familiar.

They came to a small ledge and slid down an embankment of scree. The wind picked up and swirled the rain around them like a mini water-spout, carrying with it the faint sound of maniacal laughter. Lightning cracked open the sky, revealing a cliff looming before them.

Summer sobbed.

"Now what? You got us into this! This is your fault…your stupid vision!" said the distorted girl. "Change it, if you really are some kind of prophetess!"

"Can you actually change it?" asked the shadowy man.

Winter looked around frantically. Nothing…nowhere to hide.

*Could* she change the vision?

And if she could change it here, does that mean she could change the actual event? Would it even become an actual event?

"Hurry!" shouted Summer. "Change the dream! He's coming! Get us out of here!"

"The tree!" Winter pointed to an old half-dead oak that had materialized fifty feet away. *Did I do that?*

Silence. Suddenly. As if all sound had been sucked away. The rain and wind paused, frozen in midair.

Winter slid to a stop and looked around…her three companions were gone.

A little girl stepped out from behind the old oak tree. She opened her mouth and formed words, but Winter heard nothing. Had she seen this girl before?

"What?" Winter asked, but the words seemed to be absorbed by the air, snatched away like the rest of the sounds.

The ground below heaved and rolled. Light materialized from behind the tree. Winter fell to the ground as the earth gave a violent lurch. The light grew to a blinding intensity, leaving only the dark silhouettes of the tree and girl.

The cliff was gone. The ground was gone. Only light remained. Light…and the shadows of the tree and the girl.

"Who are you?" Winter screamed. "WHO ARE YOU?"

"Help me," the girl whispered, but the delicate voice roared in Winter's ears.

Winter covered her face from the brightness with her arms.

"Help me," thundered the girl with another whisper. "What are you waiting for?"

The light surrounded Winter and consumed her.

"Help me!"

The light penetrated her mind and soul, piercing through her flesh and searing her eyes, becoming…

…sunlight streaming through her window. Winter opened her eyes and blinked. She took a moment to catch her breath. She jumped out of bed to get a pen and notebook, and began to write…recording the dream. Details came clearly the more she wrote and thought.

"There must be something here about Sandy." Winter sighed. Waiting? Didn't the girl realize she was trying?

She looked at her clock – 6:30. With an aggravated huff, she threw her notebook back onto the desk.

Kaci grunted in her sleep, and rolled over.

Winter laid her face in her palms, letting her disheveled black hair fall across her hands. After a few minutes, she rose and went to shower. First day of finals. Maybe she could get a little more studying in before her exam later that day.

*Four Years Ago*

Winter drifted down the crowded hall on her way toward English, staring at the floor and mostly oblivious to how many people she bumped into. Or at least, she didn't care. The amulet Alison had bought for her at The Moon and Willow hung around her neck. She twisted the dark amber crystal between the finger and thumb of one hand, and held her books close with the other.

Had it been almost six months already? It felt like the hole in her heart still bled fresh. Every mention of her mom resulted in ripping her soul a little further from her body.

And that night at Alison's with the Ouija board…

She twisted the amulet again. Was there a way? Could it be possible? Maybe Claire and Alison had the right idea of things. Maybe she should go talk to Madam Morial. Maybe…just maybe…there was a way to really talk with her mom just one more time.

The low din of hallway confusion crescendoed into a near frenzy. The crowd roiled around her, surging forward. Someone crashed into her and she nearly lost her books.

Winter knew what was happening without being told. Fight. Everyone always wanted to see a fight.

She joined the surging crowd, pushing forward, caught up in the collective curiosity. When she reached the central knot of people, she put a hand on someone's shoulder and tried to stand on her toes but couldn't see past the protruding heads. She fell back onto her heels.

A shoulder bumped into hers. Stacy.

"Who is it?" Winter asked.

"Claire and Alison."

Energy coursed through Winter. She strained on her toes again, stretching her neck to see. She could barely make out Claire's and Alison's heads just a few feet away in a small clearing. Winter shoved the person in front of her, and forced her way through.

Stacy grabbed her arm. "Winter, no!"

Winter shook her off. She shoved two more people to the side. She expected more resistance, but to her surprise everybody seemed more than willing to get out of her way.

"It doesn't take much to figure it out!" Claire shouted. "Did you honestly think you could trick Madam Morial? She sees right through you. She knows what you've been doing. And now we all know. Just when I thought we were becoming friends again, too. How could you?"

"You sold me out!"

"I did not!"

"Now I can't study anymore!" Alison lurched toward Claire.

Claire shoved her back. "I don't care, you've crossed a line. You broke the rules!"

Alison's face glowed red from sweat and tears. Her hair hung in clumpy strands. "What's wrong with you? Why do you hate me so much?"

"I don't hate you, but what you're doing is dangerous. It's wrong."

"But it's your fault! You're the one who found my books. You're the one who told her!"

"I didn't have to tell her, she already knew! She's been watching you from the beginning. She doesn't do black magic. She could tell. She could smell it on you. We all could!"

Alison stepped closer to Claire. "Maybe I'll use some of it on you."

"Stop it!" Winter screamed.

The jeering crowd hushed. Claire and Alison turned to her, mouths still hanging open.

Winter stepped between them and faced Alison. "Black magic? You've got to stop this right now!"

"But you don't understand. It's the only way…"

"The only way to do what? Get back at Claire?" Winter put her hands on her hips. "You need to get over yourself and realize that it's not her fault you lost Phillip…it's yours!"

"But she…"

"It doesn't matter what she tried to do. It didn't work. I want this to be over with. You're done, do you hear me? Done with this! No amount of witchcraft is going to get you what you want, it's only going to get more people hurt."

"Winter, it's not like that." Alison's red face blanched.

"Really? Because that's all you've been talking about. It's all about Alison and what she wants. You don't care about anyone else, do you? You used me! Black magic? Seriously? I can't believe you!"

"I…" Alison's voice trembled and she covered her mouth.

Winter leaned into her face. "What?"

Alison turned and ran through the crowd. Everyone let her pass in silence.

Winter spun to face Claire. As soon as she did, the smirk on Claire's face fell away. "And you!"

"I didn't do anything."

"You started all of this. You were the first. It was your idea to get involved in this garbage!"

"I don't care what you think…"

"It doesn't matter what I think or what you think. You've lost all of your best friends because of this. How much more are you willing to lose?"

"I haven't…"

"You've lost Alison, and Stacy's a Jesus Freak now. And do you really think Phillip's going to stick around to be friends once he's done screwing you?"

"Winter…"

"No! He'll move on to the next slut in line and you'll be tossed aside like Ali!"

Claire pursed her lips and looked at the floor.

"And you'll have lost everybody."

Claire looked up. "What about you?"

Winter crossed her arms. "Do you really want me to answer that?"

Claire looked back down and her chin started to quiver.

"What's more important? Witchcraft or your friends?"

Claire turned and ran away.

Winter panned around. Everybody who had moments ago been watching, somehow managed to avoid eye contact. The crowd dissolved away, flowing around Winter like a current around a boulder.

A teacher appeared at her side. "What's going on?"

Winter shook her head. "Nothing. I ended it." The corners of Winter's eyes prickled. She grabbed the amulet and twisted it. Her soul split just a little. "I ended everything."

# 29

*Present Day*

A few days later, Winter sat alone in the Union trying to finish her sandwich. She couldn't get her mind off Sophie. Or Skotos. She was missing something. Something staring her right in the face. What was it? She should be worried about her last two finals…but she just couldn't concentrate.

Why wasn't she having more visions or premonitions? Was something wrong?

Winter shook her head. Things were definitely different this year. She sighed and took another bite.

"Mind if I join you?"

Peter's voice made her jump. She looked up at him and nodded.

He slid into the seat opposite her. "You look deep in thought."

She shrugged. "Still thinking about the other day."

"A little paranoid then?" Peter smiled.

"No. I just feel like I'm missing something obvious. Like I've been handed this huge clue and I'm just too stupid to figure it out."

"Well, maybe I can help."

Winter shook her head. "I doubt it."

"What's bothering you? What do you know about it? Start there."

Winter took a deep breath. "Sophie said Skotos is watching us."

"Who's Skotos? You didn't bother to tell me the other day. And I didn't want to pursue it because of Kaci."

"Right. Sorry. All I know is what Agent Gains said before he died. He called them 'dark magic' and said they could be anywhere or anybody…not to trust anyone."

Peter nodded. "Makes sense with what Sophie said, right?"

"Yeah. Skotos is watching us and we don't know who they are."

"Did Agent Gains say anything else?"

Winter thought for a moment. "Only that Skotos was after Sandy too."

"Skotos and Xaphan, both?"

"Right. Or together. I'm not sure. I'm not sure about anything anymore." She pounded her fist onto the table. "What am I missing? It's right there. Right in front of me but I just can't see it." She grunted.

Peter pursed his lips. "Hmm…What do we know about Sophie? What does she have to do with Skotos?"

Winter shook her head. "I don't know. I mean, we suspected she was involved somehow last year but there was never anything solid. She was just really hateful. I thought maybe it was just me. But now…"

"Now you at least know she's involved, right?"

"I suppose." Winter jiggled her straw and made it squeak. "She must be involved with Skotos somehow."

"But why would she warn you?"

Winter shrugged. "I don't know. I just don't get it. It's right there…and I don't understand."

Peter leaned back. "I'm sorry I can't be more help. I'm sure God will give you something to help when it's time."

Winter shook her head and checked her watch. "I've got an exam in a few minutes. I need to be going so I can cram before the proctor gets there."

Peter nodded. "Before you go, there's something I wanted to ask you. It's actually why I sat with you."

Winter crossed her arms, hoping to play off the flush creeping through her cheeks. "What?"

"How's Kaci? I mean…really?"

All the warmth in her cheeks crashed down into her stomach like ice. She looked at the tabletop. "The same, mostly. She goes to her classes and then comes back to the room. Usually she eats there, but sometimes she goes to the Union when it's not crowded. She doesn't talk much about things."

Peter furrowed his brow.

"Why?"

"I had a class with her this term," Peter said. "We talked sometimes."

Winter nodded. "I know. She tells me about it. One of the only things that she smiles about, actually."

Peter rubbed a hand through his hair. "Well, that's promising. I was thinking of asking her out."

"If it were the Kaci from last year I would say you two are perfect for each other, I guess."

"So you think I should?"

Winter tilted her head. "She's pretty messed up, you know."

"I know. Detective Fox told me what they did to her. But I don't care about that. I know the real Kaci's still in there somewhere. I can see it when we talk."

Winter slowly nodded. "It'd probably be good for her. But she won't agree to it."

"But I can at least try, right?"

Winter shrugged. "As long as you realize how fragile she is. Don't be pushy."

"I won't."

"I mean it," Winter said. "Hurt her and you'll see what I'm capable of."

Peter looked unblinking into her eyes. "I promise I won't do anything that will hurt her."

"Fine. Maybe it'll work out." She stood, putting more force into pushing back her chair than she intended. The chair crashed over.

"I'll get it." Peter stood and reached for the chair.

"No. Let me do it." Winter rubbed her face and bent down. Heat crept into her neck and face. She wanted to run away and hide.

"It's okay, let me."

"I said no!" Winter flung the chair back up and shoved it against the table. She spun and rushed away.

# 30

As Winter sat in World Lit, agonizing over the questions, she said a prayer asking for that sporadic photographic memory to kick in. Most everything she managed to recall. But on the last question Winter drew a blank. She stared at it, trying to force the answer to rise to the surface of her brain.

She mumbled the question, hoping that adding her voice to the equation could help. "Explain how the voice and tense of the above passage helps to create mood and to further define the main character."

She ran her fingers through her hair and shook her head. *The last question of the last final on the last day of the week. Why did this have to happen now? What's wrong with me? I studied this!*

She strained her eyes toward the words on the page, holding back the blink reflex and trying to make the answer materialize by force. Her vision began to tunnel as she stared. The words on the paper blanked out. The tunneling continued until she was blind. Still no answer. No premonition. No divine revelation. No blasted photographic memory help. Nothing.

The blankness in her eyes engulfed her whole body. She fell through ivory space, wrapped in muted warmth. She tried to blink it away and return to the exam, but cool light had replaced the blankness. She could see depth and height. She wasn't in the exam room anymore. Winter reached out her hands to steady herself, but the viscous expanse flowed through her fingers like milk.

Then her feet landed on something solid. The ivory gel cracked and powdered away like dust.

And she was in the Union.

Screams. Shouts. People running and crashing through chairs. Dead bodies lay everywhere. On the floor. Slumped over tables. Blood pooled, dripped.

She covered her mouth and stepped back.

A man rounded the corner with a shotgun.

Winter turned to join the fleeing survivors, and tripped over a dead body. She twisted as she fell, slamming to her back.

The man stepped over her. Silver and black mask. He tilted his head and swung the gun into her face. "You can't stop me."

He lifted the gun, took aim, and shot. A garbled scream echoed through the rafters and choked to nothing. Then the man in the silver and black mask walked away.

Winter turned her head to watch him, paralyzed on the ground. The building began to shake. The man disappeared in a twirl of smoke and the bodies dissolved into dust. She lay on the ground alone now in the Union. No more shaking. Just emptiness and silence. The stillness of the building was overwhelming, as if the walls themselves were holding their breath.

She pushed herself up to her knees and looked around. Her mind throbbed. Her whole body numbed. Her mouth hung open, teeth chattering like the rest of her body. She didn't know what to do. Was it a vision? Was it a warning? A child laughed and the laughter echoed all around.

Winter stood, pushing through the weakness of her legs. "Hello?" Her voice came out high and cracked.

A flash of golden brown hair passed by a corner further inside the building.

Winter shuffled her feet in that direction. The premonition ignited…a sweet life-saving premonition. It restored some strength to her body and she started jogging.

The child laughed again.

Winter rounded the corner and stared into an abnormally long hall. It grew forward as she watched. A small girl waited at the other end and took off around the next corner the moment Winter saw her.

"Hey! Wait!" Winter ran down the hall, pushing to cover ground faster than the hall could expand.

The child laughed, the voice echoing all around. "Let's play hide and seek!"

Winter reached the end of the hall and turned, only to see golden brown hair flash around the next corner.

"Can you find me?" More laughter.

"Wait!" Winter rushed to the next corner but the girl was already gone. "Where are you?" Her voice reverberated down the hall, returning hollow. She cupped her hands to her mouth. "Where are you?"

A quiet voice spoke from behind. "Right next to you, silly."

Winter jumped and spun ...

Into the barrel of a gun. Xaphan pressed it against her forehead.

"I'm done with you." Xaphan squeezed the trigger.

The explosion compressed all sides of her head like a vice. She flew backward through the air.

And slammed back into the classroom. Winter jolted upright and dropped her pen. She blinked and wiped the sweat from her forehead.

The professor looked up, eyeing her. "Thirty minutes," he said.

Winter reached over and retrieved the pen. She looked back at her final question and started writing, filling out the now obvious answer while she tried to process the most horrifying vision she had ever had.

# 31

Winter wandered out of the test feeling worn and shaky. She stood at the top of the steps and looked out over the Meadow. Was anyone safe?

*You can't stop me.*

Winter pulled her trench coat tight and took the shortest route back to Devine Hall. Every small movement made her jerk her head to investigate. Every small sound made her jump.

The bodies. So many bodies.

When Devine Hall came into view, she sped up, nearly jogging. She took the side entrance to avoid the lobby. As she climbed the stairs to the fifth floor, for a moment she thought she heard the little girl's laughter. Winter stopped and listened, waiting for more. There was nothing but the pounding of her heart. She rushed up the remaining steps and found her room.

"So, how was the test?" Kaci smiled up at her from where she sat on her bed watching TV.

Winter closed the door and slumped across the room. She tossed her coat and stocking cap onto her bed and crashed into her papasan chair. "Good enough. I had a pretty intense vision near the end. It really freaked me out."

Kaci stared at her.

Winter put a hand to her forehead and closed her eyes. "Will you let me tell you about it? I really need to get this out. I promise I'll keep it sort of tame."

Kaci bit her lip and looked at the floor. "Winter…I want to help you. I really do. It's just…"

Winter looked the TV and sighed. "I understand. I'll just call Davis or Summer. Or Peter."

"Maybe you can tell me about it later?"

Winter nodded. "Sure. Just tell me when."

Kaci stood. "I guess we should start getting ready then."

"For what?"

"The CLC Christmas party, remember?"

Winter groaned. "I was kind of hoping you wouldn't want to go, so I'd have an excuse again. It was kinda nice skipping the mid-term party this year."

Kaci chuckled and brushed the hair behind her ear. Her face reddened a little.

Winter sat up, eyeing her. "Wait, is this a date?"

"No!"

Winter grinned. "Then what's going on?"

Kaci hesitated. "Peter asked if I was going."

"Oh. So it is sort of a date." That strange flicker returned. Winter sank a little lower in the chair. She crossed her arms and looked away.

"You don't seem surprised."

"Well…he keeps asking me about you."

"I think he likes me," Kaci said, her voice soft and sad.

"He's a good guy."

"I know."

"So do you like him too? I mean, is this something you're going to try?"

"I don't know if I can," said Kaci. "I don't know if I can return those kinds of feelings back to him. But…it's Peter. He's always been a good friend. And he doesn't seem to be bothered about what happened. He deserves so much better than me."

"For what it's worth, I think you're way out of his league."

Kaci laughed. "Whatever."

Winter made herself look back and smile. She'd do the right thing for Kaci regardless of that little flicker. "Give him a chance. Rather, give yourself a chance. Peter's asked me about you, because he understands what you're going through. He won't push you."

"I know."

"Will you try, then?"

Kaci nodded. "I'll at least try to try."

"Good enough." Winter stood and went to her closet. "How black should I dress?" She glanced back at Kaci for a reaction.

Kaci's eyes widened. "Um. Just dress normal, please."

"I don't do normal, remember?"

"Then don't overdo it."

Winter smiled and reached in for a purple and black top. "I'll see what I can do."

Winter and Kaci rode with Summer to the off-campus house owned by the CLC Director. When they pulled up, Peter and Davis were waiting for them on the porch.

The three girls walked together to the house. Both Peter and Davis grinned as they approached. Winter couldn't help but notice how dressed up they were.

"Good evening, ladies." Peter tucked one arm behind his back and bowed.

Winter rolled her eyes. "Hi."

"I was hoping you'd wear something a little scarier," said Davis. "I'm disappointed."

"I decided to take the night off on the outfit. But if you still want me to freak you out, I've got a great story to tell you."

Peter turned to Kaci. "I'm glad you came."

Kaci stared at the ground. "I figured I needed to get out."

Davis held out his elbow to Summer, squared his shoulders, and lifted an eyebrow. "May I?"

Summer giggled and took his arm.

Peter held open the door as they entered. Music boomed from the back and the foyer was more crowded this year than it was last year, probably because of the relocated refreshment table. As she walked over to get a drink she scanned the room for other familiar faces, but found none.

After picking up a soda, she turned and noticed a guy leaning against the wall on the other side of the room. He stared at her, unsmiling. When they made eye contact, he looked away.

Strange.

Winter shrugged it off and rejoined the group, now swelling with several of Peter's friends. Kaci seemed to be loosening up and getting some of the old sparkle back in her eyes.

Summer and Davis were entranced in a conversation of their own. Winter looked around again for someone else she might know…or maybe for a place to hide.

The guy was staring at her again. Shaggy hair…unshaved face…both ears pierced. He didn't belong here. Something wasn't right.

Winter took a half step toward him.

The guy turned and disappeared around the corner.

Winter's heart fluttered. Skotos?

"How were finals?" said Davis.

Winter stretched up to see over heads, trying to track the guy's movement.

"Winter? How were finals?"

Winter settled back down and turned to him. She took a deep breath and cleared her mind. "Fine, I guess. In self-defense I only had to demonstrate some basic techniques. Most everything else was a breeze. Biblical Theology and World Lit were a little tougher, but I think I did okay." She noticed Summer was missing. "Hey, where'd she go?"

Davis shrugged. "She saw someone she knew and bounced away."

"Figures. She does that sometimes."

Davis laughed.

"So how'd you do?" she asked.

"As good as to be expected."

"Which means?"

"I studied sufficiently and felt like I knew all the answers on the exams. So good, I suppose," said Davis.

Kaci touched Winter's elbow. "Hey. I'm going to go out back with Peter, okay?"

"Sure." Winter nodded and smiled. "I'll join you in a little bit."

Kaci, Peter, and two others Winter didn't know walked through the crowd toward the back of the house.

"She seems to be doing a little better," said Davis.

"A little. She's really trying."

"She'll get there."

"I know." She flashed him a polite smile.

"So what was that creepy story you wanted to tell me?"

Winter hesitated. "Um…I'm not sure this is a great time. But I do need to tell you about it."

"Hey Winter!" Summer bounced up. A girl with brown hair and just a little shorter than Summer trailed behind. "I want you to meet someone. This is Sadie. She's a freshman on my floor."

Sadie offered her hand. Winter reached out and took it, looking at the delicate arm. A small flash of color on the inside of Sadie's wrist caught Winter's eye. Winter twisted Sadie's wrist to see it better.

"You have a tattoo."

Sadie laughed. "Yeah, stupid graduation thing."

Winter let go. "It's a butterfly."

Sadie nodded. "It symbolizes rebirth. I thought it appropriate as I came to college. You know…a chance to reinvent myself."

Winter stared at Sadie. Butterfly tattoo. Rebirth. Reinventing. Could it be?

Sadie shifted and turned to Summer, one eyebrow raised.

"Are you okay, Winter?" Summer asked. "You're staring."

"Um, yeah. Sorry. Déjà vu."

Summer's eyes widened a little. "There's nothing wrong, is there?"

Winter shook her head. "No, I'm fine."

Sadie wrinkled her forehead and shuffled her feet. She looked around as if to escape, and then back at Summer.

Davis grabbed Winter's arm. "Why don't we go find Kaci?"

Winter nodded. "Yeah, sure. Coming, Summer? Sadie, you're welcome to join us too. Summer, why don't you bring her?" She tilted her forehead toward Summer trying to psychically project what she was thinking. Summer didn't seem to get it. So much for mind communication.

"Maybe we'll catch up in a little bit." Summer led Sadie away. Sadie leaned to Summer and whispered something. Then she shot a glance over her shoulder at Winter.

Davis tugged on Winter's arm. She followed him to the back of the house.

"What's going on?" asked Davis.

"Could she be Sandy?"

"What? Really? I don't know. Sadie…Sandy…I guess it's close enough. Did you see anything?"

"Maybe I misheard Agent Gains," said Winter. "Maybe he didn't say Sandy at all.

"That's certainly possible too, I guess."

"And there's also the butterfly. The codename on the folder I saw was Butterfly. She's got to be the one."

"But we need to be sure," said Davis. "You said you would be sure when you found her."

"I know," said Winter. "I didn't feel anything just now. But it makes sense, doesn't it?"

"A little. But lots of girls have butterfly tattoos. That's nothing special."

Winter took a deep frustrated breath as she walked out the back door. "I know. But how many freshman girls have one? I bet Summer could find out."

Davis nodded. "If you think she's the one, you need to find a way to be sure. You need a plan."

"I'm working on it. I just wish Summer would have gotten my hint and brought her with us."

"If you'd like, I'll go find Summer and let her know what's going on. You'll get your chance to talk with Sadie. So don't panic. We've been safe for this long. I doubt they're any closer to finding her than we are. A few more minutes won't hurt."

Winter sighed. "You're right. Again." She shot him a mean glare. "I'm starting to hate you for that."

Davis laughed. He pointed to a small group of people standing together laughing. "Hey, there's Kaci and Peter. You go on. I'll get Summer and Sadie."

Winter nodded as he left. She began walking toward Kaci and Peter, but a premonition flicker made her pause. She followed the gentle nudging and turned to peer into the darkness near the back corner of the house. The light shifted as the back door opened again. There in the shadows…the guy who was staring at them in the lobby. Watching again.

Winter clenched her teeth and took large strides in his direction. The guy's eyes widened when he saw her coming and he turned away.

Winter broke into a run. She rounded the corner of the house and saw him sprinting toward the front.

He passed the front corner and slowed, looking to his left toward the chattering partygoers.

Winter closed the gap.

He glanced over his shoulder and saw her coming. With two swift steps, he vaulted over the hedge at the edge of the yard just as Winter reached out to grab him.

He turned and sneered. "Don't come any closer."

"Who are you?" She pushed forward into the hedge, looking for a way to get through or climb over it. How did he jump like that?

"I mean it!" He flashed a gun above the hedge and then dipped it back out of view. "Do you see all those people behind you? They're all dead if you keep this up."

Winter turned and looked at the crowd gathered on the front steps of the house. She turned back and narrowed her eyes. "I'm not afraid of you."

The guy started to back away. Winter focused on his eyes, allowing herself to sink in like she had done a few times before. The premonition told her to. The premonition told her how.

Flash. Images streamed into her brain faster than she could comprehend. A little girl, an old tree, walking on a gravel road, a train, a shadowy man on horseback, something dragging her beneath the water.

A moment later, they organized themselves into categories and chronological order. She allowed her mind to sift through the information, pulling out bits and pieces that she needed as if she were sitting at a desk perusing a personnel file. She reached for the name and pulled the words in front of her mind's eye.

"Logan."

The guy stopped. "How do you…"

"Logan Salvina. You're spying on me. You're getting information for him. But you hate him. You feel like you have no choice, that he'll kill you if you don't. But that's not true, Logan. You always have a choice."

"Get out of my head! You don't know me!"

"I do know you. I know you were orphaned when you were a teenager. That your grandmother gave you a home, but you didn't appreciate it. I know you got into drugs. I know you joined Skotos because you thought it'd give you power. But Skotos did something…I, I can't see that. It's blocked. How's it blocked? Xaphan owns Skotos now. He owns you. You tried to get out once, but Xaphan killed your…" Winter caught her breath.

Logan swung the gun over the hedge, pointing it in her face with a shaky grip. "That's enough! I said get out of my head!"

"I'm so sorry. He's a monster, you know that, right?"

Logan started to back away.

"I can help."

"No one can help me," Logan said.

"You're wrong." Winter patted the air gently over the hedge. "I, of all people, know just how wrong you are. Look at me, Logan. Look at me. I've been there…I know where you are. And I can help."

Logan glanced behind him, and then turned back to glare at her. His face glistened with angry tears. The muscles in his cheek twisted with anger and fear.

"Just come with me." Winter reached out, palm up.

Logan held his breath for a moment and looked at her hand. Then he jerked his head up, looking back toward the house. A smile crossed his face. Then he turned and fled.

Winter watched him fade into the darkness. Then she looked over her shoulder to see what had made him smile. Summer stood on the porch with Davis.

Sadie stood nearby, staring at Winter with wide fear-struck eyes.

Winter flung her textbook at the wall.

Summer grimaced. "I'm sorry."

"How am I supposed to protect her then? I just found her and now she's gone already? The party was last night. What…did Sadie have her things packed and waiting?"

Summer shook her head. "Look at it this way. They think she's here, right? That means they don't know where she lives. She's probably safer at home than she is living here."

Winter took a deep breath. "I hope you're right."

"Anyway, there's nothing you can do."

"I know. Do you at least know when she's coming back?"

Summer shook her head. "But she at least won't be back until after the holidays, right?"

"I need to make sure I'm here waiting for her. I'll be back as soon as I can after New Year's."

Summer rubbed Winter's shoulder. "I'll try to come back then too. We can both watch her."

Winter nodded. "Thanks."

Steve was there to pick her up early the next day for Christmas break. She realized how much she had missed him the moment she saw his truck. After squeezing him tightly, she tossed her duffle bag into the back of the cab.

The next week dragged by. All she could think about was what she was going to do about Sadie. How was this going to work? How could she possibly protect her when they lived in different dorms?

Winter tried to call Stacy, hoping to get out of the house and do something fun. But there was no one home. She tried calling every day, but no answer. Maybe they had gone out of town for the holidays. Figures.

On her birthday, Winter awoke to the heavenly smell of homemade muffins.

"When did you learn to bake?" she asked as she sat at the table.

Steve shrugged. "I was getting tired of spending so much money on fast food."

Winter smiled. "You've never been the money-saving type."

"Well, I had a good reason." He set a small wrapped box in front of her. "Happy twentieth."

"Dad…this better not be expensive."

"The bad news is that it was expensive."

Winter rolled her eyes.

"But the good news is that it's something you really need."

"What could possibly fit in this little box that I need?"

Steve smiled. "Open it and see."

Winter smirked and started tugging at the black and white paper. With the paper removed, she pulled the lid up. Inside was a single key lying on a cotton bed.

Her hand went to her mouth. "Dad…Thank you, but you know I can't…"

"Come see." He stood and held his hand to her.

"I don't know if I can do this."

"Yes you can, and you will."

"I'm not ready."

"It's time you are. It's been long enough. For once I'm going to make you do something for your own good. Now stand up."

Winter bit her lip and took his hand. He led her through the house to the garage. In what used to be the empty spot next to his truck, now waited a black four-door sedan.

"I brought it in last night while you were in bed."

"What is it?"

Steve grinned. "A 1992 BMW 325i, slightly modified."

Winter almost choked. "A BMW? You're joking, right? I…I can't!"

Steve nodded. "Yes you can."

"But this must have cost a fortune."

"Actually, not so much." Steve shrugged. "You're looking at two cars. One was banged up with a blown engine, and the other had been totaled in a rear-end accident. I took the engine and a few parts from one, put them in the other, and voilà! It's the safety upgrades and new electronics that were expensive."

Winter walked toward it and set a hand on the hood, memories pulling her inside out. Her eyes started watering and she wiped them. "Dad…"

He rubbed her back. "You're a new person now. Don't let the past define you."

"I don't know…"

"Mistakes will stay in your memory forever, but you can't let them affect the future. God has plans for you, and you can't always depend on someone for a ride to get them done."

Winter rolled her eyes. "Listen to the wise father." She strolled around the BMW, tracing the smooth lines with one finger.

Steve grinned. "Custom paint job and window tinting. There's a brand new stereo system with a navigation console and MP3 jack. Alarm system with GPS locator, and hands-free Bluetooth sync for your cell phone. I've made sure all the safety features are completely updated, with modern front and side airbags and even a roll bar."

"A roll bar?"

Steve laughed. "Are you surprised?"

"Not really, I guess."

"The bar doesn't look great on the inside, but I figured it might make this easier on you. At least I had the visible part upholstered."

Winter opened the driver door and sat down, the tan leather seat perfectly conforming to her body.

Steve came over and knelt beside her. "What do you think? You'll have to renew your license while you're here."

Winter looked at the navigation console and then to the gauges. "A hundred and eighty? Dad…how fast does this thing go?"

Steve sighed. "Only as fast as you want it to. The important thing is that you feel safe in it. I didn't want you to have another flimsy toy."

Winter stared at the gauges, letting the memories seep in.

"Well?"

"It's great, Dad."

"Would you like to take it for a spin?"

Winter shook her head. "Not today. And really, thank you. I'm sorry I don't seem very enthusiastic. I love it…I really do."

Steve nodded. "It's okay. I completely understand. I knew this was going to be tough."

Winter looked into his eyes, struggling to hold back the tears. "This may sound weird, but can I be alone?"

Steve touched her arm and frowned. "Yeah, sure."

When he left the garage, Winter laid her head on the steering wheel and opened the gates to her memories and her tears.

# 33

*Four Years Ago*

Winter sat at the dining room table at the request of her dad. She held her hands together on top of the table and leaned on her elbows. She stared at her fingers, allowing her mind to wander into numbness.

Steve sighed. "I know you hate it here. And for whatever reason, you hate me. I don't know what I can do to fix this."

Winter didn't move.

"Will you please look at me?"

She cut her eyes to him, and then looked back down at her hands. "Can we just get the lecture over with?"

"I'm not going to lecture you."

Winter rolled her eyes. "Why else would you call me out of my room to sit at the table?"

Steve sighed again. "It's your birthday today, your sweet sixteenth. I was hoping that maybe a special present would help mend things between us."

"You're going to try to buy me off?"

"No. It's not like that." Steve ran his hand through his hair. "You may not believe me, but I do love you. And I know your mom would want this day to be special."

"Dad, don't…"

"No doubt she would have planned…"

"STOP IT!" She flattened her hands on the table and clenched her jaw. "It's just another day, okay? I don't want anything but to be left alone."

Steve stared at her a moment. "Okay." He slid a small box toward her. "Now that you're sixteen and you've finished Driver's Ed, we can go get your license this week."

Winter grabbed the box with one hand and slid it in front of her. She pulled the ribbon and pried the box open. Inside was a key.

She narrowed her eyes at it. "What's this for?"

"Your car."

Winter looked up at him with wide eyes. "A car? Seriously?"

Steve smiled. "Seriously."

Winter looked back down. "What's the catch?"

"Why do you think there would be a catch?"

"Why wouldn't there be?"

"Believe it or not, I'm just trying to do something good for you. Maybe you can give me a break and we can start putting things right between us."

Winter flipped the key in her hands. "Where is it?"

"In the garage."

Winter stood and walked through the kitchen to the garage door. Steve followed.

In the garage was a brand new light blue Mustang parked beside her dad's work truck. The fluorescent lights shimmered from the perfectly waxed exterior.

"Blue?"

"Could you at least try to be a little grateful? It didn't come with a spare, so I bought one. I'll have to teach you how to change a flat."

Winter walked toward the car and dragged her fingers over the hood. “Is it really mine?”

“Yes, it’s really yours.”

“Can I drive it?”

Steve shook his head. “Not until you get your license.”

“But I have a permit. I can drive with you in the car.”

Steve took a deep breath. “I want to go put flowers on your mom’s grave Christmas day. You can drive it then.”

“Forget it.” Winter flung the key at Steve’s feet and went back inside.

# 34

*Present Day*

With the restored Beamer in the garage for her birthday, Christmas was slim. All Winter got was fifty dollars in cash. After the traditional Christmas pizza, Winter drove her car for the first time to the cemetery to visit her mom. Steve rode in the passenger seat, holding tightly to the armrest. But Winter kept the car under 50 miles per hour…especially since her license was expired. She'd have to get that fixed before going back to school.

The weather was warmer than usual, but the wind still held a crisp bite. At the cemetery, Winter pulled her trench coat tight but left her stocking cap in the car. The sky was bright blue and the sun blinding, and she shoved her sunglasses tighter to her face.

With the dozen roses in her hand, she walked slowly through the rows of headstones as Steve walked in the other direction to his parents' graves. She knelt before her mother's stone and read the engraving once again.

*"So you have sorrow now, but I will see you again; then you will rejoice, and no one can rob you of that joy."* John 16:22.

She sighed and reached forward to place the roses into the vase. A warmth filled her, not of sadness or joy. Winter didn't know how to feel at that moment. She had no words. She opened up her mind and her heart, to allow God to speak if he wanted. The warmth seemed to wrap around her and a smile crept to her lips. There was no need to stay for long this year. There was no need to dwell on the past. She missed her mom, but one day they would be reunited. This Christmas would be a time to move forward in more ways than one.

Winter stood and turned to go to her new car, glistening in the bright winter sun. Not far away she saw someone standing next to a grave. Winter paused and looked closer. She recognized him. Seeing that her dad had not yet returned, Winter walked over to the man.

He saw her before she could speak. "Winter."

She smiled. "Hey, Brother Daniel."

"How many times do I have to tell you? Just call me Daniel."

Winter stepped up to him and they wrapped their arms around each other.

"How are you?" he asked.

"Great, actually. Things are so much different now, you wouldn't believe it."

"Your dad's been keeping me updated. I'm very proud of you."

Winter looked at the ground. "Thank you. I don't feel I quite deserve that."

"But it's true."

Winter turned and looked at the headstone Daniel stood before, remembering everything that he'd been through. A knot formed in her throat, shoving an aching lump through her chest. The unexpected sensation sent chill bumps across her skin. She crossed her arms.

"I…I really don't." Her voice trembled and her vision blurred. She sniffed, looking across the cemetery to her mom's grave.

Daniel put his arm around her shoulders and pulled her in close. Winter leaned into him and cried. "I'm so sorry."

"Shh…It's okay, really. It was all part of God's plan."

"I know," she whispered. "But it still hurts."

"It does." He paused and rubbed her shoulder. "Thank you. Thank you for sharing this with me. It's nice to have someone who understands."

She leaned against him until she regained control of her emotions. When she straightened, Daniel released her and smiled. She rubbed her eyes dry and looked back to her new car. Her dad was leaning against it, watching them. Winter turned back to Daniel, and he met her eyes.

She sniffled. "It's my birthday present."

He nodded. "And are you doing all right?"

"It hasn't been easy."

"It'll get easier. It was good of your dad to make you start driving again."

"I suppose." She glanced back to her dad for a brief moment. "I can't believe I was so horrible to him for so long."

Daniel laughed. "You were young. Well…younger. And you'd been through a lot."

"That's still not a very good excuse."

"I really am proud of you, Winter. You are an extraordinary person. I have no doubt that whatever you decide to do for God will have extraordinary results."

Winter stared at her feet for a moment, wondering if she should tell him her secrets. Finally, she looked up. "Will I see you at church tomorrow?"

Daniel smiled. "I'll save you a seat."

"Thank you." Winter gave him another hug. Then she walked back toward her car, leaving Daniel in silence before the grave.

# 35

*Four Years Ago*

Winter rode in the truck with her dad three days after Christmas. She had wanted to take the Mustang, but he refused to let her drive it yet. She kept her arms crossed and chewed at her cheeks. "Where are we going?"

"You'll see soon enough."

After making a couple more turns, her dad pulled into the parking lot of a church.

Winter grunted. "Seriously?"

"I figured it's Christmas time. We should try something different."

"Are you going to make me go in?"

He looked at her. "I was hoping you would."

"Forget it." Something banged on her window. Winter jumped and turned. Stacy waited outside waving her hand.

Winter huffed and opened the door.

"Hey!" Stacy said. "I can't believe you're here."

"Me either."

Stacy grabbed her hand and tugged Winter out of the truck. "Come on. Service is about to start. You can sit with me. It's so good to see you!"

Winter shook her head and pulled her arm away. "Um. I wasn't going to stay."

"Yes, we are," said Steve.

"No," said Winter.

"Hey, Winter." Ryan stepped out of the crowd at the steps of the church. He walked over to them. "I'm glad you're here. I haven't talked to you in a while."

"I didn't know you two hung out," said her dad.

Winter's eyes widened, remembering the party. She looked at her feet and crossed her arms.

"Yeah," said Ryan. "Well, sometimes."

"Come on." Winter started walking toward the church. "Let's get this over with."

Ryan and Stacy led her through the front doors to the foyer. Ryan brought her to one side where a man stood that she vaguely recognized. When he turned, she gritted her teeth for allowing herself to be dragged inside.

Daniel smiled at her. "It's good to see you again, Winter."

Winter found someplace else to look.

"Have you had a good Christmas?" Daniel asked.

Winter shrugged. "Okay."

"I know the first Christmas can be tough after losing someone…"

"Stop it." She glared at him through the hair hanging over her eyes.

Ryan and Stacy exchanged looks, but Winter ignored them.

Daniel pursed his lips together. "Why don't we talk later? Just you and me. Maybe Ryan can join us. He really does understand how you feel."

"No thank you."

"You can't ignore it forever. Sooner or later you'll have to talk about her."

"No!"

Daniel took a small step toward her.

Winter turned and stomped away.

"Are you numb?" Daniel asked.

Winter stopped.

"How long has it been since you've felt anything? Pain is good. It brings healing. But when you push the pain away, it numbs everything. And pain has a way of breaking free, whether you want it to or not."

Winter turned a little. "Just leave me alone. Maybe I don't want to feel anything."

"You don't want to feel loved?"

Pain stabbed through her chest. She shoved it down and stormed back outside.

Winter found her dad talking to someone at the bottom of the steps. "Stay if you want. I'm walking home."

"Winter, wait."

He grabbed her arm but she jerked it free. "Leave me alone."

"You can't just leave like this." She heard him stop following. "Winter." His voice farther away now.

She folded her arms, tucked her chin, and found the sidewalk.

With her back to the church, no one could see the tear rolling down her cheek. She swiped it away and summoned the numbness. It coursed through her, filling her like Novocain.

# 36

*Present Day*

The Beamer drove like a vision. Winter's eyes darted to either side of the road constantly, waiting for some random projectile to hurl itself into the road. With her cruise control set five miles under the speed limit, Winter often felt like she was in reverse with the rate at which cars passed her by. When she made the turn off the interstate onto Hoole Boulevard, her knuckles creaked from the release of pressure.

Finally, the Beamer crawled into the parking lot of Devine Hall. Winter parked it and slowly lowered her hands to her lap. She took a deep breath and tried to relax.

*I made it.*

As she got out she scanned the parking lot for Kaci's Honda Accord, but it wasn't there. She grabbed her duffle bag from the back seat and pulled out her cell phone.

"Summer?"

*"Hey! Are you back?"*

"Yeah. Just pulled in. Is Sadie there yet?" A group of butterflies took flight from the shrub bush by the front door. Winter paused to watch them before going in.

*"No. But I'm watching for her. I'll let you know as soon as she shows up."*

"Thanks."

*"Do you want to go get something to eat later?"*

"Yeah, sure. Who else is back?"

*"Um…I've talked with Davis. I don't know about Peter. How about Kaci?"*

Winter pressed the elevator call button and shook her head. "Not yet. But I talked to her this morning. She said she'd be here today."

*"Good. She seems to be getting back to her old self."*

"Yeah. Slowly. Go ahead and call Davis. I'll see if Peter's here. We'll meet up at the Raven at six."

*"Sure thing. Do you need a ride?"*

"No. I'm good. Oh…one more thing. Do we normally have butterflies this time of year?"

*"I don't know. Maybe you should look it up online."*

"Yeah. I think I might."

The Beamer rolled down Hoole Boulevard toward the Raven. Peter, Davis, and Summer waited for her just outside the entrance. She sighed and clenched the wheel a little tighter.

They grinned at her as she parked. Winter bit her lip and stared at the pavement while walking toward them.

"Nice wheels," said Davis.

"Shut up." She pushed past them and went in.

They ordered and found a booth near the back corner where the Raven was least populated.

Winter vaguely noted that the others had started talking. Why wasn't Sadie back yet? And why did she leave so quickly after the Christmas party? Did she know something was wrong? And the butterfly tattoo…was that the meaning of the FBI code word she saw? Was Sadie *really* Sandy?

Peter's hand waved in front of her face. "Hey. What about you?"

"Huh?"

"I said, how was your Christmas break?"

"Oh. Fine, I guess." She thumbed to the parking lot. "Got the car."

Peter frowned. "Something on your mind?"

Winter shook her head. "I just need to talk to Sadie. I'm not sure what to think about her yet. So much of it makes sense, but I have to be sure."

"You seemed pretty sure right after the party," said Summer.

"I know. It's just…"

The waitress arrived with their plates and passed them around.

Peter inspected his sandwich and picked it up. "You're second-guessing yourself. Maybe you should trust your instincts."

Winter took a deep breath. "I do. But I don't have a plan. I thought about it all break. If Sadie denies everything, I'm not sure there's a way to prove she's the right person. And even if I can prove it, I don't know what to do next. It's extremely frustrating."

Davis leaned forward. "Just take it one step at a time, Winter. Talk to Sadie. See what happens and go from there."

Peter nodded and swallowed. "That's the best plan you've got, anyway…that is unless you get some sort of divine intervention."

Winter rolled her eyes. "I wish."

"But you don't want to freak her out again," said Summer with a mouth full of food.

"I know. Any ideas?"

Davis shrugged. "How about be honest with her?"

"You mean tell her exactly what I'm doing?" Winter furrowed her brow.

Davis nodded. "Sure. Why not? There's no need to go into the whole prophet thing…"

"Prophetess."

"…But you could hint around at some of the stuff that happened last year…you know, things everyone already knows. Tell her you're doing a safety survey or something and see if she gives anything away. Maybe it'll be enough to spark some sort of premonition or confirmation."

Winter chewed slowly and let the idea swell like a wet sponge. "Okay."

"Okay?" asked Davis.

Winter nodded. "Yeah. Okay. I'll do that." Her phone chirped. Winter put down the last quarter of her sandwich and checked the phone. "Kaci's here. I need to go help her unload."

Peter wiped his mouth with a napkin and stood. "Hold on. Let me get her something for you to take back." He took off to the counter.

Winter watched him go. The jealous flicker no longer existed. Not since…not since getting her new car. She choked back the memories and turned back to Summer. "Don't forget to tell me when Sadie gets back."

"I won't."

"And see if you can find out what her Monday schedule looks like. Maybe I can catch her after class tomorrow."

Summer nodded. "Sure. I'll ask. We've got a dorm meeting tomorrow night anyway. Maybe you can catch her then."

Winter stood and slipped back into her coat. "Yeah. I'll be there. Text me the time." She walked over to join Peter by the take-out counter.

He gave her a warm smile. "I doubt she's eaten yet. You'll be a hero."

Winter shook her head. "Don't worry. I'll give you all the credit."

"Thanks." The cashier handed him the take-out bag and he

passed it to Winter. "Tell her I said hi, too."

Winter felt her checks dissolve into a grin. "She's coming around. Just be patient."

Peter nodded. "Thanks again."

# 37

Screams. Shouts. People running and crashing through chairs. Dead bodies lay everywhere. On the floor. Slumped over tables. Blood pooled, dripped.

She covered her mouth and stepped back.

A man rounded the corner with a shotgun.

Winter turned to join the fleeing survivors, and tripped over a dead body. She twisted as she fell, slamming to her back.

The man stepped over her. Silver and black mask. He tilted his head and swung the gun into her face. "You can't stop me."

Winter popped open her eyes and put a hand to her sweaty forehead. She took a deep, steadying breath.

"Something wrong?" asked Kaci.

"I've been having this recurring nightmare. No big deal. Don't worry about it." Winter swung her feet off the bed.

Kaci rolled over and pulled her sheets up tight.

Winter showered and left for breakfast. A group of bright blue butterflies drifted through the center of the Meadow. Winter stopped and watched them. A student passed near and the butterflies fluttered around his head. But he didn't seem to notice.

Winter walked toward the butterflies.

Another student came close and failed to notice them.

Winter sped up. The butterflies floated just ahead of her. She stuck out her hand and rushed forward.

They dissolved into blue sparkles that melted into the air.

Winter stared at the empty space, more confused than ever. Butterflies? It obviously had something to do with Sandy. But what?

Winter hurried to the religion building later that morning for her first meeting with Dr. Cook. She smiled at Dr. Cook's secretary and then knocked on his office door before easing it open.

Dr. Cook lifted his head. "Good morning. Have a seat."

Winter slipped her backpack from her shoulder and sat in the leather chair.

"How was your break?"

Winter shrugged. "Just fine. I guess."

"And how are you doing?"

"A little frustrated."

Dr. Cook nodded. "I take it things aren't going precisely as you would like."

Winter shook her head. "No. I sort of know what I'm supposed to do, I just can't find the right person."

"I'm sure you'll get it soon enough. What else are you taking this semester?"

"Intro to Greek…"

"Stevens or Warren?"

"Stevens, I think." She fished out her printed schedule from her backpack. "I've got World Lit 2, church history, another psychology class, and principles of interpretation with you this afternoon."

Dr. Cook nodded again. "Sounds like a busy semester."

Winter sighed. "I know."

He leaned forward on his elbows. "Maybe our time here will help you. That's partially why I recommended you do this directed study on the prophets. With everything you've told me, I feel like you need a deeper understanding of what the Bible says concerning what you're going through. And this way I can keep a closer eye on you. Maybe I can help."

"I'll take any help I can get."

"Have you at least got any leads?"

"One. There's this girl in Carmichael that might be the right person. I'm going to talk with her tonight. Maybe this is it."

"Nervous?"

"A little. I mean…what if she is the right person and I can't figure it out? I mean, it's not like last year. Last year things just happened to me and I didn't expect it. I got what I needed when I needed it. This time it seems God's not telling me anything. I don't understand."

Dr. Cook tapped his fingers together. "That's to be expected."

"What do you mean?" She tilted her head.

He leaned back. "Do you think God constantly talked to and revealed things to the prophets in the Bible? Often there were periods of silence, for one reason or the other. Sometimes it was to teach the prophet a new lesson about God's power and sovereignty. Sometimes it was because God didn't want the prophet to take action. In every case the silence was an integral part of God's plan for them. Ultimately silence exists because God allows it to exist. How could we ever think that God doesn't calculate silence into his plans?"

"Like Elijah?"

He nodded. "Precisely. God sent him into the wilderness to wait. He was fed by ravens by the brook at Cherith and was later taken care of by a widow. He did some miracles during that time, but never in direct relation to the larger story unfolding around him with

Jezebel and King Ahab."

"So you're saying this silence is part of God's larger plan for what's going on?"

"Exactly. Just keep waiting. Keep trying. You'll have your breakthrough soon enough."

Winter nodded.

"Now. Get your Bible and a notebook. We'll begin with Abraham…"

Winter sat in the back of Carmichael, reading about Abraham and jotting down some notes for Dr. Cook. Georgia Velasquez, the head resident of Carmichael, droned on in front of all the freshman girls gathered.

A déjà vu washed over her. Something was about to happen. Winter looked to the door, expecting to see Ayden burst in.

For a moment, Winter saw the spiky red hair. How could Ayden be…? She blinked and the red became two butterflies fluttering beyond the glass.

An eruption of chatter and shuffling made Winter look back. The girls were all dispersing. Including Ayden. Winter watched her a moment. Could she be Sandy? No. But she was something…something different.

Summer crossed into Winter's field of vision and waved, Sadie in tow.

Winter tore her attention away from Ayden back to the task at hand. Winter closed her Bible and shoved it into her backpack. She wrung her hands as she watched Summer and Sadie walk over to her.

Winter tried to smile. "Hey."

Sadie's wide eyes passed from Winter to Summer as she sat across the table. "What's going on?"

Summer sat to Winter's left.

Winter bit her lip. This was it. "I've got something pretty serious to talk to you about. And maybe a few questions to ask. I'm doing a…safety survey."

"Okay…"

Winter leaned forward. "Listen, there's been some strange stuff happening here over the past couple of years. People have been attacked, including a good friend of mine. At what point were you told about this during the admission process?"

Sadie's face stretched and her cheeks paled. "Nobody told me. I heard about it on the news. What's this have to do with me?"

"Nothing…does it? Have you heard something?"

Sadie shook her head quickly. "No."

"Do you feel safe on campus?"

Sadie looked around at the other students departing for their rooms. "I guess. Aren't the police doing something about it?"

Winter nodded. "They're doing the best they can. But I don't think they really know who's responsible. There's…um…" Winter flashed her gaze to Summer. "There's a rumor that the FBI are involved."

"Really? The FBI? Have you seen them?"

Winter averted her face for a moment, then shook her head. "No. Have you?"

Sadie narrowed her eyes. "Why would I see the FBI?"

"I don't know. Just…just part of the survey. So, have you seen anything unusual?"

"Um…I don't think so. Am I supposed to be looking for something?" Sadie shifted in her seat.

Winter bit her lip. "No. Not really. But if you do, let me or Summer know. Anything." Winter leaned toward her. "Even if it's as simple as you don't feel safe. I'll add it to the survey, okay?"

"Yeah, sure." Sadie looked to Summer. "So…can I go now?"

Summer nodded. "Thanks, Sadie."

Sadie stood and stepped away.

Winter grabbed her arm. "Just one more question. Are you Sandy?"

Sadie paused. "What?"

"Sandy. Is that your name? Have you ever gone by the name Sandy. Just look me in the eyes and tell me the truth. That's all you have to do."

Sadie jerked her arm out of Winter's grasp. She narrowed her eyes and stared directly into Winter's. "No. My name is not Sandy. It's Sadia. Are you happy now?"

"Are you sure? Are you absolutely telling me the truth?"

"Do I look like I'm lying? You really are some kind of freak." Sadie turned and rushed away.

Summer slid to Winter's side. "Well?"

Winter slouched in the chair. "I think she's telling the truth."

"Now what?"

Winter wrinkled her chin and pressed her bottom lip up against the top. "I guess we just wait. We wait for God to send some kind of breakthrough."

"So we're giving up looking?"

Winter stood and picked up her backpack. "No. We just need another lead. Keep watching and listening. Let me know if you have any other ideas. Anyone."

"Sure."

"One more thing." Winter furrowed her brows. "Have you noticed all the butterflies?"

Summer shook her head. "No. What is it with you and butterflies lately?"

"I've been seeing them all over the place. I'm not sure what it means. But if you start seeing them too, let me know."

*Four Years Ago*

Winter stood in her bathroom before the mirror, staring at her sunken cheeks and pale face. Golden brown roots showed beneath her dyed hair, which hung unbrushed and unwashed to her shoulders. Her eyes were swollen and bloodshot, with dark shadows covering her bottom lids and her upper cheekbones.

She looked down at her tools arrayed on a towel on the bathroom counter…an assortment of stud earrings, several large needles, an ice pick, and a pair of scissors.

She walked back into her room and peeked out the window. Her dad was still gone. He shouldn't be back for a few hours anyway.

Winter returned to the bathroom. She took up a needle and rolled the cold steel between her forefinger and thumb.

Such a small thing. Was it sharp enough?

She grabbed the lobe of her left ear and shoved the needle into it. The skin stretched, not wanting to give up. When the needled popped through it jabbed into her thumb on the other side.

The sting was barely noticeable.

She forced a stud through the new hole just above her existing earring hole. A single drop of blood oozed out of it, but her punctured thumb spread enough sticky blood to make up for it.

Winter took a moment and rubbed the blood from her thumb with her forefinger as she had done the needle. It was already cold. Maybe it was always cold.

She grabbed the slippery needle again and pierced her other ear, jabbing her left thumb this time. The sting was too brief. The blood not enough.

Her arms trembled and her chest ached as if someone were standing on it.

She attacked the top of her left ear, forcing the needle through the cartilage. The faint popping sound made her skin jitter. Just a little more pain this time. She chewed her bottom lip and savored it before shoving another stud in, tearing the skin and cartilage more than the needle had.

Again. The needle popped through the cartilage. The stud tore through. Again. Pop. Pain. Three studs at the top of her ear now. Two in the lobe.

Blood ran down her ear from her punctured thumb, dripping from her lobe. From the back, the blood trickled down her neck, and into her shirt.

She rubbed both thumbs against her neck and let it flow. Pain…sweet pain.

The empty space inside her ballooned out, forcing away the pressure.

She moved to her other ear with more passion and force, allowing the needle to mangle the tips of all her fingers. The blood was sticky and slick at the same time. Still, she kept pressing the needle through, making more holes and more pain.

Her neck and shoulders were covered in more blood than flesh. It trickled down her chest and back. Winter watched herself in the mirror. Is this what death looked like? Is this what it felt like?

She felt nothing. The pain had numbed.

More.

She took up a safety pin and opened it. With one hand she pinched her eyebrow, and with the other she started pressing the pin through the fold. She applied pressure slowly, trying to make the pain last as long as possible. Blood from her fingers spilled into her eye. She blinked and pushed a little harder with the safety pin. It popped through the first layer of skin and the tip of the needle rested against the inside of the second layer. She let it sit there and linger. Just a moment longer.

The pain only made her feel more empty. The more she relished it, the more hollow she became. But the fleeting moments of agony were all that reminded her she was alive.

She pushed through the rest of her eyebrow and closed the pin. Then she grabbed another one for the other eyebrow. The second eyebrow sent a sharp stab through the nerve in the side of her face. She gasped and smiled. The dripping blood from her fingers sent more blood into this eye.

She took a moment to pat her face with a towel and then studied herself again in the mirror. Not only was her neck stained red, but now blood covered her cheeks like dripping mascara. Where she had wiped her eyes, it was a solid smeared mass. Her eyebrows dripped large slow drops.

She stared at her mutilated face, savoring each dull throb. Was this all? It was so easy. It could be over soon. Everything. Her body shuddered and she involuntarily sucked enough air to keep living.

More…she needed more.

Winter took off her shirt, unbuttoned her pants, and pushed them low on her hips. Her torso was veined in sticky trails of blood, like a demonic rash. She stood on her toes and leaned forward on the counter. With one finger she grabbed the top of her navel and arranged the fold of skin on the counter.

With the other hand, she grabbed the small ice pick.

She placed the tip on the outside of her navel and pushed gently so that it held the fold of skin secure against the countertop. The tip of it stung like the needles. She smiled and put both hands on the end of the handle, pressing it against her stomach and down into the fold of skin. Winter looked back at herself in the mirror. Would this be enough?

She gritted her teeth and pressed down. The skin crunched. She screamed, and leaned in harder.

Fire erupted.

She twisted it and pushed more, forcing the tip through the final layer. She pulled the ice pick free and put one hand on the counter to steady her trembling body.

The bottom hole was too small. Now free from the surface, Winter took the ice pick and reinserted it into the first hole. It burned so wonderfully, bringing tears to her eyes. She smiled and wiggled the pick around, sending more luscious fire through her nerves. With her other hand she guided the tip to the small hole on the other side. Then she shoved the pick all the way through, rotating it to stretch the bottom hole as much as possible. She slid the ice pick down to the handle and left it dangling from her navel.

She put a hand on the counter to keep herself from collapsing. Her ears rang and her head buzzed. She peered into the mirror and watched the reflection of herself speckle into blackness. What if she died like this? What if her father found her?

She took a deep breath and her vision cleared.

She needed more pain.

With unsteady blood-smeared hands, Winter reached for the scissors. She opened them and placed one sharp edge on her wrist. One quick slice is all it would take. No more emptiness. No more pretending. Her misery would come to a glorious end. With one moment of courage, she could be with her mother again.

Winter started to cry, tears washing the blood further down her face. Her chest warmed. Feeling. She was alive. This was it. This was the answer.

One slice.

She pressed and pulled, leaving a thin line of red. Winter wept from the vice squeezing her heart and stared at the small scratch on her wrist. Blood welled up into minuscule droplets.

She pressed air through her vocal chords, forcing them into a harsh rasp. "Why?" *Why?* That one word consumed her mind. That one word crawled through her veins.

She moved the scissors a half inch and pushed a little harder. Much harder. She drew another crimson scratch and screamed as the vice around her heart tightened. Blood oozed to the surface.

Not enough.

She set both hands on the counter and leaned over the sink, shuddering like the temperature on the outside was the same as inside her chest.

Why? Why did her mom have to die? Why did her dad hate her? Why did God hate her? Why couldn't she just end it now? Why couldn't she just die?

Why?

Why not?

She tossed the scissors down and reached for the yellow-handled instrument that had so far remained untouched. A box-cutting knife. She flicked out the blade and pressed it against her wrist. She could feel the upper layers of skin splitting from just the pressure. Her body trembled, but her tears had stopped. She took a deep breath and prepared for just one more cut. This was it.

One slice.

A door closed downstairs. Footsteps…keys rattling.

Winter slammed the box cutter down and ran to the door to make sure it was locked. Then she went to the shower and turned the water on to cover up the noise. She returned to the mirror and took another long look at herself.

Coward.

# 39

*Present Day*

As the first month of the semester's classes crept by, Winter felt an ever-increasing sense of urgency. As she walked across the Meadow on her way back from class, she pulled out her cell to call Summer, slipping it beneath the edge of her stocking cap. She tried to steady her chattering teeth. "How's Sadie? Have you seen her today?"

Winter heard the sigh from the other side of the phone. "The same as she always is, Winter. She's fine as of the last I saw her this morning. Nothing's happened and she hasn't come to me."

Winter's stomach twisted a little more. Her last conversation with Sadie gnawed at her like growing bacteria. "For some reason I can't seem to get her off my mind. Maybe God's telling me something."

"But you said she wasn't Sandy."

"She's not. I don't know what this is." Butterflies swarmed from the Ancient. They floated to the Union in a long trail, dissolving into blue sparkles as the line reached the door. Winter turned to follow. "But we're running out of time. I can feel it."

"Are you all right?"

Winter hesitated. "I…I had the dream again last night. The one about the Union. This time Ayden was there. And I'm seeing more butterflies today. Lots more."

"What are you going to do?"

"I don't know. I'm working on it. I'll call you later."

"Sure. All right. Talk to you in a bit."

Winter stepped into the warm Union and let the cold trickle out of her body. She felt another nudge as she looked around. Peter sat studying on a couch. Nudge. Winter shuddered again as the warm air prickled her skin. She walked over to Peter and sat in the chair next to him where she could still see most of the Union.

Peter looked up from his book. "Hey. What's going on? You look stressed."

"I've been getting a lot of déjà vu lately, but there's nothing concrete about it. It's making me nervous. I think we're running out of time."

Peter sat back. "I'm not sure what more we can do."

"I know. Barring some change, there isn't. Maybe we're not supposed to do more." Winter scanned the Union again, waiting and hoping for some premonition to kick in. Nothing.

"What are you looking for?"

She turned back to him. "I don't know. Just a small hunch. The least I can do is follow them."

A flash of white pulled Winter's eyes back to the door. Ayden walked in with her spiky red hair stuck out in all directions. Her white, vintage-style frock coat flared out from her waist almost to her knees.

"Maybe what you should be looking for is something unusual," Peter said. "When you get these nudges, are you seeing something or someone almost every time?"

Winter's heart fluttered. "You're right. Butterflies. Always butterflies. And Ayden. I've seen her too."

Peter turned and followed Winter's gaze. "How do you know

she's not the one?"

Winter shook her head. "I don't. I guess I've never felt like she had anything to do with this…like maybe she's got a different role to play. I don't know. When I see her in a vision, it's like I'm seeing something I don't need yet." Winter stared toward Ayden. The missing something dangled just before her eyes. It seemed to slip a little closer. What was the clue? Was Ayden the clue? Could that be the reason she kept appearing in her visions?

Ayden's head turned toward them and Winter refocused on her face. They made eye contact.

Flash. Sophie. Ayden. The Ancient. Winter briefly relived interrupting the argument.

She blinked. "The AFRC."

"What about the AFRC?"

Winter didn't respond. She felt like a two-by-four had just smacked her in the face. Why didn't she think of it before?

"What's wr…"

"Shhh! I'm thinking." Pieces fell into place. Winter's heart started to beat faster.

"What?" Peter asked.

Winter turned back to him. "That's what I'm missing. The AFRC."

Peter shook his head. "I don't understand. What about them?"

Winter scooted forward. "It all makes sense now. I'm a such a moron."

"Well, hurry and tell me so I don't feel like an idiot too."

Winter took a deep breath. "Sophie's involved with the campus chapter of the AFRC. She's been trying to recruit other students. She's also involved with Skotos."

"And?"

"And…we know someone's funding the AFRC. It has to be Skotos. That's why she warned me. She's involved…but she's not really involved. Does that make sense? She's not a part of Skotos, but she's kinda working for them."

"Skotos is the AFRC?"

Winter shook her head. "No. Skotos is funding it, that's all. And Sophie's gotten too involved. Maybe it's scared her."

Peter nodded. "And Xaphan has Skotos on a leash."

"Exactly. It's all linked for one purpose. To find Sandy."

"Okay. So how does that help us?"

Winter shook her head. "I'm not sure. But I bet the AFRC can give me a clue…something that will lead me to Skotos, maybe even give me enough information to find Sandy. Anything linked to Xaphan or Skotos is a clue to Sandy."

"I'm not sure about that." Peter narrowed his eyes. "Finding Skotos may be just as dangerous as finding Xaphan."

"Doesn't matter. If I can't find Sandy, then I can at least stop everyone else from finding her, right? If I find Skotos or Xaphan before they find Sandy, then I can put an end to all of this. Maybe I don't have to find her after all."

Peter shrugged. "Maybe."

Winter grinned. "So I've got to get into the AFRC. There's something there. I know it. That's the connection I've been missing."

Peter nodded. "All right. So that's the connection. What's your plan, then?"

"Do you know where the AFRC Chapter office is?"

Peter shook his head. "Sorry."

"I'm sure it wouldn't be that difficult to find out," Winter said.

"How are you going to get in?"

Winter shrugged. "Well, I figured out last year that locked doors didn't seem to be an issue. I'll go there sometime at night."

"You mean, break in?"

Winter hesitated and her jaw tightened. "We have to protect Sandy. If God doesn't want it done this way, then he'll stop me."

Peter raised his eyebrows. "Winter, I think you know this isn't the way God would have you do it. There has to be another way."

Winter clenched her fist and looked away.

"Look," said Peter. "Why don't we case the place for a couple of days, and find out how many people work there and at what times. Maybe we can find an opportunity to go in legally for you to get what you need."

Winter glared at him. "But wouldn't it be stealing if I took something? Or is stealing okay with you, so long as I don't break in?"

Peter sighed. "You won't need to steal anything, just get the info. I thought you had a photographic memory? Just figure out a way to get in legally and let the prophet stuff help you out."

"It's not a photographic memory. It doesn't work like that."

"Okay, then take pictures with your phone."

"You don't make this easy."

Peter smiled. "Just trying to keep you honest."

Ayden crossed in front of them again, leaving with take-out.

Winter grinned. "Maybe there's another way." She shoved the stocking cap back onto her head and followed Ayden out the door.

# 40

Ayden was only a few yards away. Winter pulled her open coat tight with one hand and sprinted after her.

"Hey." Winter slowed and fell into step beside Ayden.

Ayden turned to her briefly. "Hi."

"Can I talk to you?"

"I guess." Ayden firmed her lips and sped up a little.

"There's no easy way to explain this, but I need your help."

"Really? How so?"

Winter grabbed Ayden's arm and stopped.

Ayden turned to face her, narrowing her eyes.

"Someone's in trouble, and I think you can get me some information I need." Winter let her arm fall back to her side.

"Well, you're going to have to do better than that if you want my help."

Winter took a deep breath. "I have reason to believe that the people supporting the AFRC chapter may have an ulterior motive to find a particular student."

"Why would they want to do that?"

"Well…that's complicated. But I believe they want to hurt her."

"Who is she?" Ayden crossed her arms.

"I don't know," said Winter. "But I think the AFRC might."

"And who are they?"

Winter sighed. "That's complicated too."

"Sounds like you've got a complicated problem then." Ayden turned her head and looked down the sidewalk. "I'm sorry. I can't help you."

Winter took half a step closer. "Look...I'm trying to help someone in trouble. If I told you who these people are, then you might get in trouble too. I'm very frustrated and I could use a break right now."

"How exactly am I supposed to help?"

"Sophie asked you to join AFRC, right? I thought maybe you could buddy up to her and ask who's funding them. Just a name. That's all."

"How's that supposed to help you?"

Winter shrugged. "Just the next step. I could go talk to the sponsor. Maybe get another clue."

"I don't think so."

"What?"

"That's a no, in case you misunderstood. I'm not going to help."

Winter crossed her arms. "Are you always this rude?"

"I'm the one being rude?" Ayden grunted and walked away.

Winter jogged to her side. "Why won't you help?"

"I don't like Sophie. She's a skank. End of discussion."

"Well, I should think you two would get along great then."

Ayden took a deep breath and cut her eyes to Winter. "I suppose I deserved that."

Winter nodded. "I know the feeling. Sorry."

"Listen, I don't want to get involved with the AFRC in any way. I'm sorry, but you've got the wrong girl."

"You're the only one who can help me."

"Are you sure about that? Why are you even getting involved in something like this? If this girl is in trouble, why don't you just call the police?"

Winter looked away. "It's complicated."

"Yeah, so you've said. Listen, take my advice and stay out of it. And if you insist on being involved, you should probably just figure out a way to do it yourself."

Winter clenched her teeth. "Easier said than done."

Ayden shrugged. "Not my problem. And at the risk of sounding rude again, I really need to get back to the dorm so I can study. So…"

"Yeah, sorry."

She stopped and watched Ayden walk away. Winter turned and drifted along the sidewalk toward the library.

Do it herself? That would be great if she could figure out how to control this prophecy gift. Winter crossed her arms and slowed down. She thought of the dream she had last semester of the tree, and the girl who asked why she was waiting to help her.

Was she waiting? What does it take? What's the difference between last year and this year? Was God waiting on *her*?

Premonitions were guides and danger warnings. Dreams came on their own. Visions were usually sparked by something. But what? Objects, eye contact. Was that really necessary? Could visions come without help?

Maybe she'd been looking for crutches this whole time. Purpose. Intention. Faith. That's all she needed.

Purpose she had plenty of. But what of intention? Had she really been trying to have visions? Had she been praying for them? Her cheeks warmed despite the cold air. No. She hadn't really done any of those things.

And what of faith? Winter bit her lip. Did she really know what that word meant?

She stopped halfway down the sidewalk to the Ancient. She stared at the old tree and prayed. She prayed for faith and direction.

For purpose and intention. She prayed for a breakthrough in finding Sandy. And she asked forgiveness for not praying enough. When she had finished, she started walking again.

A student came toward her on the sidewalk, a guy with blonde hair. *Purpose. Intention. Faith.* As he passed, Winter made eye contact.

All colors swirled and twisted, changing into different shapes and patterns. She was at a bar, with a loud group of guys. They were laughing and playing some kind of game. Her hand reached for the beer glass in front of her. No, not her hand, a guy's hand. It lifted the glass to her face.

The colors morphed back into the Meadow. The guy had passed by. Winter quickened her step, passing beneath the Ancient. Just before she reached the library, a girl came by. She made eye contact. *Purpose. Intention. Faith.*

The world changed and the colors shifted. She stood at a podium in front of a crowded classroom. All eyes were staring at her. She wrung her hands briefly and then straightened the notes on the podium.

The Meadow returned in a flash and swirl of color. The girl had walked by. Winter smiled with one side of her mouth. It was working. She jogged up the steps to the library.

A silent crowd gathered in the study room, poring over heavy books. Winter stood in the center aisle between the tables, waiting to make eye contact.

*Purpose. Intention. Faith.*

As each person looked at her, the world heaved and sent her to another place. With each connection she saw small glimpses into their lives. Each time she returned to the library, everything tremored for a moment, almost sending her to the floor. She planted her feet and continued, adrenaline surging through her at the new liberation of her visions.

*Purpose. Intention. Faith.* That's all it took. That's all it's ever taken. She knew that now. Winter raised her chin and laughed. More people, more eye contact, more visions. They came easily, as if she had been doing this her whole life.

A premonition washed over her. She smiled, recognizing the familiar guide that had been so absent this year. She began moving, following the premonition. She crossed the library to the main hall, moving around furniture, and weaving through distracted patrons. The premonition showed her where each person would step, and where she should step so as to move effortlessly and fluidly past. She walked the way she was supposed to do it. As if it were memory. This had all happened before…or so it seemed.

Winter looked up, guided by the premonition. Sophie sat with a couple of friends at a table near the corner. She knew Sophie would look at her…knew she would make eye contact. All Winter had to do was move a little closer and stand between two certain tables. She stepped forward and moved to the side, placing herself exactly where the premonition guided.

Sophie looked up. The connection was made.

Winter dove into the vision, pushing past the swirling colors and landing in Sophie's body and memory. She was at a desk. Papers lay in front of her – letters and check-stubs. Sophie's hands grabbed them in one quick motion, and squared them on the desk. She reached into a drawer…top drawer on the left. She lifted a false bottom and pulled out a small key on a plastic coiled key ring. Sophie stood and walked to a filing cabinet. Using the key, she unlocked it. Then she opened the second drawer. She flipped through the folders until she found one near the middle marked "Contributions." She opened the folder with two fingers and slid the papers in.

The Library came back in a flash. Sophie had looked away, the connection broken. Winter smiled. The premonition faded and she turned to leave.

Breakthrough.

# 41

*Four Years Ago*

Winter stomped through the hall, parting the crowd around her with the merest glimpse of her cold stare. They averted their eyes, stepping away as far as they could. A murmur bubbled in her wake, but she ignored it.

Her new piercings felt like numb spots on her ears and face. The belly ring burned as her shirt rubbed across it. She ground her teeth tighter, pushing the pain into the familiar hollow growing inside of her.

Winter made it to her locker, smashed one palm against the neighboring locker and reached to spin the lock with her other hand. She flung it open, slipped off her backpack, and exchanged a couple of books. As she slammed the locker closed, someone touched her on the shoulder.

She spun, fist clenched at her side. "What?"

Ryan stood there, face soft and eyebrows furrowed. "Are you all right?"

She jutted out her chin. "Why wouldn't I be?"

He looked around the hall.

Winter followed his gaze to the other students whispering and stealing glances in her direction.

He turned back to her. "It's just…you haven't been very social lately."

"So?"

"So, I thought maybe you might want to talk."

Winter crossed her arms and pulled them tight. "I have nothing to talk about."

Ryan frowned. "Did you do the piercings yourself?"

"Yeah."

"Did it hurt?"

Winter shrugged.

Ryan sighed. "I'm worried about you."

"Don't be."

"You're going down a very dark path. You need to step away from yourself and take a good long look at who you've become."

"What's wrong with who I've become? Maybe I like it. Maybe I haven't changed that much." She looked away from his constant stare and shuffled her feet.

"Yes…yes you have. Do you even remember who you were before you moved here?"

"Yeah. I was naive and immature. I've grown up."

"No. It's not that. It's…"

"What?" She narrowed her eyes.

"Look around you. What do you see?" Ryan gestured to the milling crowd.

"I see a bunch of idiots walking around."

"And are any of them looking over here?"

Winter gazed again at some of the nearest faces. Every head tilted to the floor the moment they saw her looking, not one made eye contact. She bit her lip, a small pain stabbing her chest this time. "What's your point?"

"They're scared of you."

Winter blinked and looked at the floor. "W...why would they be scared of me?"

Ryan took a deep breath. "Everybody knows that Claire's a witch. Everybody knows that Alison hates Claire, and that she's been playing with magic to get her back. Most everyone is afraid of them...afraid of what they might do to anyone they don't like."

"Most everyone?"

"I'm not, at least. But a lot of the people here realize how dangerous this magic stuff is, and it scares them. Heck, the magic stuff scares me a little, even if Claire and Alison don't. It's dangerous and it's not right."

"But I'm not fooling with magic. I told them to leave me out of it. So what does this have to do with me?"

"The whole school is afraid of Claire and Alison...but the only thing Claire and Alison are afraid of is you."

Winter shuffled again. "W...what?"

"Half the school saw you get between Claire and Alison the other day. They saw you stand up to them and put them in their places. You yelled at them, tore them down, and they stood there and took it. Half the school saw Claire and Alison run from you."

Winter bit her lip and looked around again. Still no one would look at her.

Ryan stepped closer. "They know what Claire and Alison are, and it scares them. But what are you? What are you that those two fear you? That's why no one will look at you...that's why no one will talk to you."

Winter unfolded her arms and refolded them to hold her elbows. "That's...that's stupid. It's..."

"Do you even pay attention to people when you walk down the hall anymore? I've seen you. You walk like they're not even there."

"No I don't."

"Yes you do. You run over people and curse at them like it's their fault. Like it or not, Winter, most of the school is afraid of you…and I think you like being left alone."

Winter looked away. "Why do you even care?"

"Because no one should be by themselves."

"You can't fix me."

"I'm not trying to. But I remember how fragile you were when you came here. You thought no one noticed you then and it hurt. Now you want to not be noticed and you want to hurt."

"So?"

Ryan leaned against the lockers. "This is not the real you."

"What would you know about the real me?"

"I know some. Like right now, the way you look away and fidget because I told you what everybody else thought. Deep down it bothers you."

She balled her fists and leaned toward him. "You don't know that! You don't know anything about me!"

"Sure I do. We're a lot alike."

"No we are not!"

"We both lost our mothers…people who loved us very much."

Winter roared and pounded both fists into the lockers. Stillness fell through the hall like ash. Then the crowd surged away.

Ryan took a step back. "I'm sorry."

She leaned forward and rested her head against the cold metal. "Just leave me alone," she whispered.

Ryan rested one hand on her back. "Winter, you don't have to be alone."

The hollowness deep inside of her bubbled up into her throat. It crept into her sinuses and the back of her head. It clawed into her muscles and made her tremble. It leaked out of her eyes and ran down her cheeks.

The tardy bell rang. Winter ignored it.

Ryan's hand left her back. A moment later he pushed a piece of paper into her hand. Then he left.

Winter lifted the paper to where she could see it beneath the draping of her black hair. With her other hand, she slowly unfolded it. She blinked to clear her vision.

It was Ryan's phone number.

# 42

*Present Day*

"How do I look?" Kaci asked.

Winter darted her eyes over Kaci's turtleneck, blue jeans, and thick makeup. She sighed. "You look pretty. But you're still hiding."

"Just be glad I agreed to do this again."

Winter smiled and continued brushing her hair. No matter how much she wanted to concentrate on making this group outing fun for Kaci, her mind kept returning to what she saw in Sophie's eyes. She needed to get into the AFRC office, that much was for sure. But how?

"Winter?" Kaci asked.

"Sorry. Just thinking. What did you say?"

"Um…I was just thinking about changing shirts. I know you're right, of course. And I don't want to hide so much. But I just…"

"I think a different shirt is a great idea."

"You don't think people will stare at the scar?"

Winter shook her head. "Probably not. It's really not that bad. But why don't you put a little base and powder over it, if it'll make you feel better."

Kaci's eyes lit up. "Yes. I'll do that." She turned to her closet to retrieve another shirt.

Forget what Peter said, maybe she should break into the AFRC. No. It wouldn't be right. Maybe she should find Sophie again. But Sophie would never cooperate. If only Ayden wouldn't be so stupid. Maybe someone else could help. What about Sadie?

"How does this look?"

Winter turned to see Kaci wearing a light blue, long-sleeved tee. "It looks great."

"Okay. I'm almost done. Let me just put a little something on my neck."

Sadie probably wouldn't talk to her anymore. Winter sighed again. One big breakthrough, and now she couldn't even follow up on it.

Winter waited for Kaci to finish with her make-up, and then they went together down to the lobby. Peter was waiting for them already, grinning like a toddler.

"You two look nice," he said. He held open the door for them.

Winter smiled.

"Thanks," said Kaci.

Peter adjusted his leather jacket and fell in step beside Kaci, as Winter led them to her car. He followed Kaci to the passenger side and opened the front door for her. Then he dutifully climbed into the back.

Winter hesitated, suppressing the screaming memory that tried to surface.

"What's wrong?" Kaci asked.

Winter took a deep breath and pushed her thoughts back toward Sophie. "Nothing. I'm fine."

She drove them off campus and into Cherithville. Peter and Kaci talked constantly. Winter focused so hard on Sophie that by the time they reached the bowling alley, she couldn't remember driving there.

Winter found a parking spot across from Summer's Bug. Summer and Davis waited for them by the entrance, standing shoulder to shoulder.

Winter smirked. Maybe one of them would actually make the first move tonight.

As they bowled, she watched Summer and Davis trying to hide their budding relationship, and Kaci and Peter laying the foundation of what seemed to be a new one. It warmed her inside. It warmed her…in a hollow way. She had felt that way once. Tears formed in her eyes.

"You're up, Winter," said Peter. "This is it. You're the last frame of this game."

Winter stood, took up the dark purple marble-finished bowling ball, and hurled it down the lane. Six pins fell. She waited with her hand over the air blower, listening to the laughter and happiness behind her. They had no idea how she felt…no idea.

The ball came up. She grabbed it and hurled it again. Gutter-ball.

"Aww…too bad," said Summer.

"Looks like I win," said Peter.

"Whatever," said Davis. "I'm just warming up. I'll get you the next game."

Winter turned and walked back to the seat where her shoes waited. She started changing shoes. The entire night she had watched Summer and Davis tiptoe around what was obviously a mutual crush and Kaci and Peter hitting it off in what was sure to become another one. It was time she got out of the way.

"Are you not playing anymore?" asked Kaci.

Winter smiled, hoping the gesture might fill some of her emptiness. She simultaneously wanted to congratulate Kaci and wanted to run and cry in a hole somewhere. "Um, I think I want to go on back. I've got a paper I need to work on."

"Come on. Don't be that way. You can take one night off from homework."

"Really, I'm not feeling great either." The face Winter had been pushing back all night came floating forward in her mind. Ryan. She tensed and shoved the image away. "Summer, do you have room to take Kaci and Peter back?"

"Yeah, no problem."

"Are you sure you don't want to stay?" asked Peter.

"No. I need to go." She stood and grabbed the rental shoes in one hand. "I'll see you later," she said to Kaci.

"Okay, then. Good night," said Kaci.

Winter turned away from them and walked toward the counter while the others spoke their goodbyes to her back. She held up a hand to acknowledge them, but didn't turn around.

Her anger and grief warred within her during the drive to campus. It was a strange turmoil that left her feeling mostly empty. She didn't know what to feel anymore. Why did the others get to be so happy? Why not her? It wasn't fair.

Winter forced her mind back to Sophie and the question of how to get into the AFRC.

*What do I do now?*

*"Sophie,"* a voice whispered in her car. Winter jumped and twisted to look in the empty back seat.

Her heart drummed and she spoke the words aloud this time. "What do I do now?"

*"Sophie,"* said the voice.

"Great. Now I'm hearing voices. Listen, whoever you are. Either I'm crazy or you're real. Either way, that answer means nothing to me. I need a little more than that, please."

*"Sophie."*

"Seriously, stop it you creepy disembodied voice. I mean it. Shut up. You're not helping."

*"Ryan."*

Sharp pain erupted from Winter's heart and stabbed out into her arms and legs. She slammed the brakes and screamed. Her throat constricted. She tried to inhale, but her lungs refused air. The trembling in her body only allowed quick shallow breaths. Someone honked behind her so she inched her car to the curb.

She squeezed the steering wheel and laid her head on it, trying to slow the palpitating of her heart and the rasping of her breaths. All the emptiness that she had tried to avoid suddenly consumed her from the inside out. She lifted a leaded arm and released her clenched fist to fall on the dash.

*"Sophie."*

"Leave me alone!"

*"Sophie."*

Winter lifted her head. She rubbed the cold fog from the windshield with the cuff of her coat. The Raven was only about half a block ahead. The door opened and Sophie walked out with two of her friends.

Winter sat up straight, heat spreading where ice had just been.

Sophie laughed, waving to her friends. She got into a car and started driving toward campus.

Winter lifted her foot off the brake and followed.

# 43

Winter followed Sophie to Boon Hall, the twin dorm that stood next to Devine, and parked. She stood behind her open car door to watch Sophie from across the street.

Sophie took a long time to get out. When she did, she went straight to the back of the car and opened the trunk. She pulled out a briefcase and walked away from the dorm toward the Meadow.

Sparks ignited in Winter's mind, morphing into guiding images and inaudible voices. The future stretched out before her like a movie. She let the premonition be her guide, gliding through the parking lot at the perfect speed and in the perfect path to follow Sophie without being seen.

Sophie went to Upton Hall, the faculty offices building next to the Arts Plaza. Winter took a step into the Arts Plaza and watched from behind a column. Sophie jogged up the steps and danced her fingers over a numeric keypad lock.

When the door closed, Winter ran to the keypad. She peeked through the sidelight of the door, but Sophie had already gone. Stupid really. The premonition already told her that. Sophie was almost to the second floor by now.

Winter stared at the keypad, letting the images and memories of the premonition float to the front of her mind's eye. Her fingers danced like Sophie's and the lock clicked.

Winter jogged to the end of the hall and entered the stairwell. She slowed in the cavernous space and ascended on her toes. At the top, Winter peeked through the small window in the fire-door knowing already that the AFRC's office was just on the other side to the right. The door was open and the light on.

Winter waited and watched.

It's what she was supposed to do.

A moment later, Sophie emerged and went further down the hall to another room.

She left the door wide open.

The premonition goaded Winter to action. She eased through the fire-door and moved to the office, still walking on her toes.

Only the front room was fully lit. A desk sat in the middle, guarding the passage to the inner office. Sophie's briefcase sat on top of it. Shelves lined one wall, but only a handful of books and a few stacks of paper occupied them. Winter skirted the desk and went into the back office, lit only by a single lamp. It wasn't much different than the other office except three filing cabinets stood beside the bookshelves and a fake plant sat in the back corner.

Winter followed the vision she had when she made eye contact with Sophie in the Union. She let the premonition bring it up like a photograph.

Huh. Maybe that's how it worked. Maybe not a photographic memory at all…just a function of the premonition.

She rounded the desk and grabbed the drawer. When she lifted the false floor she found the key as expected. Winter snatched it up and went to the filing cabinets. She slid the key in.

Winter froze. Footsteps sounded in the outer office, followed by shuffling around on the outer desk. Winter slid sideways to the corner nearest the door and slunk into the shadows. A second later Sophie walked in and placed the briefcase on the desk. She turned opposite Winter and walked out, never looking in her direction.

*Score one for dressing in black,* Winter thought.

The light went out in the other room, and the exterior door clicked.

Winter waited a few minutes, taking shallow breaths and straining to track Sophie's footsteps, but she couldn't.

Winter slipped to the window and peeked through the blinds, squinting against the brightness of the street light. The window faced opposite the Meadow and Sophie was nowhere to be seen.

Winter bit her lower lip and crossed the room to close the office door. She pulled open the second drawer and started flipping through the folders searching for the one marked "Contributions" as she had seen in her vision. It was there, near the middle.

Winter yanked it out and went to the desk.

"Come on…what am I looking for?" The folder contained only check stubs and letters.

"There's nothing here!" She flipped through them again. The letters all had different names and addresses, nothing that could be a clue. She picked up a check stub and looked closer, reading the address. Then she picked up the rest and flipped through them. "Mordensfield Savings and Loan…Mordensfield Savings and Loan…these are all from the same place."

Winter held one stub to the light, staring at the bank watermark. *Why does it sound familiar?*

The briefcase. Winter tossed the check stubs aside and reached for the briefcase. The latches popped open on the first try. She lifted the lid.

A legal dictionary and some legal documents. Winter tilted her head and leaned in to better see the letterhead. Johnson Legal Associates, LLC. Mordensfield.

Keys rattled in the hall. Sliding of a key into a lock. The exterior door opened. Light shone through the crack at the bottom of the office door.

Silence. Winter closed the briefcase and slid the folder into a stack of papers on the desk. She crumpled the one check stub still in her hand and shoved it in her coat pocket.

"Who's here?" Sophie called from the other room.

Winter instinctively thought about flipping the lamp out. But she knew Sophie would notice.

The door opened.

Winter slid back into the corner and closed her eyes, holding her breath.

*God hide me!*

Sophie stepped in and paused. She scanned the room, looking past Winter without seeing her. Sophie walked around the desk and looked underneath. "Hello?"

Winter dared to move her arm. Sophie did not react. Winter took a step toward the door. The sleeve of her trench coat brushed the wall and Sophie looked up at the sound.

"Who's there?" Sophie spun around, eyes darting to every corner and shadow. Her face paled and she held her arms up at her sides as if to keep her balance. She jumped to the window and peered through the blinds. "This isn't funny!"

Winter took two large steps and slipped through the office door. As she reached the outer office she paused and looked back. Sophie had her arms crossed over her chest, with one arm up, holding a cell to her ear.

"Hello? Security?"

Winter smiled and stepped into the hall. She reached back for the doorknob and slammed the door.

Sophie screamed.

# 44

*Four Years Ago*

Winter glanced up from her notebook where she jotted down notes in the library. Ali sat across the table from her, scanning an encyclopedia and writing notes of her own. Ali brushed her faded black hair behind one ear. Her blonde roots gleamed near her scalp again.

Winter pursed her lips and threw down her pen. "Why don't you hate me?"

Alison looked up and blinked. "What do you mean?"

"I'm a horrible friend. I yelled at you in the hall. And despite the fact that you hate Claire, I still talk to her."

"So?"

"You still hang out with me like nothing's wrong. Why don't you hate me?"

Alison narrowed her eyes. "Why would I hate you?"

"Why not? Everyone else does. You and Claire both treat me like I'm in charge. Why?" Winter leaned forward on her elbows.

Alison looked around and sat up straight. She tapped her pen on the table. "I'm not sure I know what you're talking about."

Winter took a deep breath. "There *is* something going on. What is it? Tell me."

"Winter, calm down. It's nothing."

"Then why won't you answer my question?"

"I…I…"

"Ryan says you're scared of me. Is that true?" Winter leaned back and crossed her arms.

Alison stared at the table. Her face flushed and the pen stopped tapping. At that moment the bell rang. Alison grabbed her books and fled.

Winter snatched up her things and shoved them into her backpack. She stormed through the crowded hall searching for Claire. This time Winter noticed the crowd parting before her. She caught hidden faces and the nervous glances. And it made her blood boil even more.

Winter found Claire near her locker.

"Claire!"

Claire turned. Her eyes widened and darted in every direction as if she were looking for a way to escape.

Winter clenched her teeth. "Don't you dare run away! I need to talk to you." Winter stopped inches from her and leaned into Claire's face.

Claire looked at the ground.

"I want to know what's going on, do you understand? I want to know why you and Alison listen to everything I say and why the both of you won't dare talk back to me, even though I'm *not* the one who is a witch!"

Claire jerked her head up. "Shh!"

"I will not! What have you done? Did you put some kind of spell on me?"

"Not here, Winter. Please be quiet."

Winter narrowed her eyes. "I want to know."

Claire sighed. "Okay. But later."

"No. Now."

"I have Biology."

"Skip."

Claire looked around and her shoulders slumped. "All right."

Winter grabbed Claire's arm and pulled her toward the exit. They went to the far side of the football stadium to a secluded spot beneath the bleachers. Neither spoke.

When they were sufficiently hidden, Winter turned on Claire. "You and Alison are scared of me. Why?"

Claire dropped her backpack and sat next to one of the stadium supports. "It's complicated."

Winter glared down at her. "Is it a spell?"

"No."

"Then what?"

"You're…protccted."

Winter blinked and her arms dropped. Her anger simmered. "Protected? What do you mean?"

"It's difficult to explain. Ali doesn't really know what it is because she got kicked out, but she knows enough to be frightened. I'm not even sure I can explain right."

Winter sat down facing Claire. "Then try."

"You have…something around you that's bright white."

"Like, I'm glowing?"

Claire shook her head. "No. It's not you. It's around you. It's…following you."

"Like an aura?"

"No. Not an aura."

"Then I don't understand. You're going to have to explain it better." Winter tried to put venom into the words, but they came out softer than she wanted.

Claire looked at her and smiled. "Let's see…Imagine bumper cars."

"Okay…"

"Each person is like a bumper car. Everyone has a rubber shock absorber surrounding us…that's our aura. Follow?"

"I think so."

"We also have this wire thing connected to the ceiling…this is how we get our spiritual power."

Winter tilted her head and frowned.

"Listen, it's not a perfect analogy, but it works for what I want to explain, okay?"

"Okay."

"You don't have a bumper…at least not one we can see."

"I don't have an aura?

"You might. It just can't be seen.

Winter twisted her mouth and hunched up her eyebrows. "That doesn't sound like protection. Why don't I have one?"

Claire leaned forward on her knees. "Your aura can't be seen because you have things around you."

"Things?"

"Yeah…they're not bumpers, more like sledgehammers. And they're not plugged into the spiritual power like the rest of us, they're powered by…um, solar energy?"

"Solar energy."

"Yeah. It's more natural or pure, if that makes sense."

Winter scrunched her eyes. "So, let me get this straight. Where everybody else is in a bumper car, my car has no bumper."

"Right. Or at least it can't be seen…"

"…because I have solar sledgehammers all around me…"

"…that are prepared to destroy any bumper car who tries to hit you."

"Right." Winter blinked at Claire for a moment.

Both girls started laughing.

"That's dumb!" Winter said.

Claire shook her head. "It may be dumb, but it's the best I can do."

"So what is it really?" asked Winter.

"I don't know. Neither does Madam Morial. She says it's kinda like the aura she sometimes sees around Christians, except it's not an aura."

"It's something surrounding me," Winter said.

"Yes. It's some *thing* or *things* protecting you."

"Is that why they wouldn't let me stay for your induction? Is that why they freaked out?"

Claire nodded. "I think so."

"But how come she didn't freak out when I went to the store with Ali?"

Claire shrugged. "I guess they didn't want whatever it is around you messing up the ceremony. Not much danger in a store, really. Madam Morial doesn't hate you or anything. She'd like to study you, if you'd let her."

"Whatever. So, is this also why you and Alison are scared of me?"

Claire looked at the ground and rubbed her fingers. She scrunched her forehead in thought. "I'm not scared of *you*. I'm scared of whatever it is that's around you. Madam Morial warned me to be careful. Alison…well, she's probably scared of you because she thinks you're more powerful than her."

"That doesn't make sense. I don't care about witchcraft."

Claire raised her eyebrows. "You do know that Alison is still messing with black magic, don't you?"

Winter looked at her hands.

"She convinced Madam Morial to let her study, but secretly she'd been learning black magic. Madam Morial banned her. She hates me, Winter. She may have pretended to get over the whole Phillip thing, I don't know. But I'm the one who told Madam Morial what she'd been doing. I think she's going to do something stupid."

"Don't try to turn me against her."

"I'm not. She's your friend, and I respect that. Maybe…maybe you can help her."

Winter met Claire's eyes. "I don't want to help anyone."

"Scared or not, you have influence over her. Think about it. If she does something stupid, it's going to be to try and hurt me."

"She wouldn't go that far."

"You'd be surprised."

Winter shifted on the ground and grabbed her things. "I should go," she said as she stood.

"Please, Winter. Say something to her."

Winter glared at Claire, and then walked away.

# 45

*Present Day*

Winter ran back to Devine, working up a sweat despite the freezing air. She slung off her coat and collapsed on a couch to wait in the lobby for the others to return from bowling.

What was Mordensfield? What did it have to do with Sandy?

At almost midnight, Peter and Kaci came in. Winter stood and rushed to them.

"Hey, Winter," said Kaci. "You're still up."

"I wanted to talk to everybody. Where's Summer and Davis?"

"Summer dropped off Davis and then dropped us off by the side of the building. She's probably back at Carmichael by now."

Winter huffed. "Well, this can't wait. It'll be just you two."

Kaci looked at the floor. "Um. Do you mind?"

Winter rolled her eyes. "Whatever, Kaci. Go. I'll just talk to Peter then."

Kaci's shoulders slumped. "Sorry. I'm trying. I'm just not ready."

Winter clenched both fists and grunted. "You know, Kaci? You're not the only one who's been through a load of crap! I'm trying to be patient with you…I'm trying to understand. But at some point, you need to start being a friend again and start actually listening to me. Things are still happening around you. Stop ignoring it!"

Kaci's mouth fell open.

Winter reached out to her. "I'm sorry. I didn't mean to snap…"

Kaci put a hand to her mouth and ran to the hall.

"What's wrong with you?" Peter loomed in front of her.

Winter shook her head. "I…I don't know. It just came out."

"Even if you're right, how can you talk to her like that?"

Winter ground her teeth and glared. "Don't worry. I'll fix it."

"You'd better."

Winter huffed and turned to walk away.

"I thought you had something to tell me."

"Are you sure you want to hear it?"

Peter crossed his arms. "Just because you're being a jerk, doesn't mean I'll be one too."

"Forget it."

Peter grabbed her shoulder. "No. Tell me. It may be important."

Heat radiated up Winter's neck and warmed her cheeks. She shrugged him off and stomped to a table. "A name…a town I think. Mordensfield. I got this from the AFRC office. All of them had the same town. Legal documents too. Whoever's funding the AFRC is from here." She pulled out the crumpled check stub and tossed it on the table.

Peter picked up the check stub and studied it. "I've heard of this place somewhere."

"I was thinking the same thing," said Winter. "It sounds familiar and I can't figure out why. Do you know how to find out?"

"Well, probably a simple internet search would suffice."

Winter nodded. "I'll grab my laptop and be right back."

She ran to the elevator and went up, boots squeaking on the waxed floors. Kaci wasn't in the room. Part of Winter was grateful for that. She snatched her laptop off the desk and ran back out.

Heart pounding, she slowed her steps and caught her breath as she neared Peter again. She set the computer down, flipped it open, and pressed the power button.

Her anger dissolved. A flush crept up her cheeks. "I'm really sorry about what I said to Kaci. And I'm sorry I upset you too. I promise I'll apologize just as soon as I see her again."

Peter nodded. "Good. But you were right, really. Kaci keeps to herself too much. It's not healthy. Is she doing any counseling?"

"Not that I know of. I imagine she did over the summer. But I'll have to call her mom to be sure."

"Maybe more space and time will help. I don't know." He picked up the check stub again. "So you think this is it, huh? The big break you've needed."

"It's something. God led me to it, I'm sure of that. So it has to help." Winter leaned closer to the computer. "Here we go." She put her finger on the touchpad and moved the cursor around. "Are you ready?"

Peter slid the chair to her side. "Let's do it."

The search page opened and she typed in "Mordensfield."

"Are *you* ready?" Peter asked.

She paused and turned to him. "Of course. I've got to know."

"All right, let's see what we get."

Winter went back to the computer and clicked the search button.

Results popped up almost instantly. Winter scanned some of the title lines.

*Mordensfield Massacre*

*Tragedy in Mordensfield*

*Mordensfield: A Community Broken*

*Mordensfield School District Under Federal Investigation*

*Surviving Mordensfield*

*Preventing Another Mordensfield*

"My God," she said.

"No kidding. Wow. I wonder what happened. Click the first

one."

Winter did and the article pulled up. They sat in silence as they read. Winter put her hand over her mouth as she read further.

"Five dead. One teacher and four students," said Peter. "Geez, they were first graders! I remember this now. I was in fourth grade. Parents freaked out and kept their kids at home for days. We were all terrified."

Winter nodded. "Yeah. I think I remember it too. I would have been in second grade."

"But what does this have to do with…"

"That's her!" Winter placed her finger beneath one of the last lines. "*Sandy Wilson was the only survivor.'* This is it! She was there!"

"Look there's a picture." Peter pointed to the bottom of the screen.

Winter scrolled down. A little girl with long straight hair looked at them, smiling for a school picture.

Winter sat back in the chair, deflated. "That's not her."

"What? You just said…"

"I'm talking about something else. It's the Sandy we're looking for, yes…but that's not the little girl I've been seeing."

"You've been seeing a little girl?"

Winter glared at him.

"You tell me everything else, why not this?"

"Because…I don't want to, okay?"

"Yeah, sure. Whatever."

Winter leaned on the desk and pointed to the computer. "So how does this help?"

"Well," said Peter, "this happened years ago, and she was six going on seven at the time."

"Twelve years…she's the connection. When Erickson and Xaphan said over ten years, they both meant this. Her. They've been hiding her for twelve years, and he's been hunting her the whole time."

"She'd be eighteen going on nineteen now. A freshman."

Winter looked at the ceiling in thought. "But we visited all the possible freshman Sandys."

"Then I guess she doesn't use the name Sandy anymore. What about Sadie? Is this her?"

Winter sighed. "Maybe. But she adamantly denies it. On one hand it kind of makes sense, but on the other...my instinct says she's definitely not."

"Is instinct a part of prophecy too?"

Winter rolled her eyes. "Sometimes. What about this picture? Can we use it to make her look older? Then we could easily get Summer to check the girls in her dorm with the picture."

Peter frowned. "Age progression? We'll have to talk to Davis to see if there's any software we can get a hold of without involving the police."

"Well, what else is there?"

"The town. We could go visit. Maybe there's someone there who keeps in touch. Or maybe we could track the AFRC financial stuff...find Xaphan or Skotos like you said."

"But I wouldn't know where to start," said Winter. "Maybe the savings and loan bank, or the law office. Probably won't get us very far though."

"Well, what about this guy?" Peter pointed back to the screen. "It says here that Gerald Bevaldi warned the FBI twelve hours before the shooting. They arrived while it was still happening and almost caught the guy."

"Do you think he might know something?"

Peter shrugged. "If he warned the FBI, he knew something then. Maybe he can help now too. I think it's probably the best lead you've had all year."

Winter nodded. "Okay, so how far away is Mordensfield from here?"

"Look it up."

Winter pulled up another window and mapped Mordensfield from Cherithville. "It's about an eight-hour drive."

"Maybe we could make a weekend trip."

"We?"

Peter raised his eyebrows. "Um, yeah. You don't expect to go alone, do you? I thought you'd have figured this out by now. This lone ranger thing you've got going is getting old."

Winter shrugged. "Whatever."

"I'm sure Davis and Summer will come too. Wish we could get Kaci to come. We could make a nice trip out of it."

Winter stared at the first-grade school photo of Sandy. "Where are you?" she whispered. She turned to Peter. "When should we go?"

Peter twisted his lips. "How about sometime during spring break? That's just a few weeks away."

Winter sighed. "I hate waiting."

The weeks dragged by. With two papers due the week of midterms, Winter spent most of her spare time alone in the library. The week before spring break brought with it the standard stress and cramming of major exams. Winter breezed through most of them, feeling much more prepared and comfortable with the process this time around.

After her last test on Friday, she came back to her room to find Kaci already packing for spring break. Winter pulled a soda from the micro-fridge and collapsed onto her papasan chair.

She popped open the can. “I wish you’d come with us.”

“Sorry. I know I’ve not been much help, but this time it’s really more about the fact that I miss my mom.”

A twinge of jealousy forced Winter to look away.

“Oh. Sorry,” said Kaci. “I didn’t mean...”

“Forget it. After the way I treated you, I deserve it. But it’s okay. I understand how you feel.” She looked back to Kaci and tried to smile.

Kaci zipped up her suitcase. “I won’t be gone the whole week.

I'll probably come back Wednesday or Thursday."

"We should be back by then."

"Well, I guess I'll see you later. Be careful. I promise when I get back, I'll do better. Okay?"

"Oh, you're leaving now?" Winter stood and set her soda on the desk.

Kaci nodded. "I have to if I want to make it by dark." She pulled the suitcase from the bed and stood it on the floor.

Winter crossed the room and hugged her. "Don't worry about us. You be careful."

"I will."

They left early Monday morning, taking Winter's car. Peter insisted on helping her drive and Winter was glad for the breaks.

An hour before reaching Mordensfield, the GPS directed them off the freeway and onto a two-lane highway. Trees marched by on either side with the occasional break to showcase a field or farmhouse.

Winter kept her eyes on the horizon ahead. A shadow seemed to grow, hanging low above the trees. Clouds consumed the sun, giving the world a deathly haze. The shadows beneath the trees deepened and blurred. All of nature seemed to cower.

"What's that?" asked Summer from the back.

"I don't know," said Winter.

"Maybe it's a storm," said Davis.

"Yeah, maybe."

Winter felt a heavy tingling in her stomach…a dread she could not explain. She stole a glance at Peter in the passenger seat. He looked at her and frowned. Winter checked the mirror and saw Summer huddled next to Davis, her face as gray as the sky. Winter gripped the steering wheel tighter and took a deep breath.

A few minutes later, the trees thinned out to give room for the first fledgling buildings of the town. A faded welcome sign passed by.

*Welcome to Mordensfield. The Heart of Happiness.*

"Some slogan," said Peter.

Few cars were on the road, and even fewer people walked the sidewalks. Most of the businesses seemed to be long gone, with dark empty windows and vacant parking lots. They passed one church on the main road…windows and doors boarded tight.

"The whole town is dead," said Peter.

"It's more than that," said Winter.

Peter raised an eyebrow at her, but she just clamped her jaw and looked back to the road.

"I don't want to stay here," said Summer.

Winter shook her head. "No, of course not. Look on the GPS. There's another town about twenty miles away. It looks bigger too. We'll get our hotel there."

"So, what do we do now?" asked Davis.

Winter slowed and leaned forward, peering down both sides of a cross street. "There." She pointed to the right and turned. A moment later she pulled into the parking lot of Mordensfield Savings and Loan.

Winter parked the car and turned in her seat to the others. "The way I see it, we've got four possible leads. This bank is the first…they probably close in about thirty minutes. There's also the law office, but I'm not sure I even want to try them. Then we'll have the school and Gerald Bevaldi to find tomorrow. If we can't get a lead to Sandy from those three things, then maybe one of them will lead us somewhere else. I might even relent and go see the lawyers."

"What are we looking for here?" Davis nodded to the bank.

Winter pulled out the check stub and studied it. "I have an idea. I think I can find out the name behind this check. If I can do that, we'll add that name to our stops tomorrow." She opened her door.

"I'll be right back."

"Wait a second." Peter opened his door. "You're not going anywhere alone."

"I'm good waiting, by the way," said Summer. "Please lock the doors when you go."

Winter shook her head and held up her key ring. She pressed the lock button and the Beamer beeped. She led Peter to the door and went in.

Only a single teller occupied one of the four booths. A second stood before a plexiglass window, helping a customer in the drive-through line. A third employee sat behind a desk in the corner. There were no other customers inside.

Winter and Peter crossed the tile floor, passed through the velvet queue line, and approached the lone teller. The middle-aged lady looked at them over the top of her glasses.

"Can I help you?" she asked, her voice flat and uninterested. She looked back down.

Winter slid the check stub toward her. "I need to verify the name on this account."

The teller took the stub and glanced it over. "Are you one of the account holders?"

Winter shook her head. "No, I'm not."

The teller slid the stub back. "We are not allowed to look up information on accounts unless the account holder is present."

"Please? I really need to know."

"May I ask why?"

"I…uh…I want to send them a thank you note. This check was an anonymous gift," Winter said. She cringed inside at the lie.

The lady studied them a moment. "This stub comes from a business account."

"So?"

The lady narrowed her eyes. "I'm sorry. But bank policy does not permit me to give out personal information of any kind on our account holders. I cannot help you."

"Can you make an exception?" Winter asked.

"No."

"But…"

"I'm sorry, but I'm going to have to ask you to leave. We're closing."

"Come on." Peter grabbed her arm and guided her away. "Let's go."

As they walked back to the door, Winter glanced over her shoulder. The two tellers whispered together and pointed after Winter. The employee at the desk stared at Winter, holding a phone to his ear. His lips moved. A flicker of premonition made her want to run. She gave Peter a gentle push through the door and jogged past him to the car.

When she and Peter had gotten in, Winter locked the doors and pulled out of the parking lot.

"Well?" Davis asked.

"Nothing," said Winter. "But for some reason I think we should get away from here."

"What's going on?" asked Summer.

"I don't know." Winter turned back onto the main road. "But they saw right through me. Somehow I think they knew what I was after."

"Now what?" asked Davis.

Winter sighed. "Well, we're not getting anything from the bank. Let's go to the next town for the evening. Tomorrow, we'll find the school and Bevaldi."

Once outside the city limits, Winter floored the gas. They had to get away from there. Now.

# 47

*Four Years Ago*

Winter picked up Alison for a trip to the mall during spring break. She had been putting off Claire's request to talk with Ali, choosing instead to ignore the problem and try to act a little nicer to everyone. But it nagged her every time she spoke with Ali.

As they sat in the food court, Winter couldn't take it any longer. She finished her sandwich and stared at Ali. "Will you be honest with me?"

Ali shrugged. "I guess."

"I talked with Claire. She said you were still doing black magic, even after getting banned by Madam Morial."

Ali stared at her.

"Well?"

Ali looked at her food. "I still look at it a little."

"Have you been doing it, though?"

"Winter, there's some stuff you don't understand about magic."

Winter looked away and crossed her arms.

"I know you don't care to hear it, but you need to at least know how it works."

"Okay, so tell me."

"Do you know about the three-fold law?"

Winter shook her head.

Ali took a deep breath. "It means that whatever I do will come back on me three-fold. If I do black magic and hurt someone, then it comes back on me three times. It's the same with good stuff."

"Kinda like karma?"

"Sort of. Does that make you feel any better?"

"No."

Ali leaned back and gestured with her hands. "I can't do anything to hurt Claire without it coming back on me. Three-fold." She laid her hands on her chest. "That's a law in magic."

Winter took a deep breath and let the pressure fall from her shoulders. "So you don't want to hurt Claire?"

Ali sighed and clenched her teeth. "I'd love to hurt her. But I'm trying to wait for the three-fold law to catch up to her. I don't want to take the chance of doing something dumb myself and having it come back to bite me."

Winter narrowed her eyes. "And if the law doesn't catch her?"

Ali shrugged. "I don't know." She looked behind Winter, and smiled. "About time."

Winter turned and saw two guys walking up to them. They were both dressed in baggy clothing, with long black hair. One had piercings all over his face and the other just had a smirk.

The one with the piercings grabbed a chair and turned it around backward. He leaned it close to Ali and took a moment to cram his tongue into her mouth. When he released her, she blushed and looked at the table.

"Winter, this is Chase." She nodded to the guy at her side. "And this is his friend Louie."

Louie pulled up another chair and sat at the middle of the table. He leaned toward Winter and smiled.

Winter looked away and pulled her arms tighter against her chest.

"You want to go for a walk?" Chase asked. He stared at Ali like a dog staring at meat.

Ali giggled and stood. "Come on, Winter."

Winter stood up slowly and took a step away from Louie. "Um, I think I should go."

Ali groaned. "Are you serious? Come on, have some fun!"

"I don't think so."

"Fine." Ali looked at Louie from toe to head. "I think I can handle them both."

Winter rolled her eyes and walked off.

When she pulled into the drive at home, her dad's truck was gone.

"Dad?" Winter drifted through the vacant house to the kitchen. She set her keys on the bar. A scratchy note lay there waiting for her. It said, *Call ASAP.*

Winter pulled out her phone and called her dad.

*"Hello?"*

"It's me." Winter walked to the fridge and opened it. She stuck her head in to search for a snack.

*"Hey. I'm at the hospital."*

"Why? What happened?"

*"My father's had a stroke."*

She closed the fridge and sat at the bar. "Is he okay?"

Silence.

"Dad?"

*"No. He's in the ICU. They don't think he's going to make it. His body's starting to shut down."*

"Do you want me to come up there?"

*"There's nothing you can do. I'll call you if there's any change."*

"How late are you going to be?"

*"I'm not sure. Don't wait up. And don't go anywhere without calling first."*

Winter jutted out her jaw, but didn't release the smart-aleck comment flirting in her head.

*"I've got to go. I'll update you later, okay?"*

"Yeah, sure. Whatever."

*"Bye."*

Winter took the phone from her ear and pressed the end button.

She went to the freezer and dug out the chocolate ice cream. She scooped out a big bowlful and curled up on the couch to watch TV.

Part of her wanted to be able to feel something for her dad, maybe even feel sorry for him. But the other part, the stronger more dominant part, just didn't care.

She never knew that grandfather very well anyway.

Winter took a big bite of ice cream and smiled at the TV, letting the thoughts about her dad and grandfather fade into the void.

# 48

*Present Day*

Winter floated in the darkness, sight without any other senses. Light faded into being, illuminating bushes and small trees standing as silhouettes. She began to move, a body beneath her as a detached vehicle. The world bobbed with the forward movement. A hand reached out and parted the branches of a bush…a man's hand.

A parking lot lay just beyond, bordered by a three-storied motel. A streetlamp flickered. She flew through the parking lot, propelled by the body holding her sight captive.

Winter was carried up the stairs to the second floor, to a maintenance room near the elevators. The hand reached out again and opened a breaker box. It flipped several switches, and then the head turned Winter's sight back to the darkened balcony.

"Winter," said a child's voice.

Something pulled at Winter's eyes like muscles being stretched to a near breaking point. She wanted to scream, but had no mouth. After only a brief moment of pain, the tension released with a snap. The body walked away from her floating eyes. It was a man wearing all black.

"Winter."

Somehow she turned to the voice, like a cork turning in water. The little girl stood in the shadows. Not Sandy. The *other* little girl.

The girl stepped into a beam of light cast by a nearby streetlamp. "Wake up."

Winter's eyes popped open and she blinked at the ceiling, illuminated only by the faint green glow from the LED light on the smoke alarm. Her heart fluttered. She flexed her fingers experimentally and moved one arm. The numbness of deep sleep throbbed with the beginnings of wakefulness.

Winter rolled her head to look at the alarm clock on the nightstand between her bed and Summer's. Three in the morning. She sighed, trying to clear her head and bring back the details of the dream through the fuzziness of her brain.

A soft click brought her body to full alertness. She shoved herself up straight and strained her eyes in the darkness.

Too dark. Winter peered at thick curtains. The ethereal radiance that usually framed the curtains…was gone.

All was black outside.

The premonition flipped images through her mind, incorporating the dream sequence into her own real-time awareness. The data stream coursed through Winter, playing out every action that was about to happen. She took a deep breath, letting it process.

Another click. Time was up. Enough studying. Only five seconds left.

One. Winter lifted her legs and kicked to roll out of bed as silently as possible to the side between her bed and Summer's, landing toes first into her boots waiting on the floor.

Two. She grabbed the extra pillow and shoved it beneath the sheets as she crammed her right heel down into the boot.

Three. With one hand she slid the lamp to the front corner of the nightstand that was nearest Summer. With the other she grabbed the alarm clock and stood it on end against the lamp. Left heel down.

Four. She took two steps to reach the opposite wall.

Five. Two more steps and she was in the corner behind the door.

Another soft click. The door eased open. A small sliver of light shone in, followed by the soft padding of feet.

Winter held her breath as a gloved hand came into view holding a pen-light. The light flicked over Summer's blond hair, and then moved to Winter's bed. There the light stayed as the intruder moved in.

A surge of adrenaline flooded Winter's legs and arms. She clenched her fists.

The intruder's foot and body came into view. The other hand lifted, and Winter saw a faint glint of light off a long black cylinder. He took several steps into the room, leaving the door wide open.

When his entire back was exposed, Winter slipped behind him.

The man raised the gun to her bed.

Winter wrapped her hands around his neck and pulled. At the same time, she shoved her knee into his back.

The gun arm went wild. A muffled gunshot, like the sudden release of air.

Something shattered.

Winter grunted and pulled harder against the man's chin.

Summer screamed.

The man crumpled backward over Winter's knee, slamming his head into the ground. The pen-light rolled across the floor.

Winter twisted and dropped her knee onto the gun arm.

The man cursed and slung his other fist.

She leaned back out of reach, falling to her backside.

He swiveled to one knee, swinging the gun back to her.

With one booted foot she kicked at the gun hand, shoving it away. The other boot heel connected with his face.

He fell back, rolling, and came back to one knee. The gun swung in her direction.

Winter blinked. The premonition flashed again through her mind…did she forget something?

The man smiled and squeezed the trigger.

Click.

Winter launched herself at him and shoved the palm of her hand into his nose. He grabbed his face and stumbled backward through the door and onto the balcony.

"Hey!" came Peter's voice.

The man turned to Peter's voice and then ran the other way.

Winter crawled backward, panting, until her back rested against the wall.

Peter and Davis rushed into the room. Davis went to the hysterical Summer and wrapped her in his arms.

"What happened?" Peter knelt at Winter's side, eyes wide and face pale. "Are you okay?" He looked to Summer and Davis. "Is she okay?"

"Yeah. Near miss though. Looks like the bullet hit the clock." Davis's voice wavered.

Peter turned back to Winter. "Where are you hurt?"

"I…I'm not." Click. Her body trembled. Click.

"Are you sure? What happened?"

The gun. Click. "I…I don't know." She rubbed her arms. "I'm cold." Click.

Peter frowned. "You're sweating." He held out his hand. "Come on."

Winter tried to stand, but the room tilted and she fell back down. "No…I need to sit. I'm dizzy." Click.

Peter looked to the others. "Davis, she's going into shock. How's Summer?"

"About the same."

Peter leaned closer to Winter. "We've got to get you to our room. You're not staying here. Do you think you can walk if I help?"

Winter stared at him, trying to process his words, now distant…disconnected. Her mind and body seemed to float in opposite directions.

Peter slipped one arm behind her back and pulled. Winter pushed with her feet and leaned against him. Stars erupted before her eyes.

"Okay?" asked Peter.

"For now. I think I might throw up."

Davis crossed in front of them with Summer leaning against him.

"You can do it," said Peter. "It's just a couple doors down. You can lie down there. I'll come back and get your things."

Winter nodded.

Click.

# 49

Winter closed her eyes and tried to sleep, eventually passing out from exhaustion. An old man in a motorized wheelchair stared back at her in her dreams and she jolted herself awake. Summer grunted at her and Winter rolled over, scooting to the extreme edge of the bed.

Peter sat in the armchair by the window with his eyes closed. As Winter watched, he cracked them open and smiled.

"Trouble sleeping?" he whispered.

Winter nodded. "Not much use in it really. What happened to the police?"

Peter grunted. "They said they didn't have anyone available to respond right now…that they'd send someone in the morning, since there wasn't any imminent danger. What kind of psychotic place is this? And we're *outside* of Mordensfield."

"Same county. Same crazy rules. I'm not surprised. Skotos probably owns everything."

He opened his eyes completely. "How are you now?"

"Still a little shaken up. It's weird. That's never happened to me before."

"What? Someone trying to kill you?"

Winter slipped her legs out from the covers and sat up. "No. The panic attack. Not like that, at least. I don't know what happened."

Peter shrugged. "It's understandable."

Winter took a deep breath. "I guess all those other times were about someone else, you know? I was only in trouble because I was trying to save someone or it was about something different. But this time…"

"This time it was just about you."

"Yeah. And there I was on the ground, he was completely out of my reach, and no one was coming to save me. I was helpless. I was alone." She looked at the ground.

"What happened?"

"Nothing. The gun just clicked."

Peter smiled. "Guess you weren't alone."

Winter looked up and returned the smile. "Guess not. But still…it was me. I was the target this time, you know? I've become so used to worrying about someone else, I never thought it would be me. I panicked. I lost control. I mean…what's that say about me? How can I do this if I can't face the possibility of my own death?"

"It says you're human like the rest of us. You're not a superhero, so don't act like one. And death is inevitable for everyone. I'm sure God will keep you around long enough to get your job done…even if part of that job is dying to save someone else. So don't cheapen death. It has just as much purpose as living."

Winter let the words sink in, twisting her lips and nodding. "I guess you're right. This probably won't be the last time before all this is over."

"Probably not. But you'll do fine, I'm sure."

"Thanks." Winter stood. "I'm going to go catch a shower before Summer wakes up. She'll use all the hot water."

The steam helped to clear Winter's head, though the hot water reminded her just how tired she was. When she came out, everyone else was awake and watching a local news broadcast. Summer jumped up and claimed the vacated bathroom.

When each of them had had their turn in the bathroom, they checked out and stopped a few blocks away for breakfast and coffee. Peter insisted on driving back to Mordensfield. Maggots crawled in Winter's stomach as the shroud of haze grew on the horizon.

Winter turned so she could see everyone. "Whatever happens today, we stay together, got it?"

"I don't think you'll get any argument from us," said Davis.

They passed the first collection of houses marking the beginning of town.

"Where to first?" asked Peter.

Winter dug in her pocket and pulled out a scrap of paper. "I'll put this in the GPS. It's Bevaldi's address…or at least the one I found in the phone book."

She tapped the data into the GPS screen. The guiding voice from the navigation system instructed them to make a right. After a few more turns, they drove by an old complex of buildings. A tall fence with razor wire along the top ran round it. Inside the fence, grass and bushes grew uncontrolled. Most windows in the long low buildings had long been broken.

As they passed, they stared at it in silence. A faded sign beside the largest of the buildings confirmed Winter's unspoken suspicion.

Mordensfield Elementary.

"We'll come back later," Winter said quietly.

One final turn and they arrived at the address. As they climbed out of the car, Winter looked back at the abandoned school, still easily visible.

The old brick house had no porch. A blue tarp shrouded one corner of the hipped roof. White steel poles supported the flat roof of an attached carport, covering a faded van. The unkempt grass and bushes matched what they had just seen at the school.

Winter led the others to the front door and knocked. After a few silent seconds, she knocked a second time.

A flick at the curtain next to the door. "Go away!" yelled a gruff voice.

"Mr. Bevaldi, we need to talk with you, please."

"Why can't you people leave me alone?"

Winter crossed her arms. "I promise we won't take much time. We just have a few questions."

"No!"

"It's about Sandy."

Silence. "I don't know where she is," he said with less force.

"Please! We need your help. She's in trouble…"

Silence. Locks on the door began to scrape and slide. The door opened a crack and pulled tight against a chain. An old wrinkled face looked back at them from just above the doorknob.

"Are you saying that you do *not* intend to kill her?"

Winter looked down at the man and blinked. "Kill her? Who do you think we are? We're trying to save her."

The eyes flickered from Winter to the others. "Show me your forearms…all of them."

Winter shoved her sleeves up and presented her forearms. She turned and urged the others to do the same. Bevaldi scrutinized each arm in turn and grunted. The door closed. There was some scrambling behind the door, and then the sound of the door chain sliding. After another loud grunt, the door opened all the way.

"Come in." He turned his motorized wheelchair away.

Winter hesitated with one foot over the threshold. Was this a good idea? She glanced back to Peter. He nodded, urging her forward.

Bevaldi led them to the far side of his living room before turning back to face them. His beard was stringy and white. The hair on his head was sparse. He wore a flannel shirt and blue jeans. "Sit. Tell me what you want."

Winter sat on the couch nearest Bevaldi. Summer and Davis sat beside her. Peter took the chair against the wall.

"Um," she said, "your name was in the news article about the shooting."

"Yeah, so?"

"So, the reports said that you had been tipped and that you tried to warn the police. And we thought you might be able to help us."

The man stared at them. Winter shifted in her seat, looking at Peter and hoping he would jump in.

"How am I supposed to help you?" Bevaldi asked.

Winter fidgeted with her hands. "It's like this. We know that Sandy is at our school…we know because the federal agent who was watching over her told me that much. Xaphan killed him trying to find her."

At the name Xaphan, Bevaldi grunted yet again.

"The…the only problem is, we don't know who Sandy is. All we know is that Sandy was her old name, and we think the FBI changed it. She could be anybody."

Bevaldi narrowed his eyes. "I already told you, I don't know where she is."

"I don't want to know where she is," said Winter. "I want to know *who* she is."

"Why?"

Winter looked at the others and then back. "So we can protect her."

The old man crossed his arms. "So you're the new prophet, huh?"

Winter blinked and sat up. "Um, yeah. How did you..."

"I know, because I was the old prophet."

# 50

*Four Years Ago*

Winter refused to ride with her dad to the funeral home, but agreed to come an hour before the funeral began. She parked her Mustang and wrapped a black wool jacket around herself.

Winter slammed her car door and stared at herself in the tinted windows. She almost looked normal…like everything was perfect. Like nothing had ever…

Why'd she have to come to another stupid funeral?

Winter scowled and the illusion of normalcy shattered. She crossed her arms and stomped through the parking lot to the front doors.

A handful of elderly people mingled in the lobby. Winter walked to the threshold of the viewing room, hoping she could see her dad without going in. He stood talking with someone she didn't recognize.

Steve paused to glance at her. He gave her a small smile and waved.

Winter flicked her fingers at him and walked away. She went to another room and found a vacant corner to sit in and wait. After a half hour, Winter heard a younger voice from the lobby…a voice she thought she recognized. She thought about going to investigate, but then Ryan turned the corner.

"Hey," he said. "How are you?"

Winter shrugged and leaned back in the chair. "Fine, I guess. What are you doing here?"

He sat in the chair next to her. "Your dad called my dad. My dad wanted to come, so I came too."

"Why?"

"I don't know. I thought it might be kind of nice if you had a friend."

"I have friends."

"I know you do. But I figured this wasn't the kind of old-people party they'd show up for."

Winter smiled. "Well, I'm having a blast. Have you had any of the punch?"

Ryan laughed. "Not yet."

Winter's dad stuck his head around the corner. "Winter, can you come here, please?"

"Why?"

"I want to introduce you to someone."

She rolled her eyes and stood. Ryan stood too and followed just behind her. Steve led them to the viewing room and toward the casket where Winter's grandmother stood talking with a lady Winter didn't recognize. A cold lump grew in Winter's throat at the sight of the casket. She looked at the floor.

"Winter, this is your great-aunt Helen. I don't believe you've met her before. Aunt Helen, this is my daughter I've told you about."

Winter looked up at the introduction. The older lady wore formal black. She pressed her lips together and offered her hand in a dainty fashion. Winter squeezed it then crossed her arms again.

"She looks remarkably like Marie, doesn't she?" said Aunt Helen.

Steve nodded. "She does."

"How do you stand it?"

Winter's eyes widened.

"She's not Marie at all," said Steve.

"Well, that's good to know. It would be horribly inconvenient otherwise."

"What?" said Winter.

Steve furrowed his brow. "Aunt Helen, Winter and her mother were very close. I'm sorry, Winter. Aunt Helen likes to speak her mind. We've warned her to behave."

"Oh, pish posh! I will say whatever I like, thank you very much."

Winter clenched her teeth and Ryan rubbed her back. She shook him away.

"Well, I say good riddance," said Aunt Helen.

"Are you talking about my mother?" Winter shouted. She took a step forward, leaning in.

"Calm down, child!"

"Winter!" said Steve.

"Dad, are you going to let her talk about Mom like that? Come on!"

"Why wouldn't I talk about her like that? The woman was a harpy."

Winter clenched her fist and took another step. Ryan grabbed her shoulders, tugging back.

"That's enough, Helen!" Steve stepped between them and faced Winter. "Maybe you should go back to the other room."

Winter pointed past his shoulder. "Tell her to apologize!"

"I will not apologize," said Aunt Helen.

"Winter, go to the other room. I need to talk with your aunt a minute."

Ryan pulled harder and Winter stepped away.

As Winter turned Aunt Helen said, "You never told her, did you?"

"No," said Steve. "And I'd appreciate it if you…"

Winter spun back around. "Told me what? Dad! Told me what?"

"Winter…" Steve looked at the floor.

Aunt Helen flapped her shawl. "Well, if you won't tell her, I have no problem doing it."

"Helen, that's enough!" said Steve.

"Tell me what?" Winter stepped closer. "Whatever it is, tell me!"

Steve sighed. "It's about why your mother and I separated."

"You told me it was because you stopped loving each other. Was that a lie? Tell me!"

Steve shook his head. "No. It wasn't a lie."

Aunt Helen shook her head. "But it wasn't the full truth either."

"Helen, she's my daughter, I'll tell her." Steve stared at the carpet and clenched his jaw.

Winter turned to Aunt Helen and raised an eyebrow.

Aunt Helen blinked at her and looked at Steve, hesitating.

He wouldn't look up.

Aunt Helen reached out and put a gentle hand on Winter's arm. "Your mother had an affair, dear."

Winter's face and arms went suddenly numb. Her knees trembled. "That's a lie…Dad, tell her that's a lie!"

But he still wouldn't look up.

Ryan tugged at her harder than ever. She could hear him speaking into her ear, but she wasn't listening.

"Dad?" A knot solidified in her throat.

Steve looked up, eyes glistening. "I'm sorry. It's the truth."

The fight in Winter vanished. Her arms flopped to her side. Her legs nearly buckled and she would have fallen if it were not for Ryan wrapping an arm around her and pulling her away toward the other room.

"I've got to get out of here," she mumbled.

Ryan steered her to the door. "Come on. I'll drive."

She let him lead her to his car. The emptiness inside her bubbled and pushed up like vomit. He let her in and she sat staring at the dash. He got in and cranked the engine.

"Where do you want to go?"

She turned her head slowly, knowing she had nothing to say. Anger and loathing, fear and misery, all roiled together in the hollowness of her life, mixing into the acid rising through her body and eating at the lump in her throat. A tightness she wore across her skin seemed to snap into vapor. The stone encasing her heart shattered like glass.

Her jaw slacked. Lips parted. Sight obscured. And everything erupted.

Ryan wrapped her up with a tender embrace, placing one hand on the back of her head and holding her tight against his chest.

# 51

*Present Day*

Winter's heart started to flutter. "What? What do you mean, the old prophet?"

"Do you think you were the first?"

Xaphan's words from the dark cellar last year came floating back to her. *Your God has already sent several much more powerful and confident prophets to stop me.*

"And a fat lot of good it did me, too." Bevaldi shook his head.

Agent Gains sitting across from her in the apartment office. *He always kills the prophet. It's a game…*"But you're not dead," she said.

"Not for lack of trying. Just look at me. I'm not good for anything anymore. I might as well be dead." Bevaldi rolled over to the window and peered out. "Do you realize how dangerous it is for you to be here?"

The four of them looked at each other. "Yes, we do," said Davis.

Bevaldi looked back and nodded. "What you've got to understand is that there's more than one party looking for Sandy."

Winter sat up. "We know. Skotos. I've spoken with one of them.

They're working with Xaphan now."

Bevaldi sighed. "That's unfortunate. It wasn't like that in the beginning. Together they may be unstoppable."

Peter leaned forward. "So you know exactly what's going on? You know why they want her?"

Bevaldi nodded. "Maybe I should just start at the beginning." He rolled closer to them and leaned forward in his chair. "About twenty years ago, this crazy old evangelist by the last name of Smith had a near-death experience. When the doctors brought him back, he began telling these wild stories that turned into a prophecy. Now, I don't know if anything he said is true or not, but that's not the point. They were taken to be true by some dangerous people."

"What did he say?" asked Summer.

"I'm getting to that, blondie. This old man says that the end is coming, right? He says that before the end can come there must be a great revival. And that this great revival will begin with a woman. He said she won't use many words, but because of her millions will come to Christ. And then he says that this great woman will be born in a little over a year."

"Sandy?" asked Winter.

Bevaldi nodded. "That's right. She's the one."

Peter whistled. "Wow. The end?"

"Not until the revival. Smith was the first prophet. He spent the next two years searching for this child, until Xaphan found him and put a bullet between his eyes. Two days before he was murdered, he came here..." Bevaldi gestured to the front door. "…knocked on my door, and told me everything. I'd never seen the man before, but he said I was supposed to be the next prophet and that I needed to find and protect the child. They found his body a hundred miles away. I think he knew his time was up."

"What did you do?" asked Winter.

"I knew a family around here…knew they had a baby girl about the same age I should be looking for. The Wilson family. So I watched them. The kid didn't seem anything special, but I started to have these dreams about her and weird stuff started to happen. Animals disappearing. Strange people hanging around town. Normally nice people committing crimes. Had my first run-in with Skotos then. That's how I found out Xaphan wasn't the only one looking for Sandy."

"What do they want with Sandy?"

"Well, Xaphan wants her dead, obviously, if she's going to bring about the second coming of Christ, or whatever. Satanist and all that. But Skotos wants to turn her. They couldn't care less about what she's supposed to do, and want to turn her to do those same things for their cause. Does that make sense? If she's going to bring about the end of the world, it might as well be how they want it to happen. Skotos runs this town now. Nothing happens without them knowing. Guess they figure she'll eventually come back."

Winter looked out the window to the school, and her heart ached. "So what happened? It must have been horrible. How'd they find her?"

Bevaldi looked away. "Yeah. I'll never get the images out of my head. If I had only been an hour faster, maybe even thirty minutes." He shook his head. "It was probably my fault."

Peter furrowed his brow. "How?"

"I kept sticking my nose in Skotos's business. Once they figured out who I was…that I was the new prophet…they decided Mordensfield was the right town. They stopped looking, started following me around…watching me. I led them straight to her and didn't even know I was doing it."

Winter bit her lip and made eye contact with Peter. "How did you find out it was about to happen?"

Bevaldi shrugged. "How do you find out about things? Must have been a dream of some kind. I tried to warn the cops, but they didn't care. Called the FBI, but it wasn't until I mentioned Skotos and Xaphan that they started listening. Guess they thought I was crazy.

Took them hours to get here."

"She's in trouble again. Can you help us?" asked Winter.

Bevaldi shook his head. "I told you, I don't know where she is now. The FBI took her and she disappeared. Other prophets popped up after me to lead Xaphan and Skotos away from the trail. I suppose it helped. Now they're all dead and I'm lucky to still be alive. Lost my family, though. Xaphan seemed to enjoy the game. Sick bastard."

"And now it's just me."

He nodded. "Now it's you. Seems your job's a little bit bigger than ours. The first prophetess. I hope you have better luck."

"Why do you stay here in Mordensfield? Why not move away?" said Summer.

"Because there's nothing left for me to do. And I want to stay where I can be reminded of my failures."

Winter leaned forward. "Do you think we could…"

"You want to go to the school, huh?"

Winter nodded.

Bevaldi sighed. "I suppose it's only right. Maybe it'll spark that next vision you need."

Peter stood. "How do we get in?"

"There's a hole in the fence near the far corner. I go there sometimes…to pray, sort of."

Winter stood, her heart aching now for the man in the wheelchair. "You don't have to come with us. I think we can find it."

Bevaldi shook his head. "No. There are some things I should show you." He started moving his wheelchair to the door and they followed.

Bevaldi didn't look back as his chair sped toward the school. Winter and the others had to jog to keep up. He led them down a sidewalk to an old beaten path that ran beside the school fence. As they neared the far corner of the enclosure, the path turned and ran beneath a curl in the chain-link. Bevaldi slowed and maneuvered his way through the breach.

Winter ducked her head and followed.

He aimed for the nearest entrance, a set of rusty double doors at the end of a wing. About thirty yards from reaching the doors, he stopped.

"That's the way the gunman fled." He pointed to a grove of trees to their left. "There's an old creek bed he followed beneath those trees. The cops think he had a getaway car stashed about a hundred yards away." Bevaldi turned and pointed to an unassuming patch of grass nearby "And that's where he put a bullet through my stomach and into my spine." He wheeled away, electric motor humming.

Winter stared at the half-withered grass. Peter stepped to her side. "What are you thinking?"

Winter shrugged. "I'm not sure."

They caught up to Bevaldi as he reached the doors. Peter grabbed one and jerked it open for the others.

The whir of the wheelchair sounded irreverent inside the abandoned hallway. They contracted into a tight cluster, almost hanging on to each other for support, as Bevaldi slowly rolled ahead of them.

A thick layer of dust clung to everything, except where wheelchair wheels had carved tracks. Bevaldi rolled almost perfectly across the well-worn path. The air stunk of mildew and decay. Deep shadows clung to the corners where sunlight couldn't touch them. Gray light spilled into the hall and twirled through the dust like holy radiance from open doors and abandoned classrooms. With each classroom they passed, Winter expected to look in and see dead bodies. But there was never anything but old desks.

Bevaldi led them through the first hall, turned, and stopped at a wall of glass windows. The office beyond was mostly dark, but the interior offices entombed sacred light. He went in and led them to a back room.

"This is where they brought Sandy afterward. At least, that's what I was told. She left with the FBI from here and disappeared. Her parents were found dead at their home."

A towel lay in the corner, half of it tan with age, the other half black with decay. A wooden chair was next to it. Black streaks ran down its legs and black spots covered the floor beneath it.

"Did they…did they not even clean up?" Peter asked, his voice shaking.

Bevaldi rolled back into the hall. "No. Once the bodies were removed and evidence collected, nobody came back."

"But that's…" said Davis.

"I know," Bevaldi said. "Can't be helped. That's what happened. The town was so broken, they couldn't even deal with it. Put up the fence and had a new school built by that fall. This place was just left to rot."

He made another turn.

Butterflies floated near the end of the hall, by the dry-rotted remains of police tape on the floor.

Winter grabbed Summer's arm. "Do you see them?"

"See what?" Summer gave her a blank stare.

Winter pinched her lips and watched Bevaldi follow the wheel tracks in the grime to the room closest to the tape. As he neared the butterflies, they dissolved like glitter in the air.

Bevaldi rolled in and stopped just inside the room. Winter and the others filed in beside him.

Most of the desks were turned over and scattered. A few decaying book sacks hung in a row of cubbies against one wall. Black patches dotted the floor, as if someone had poured a thin layer of dark paint in random places throughout the room.

"Four kids died here, first graders…they were seven." Bevaldi started pointing to each black spot one by one. "Lucy Asbury…Jason Long…Amanda Green…" His voice cracked and he coughed.

A sob burst through Winter and she realized she had been crying. She wiped away the tears and turned to the others. Summer leaned onto Davis's shoulder, face red and wet. Peter's eyes were wide and glistening, jaw tight and skin flush.

With obvious effort and a strained voice, Bevaldi continued. "Little Billy Warren. And there, that's where the teacher Connie Morgan died. She was shot in the back. And as she fell, her dying act was to land on Sandy and shield her."

Winter bit her lips together and drifted toward the stain of Connie Morgan's blood. Connie…the woman who saved Sandy's life. *Would I do the same?* She knelt and reached out, the blood beckoning like a magnet. She placed a finger on the stain.

The world twisted and swirled with a kaleidoscope of color. Winter plummeted into the vortex.

A single tulip, small and unblossomed, stood above a field of emerald grass. The young bud filled her vision, until she could see little else but the immediate surroundings. The tulip glistened with dew, making the veins of pink shimmer like precious jewels.

The wind began to blow, slowly at first but swelling into a near gale. The tulip bent to the ground, until the fragile stem folded beneath the pressure and the flower fell.

The wind died away. Winter wanted to reach out to the tulip and hold it up. But strong hands reached down first. The fingers were callused from heavy labor, yet they touched the flower with the gentleness of a loving father. As they lifted the young flower back into place, the palm of one twisted toward her and she saw clearly a large white scar in the middle.

Winter held her breath.

The hands held the flower steady and lovingly, until the stem strengthened and it could stand again on its own. Winter watched as the flower began to grow tall and radiant. The petals opened with a simple beauty that warmed Winter's heart. The tulip radiated love and compassion.

Then an ugly black boot appeared and crushed the flower. Winter screamed and reached forward, but the hands returned. One hand caressed and lifted the flower. The other hand reached for her.

The fingers wrapped around her hand. The warmth and softness of the touch brought a deep longing and overwhelming sense of unworthiness to her soul. She wanted to weep and to laugh all at once. She wanted to rush forward and embrace the hidden man behind those hands. Yet at the same time she wanted to hide her face.

The hand pulled her forward, and placed the broken flower in her own hands.

"You must help her," said a voice…a voice she recognized. A voice that had spoken to her before.

"How?" she whispered.

The hands guided hers. "Hold her up, so she can grow again."

The limp flower collapsed like a piece of yarn. She tried her best to keep it straight, but it was almost impossible.

"It's so broken," she said.

"So were you once."

Winter sniffed back tears. "I don't think I can."

"I believe in you."

She adjusted her hands to catch the flower as it leaned another direction. "Will you help me?" she asked.

The hands reappeared and covered hers. "Of course."

The stem began to firm in her palms, slowly and delicately, and not quite as strong as it once was. New petals sprouted to replace the fallen ones, petals more beautiful than the old. Winter smiled and sighed. That's when she realized that the loving hands were gone, vanished without her noticing.

"Wait! Where did you go? I need you!"

"I'm always here, my love," said the voice, but the hands did not reappear.

"I…I can't find her." All the desperation from the past year danced from her voice. She gazed at the still strengthening flower, feeling more helpless than ever. "I'm sorry. I don't know how to find you."

The voice laughed, a strong and merry chuckle that embodied all the sounds of rushing wind, pouring rain, and thunder at once. But it sang out with the delicate honesty of a child. "My dearest Winter…you already have!"

A second flower sprouted from the roots of the first. Its color even brighter, its stem stronger. It glowed with a power that she didn't understand.

"What is this?"

The voice laughed again, and joined with it this time was the tinkling of little bells, as if the stars themselves shared the joke. "That one is not for you to tend, my love. Tend the first, the broken one. Without it, the second cannot grow."

"I don't understand."

The voice laughed a third time, and all of creation joined with it. "You don't have to! But you will. When you are ready. Now go. Take care of my garden."

The flower and the field pulled away. The deep colors and sounds swirled together into the same longing she felt when she heard the voice. She didn't want to go. She wanted to stay there…forever. Winter reached back out to the fading flower and cried out with a sound too instinctive to contain words.

She blinked. And found herself back inside the classroom, one finger still touching a forgotten bloodstain.

# 52

Winter watched the grass line at the edge of the road, replaying the vision in her mind and gently chewing the end of one finger as Peter took the first driving shift back to Cherithville. They all sat in silence as the dead town passed by.

"So now what?" Davis asked.

"Now, we find her," said Winter.

"But how?" asked Summer. "We didn't exactly find out anything new here."

"Yes, we did. I had a vision when I touched the blood." She turned back and glanced over her shoulder at Summer.

"Well…tell us about it," said Peter.

"I can't. It was…um, personal. But I know one thing for sure now about Sandy."

Peter stole a glance at her and looked back to the road. "Again with the personal."

Winter shot him a glare.

"What was it then?" Peter asked.

"That I've already found her."

"So you know who she is?" asked Summer.

Winter shook her head. "No. But I think we can figure it out. What do we know? Let's start at the beginning."

"She's a freshman," said Davis.

"And you've already found her," said Summer. "Which means she's probably one of the ones we've talked to."

"But if the FBI immediately took her away and she disappeared, then it's probably safe to say she doesn't go by Sandy anymore," said Davis.

Winter nodded. "Right. That leaves us only one obvious choice. Sadie."

Peter glanced at her again. "But I thought you said Sadie wasn't the one."

"She says she's not. I thought I was sure, but maybe I'm wrong. She has a tattoo of a butterfly, which matches the codeword I saw and all the butterflies I've been seeing. And she left almost immediately after the Christmas party when that Skotos guy was watching her. She's the only one who fits everything. It's got to be her."

Peter shrugged. "I still don't understand why you won't consider Ayden. She's shown up in your visions."

"I told you. There's…something else about her. It's not this."

"Besides," said Summer, "she's too old. She told me she took a year off before coming to college."

"I guess that settles it, then," said Peter.

"Okay, so it's Sadie," said Davis. "What do we do?"

Winter shook her head. "I'm not sure. Maybe I can talk to her again. If I tell her a little more about what's going on, maybe she'll come clean. If she knows who I am and what I'm supposed to do, she'll want me around right?"

"I don't know," said Davis. "I think you've got a major problem."

Winter frowned. "What?"

"Weren't you listening to Bevaldi? Remember what happened

last time? He led Skotos straight to her. Sophie said you're being watched."

Winter slouched into the seat. "I didn't think of that."

"Then we can't involve her just yet," said Peter.

"What are you suggesting?" Winter asked.

Peter shrugged. "Watch her. Figure out her schedule and one of us can try to be nearby at all times. But don't commit and don't get too close. Don't act like anything has changed. If Skotos comes after her, you'll know exactly where to go to stop them and they won't be expecting you."

"Protect her by ambush," said Davis. "I like it."

"And what if she comes to me and admits everything?" asked Winter.

"Then tell her to pretend like nothing has changed," said Peter. "Maybe get her to start asking around about Sandy. If she's on our side, Skotos will think Sandy is someone else. Does that make sense?"

Winter nodded and smiled. "I'm so glad you're helping."

Peter grinned. "You're welcome."

"I think this might actually work," said Davis.

"Are we done yet?" asked Summer. "I want to nap."

Winter nodded. "Yeah. I think we're okay for now. Go ahead. I think I might nap too. Peter, wake me when you need a break."

Winter reclined her seat a little and turned her head toward the window. She let her heavy eyes close and drifted into visionless sleep to the drone of the road noise.

# 53

*Four Years Ago*

Winter sat in the back of Chase's car beside his friend Louie. She stared at the top of Alison's hair sticking up just beyond the headrest, trying to ignore Louie staring at her. Ali giggled and leaned her head on Chase's shoulder.

All Winter could think about was going home. But Ali had insisted. A party was just what Winter needed, so she said. Something to take her mind off things again. A double date.

Winter closed her eyes to reinforce her numbness. She stole a glance at Louie and he grinned, brushing his stringy hair from his face. Winter clenched her teeth and turned to stare out the window. Her hip already rested against the door, but she pushed it in a little tighter. Maybe the door would open so she could just fall out.

Chase found a place to park on the crowded street outside the party. The teens hanging out on the lawn watched them. Winter didn't wait for anyone else to get out, and opened her door first. Louie rushed around the car to her side, but Winter crossed her arms and stomped toward the house.

Alison grabbed her arm just before Winter went in. "You need to lighten up," she whispered into Winter's ear.

"Not exactly my ideal date, is it?"

Ali smiled. "Relax. Go have a couple drinks. Loosen up. It's not so bad."

Winter sighed. "Fine."

Alison took her to the back of the house where they found the beer cooler. They each took one and walked back to the main room. After a few sips, Winter smiled and walked around the room searching for people she knew. Whenever she saw Louie coming toward her, Winter stuck her nose into the nearest conversation and ignored him.

By her second beer, she didn't mind Louie hanging around her so much. At least he wasn't trying to suck on her face like Chase had been doing with Ali. Maybe Alison had been right about having a little fun. Winter allowed herself to laugh and dance to the steady thumping of the music, moving with the mass of flesh gyrating in the living room.

The time flew. The music grew louder. The dancing faster. The crowd more dense. Winter held her drink up above her head to keep it safe and allowed Louie to drape his arms around her waist.

He gently pulled her, guiding her through the party. He took her to a corner and maneuvered her against the wall.

She smiled and draped both arms over his shoulders, letting her hips keep rhythm to the music.

Louie leaned in and kissed her on the neck, sending a flurry of tingles through her buzzing skull. He worked his way up to her cheek and then across to her mouth. She kissed back, letting herself plunge into the passion of the moment and the electricity Louie propelled through her body.

His hands moved up her back and then down beyond her hips. One hand slid around her thigh to the front.

She grabbed it and moved it to the back. "No."

"What's the matter, not drunk enough?" He reached again.

"I said no."

"Aw, come on. Just have fun with it." He reached again, this time bringing his other hand across her chest.

She shoved him with both hands. The electricity dissipated. "I said no!"

"Lighten up." He stepped back to her, pushing her against the wall, and grabbing her crotch.

Winter twisted her legs and tried to push at him with her elbows. "Get off me!"

"What's wrong with you? You need to loosen up like your friend!" He grabbed both her shoulders and shoved her against the wall so hard her head thumped. He thrust his hips against her, spreading her feet with his own.

She twisted again and brought her knee up as hard as she could. She only managed to slam into his thigh, but he backed up far enough so she could get her hands on his chest and shove as hard as she could. He came back at her and she slapped him with so much force her hand stung.

The roiling bodies closest to them stopped dancing to stare.

Louie put a hand to his cheek and glared at her. He growled and drove her back into the wall. Her head slammed again and she crumpled to the floor. He leaned over her and roared, and then walked away. The nearest partiers went back to their dancing like nothing had happened.

Winter sat and hugged her knees for a few minutes, trying to rebuild the numbness despite how slippery the alcohol had made it. When the trembling stopped, she eased to her feet and walked as quickly as she could to the open door.

No one seemed to notice her.

Winter found the sidewalk and walked in the direction that Chase had driven from. She turned at the first cross street. As soon as she was out of sight of the party, she took out her phone and stared at it.

Her dad's number was the only one still programmed into it. She cursed and shoved it back into her pocket, wrapping her arms back around herself and speeding up.

She wanted a shower…wanted to scrub the filth from her flesh. She felt contaminated, like raw meat left to rot. But the foulness penetrated her skin, muscle, and bone, invading her comfortable void and infecting her numbness. She was decaying from the inside out. And no shower would help.

A car turned the corner ahead, flooding Winter in a bright light that made her cringe. It slowed and the window rolled down.

"Hey. Need a ride?" Ryan said.

"What are you doing here?" She kept walking.

The car started to back up. "Oh, you know me. Where there's a party I'll be there to drive."

"Could you just leave me alone?"

The car stopped. Ryan jumped out and ran to her side. "Hey. Did something happen?"

"No." She turned and glared at him.

"Where are you going?"

"I don't know."

Ryan frowned. "You know, I'm not trying to get you to like me or anything. So stop treating me like a jerk. You want me to forget what happened at the funeral? Fine. You don't want to tell me what happened at the party? Whatever. But you should at least realize that there's someone standing in front of you actually trying to do something for you instead of take something away."

Winter looked at her feet.

"I thought you'd have realized by now that you're not alone."

"I like being alone," Winter said.

"I know you do. But you're not. Not tonight. Let me help."

She looked up. "You like being the hero, huh? Rescuing poor, sad Winter. I don't need a hero. Why don't you go rescue someone else? Give up on me. I'm not worth it."

Ryan shook his head. "I'm not trying to be a hero. Just a friend. And you're worth at least that much."

Winter looked at his car, tapping her foot.

"Do you need a ride?"

She started walking to the car. "Fine. But I don't want to talk. Just take me home."

# 54

*Present Day*

When Sadie returned after spring break, Summer easily got her class schedule from her. With that the others found ways to station themselves so that Sadie was almost always watched, at least from a distance.

Winter walked with Kaci one afternoon to the Union for lunch. She made sure to be in the Meadow at this time every Tuesday and Thursday because Sadie always crossed the Meadow going back to Carmichael.

As they neared the Ancient, Winter spotted Sadie coming down the steps of Ingram Hall.

"Can you believe him?" Kaci said. "He asked me out again."

"And let me guess," said Winter, "you told him no again."

"Of course."

"But why are you doing that? You get along great, otherwise. Especially in our group things. Those are practically dates anyway."

Kaci sighed. "I just can't. Not now. Not one on one."

"He's really nice, you know."

"Yeah, I know," Kaci said. "And maybe if…" She sighed. "I don't know. I'm just not ready."

"He knows that."

Sadie turned into the middle of the Meadow, deviating from her normal route. Winter frowned. In a few moments, Sadie would pass by them on the same sidewalk.

"That I'm not ready?" Kaci asked.

"That you're not blowing him off because of him. I don't think he's going to give up on you."

Kaci shook her head. "I don't understand that. What does he see in me? I mean…how could he possibly like this?" Kaci waved her hand down her body. "I'm not worth it."

Winter laughed. "Kaci, there's nothing wrong with you. I wish I could convince you of that. You're more than worth it…at least Peter thinks so. Don't cut yourself short. Nobody sees you any differently than they used to."

Kaci grunted. "Well, I do."

"At least you're getting out more with me. That's something."

"But for the record, I don't like it."

Sadie slowed just in front of them. "Hey, Winter. Can I talk to you?"

Winter shrugged. "Yeah, sure."

Sadie glanced at Kaci.

"I'll go on ahead and save you a seat," Kaci said.

"Okay. Meet you there in a second." Winter turned to Sadie. "What's going on?"

"I've been thinking a lot about what you said last time…about letting you know if I see anything."

"Yeah?"

Sadie looked around the Meadow. "I think people have been watching me."

Winter took a deep breath. "Are you sure? What did they look like? Not other students?" Had Sadie seen them?

Sadie shook her head. "No. Well…maybe. I don't know. Just random people. They just stand around and stare. And when I look at them, they turn away. Why would people be watching me?"

"I don't know. Can you think of any reason? Is there anything you want to tell me?"

Sadie shrugged. "Not really. I mean…I made some enemies in high school, I don't exactly have a clean past."

"I completely understand."

"But why would someone follow me here?"

Winter crossed her arms. "Was there any one thing that happened to you that stands out? Think really hard. It may be something from first grade."

Sadie stared at the ground. "I honestly can't remember anything."

Winter sighed. "Let me know if you do. That might help."

"But what am I supposed to do, now? If these people really are watching me…I'm scared."

"Did you call security?"

Sadie blinked at her. "No."

"If you see someone like that, call security. Then call me, okay?"

Sadie nodded. "I can do that. Thanks." She took a step to leave and then turned back. "Why did you ask if my name was Sandy?"

Winter bit her lip. How much should she tell her? "Because…I think some of these people are looking for someone named Sandy. Or rather, someone who used to be called Sandy."

"And you think that's me?"

Winter shrugged. "Maybe. But if you say you're not…"

"I'm not. Honest. But who is it?"

"I don't know." Winter shook her head. "I think she's a freshman at Carmichael and she was originally from a town called Mordensfield."

"That's where there was a school shooting when we were kids."

Winter tilted her head. "That's right. Are you sure there's nothing else you need to tell me?"

Sadie shook her head. "Are you trying to find this girl?"

Winter nodded. "It would be nice. The authorities would know who to protect. Maybe they could catch these people if they knew exactly what they were up to."

"Maybe I can help you, then."

"Are you sure?" Winter shifted her weight to her other leg.

Sadie twisted her mouth. "If you find the right person, it might help catch these pervs, right? Which means they'll stop watching me. So, yes. I want to help. What can I do?"

Winter shrugged again. "Just listen…ask people about their childhoods. Maybe you'll get a clue. Let me know whatever you find out."

Sadie smiled. "I will. I promise. I've got to go. See you around."

"Later."

Winter watched Sadie walk away toward Carmichael. Why wouldn't she just admit she was Sandy? Why the big act? When Sadie turned out of the Meadow, Winter set her face to the Union.

That's when she saw Sophie watching her by the administration building.

Winter held her breath.

Sophie turned and started running down the side of the building away from the Meadow.

Winter sprinted across the grass, past the administration building, and to the parking lot on the other side.

Sophie was gone.

Winter turned back. She could still see the place where she had spoken with Sadie. And she could see the sidewalk that Sadie had walked down. But Sadie was long gone too.

Winter sighed. "Great."

Logan stood before her on the other side of the hedge. His eyes moved from Winter and focused beyond her. Winter turned.

He was looking at Sadie.

Whispers. Whispers all around. Low. Inaudible.

Flash.

Winter watched Sadie walk away from her in the Meadow. She turned this time to where Sophie was standing.

She was looking at Sadie.

More whispers. Fast. Urgent. Growing. Unifying. Solidifying into two words. "Wake up."

Winter bolted up and looked around the room. The whispers lingered in her ears, but faded to be replaced by a sinking premonition. She had to get to Carmichael.

Winter jumped out of bed and fumbled on the desk for her phone.

Kaci stirred. "What's going on?" she mumbled.

"I don't know," Winter said. "Something's not right. I need to call Summer." She put the phone to her ear.

Kaci sat up. "Here? Now?" Panic flooded out of her voice.

"Not here. At Carmichael." She snapped her phone shut. "And Summer's not answering."

"Are you sure it's not here?" Kaci backed against the wall on her bed and pulled her knees in tight.

"Yes, I'm sure. You're safe. But I need to go check on Summer."

"Winter…"

Winter sighed. "Don't worry, Kaci. I'm sure nothing's going to happen to you. Don't let anyone in, okay? I have my key."

Kaci watched with wide eyes as Winter dressed.

"I'll be back soon. Just call if you think there's a problem."

Kaci nodded.

Winter closed her eyes a moment and turned back. "I won't be long. I promise. Don't worry. Everything's fine."

Winter ran down the hall and down the stairs. She didn't slow until she reached her car. It roared to life and she floored it leaving the parking lot. Half a block from Carmichael, Winter slowed and turned off the headlights. She parallel parked on the street. Everything appeared quiet and normal.

She kept to the shadows as much as possible and crept to the side door. The lights were out on the card reader. She tried the door, and it opened easily. Inside, the hall lights were out as well, leaving only the glow of the exit sign. She turned to the stairs and sprinted up to Summer's floor. Everything was dark. What happened to the power?

She paused before opening the stairwell door, letting the premonition fill her with the next few seconds. This was it. It was happening again.

Winter pushed open the door and rolled her feet onto the carpeted hall. She guided the door back closed, staring into the deeper darkness further in where the exit sign light could not touch.

She closed her eyes and took a deep breath. When she opened them again, her eyes had adjusted enough to discern shapes and patterns.

Winter stepped forward…heel to toe. A door stood open about two-thirds of the way down the hall, faint red light reflecting from the metallic handle. She quickened her step. Whose door was that?

A dark figure stepped out. A body slung over its back. It turned away from her, swinging the long black hair of its captive.

Winter planted her feet, thunder rising in her ears. Heat spreading through her arms and legs. Skin pulling tight. The premonition outlined every movement and breath. "Let her go!"

The figure stopped. It turned. Muscular arms and shoulders outlined in the red light. A silver and black mask flashed. His head tilted.

Winter tensed, waiting for his next move…premonitioning her own.

He turned back away and rushed for the stairs in the middle of the hall.

At the same time Winter spun back to the staircase at the end, jumping them four steps at a time. She burst out of the stairwell door and turned just in time to see the man burst from the other stair door.

"Put her down!" Her voice rolled down the hall, building into a greater volume than her mortal voice could create.

The man took one step, readjusted the girl on his shoulder…and charged.

Winter ran forward and met him halfway, letting the premonition feed the next few seconds to her like streaming data.

He slung his fist and she twisted away using a move she learned in self-defense class. Winter crouched and slammed her palm into the cap of his knee. He stumbled backward, putting one hand to the wall for balance. Winter stood and spread her feet into a defensive stance.

The man rushed forward with one arm held out stiff. Winter ducked away, planting her palm into his stomach. But he didn't stop. He didn't hesitate. He plowed over her, tossing her against the wall like a paperweight.

Winter slid to the floor, holding the back of her head. As he stepped past her, she lunged forward and grabbed his ankle. He planted the foot she held and turned back to kick her with the other.

In that moment of pause, Winter rolled, planting one foot and one knee on the ground. She launched forward, shoving the heel of her hand into the center of the mask.

The man stumbled back with both hands clawing at his face. His prey tumbled to the ground. He kept one hand on the mask, and with his newly freed hand he reached down and pulled a knife out of his boot.

Winter stepped back to the wall. She looked around, letting the premonition guide her. Where was it?

He charged forward.

There!

Winter spun. With one hand she deflected the knife. With the other she reached for the red box hanging on the wall just a few feet away.

The dorm filled with the shrill throbbing drone of the fire alarm, piercing every dark corner and every room of the building. Safety lights strobed through the shadows. Voices shouted. Some screamed. Life awoke behind the closed doors.

The man in the silver and black mask ran to the open door at the end of the hall and fled into the night.

# 55

Winter fell to the side of the fallen girl. Other girls rushed into the hall in their pajamas. Winter rolled the girl over…Sadie.

"What's going on?" someone shouted.

Winter reached for Sadie's neck and prodded until she found her pulse. A crowd gathered around her, blocking the feeble light spilling out from the rooms. "She's still alive. Is anyone calling 911?" Winter shouted to be heard over the alarm.

"I will," said a girl a few feet away. She ran toward the exit.

The other girls began to mumble and cry.

"Winter, what's going on?" Summer knelt beside her.

"Someone tried to kidnap Sadie. I was almost too late."

"Why is she here, Summer?" someone asked.

"Everything's fine, go outside like you're supposed to," Summer shouted. "Go!"

The freshman girls turned to file out into the cool night air. Two other RA's joined Summer and Winter beside Sadie.

"Let's get her to the lobby," one of the RA's said as she grabbed Sadie's feet. "And see if Georgia can silence the alarm."

Winter shifted around and grabbed Sadie by the shoulders. Through the blaring alarm and flashing safety lights, they hauled her to the end of the hall and to the nearest couch in the lobby. As they draped her down, the alarm went silent and the lights came back on.

Georgia Velasquez marched toward them from a utility closet near the lobby desk. "What happened?"

Winter looked at Summer for support, but Summer just shrugged. Winter turned to face Georgia. "I…I saw someone suspicious come into the dorm, so I followed. The outside lock was disconnected and the lights were out. He had Sadie over his shoulders. I had to pull the alarm to get him to drop her."

Summer stepped beside her and rubbed Winter's back. Winter crossed her arms and waited.

Georgia nodded. "Has anyone called the police?"

"One of the girls said she was, but I don't remember who," said Summer.

"Will one of you call too, just in case?"

"Sure," said one of the other RAs. She ran over to the lobby desk and picked up the handset there.

Sadie groaned and rolled her head.

Summer knelt close beside Winter and leaned her head over. "Now what?"

Winter looked down at Sadie. "Now, we stop playing this stupid game. I'm calling Agent Erickson. Someone's going to tell me the truth tonight."

Winter jerked the phone from her pocket and punched out a text. *Sandy's been attacked at Carmichael.* She looked up at Summer. "There. He'll be here in just a few minutes. I'm going to go wait outside."

Summer nodded. "I'll stay here."

Winter walked outside. Sirens were already nearby. She drifted to the shadows beside the door and leaned against the brick wall. It wasn't long before a fire truck came flying toward the building. It stopped just in front of the lobby and three fully dressed firefighters jumped out. One of them spotted her.

"What's going on?"

Winter nodded to the lobby. "No fire. A student was attacked."

He nodded and two of them rushed inside. The third grabbed a large bag and followed.

Another siren wailed nearby. A single car with grill lights and a dash light screeched around the corner.

Winter smiled.

The car parked just behind the fire truck and Agent Erickson popped out. "Where is she?"

"In the lobby."

"Is she hurt?"

Winter shook her head. "I think she's just drugged."

"Is he still here?"

"It wasn't Xaphan. Some guy in a mask. He's gone now."

Erickson pulled the door open and went in. Winter followed him, keeping her arms crossed.

As soon as he came close enough to see Sadie, he stopped.

"What's wrong?" Winter asked.

He spun to face her, his forehead furrowed. "You said…" He clenched his jaw. "You tricked me."

"What? No. What are you talking about?"

He shook his head and pushed past her.

Winter ran after him. "What's going on? What are you talking about?"

The ambulance arrived, pulling just ahead of the fire truck. Paramedics pulled out a stretcher and wheeled it to the door.

"Agent Erickson, wait!"

Erickson stopped just short of his car. He pointed back to the lobby. "Your text said Sandy had been attacked!"

"Exactly. So why aren't you doing anything?"

"Because that's not Sandy."

Winter held her breath. "What? Can't be. I was sure."

He stepped closer to her. "I can't stop you from sticking your nose where it doesn't belong. But now you're endangering innocent people. I think you should stop and think about that. How many more people are going to be hurt because of you?"

Winter felt like a frozen knife pierced her heart. "I…I'm sorry."

"I should have never brought you back into this. But Gains trusted you…" He jabbed his finger to the lobby. "And now this happens. If you keep this up, I'll find a reason to have you arrested. Is that clear?"

Winter clenched her lips and nodded.

"Now, before I go. What did this attacker look like? Tell me everything."

"Um…he had a silver and black mask."

"Is that it?"

"Tall…kind of muscular."

Several police cars screamed toward the dorm, lining up behind Erickson's car.

Agent Erickson took a deep breath. "Listen. I understand why you feel you need to do this. And I wish I could help. But I can't. The less you know the better, because the less you know the less likely it is you'll lead them to her. Do you understand? We can't have them getting the real Sandy."

"Why can't you just tell me?"

He shook his head and turned away. "I'm sorry."

Erickson went back to his car and left.

Winter retreated into the shadows and sank to the ground. She laid her head on her knees, allowing the full weight of Erickson's words crash into her soul.

She had been wrong. Again. And someone else had been hurt. Like last spring at the silo, when it should have been obvious that Jennifer had been killed in the bell tower. Now Sadie. Could the real answer be staring her in the face this time too? Or should she just give up before she did any more damage?

Winter prayed. And cried.

A flicker of premonition sparked through her mind and was gone. She lifted her head and peered beyond the pulsing lights of the emergency vehicles.

Sophie stood watching from the other side of the parking lot.

# 56

*Four Years Ago*

The bell rang. Winter abandoned all her books in her locker and joined the current flowing into the parking lot. Before she could even reach her car, a line of traffic had already jammed all movement out of the school gate. She rounded the back end of her Mustang and stopped with a sigh.

Her rear tire was flat.

"Great." She crossed her arms and leaned against the trunk. She fumbled in her pocket for her phone and tried calling her dad, but only reached his voice mail.

Winter looked around, gnawing at her bottom lip and wondering if anyone would bother helping. Most everyone acted as if she didn't exist. The perfect result of trying to push everyone away all year. The few people that did look her way just laughed. She clenched her teeth and stared at the ground.

"Are you okay?" asked Stacy.

Winter turned to see her leaning with one arm out of her car window.

"Flat."

"Hold on." Stacy pulled into the recently vacated spot next to Winter's car. A moment later, Stacy stood beside her. "Do you know how to put on your spare?"

Winter rolled her eyes. "No."

Stacy leaned beside Winter. "Me either." She pulled out her phone and made a call. "Hey, it's me. Winter has a flat. Yeah. Can you help? Awesome! Um…near building B. Yeah, I see you." She started waving her hands. "See us? Okay. Bye."

"Who was that?" Winter asked.

"Ryan." Stacy stuck the phone back in her purse.

Ryan waved at them as he drove by. He doubled back through the parking lot and parked a few spaces down.

"Hey," he said as he jogged over. "Do I need to teach you girls how to change a tire?"

Stacy laughed. "That's what boys are for. Duh."

"I suppose we have to be useful for something. Winter, can you pop your trunk?"

Winter took her keys and pressed the trunk button on the remote. Ryan dove beneath the lid and started rummaging around. He came out with a jack and the spare tire.

Alison drove by glaring at them. A smirk covered Alison's face.

"She did it," Winter whispered.

"What?" asked Stacy.

Winter's cheeks warmed. She clenched her fists. "Alison! She did this to my tire!"

"Why would she do that?" asked Ryan as he went to his knees to maneuver the jack into place. "Isn't she your friend?"

"It's probably because I wouldn't sleep with her boyfriend's friend at the party. I can't believe this!"

Ryan smiled. "So that's what happened. Still not something a friend would do though."

"Shut up. I need to sit." Her head spun.

"Well, don't sit here. I wouldn't want the car to fall on you."

Winter and Stacy sat with their backs to Stacy's car and watched as Ryan slid the jack under and cranked the car up a little. He slid the tire iron onto a lug nut and pushed down his weight.

"Are you okay?" Stacy asked.

"I don't know anymore. It's more than just the stupid party. It has to be."

"What's going on?" asked Ryan.

"It's Ali and Claire…they've been doing all this witchcraft."

Ryan laughed. "So? The whole school knows that." He set down the tire iron and cranked the car higher.

"I don't know who to believe anymore. I thought Claire was doing all this stuff to Ali, but Claire says she wasn't. Now Ali's been messing with black magic and hates Claire. I just don't know what to do." Winter laid her head on her knees.

"Who do you trust?" asked Stacy.

"I don't know."

"But they're both your friends, right?"

Winter looked up. "I thought so. If Claire's right, then Ali's trying to hurt her and Ali's been using me. If Ali's right, then it's the other way around. I don't know what to do."

"Witchcraft is nothing to play with." Ryan leaned into the tire iron until the first lug nut popped. "Somebody's going to get hurt. You better make sure it's not you."

"But what should I do?"

Stacy touched Winter's arm. "Some of this stuff is real, you know that, right? There are real spiritual powers out there, and witchcraft messes with that stuff."

Winter shook her head. "Don't…"

"There's a spiritual power greater than all that," said Ryan as he spun off the last of the lug nuts.

"I said don't! I don't want to hear any of your preaching!"

"Sorry." Ryan slammed the top of the tire with his palm, and the tire broke free from the wheel hub. "I think the first thing you should do is talk to them. Confront them with what the other person is saying. If that doesn't work, then keep pushing. I have no doubt that you could get them to tell you anything."

"That's not true," said Winter.

"He's right," said Stacy. "If one of them is planning to hurt the other, then you can stop it."

"Maybe."

Ryan settled the spare onto the car and starting putting the lug nuts back on. "You know, doesn't it get tiring constantly wondering if a friend is being genuine or not?"

"Sometimes."

Ryan lowered the car a little and started tightening the tire.

"Wouldn't it be great if you had friends that you didn't have to doubt all the time?"

Winter sighed and watched Ryan lean into the last two lug nuts. "But nobody else wants to put up with me. I've pretty much ran everyone else off. They're the only friends I have left."

Ryan twisted the release on the jack and the car dropped back onto its suspension. He grabbed the jack and iron, and returned them to the trunk. After hoisting the flat tire into the trunk, he slapped his hands together and grinned. "Maybe it's time you started looking for some new ones."

"Your hands look horrible," said Winter. "And you're getting that stuff all over your clothes. I'm sorry."

Ryan shrugged. "I don't mind. It'll wash off and I can always change, know what I mean?"

Winter twisted her jaw and avoided eye contact with him.

"He did better than I could." Stacy stood and offered a hand to Winter.

Winter grabbed it and rose to her feet. "I've got to go. Um…thank you."

Ryan smiled. "Sure. Anytime. Glad I could help."

Stacy put an arm around her and pulled her close. "We'll pray for you."

Winter clenched her teeth. "Yeah." She pulled away and hurried to get in the car.

"Can I ask you a question?" asked Ryan before she could close the car door.

She paused with one foot still on the ground. "I guess."

"Will you go to prom with me?"

Winter blinked and stared at him. Ryan raised his eyebrows as if to prompt a response.

So she slammed the door and sped away.

*Present Day*

"It's not my time yet," Winter said. Rain pelted her head. Lightning flashed. Running. Running. Running.

She stopped and looked around. Darkness engulfed her like a blanket. Her heart raced, and the drumming echoed in her ears.

"You must be strong now," said the voice of a little girl.

Winter spun around, slinging her wet hair. There was no one there. She moved her feet up and down, restless to run. Her arms wanted to strike out. Every muscle felt as tense as a bowstring.

Whispers. She spun around again.

Whispers. "Where are you?" Winter shouted.

Whispers.

She turned again and found the man in the silver and black mask standing before her. He struck out with fingers like daggers and punctured her chest.

Winter's body seized and she gasped for air. The man twisted his hand and then pulled away, holding her beating heart in his black gloves.

The heart beat faster. And faster. Winter tried to breathe, but the fear consuming her left no room for air.

The man squeezed. Winter screamed and fell to her knees.

Laughter. Deep and dark. It made Winter…angry.

She clenched her teeth and pushed herself back to her feet.

"What a waste your heart is," said a deep voice behind the mask. "Your time is almost up. And your pitiful heart will be mine to rip out."

Winter narrowed her eyes and balled her fists. "My heart was ripped out long ago." She flexed her hand and a knife materialized in her grip. She swung out, connecting to his neck.

But the man in the silver and black mask was gone. Kaci stood there instead, eyes widened in betrayal. The knife sliced through her neck, tracing the path of the scar. Kaci's eyes stilled and darkened. She pitched backward and slammed into the ground.

Winter felt her heart rip out. Again.

Winter awoke panting, all muscles tensed. She rubbed her heavy eyes with the heels of her hands and tried not to cry out as she longed to do…She might wake Kaci.

She propped onto her elbows and glanced over at Kaci still sleeping soundly. *It was all my fault. If only I had paid attention to my premonition, Kaci wouldn't have been hurt.*

Tears caressed her cheeks. "I'm sorry," she whispered.

Kaci stirred and Winter bit her lip.

Something shuffled outside the room.

Flash. A premonition surged through her at full force. She stared at the door…waiting.

A piece of paper slipped through the crack. Soft footsteps walked away.

Winter swung her legs off the bed and went to pick up the paper. She unfolded it and read.

*They've found her. You're out of time. He's coming today. I'm sorry about Sadie.*

Winter's muscles tensed and cold spread through her arms and legs. Out of time. Her pulse spiked and she trembled. He's coming today. The premonition screamed.

Hurry.

Winter threw on the nearest mostly-clean clothes she could find, being careful not to wake Kaci. She grabbed her cell phone and headed for the door.

She paused and looked back at Kaci. "I'm sorry. I'll make this right." She eased the door closed and sprinted down the hall with the phone to her ear.

*"Hello?"* said Summer.

"We have a problem."

*"What's wrong? It's six thirty. Today's my one day to sleep in."*

"We're out of time," Winter said. "We have to find her today. They're coming."

*"Are you sure?"*

"Yes, I'm sure. I'm heading your way, get dressed."

*"Winter, you're scaring me."*

"Am I? Good."

*"What about class?"*

"You're skipping today." Winter hung up as she exited the lobby, and ran to her car. The restless energy coursed through her twice as intense now. She wanted to stomp on the gas, but restrained as best she could.

As she rounded the corner to the back part of campus, a little girl stood watching her from the steps of a building. Winter slammed the brakes and the car skidded to a halt. She looked back, but the girl had disappeared.

Winter gripped the steering wheel tighter and this time pushed the gas all the way to the floor.

She double-parked in front of Carmichael and ran to the lobby. Summer came in at the same time, dressed, hair fixed, and makeup perfect…as always.

"Come on, we've got to wake everyone." She grabbed Summer's arm.

"Calm down," said Summer. "Let's talk first. What's going on?"

Winter shoved the letter at Summer. "Someone left this. I think it was Sophie."

"Maybe you should find her."

"Maybe. But Sandy's here. I need to find Sandy."

Summer shook her head. "Shouldn't you just call Agent Erickson?"

"No. After last time, he'd probably arrest me. We're on our own for now. Let's find her and get her safe first."

"So what do you want to do?"

Winter crossed her arms. "We know her. We've found her already. Who do we know?"

Summer smiled and shrugged. "I know everyone."

"Who do *I* know? Come on. What freshmen have I interacted with?"

"Sadie. But she withdrew for the year. She's not here."

"Who else?"

"Sandy, you helped her move in."

"No." Winter turned and paced a few feet away. "Who else?"

"I don't know, Winter. Why are you asking me?"

"Who am I forgetting?"

Summer shrugged. "What about Ayden?"

"You said she was too old."

"What if she lied?"

Winter stopped pacing. Scales fell from her mind, lifting a shadowy veil. What was it about Ayden? Was she Sandy? How could that be? She was supposed to be meant for something…else.

Something Winter didn't need yet.

Unless she was both.

Winter spun to face Summer. "I've got to find her. Now."

"Do you think she's Sandy?"

Slow warmth spread through Winter's body like the rising of the tide. "Yeah. I think so. Where is she?"

"In her room, probably."

"Take me there."

Summer led Winter back into the dorm area, through the hall, and to Ayden's door. She knocked.

A moment later, a sleepy-faced girl with brown hair cracked open the door. "Yeah?"

"Is Ayden here?" Winter asked.

The girl looked behind her and shrugged. "She must have gone to breakfast already."

Winter grunted. "Thanks."

She turned and rushed to the exit, Summer following close behind. Outside, Winter scanned the tops of the trees and buildings. "She could be anywhere right now."

"Where do we go first?" Summer asked.

"The Union." Winter's cell phone rang. She pulled it out of her pocket. "Hello?"

*"It's Agent Erickson. Something's happening."*

"I know."

*"You know? What do you know?"*

"Nothing really. But I know they're coming for her today."

Silence. *"There's been…movement. We have reason to believe he's coming into Tishbe this very moment. I'm gathering some people to intercept, but he may already be there."*

Winter widened her eyes at Summer.

Summer's face paled. "What's going on?"

"Is it Xaphan or is it Skotos?" Winter asked.

*"How do you…"* Erickson said. *"It doesn't matter. We think he's*

*running Skotos now anyway."*

"I know that, too."

Silence again. *"Maybe Gains was right about you."*

"So what do we do?"

*"Have you found her?"*

"Yes."

*"Then stay with her. Don't leave her side until I get there. Keep her safe. Can you do that?"*

"Of course I can."

*"Good. Do it. Now."* He hung up.

*Four Years Ago*

Winter put the finishing touches on her makeup and looked at herself. It wasn't as black as normal. Even though her dress was black, it was more formal than anything else. She left most of her piercings empty, mere freckles on her skin. The only thing that broke the illusion was her boots.

Winter lifted her golden locket and traced the silver inlay of her name with her eyes. It was her mom's final gift to her. She clasped it around her neck and smoothed it over the top of her dress.

Winter's hair hung just over her shoulders in gentle waves from where she had used a curling iron. She still didn't know why she did that. She brushed her hair behind her ears and started putting in a pair of her mother's earrings.

Could it be? Could Ryan really…

Something small stirred in her chest. Something like…life. It warmed her a little, and she smiled. A real smile.

"You look beautiful," said her dad.

Winter turned to find him leaning against the door frame,

watching her. She looked down and felt her cheeks flush.

"What do you want?" she said, trying to force her face and voice flat.

Steve sighed. "He's here." He turned away and left.

Winter looked back at the mirror and took a deep breath. That flicker of life stirred again, and she bounced once before leaving the bathroom.

Ryan waited for her just inside the door. His hair slicked back, he wore a gleaming tux and carried a rose corsage in his hand. She stopped near the bottom of the stairs when she saw him, unable to hide the grin that erupted across her face.

Ryan watched her like a sailor would watch a siren.

Winter crossed toward him, watching the floor. What could he possibly see in her? What was there to like? The flicker of life grew a little, bubbling out of her mouth as a shy chuckle.

He grabbed her hand and squeezed. "You look amazing."

Winter met his eyes briefly and then looked back at the ground.

He gently took her chin and lifted her face back to him. "I'm serious."

She grinned. "Thanks, I guess."

Ryan slipped the corsage onto her wrist and turned to offer his elbow. She took it and Ryan led her through the door.

"Have fun," said Steve.

Winter glanced back over her shoulder to where her dad waited in the kitchen doorway. For the first time in a very long time…she smiled at him.

# 59

*Present Day*

Winter shoved the phone back into her pocket and turned to Summer. "Do you know where Ayden's first class is?"

Summer shook her head. "No."

"See if you can find out from her roommate. Find out from someone…anyone. Go to her class and wait until I call. If I miss her, then you might intercept her there."

Summer nodded. "Okay."

"Go! We're out of time. He may already be here."

Summer ran back inside.

Winter faced in the direction of the Meadow. She clenched her teeth and let the adrenaline fill her legs. Then she shot forward as fast as she could.

She crossed the road and found the sidewalk taking her the shorter route beside the Chapel. As she entered the Meadow, Winter jerked to a complete halt.

The Ancient swayed violently. Each leaf fluttered in unison as if they were a swarm of insects pulsing in an evolving formation. Even the thickest limbs bent like rubber.

A few students crossed the Meadow, but none seemed to notice the curious movement of the Ancient.

One guy passed beneath the tree without a hint of concern. As he cleared the tree's reach, it lurched even more, bending and creaking toward the ground. The topmost branches fell ever closer to the earth.

Winter drifted toward the Ancient. What was happening?

The branches brushed the ground like a giant feather-duster. Dirt swirled into the air as the limbs gouged it and fanned the dust away.

Winter stopped and watched the dust cloud. After a minute or two, the tree rocked back into an upright position. The limbs twirled into their proper places. And then the tree went still.

The breeze carried the dirt and dust away. The little girl stood over a bare spot in the grass. She was crying.

Winter held her breath. But the girl did not run away or disappear. This time she was real. Winter eased in front of her. "What's wrong?"

The little girl wiped her face and pointed to the ground. Bones lay exposed in the dirt. "They're dry," said the little girl.

Winter reached out to her.

The girl stepped back beyond Winter's reach. "You have to make them live."

"How?" asked Winter. "What do I need to do?"

"Prophesy to them, Winter. Speak to them. Teach them to live again."

"I don't know what to say."

"You have to help them! Please!"

"Who are you?"

The girl took another step back, shaking her head.

Winter bit her lip, studying the little girl. In many ways, she looked like the school picture of Sandy. But her hair was all wrong and her eyes were different. She was like Sandy…but she was not Sandy.

Winter looked down to the bones. She reached her shaking hand to them. As she brushed one with a single finger, an overwhelming sorrow consumed her. It filled her bones and muscles…collected in her stomach and chest…erupted from her mouth and eyes.

"What do I do?" Winter asked the little girl again. "I'm not good with puzzles…tell him that!" She tilted her head to the sky. "God, I'm not good with puzzles! Just tell me what to do, please!"

The little girl took a small step toward her, face softening. She reached out her little hand to Winter. "It's the puzzle that makes you strong enough to handle the answer."

"I can't!"

"You must."

"What's going on here?" A female voice behind Winter.

A voice Winter recognized.

The little girl's eyes flitted to beyond Winter's shoulder.

Winter turned.

Ayden stood behind her, glancing back and forth from Winter to the little girl.

Winter's pulse quickened. "Can you see her?"

"The girl?"

Winter turned back. The girl looked at Winter and then Ayden. She took two quick steps backward.

"No, wait!" said Winter.

"Who is that?" asked Ayden.

"I'm sorry," said the girl. "You must be strong now." She turned and ran away toward the administration building.

"Come back!" Winter jumped to her feet.

"What's going on?"

Winter grabbed Ayden by the arm. "We have to catch her."

"Is she lost?"

"Come on!"

Winter sprinted after the little girl, but no matter how she pushed herself she could not catch up. The girl led them between the buildings and turned the corner.

Winter reached the corner and stopped. She scanned the street and parking lot in front of the administration building, but the girl was gone. Dr. Cook was walking to his car. He spotted her and waved.

"What's that all about? Where'd she go?" Ayden huffed up to her side.

"You mean you could really see her?"

"Why wouldn't I? Where'd she go? Where's her mother?"

Winter stepped closer. "Are you Sandy? Tell me! Is that your name? I have to know."

Ayden rolled her eyes. "No one's called me that since kindergarten. My first name is Sandra, and I hate it. I've been using my middle name since I was old enough to tell my parents I wanted to. How did you know?"

"But you're too old! You took a year off!"

"I graduated early. What's wrong with you?"

Winter scanned the street again. At the corner of a far building a man in a baseball cap leaned against the wall, staring at them with a taut face. There was something familiar…

Then it hit her. The CLC party. Logan. Winter stepped toward him and he shook his head.

Sophie stepped from behind him to his side. She looked at Winter with wide eyes. "I'm sorry," she mouthed.

Logan and Sophie turned and disappeared behind the building. Winter scanned the shadows, searching deeper, and found others lurking. Staring at her.

The pit of Winter's stomach dropped away, leaving a hollow vacuum. "Oh, no…It's starting."

"What?" asked Ayden.

Winter turned back to her. "You. We have to get you out of here now!"

Ayden blinked. "Me?"

"Yes, you. Now go! Run!"

Winter looked back to the street.

The man in the silver and black masked stepped around the corner where Logan and Sophie had stood. Dr. Cook looked up from putting his briefcase in his trunk.

The man lifted a shotgun. Pointed it at Dr. Cook.

Explosion.

Dr. Cook collapsed onto the ground. Screams filled the air. People ran like frightened sheep.

The man turned toward Winter and swung the gun forward.

*Four Years Ago*

They took Winter's car because it was the nicest. Ryan drove. Winter felt like she was dreaming as he smoothly navigated the roads and brought them to Trenton Hills High School. She stole glances at him in the dim light, trying hard not to stare.

He parked the car, and she reached for the door handle.

"No, no," he said with a grin. He hopped out and ran around the nose of the car to her side. As he opened her door, he extended a hand to help her out.

She grabbed it and stood. "Why are you doing this?"

He offered his elbow again. "Why am I doing what?"

"Why are you being so nice to me?"

He shrugged. "Why would I *not* be nice to you?"

"Because I don't deserve it."

"I think you deserve much more than a nice date."

She leaned into him as they walked and smiled at the ground. "Thank you," she said.

"For what?"

"For seeing through me."

He laughed. "The real Winter is quite beautiful, you know."

She blushed and was thankful he couldn't see it. She tried to find words for a modest response, but could think of nothing. "Mmm…"

He patted her arm.

At the door to the gym, a teacher checked them off the reservations list. They were ushered to a corner of the gym lobby where they waited their turn to have their picture taken beneath an arch of blue balloons and flowers. Winter stood dutifully, holding Ryan's hand, and smiled for the camera.

The photographer held out a claim ticket to Ryan. "You two are a beautiful couple."

Ryan led her to the gym, now transformed into a fairytale. Fabric and lights had been draped from the center beam to the walls, covering the ugly ceiling with sparkling beauty. A portable water fountain stood in the center, gently refracting the glimmering light shining from the newly materialized stage at one end of the gym floor. On that stage, musicians in tuxedos created soft jazz rock.

A few couples danced around the fountain, but most sat at the white-clad candle-lit tables or stood around in small clusters. Ryan and Winter glided across the paper black and white checkered floor to one of the tables along the wall. He took a chair in his hand and slid it back for her.

"Would you like something to drink?" Ryan asked.

She nodded and gathered her skirt to sit.

As he walked to the refreshment table, Winter panned the darkened room for anyone she might know.

"Winter?"

Winter turned and saw Claire rushing toward her. She stood and gave Claire a hug.

"You look awesome!" said Claire.

"Thanks."

A guy she barely recognized from school stepped up behind

Claire. "Winter, this is James."

"Hi, Winter." James extended his hand.

Winter reluctantly offered her own and he gently squeezed it. She turned back to Claire. "I wasn't expecting to see you."

"Same here," said Claire. "Who are you with?"

Winter looked over her shoulder to the refreshment table, where Ryan was ladling punch. "I came with Ryan."

Claire grinned.

"Ryan's a good guy," said James. "He's top of our class. I was wondering who he asked. He wouldn't tell anybody. It drove the girls crazy."

"What do you mean?" asked Winter.

"He probably could have come with anyone he wanted," said James.

Claire reached over and squeezed her arm. "And he asked you. Cool!"

Winter felt her cheeks warm and she looked over her shoulder again. Ryan was coming toward them.

"Hey, James. What's up?" Ryan shook hands with James.

"Not a lot."

"Can we sit?" Winter asked Ryan.

"Uh, sure." Ryan clapped James on the shoulder. "See you later, man."

"Have fun!" said Claire as she and James walked to the dance floor.

For the next hour they alternated between sitting with some of Ryan's friends, talking with Ryan's friends, and occasionally dancing. The surrealness of everything made Winter's head spin. Somewhere in the back of her mind she thought it was too good to be true, and dreaded the moment when everything would come crashing back to her miserable reality. She felt oddly…normal. What would life be like if every day were like this? Could she dare to let herself be happy?

The spark of life inside of her grew little by little despite her efforts to suppress it. Her heart felt like it was growing too big for her chest. Was it real?

Winter looked up into Ryan's eyes as they danced. Was *he* real?

"What?" he asked.

She smiled and shook her head. "Nothing."

The song ended.

"I need a break," Winter said.

"Sure." Ryan took her by the hand and led her back to the table.

When they sat, Winter leaned her cheek onto her propped-up arm and stared at Ryan. "Why is it that you and your friends are so nice to me?"

"Nice compared to what? I don't see my friends as being anything extraordinary."

"But they're different. You're different. You're not like the other people who look down on me, or like my friends who are just as likely to stab someone in the back as they are to smile at them. As horrible as I've been all year, you still see me like I'm normal. I don't get it."

Ryan nodded.

"It's just that you and your friends are not like everyone else. You're…happy. You're…nice. And somehow, I don't know…I kinda like that."

Ryan squeezed her hand. "And I like you."

Winter shook her head. "But why? I'm so screwed up, why me? You can have any girl you want. What makes me different?"

"Because I understand you. As much as you hate me to say this, we're a lot alike. Of all these people in this room, you're the only one who understands what I've been through. The difference between you and me is very small."

"But how? How do you stand it? Doesn't it make you want to die? Why can't I be like you? What's the difference?"

Ryan nodded. "I think I know."

Winter leaned forward. "So there is something?"

"Yeah," he said. "But I don't think you're going to like it, and I don't think you're going to want it."

"Why not?"

"Because you've told me before."

Winter crossed her arms. "Well, I certainly think I want to know now. So why don't you try me?"

Ryan grinned and took a deep breath. "It's God."

"What?"

"Me and all my friends that we've been hanging out with…we're all Christians."

"Stop it."

"See, I told you that you wouldn't want to hear it."

She narrowed her eyes at him. "Are you saying that's the only difference?"

He nodded. "Yeah. That's the difference. That's what you see…that's why we're so happy. And that's the thing you just said you wanted."

Winter looked away, her face heating up. Inside, anger and misery collided. She didn't know what to think. How could a God who had caused her so much pain make others so happy? It wasn't fair.

"Well, now I'm changing my mind," she said.

"Why? What has God done to you?"

She felt tears swelling in her eyes. "I don't want to talk about it, okay? God hates me."

"No he doesn't. God loves you."

"Really? Then why did he take my mom away? WHY?" Winter clenched her teeth and stared at the wall.

Ryan squeezed her hand again.

The anger and misery smoothed away.

"We all die, Winter. It's just a matter of when. The real question is whether or not you're ready for what happens afterward. That's where God's love shines. And that's why me and my friends are so happy. We're ready."

"But what about now? Why does it have to hurt? What about

me?"

"Would you rather God stop all evil? That would take away our free choice. And that would mean God isn't good. You can't have it both ways. A little pain now…and then an escape later. That's God's plan."

"I just don't know…"

"Winter, I'm not going to ask you to be a Christian or anything. If that's not what you want, then fine. But remember…I know how you can have what I have. I know how you can have hope instead of guilt. And I know how you can be happy again. When you're ready, just ask."

She finally looked back at him, and gnawed her cheek. "Okay."

"Would you like to dance again?" He smiled and offered his hand.

She grinned, melting inside and head buzzing again. "Sure."

*Present Day*

Winter couldn't move. She couldn't think. The end of the shotgun drew her gaze like a moth.

The gun swung away. Another explosion sent another victim crumbling to the ground.

The spell broke. Winter spun, the chaos revolving around her like slow motion. She reached for Ayden. But Ayden was already gone.

Another shot. Winter tensed and then crouched low. She sprung forward, running back toward the Meadow and scanning for Ayden's red hair. She rounded the corner of the building and paused for a thorough sweep of the Meadow. No sign of Ayden. She flitted her eyes to doorways and shadows, anywhere Ayden might be hiding.

Nothing. Ayden…Sandy. Where did she go?

Winter looked back between the buildings. Campus security had shown up, weapons drawn, and were trying to shepherd people away from the scene. But the man in the silver and black mask had disappeared.

One guard knelt over Dr. Cook's body. Blood spread across the pavement and trickled toward the drain.

Winter's vision lurched as hard as her stomach. She crumpled to the ground, leaned over, and vomited.

Ringing rolled through the Meadow as the fire alarms in each building erupted in sequence. People poured out.

Winter waved her arms. "No, no, no! No! Go back!" But no one heard her. As more people emerged and turned to watch the buildings for smoke, chills crawled over her skin. The Meadow filled, but there was no fire and the alarms had nothing to do with the shooting. How could they? There hadn't been enough time.

It was part of his plan. Trigger the alarms. Draw out the crowds. And kill them all if necessary.

She looked back around the corner. Security swarmed the Meadow, faces frantic and white.

"No!" Winter grabbed her phone and dialed Summer. "Summer!"

*"What's wrong?"*

"He's here. He's found her. And he's already killed three people."

*"What?"*

"We were right. It's Ayden. Summer…I lost her! We have to find her, go look in her room!"

*"I just came from there."*

"Go back. She ran and may be going back."

*"What about him? Where is he?"*

"I don't know. He disappeared. He probably saw which way she went. Be careful. If he can't find her then something horrible is about to happen. I can feel it. Hurry! I'm going to the Union."

*"Okay, I'm going now."*

"Call Davis. Get him to help you."

*"Okay."*

Winter hung up. Her premonition screamed at her, but gave her little foreknowledge of what to do next. The Meadow was full to capacity now. Cattle ready for slaughter.

Winter pushed through the crowd and called Peter.

*"Winter, where are you?"* he asked.

"In the Meadow."

*"I'm at the Union. Can you get there?"*

"Yes. I'm coming now. Whatever you do, stay inside! It's Xaphan…I mean, the man in the mask that works for him. He's killed at least three people. It's all happening so fast and these stupid people won't get back inside! No one knows yet…they think there's a fire."

*"Are you serious?"*

"He's after Ayden. She's the one. Watch for her, she may be coming that way."

*"Okay. Hurry. I'm waiting."*

Winter shoved her phone into her back pocket. She plowed through the crowd, both arms ahead of her. A few minutes later she reached the steps of the Union. Peter stood at the top waiting.

"I haven't seen her. Now what?" he asked.

"I…I don't know."

"Where else could she have gone?"

"Just give me a moment to think." She closed her eyes and tried to tune out the shouts of chaos all around, tried to force some sort of vision to materialize out of the screeching premonition.

Peter grabbed her arm and squeezed.

"Winter?" said Ayden.

Winter opened her eyes.

Ayden stood at the bottom of the steps looking at her. Her face was pale and her eyes wide and bloodshot. "What's happening?"

"Quick," said Winter. "Come here. We have to get you inside."

"Me?" Ayden took the first step up.

More gunshots like thunder rolled through the Meadow. The masses began to roil and fill the air with piercing shrieks. People rushed past Ayden and into the Union.

The man in the silver and black mask walked down the sidewalk toward Ayden, a semi-automatic in his hand and the shotgun strapped across his back. Everyone who came near his path fell beneath a quick burst of the gun. Bodies lay scattered in his wake, some crawling to take cover and some no longer moving.

"Hurry!" Winter shouted.

Ayden ran up the remaining steps as the concrete near her feet splashed with broken rock at the sound of more thunder. Peter grabbed Ayden and pulled her inside as Winter held the door open. They ran across the room, past frightened students huddling behind tables and couches.

Winter's phone rang.

*"It's me,"* said Summer. *"I'm at the Music building and I can't leave. There's too many people. Was that a gun I heard?"*

"The Music building! What are you doing there?"

*"Ayden's supposed to be in Music Appreciation, but I can't find her."*

"Never mind. Stay there! Ayden's here. Get inside. Where's Davis?"

*"He was in the Meadow coming to meet me. What's happening?"*

"Just get inside!" She hung up and felt a stab in her stomach at the thought of Davis lying in a pool of his own blood.

Winter led them down the hall toward the post office, fire alarms compressing her ears.

"What's happening?" asked Ayden.

"That guy is after you."

"After me? Why would he be after me?"

"Because you're Sandy. Peter, we have to hide somewhere."

"There aren't many good places to hide here," Peter said. "We need to get out!"

"I don't understand," said Ayden. "What has my name got to do with anything? What's he want with me?"

"He wants to kill you, Ayden. Now shut up!"

Rapid gunfire nearby. Screams in the Union.

Winter spun to look down the hall toward the eating area. People ran past the hall. Another burst of the gun. A girl collapsed. "Peter, where do we go?"

"There's nowhere to hide here. All the offices are locked, and if we go into a classroom we'll be trapped."

"Then what do you suggest?"

"Winter…" whimpered Ayden.

Peter pointed to the hall corner. "Let's try to double around through the halls and make the other exit."

Winter nodded.

They crept further down the hall to where it teed. The left went to a stairwell and the right went through the office corridor and then turned to go back to the main Union area. They eased past the offices, trying to be as quiet as possible. Screams and shouts still floated toward them from the Meadow, but the gunfire in the Union had ceased.

A click from behind them made them turn. The man in the silver and black mask rounded the corner, taking long strides.

Ayden screamed.

The man leveled the shotgun.

Peter tackled Winter and Ayden, shoving them down onto the floor. A concussive roar bounced from the walls and pressed against Winter's back.

Something hot stung Winter's arm, making her cry out. She looked down to see a dark crimson piercing, leaking tendrils of blood. She pushed up with her other arm, scrambling to find traction beneath her feet.

Peter yanked Winter and Ayden to their feet and pulled them toward the entrance.

The pounding of boots quickened behind them. Winter stole a look back and tripped over a body, landing in a pool of blood. She glanced around the Union. People lay dead everywhere…just like her dream.

"Come on!" Peter grabbed her arm and pulled her across the

floor until she stood.

Just before they reached the glass doors, another cock sounded and another boom thickened the air. The door beside them exploded with a rain of shattered glass. Ayden fell to the floor clutching her leg. Peter dragged her through the door.

The crowd in the Meadow had thinned…hopefully back inside. But a few hovered over the fallen bodies.

"This way!" Winter jumped down the steps and faced the music buildings on the other side of the street.

Ayden scrambled to her feet and clung to Peter as they followed.

"Winter!" someone shouted.

She turned. Davis ran toward them from the Meadow.

"Davis! Get out of here!" Winter screamed.

"Come on!" Peter lifted Ayden's arm over his shoulder.

"Wait for me!" Davis reached the foot of the Union steps.

The Union doors flew open. The man in the silver and black mask emerged. He looked briefly at Davis, and then at Winter, Peter, and Ayden. He cocked his shotgun and swung it to Ayden.

Winter couldn't move again. Her whole body went numb and she stared at the gun like she had before.

Davis roared, launching up the steps. He slammed his shoulder into the man, bringing them both to the ground. The shotgun fell out of the man's hands.

"Winter!" shouted Peter, pulling Ayden toward the service road.

Winter shook the scales from her mind and grabbed Ayden's other arm, and they barreled across the service road to the Arts Plaza. Winter heard a muffled cry and she turned. The man in the silver and black mask stood at the top of the steps…watching them. He stooped and picked up his gun.

*Four Years Ago*

Winter laid her head on Ryan's shoulder, closed her eyes, and let the golden smile seep through her whole body. It was near midnight and the prom would soon be over. The fairytale would end and she'd have to go back to her normal life. But not yet. Just one last dance to be happy.

Maybe…maybe she didn't *have* to be a freak anymore. Maybe everything could stay just like this.

The soft piano and baritone voice added a magical luster to the prismed light twirling on the floor. Other couples swayed around them, cocooning them in mutual privacy.

Winter lifted her head and looked up at Ryan. His eyes…his smile…

The flicker of life in Winter's chest blossomed. She smiled wider than she thought possible, and he smiled back. He really did care about her. She could see it now…see it in his glistening eyes.

He leaned forward and she let her eyelids fall shut. His soft lips gently touched hers for only a moment, and then he wrapped her tighter in his arms.

Winter sighed and laid her head back on his shoulders. Maybe she didn't have to let this go. Maybe it could be like this forever.

A murmur spread through the dance floor. Winter turned to see what was happening, and her stomach sank. The happiness fled.

"Oh, no. Not now. Please, not now."

"What is it?" asked Ryan.

"It's Alison."

Alison stalked through the crowd wearing a dirty white dress, looking as if she had been lost in the forest for the past few hours. Her make-up streaked across her face, and her frayed hair jutted out everywhere.

"Where is he?" she was mumbling. "Where is he?"

Alison spotted Claire and stomped toward her. "*Where is he?*"

James took half a step in front of Claire, but Claire pushed past him and faced Alison. "He's not here. He broke up with me, the same as with you."

"LIAR!"

Winter took a step toward them, but Ryan held her arm. She looked back at him.

"Don't," he said.

"I have to. They're my friends."

Ryan firmed his jaw and nodded.

Winter walked through the crowd to Claire and Alison, Ryan following and refusing to relinquish her hand.

"Ali, what's going on?" she asked.

Alison turned to face her. Her chin quivered. Her voice dropped. "Where's Phillip?"

"He's not here. What happened to you?"

Alison's eyes widened with confusion. She clutched the sides of her head and looked at the ceiling. "I…I don't know." She started to cry. "Culsu."

"Culsu?" Claire took a small step toward Ali and stretched out a calming hand. "Ali, what have you been doing?"

Alison looked around, seeming to notice the other couples for the first time. She blinked and focused on Winter.

"Where am I?"

"This is prom," said Winter. "Why are you here?"

"I don't remember."

Claire stepped closer to Alison and gave Winter a frightened, knowing look. "Ali," she said quietly, "what spells have you been trying?"

Alison screamed. "I don't remember. What's happening to me? Where's Phillip?"

"Have you been invoking spirits?"

Alison's face suddenly twisted. She bared her teeth and hissed. "Leave Culsu alone!" She shoved Claire backward, and then her face shifted again, softening with wide-eyed confusion. "Oh, no…" she moaned. "Phillip…"

"Do you know where he is?" asked Winter.

"I don't know…I don't…"

Alison lifted a trembling arm, and for the first time Winter saw that she clenched something in her fist. Alison held her hand out and slowly opened her fingers. A bloody pair of scissors fell to the floor.

"Where is Phillip?" asked Claire.

Alison's face changed again, wrinkling with pursed lips and narrowed eyes. "He's dead," she growled.

Ryan tugged at Winter and she stepped back with him. "Claire, what's wrong with her?" Winter asked.

"She's gone too far," Claire said.

"Is she telling the truth? Is Phillip dead?"

"I don't know!"

Alison crumpled to the floor and rocked herself. "Leave me alone…leave me alone."

Silence filled the gym. Winter panned around. Everyone had stopped dancing and was staring at them.

Winter stepped toward Claire, and Ryan pulled her back again. "Claire! Make it stop!"

"I can't!"

Alison looked up at Claire, her face changing again. "This is all your fault! You're the reason he's dead! You're the reason he left me!" She lurched to her feet, staggering. She faced Winter and pointed at Claire. "Can't you see? She's the reason all this stuff has happened to us! It's all her fault!"

"No it isn't!" said Claire. "You've done this to yourself! You're messing with stuff you shouldn't."

"SHUT UP!" Alison roared. She put her hands over her ears and whimpered. "Culsu won't shut up…"

Claire eased closer to Winter. "Winter, we have to calm her down. Help me." She reached out slowly and stepped toward Alison.

Alison backed away, her face changing to rage again. "Look at her! She's trying to kill me now like she killed Phillip! She'll kill you too! She'll kill everyone!"

"I didn't kill anyone," said Claire.

"You killed Phillip!"

"If Phillip's dead, it's because of you, not me." Claire looked back to Winter. "Help me."

Alison took another step back, face turning to Winter too. "Winter, stop her! She's going to hurt me!"

"Please, Ali, just calm down. Winter…help."

Ryan pulled harder at Winter's arm. She looked into his soft eyes and he shook his head. Winter turned back to Claire and Alison. Both stood still now. Both watching her…waiting for her choice.

Ryan laid a hand on Winter's shoulder and she reached up to grab it. Winter looked into Claire's eyes, into Alison's, and shook her head. "No." She turned and walked away with Ryan.

There was a brief scuffling behind her. Winter glanced over her shoulder as Alison collapsed onto the floor crying again. Claire stormed out of the building with James in tow. Chaperones had finally arrived from the lobby, kneeling beside Alison.

Ryan put both arms around Winter. "Would you like me to take you home?"

"Please?"

He smiled. "Come on."

# 63

*Present Day*

Peter led the way, bursting through the front doors of the music building with one arm. “Lock the door!”

A guy ran out of the office. “What’s going on?” He took one look at Winter’s bloody arm and Ayden’s bloody leg, and ran back in the office.

Peter walked them to a wall and eased Ayden to the ground. “We’ve got to wrap her leg with something.”

Ayden leaned her head against the wall with her eyes closed. Her forehead pinched as she sobbed with an open mouth, pulling in shallow bursts of air. Her red cheeks gleamed against the rest of her pale face.

The guy came out, ran to the door, and spun a key in the lock.

“Do you have any towels here?” asked Peter.

The guy shook his head.

“Old shirts? First aid kit??”

He ran back into the office.

“How’s your arm?” Peter asked Winter.

Winter clenched her teeth. "It hurts."

Peter nodded. "We need to wrap it too."

"We can't stay here," she said. "He's coming."

"I know." He reached down and took Ayden beneath her shoulders, hauling her back up. "Where's that first aid kit?"

The guy ran out with a small white box.

Peter snatched it from his hands. "Listen to me. You have to get everybody in this building out of here. Do you have a back door?"

He nodded. "Yeah. Several."

"Good. Leave. Now. There's a gunman out there shooting everybody, and he's after us. If you can't leave…hide."

The student's eyes widened and he ran back into the office.

"Come on." Peter draped one of Ayden's arms over his shoulder and dragged her down the hall.

Summer appeared around the far corner at a full run. She slid to a halt and covered her mouth with both hands.

"Summer!" Winter shouted.

"Oh my God…what happened?"

Winter grabbed her arm. "We need to get someplace safe."

Summer nodded. "This way." She turned and jogged to a set of double doors.

Ayden whimpered. "I can't…"

"Yes you can," said Peter. He hoisted her higher onto his hip, lifting her mostly off the ground.

Summer led them into a darkened room. One hidden light illuminated ropes, and chairs, and an assortment of junk.

"What is this?" asked Winter.

"It's the side entrance to the auditorium," Summer said.

"Is there any place to hide?" asked Peter.

Summer nodded. "You can go up to the sound and lighting booth, or down beneath the stage."

Peter grabbed a chair and sat Ayden in it. "Good." He dumped out the first aid kit onto the ground, and grabbed a gauze pad and medical tape. He ripped a large gash in the fabric over her thigh.

Winter snatched a broom from the wall and slid the handle through the push bars of the door. "That's not going to last long…"

A nearby gunshot sounded. Glass shattered. Someone screamed.

Peter slapped the pad over the black, bleeding hole in Ayden's leg and quickly wrapped strands of tape over it. Then he shoved another gauzed pad and the tape into Winter's chest. "Do it as we go."

Another gunshot in the hall. Closer.

Peter grabbed Ayden's arm and yanked her to her feet. "Take her," he said to Summer. "Hide. Stay quiet. He thinks she's with us, so we'll lead him away. Then get out, got it? Get as far away from the school as possible."

Summer nodded and took Ayden's hand.

Winter held the pad to her arm and kicked the contents of the first aid kit toward the sound booth entrance. "We'll get him up here. I'll figure something out then."

Peter nodded.

Summer stared with wide eyes back at the double doors.

"Go!" Peter pointed over Summer's shoulder.

Summer tugged at Ayden's arm and they ran across the stage into the darkness.

A crash from a nearby door in the hallway. Followed by another. Heavy boots thumped in the hall.

"Come on." Peter eased open the door to the sound booth and the hinges squeaked, echoing like a screeching bat in the empty theater.

The stage doors rattled. Ice crystals cracked through Winter's chest. She jumped through the door after Peter.

Peter eased the door against the jamb without fully closing it.

A blast tore through the doors, splintering the broom handle. Then one of the doors burst open.

Winter held her breath.

Peter tapped her on the shoulder and pointed up. They crept up the stairs until they reached the sound booth overlooking the stage. Winter eased to the window and peered out.

Nothing.

Peter tapped her on the shoulder again and gestured to an iron ladder. They eased over and Winter followed him up at least another fifty feet to the theater ceiling, her punctured arm shrieking each time she had to put her weight on it. At the end, they exited onto a catwalk that spanned the entire width of the auditorium. Lights and wires hung from a network of railing just in front of the walkway. Platforms at either end held spotlights.

Winter paused, wondering if the killer would take the bait. She heard footsteps below and eased around Peter until she could see the stage.

The man in the silver and black mask paused in front of the empty first aid box. He followed the trail of stuff with his head. Then he looked up, making eye contact.

Winter jerked back into the shadows.

More footsteps. The squeak of hinges.

"What now?" whispered Peter.

Winter leaned over to look down the ladder into the sound room. "Get ready to go to the other side of the catwalk."

The footsteps returned to the stage. Winter held her breath and fought the urge to look back out to see what he was doing.

There was a loud stomp.

A frightened squeak floated through the room.

"No…" Winter leaned back out to look at the stage.

The man walked softly, gun pointed at the floor.

"Hey!" she shouted.

He turned and swung the gun up.

Winter spun away as a lighting module exploded.

A muffled scream filled the sound void that followed the gunshot.

"It's not working. We have to do something!" Winter rushed for the ladder, almost slipping on the first steps. She slid four or five steps at a time, clenching her teeth against the searing pain coursing through her arm. At the bottom, she jumped the last five feet.

Winter slammed into the door, but it wouldn't move.

"He jammed it!"

Another scream. Two screams.

Winter pounded the shoulder of her uninjured arm into the door and nothing happened.

"The other side," said Peter from the ladder.

She nodded and followed him back up. Winter tensed, waiting to hear the next gun blast.

They reached the lighting platform and Winter ran onto the catwalk. Another light exploded and she dropped to the steel deck. Winter peered over the edge to the stage. The killer herded Summer and Ayden to the double doors, their hands bound with medical tape and their faces covered in blood. Ayden fell to her knees and the man shoved the barrel of the gun against the back of her head.

"Go!" shouted Peter.

Winter crouched and ran as fast as she could. Another shot sent sparks flying from the grate just in front of her. She reached the other end and pressed into the shadows.

"I have her," said a deep voice. "You can't stop me."

The same voice and words Winter had heard in her dreams. Over and over…

"If you want her back, you'll have to come find me."

Winter found the other ladder and jumped down it several rungs at a time. The last jump jarred her knees and she almost fell.

She heard Peter land as she reached the top stairs leading to the stage. Winter leaped over half the landing, stumbling briefly before jumping the rest of the way. She hit the bottom and crashed to her side, landing on her injured arm. Winter clenched her teeth and whimpered.

Peter was at her side. He grabbed her by the arm and pulled her up. The door opened easily, but the theater was empty.

"He's getting away!" Winter ran across the stage and slammed into the bar on the double doors. She looked both ways in the hall, but it was empty too. She ran to the front of the building and through the shattered glass doors to the courtyard.

Chaos reigned on campus. Sirens wailed in the distance. But the man in the silver and black mask was gone.

*Too late…*

Peter huffed to her side.

"They're gone, Peter! They're gone! Summer! Ayden!" She turned and shoved him in the chest. "We shouldn't have split up! It's your fault!"

"Hey! Getting mad at me isn't going to help. What do we do now? Think! He can't have gotten far yet."

Winter searched for her premonition, but the buzz of confusion blocked most of it out. She took deep breaths, trying to summon it back.

"Winter? What do we do?"

Winter let the images swirl in her mind, colliding and taking shape. Summer hugging her at the beginning of the semester. Ayden apologizing after the encounter with Sophie. Kaci running through a field.

Not that. Never again. *Never.*

Energy pulsed through her. Strength returned to her legs and arms. Clarity washed through her mind. The premonition swelled, activating like the winding of a clock.

"My car," she said. "We have to follow."

"But we don't know where they went."

Winter narrowed her eyes. "I can find them."

*Four Years Ago*

Ryan led Winter the long way around the crowd to better avoid Alison. The quiet cool outside felt like a sanctuary. A few stars twinkled overhead, barely visible beyond the light of the streetlamps. Crickets chirped in the shadows.

Winter held tight to Ryan's hand and bumped against him as they walked. "Thank you."

"For what?"

Winter shrugged. "For giving me another choice."

Ryan transferred her hand to his free hand and put his arm around her. He kissed the top of her head.

They reached Winter's car and Ryan opened the passenger door for her. Before she sat, Winter watched Claire's car drive out of the parking lot and speed away.

Ryan eased her door closed and walked to the other side. He got in and grinned at her. Then he leaned over, brushing her lips again with his.

Winter giggled.

Something boomed into Ryan's door, jolting the car. Winter squealed.

Alison stood outside the window, her face red and smeared like a dead harlequin. She narrowed her eyes and bared her teeth. "Get out!"

Winter touched Ryan on the shoulder. "Just go. Let me talk to her."

Alison bent over, sliding a hand down her leg. She straightened and leveled a pistol at the window. "Get out!"

Ryan held up his hands. Keeping the gun pointed with one hand, Alison grabbed the handle with the other and flung open the door.

Ryan climbed out, keeping both hands up and backing away from Alison.

Winter opened her door and set one foot on the ground.

Alison swung the gun to Winter. "No! You stay! You have to drive! Get over here."

"I'm staying with Winter," said Ryan.

"It's okay," Winter told him as she walked around the car, her voice shaking.

Ryan shook his head. "No. I'm not leaving you alone."

"Fine!" said Alison. "Get in the back."

"Why are you doing this?" Winter trembled. Cold beads of sweat rolled down her forehead.

Alison pointed down the road with the barrel of the gun. "We have to catch her. Don't you understand? She killed Phillip."

"I don't think she did."

Alison leveled the gun at her. "I don't care what you think. Drive!"

Winter eased into the driver's seat as Ryan scrambled into the back. Alison kept the gun trained on her as she moved around the front of the car to the passenger side.

Her hand shook with the key as she struggled to turn the ignition. The Mustang roared to life. "Please..." Winter's voice cracked.

"Don't do this."

Alison moved the gun closer to Winter's head. "Go!"

Winter whimpered and put the car into gear. She gently pressed the gas.

"Faster!"

Winter pressed harder, propelling the car out of the school parking lot and onto the road.

"Turn here."

"I don't know this road!"

"It'll get us to her house faster."

"Alison..."

"DO IT!"

Winter turned down a small country road. Her chest shuddered, ragged breaths pushing tears onto her cheeks.

"Ali," said Ryan. "Let Winter out, I'll drive you."

"Shut up!"

"Please, let me do it."

"NO! It has to be her!"

"Why?" croaked Winter.

"Because you're protected. With you driving we can go faster."

"No...that's not true."

Alison placed the gun on Winter's temple. "If you don't press the gas more, I'll blow your head off."

Winter cried out and floored the gas. As the speedometer crept higher, Winter cried more.

"Faster!"

The car leaned deep into each curve. The tires protested. Winter eased off the gas and Alison pressed the gun harder into her head.

"That's enough," said Ryan. "She can't handle it, can't you see that? We're going to crash. I'm the better driver. Let me do it."

Alison turned the gun toward him. "Faster, Winter. Or he'll die first."

Winter's hands shook violently on the steering wheel. "Stop it!

Just stop it!"

The needle passed sixty.

A sharp left-hand curve loomed ahead. Winter cut into the inside lane to take the corner. As the car slung around the bend, headlights blazed in her eyes.

Winter screamed. She twisted the wheel away and the oncoming car thundered into the back end of the Mustang.

Screeching metal. Shattering glass. Winter's head slammed into the door window.

The car spun, flinging Winter forward, seatbelt raking across her throat. The tires shrieked as the world twisted around.

The car lurched sideways. A brief hush. As the car slammed back into the ground, the roof crumpled toward Winter's head. The rattling boom pounded her ears. Airbag thrust into her face. Crushed glass flew like confetti.

Lurch. Slam. The tires chirped again on the pavement, shoving Winter into the seat.

Lurch. Slam. Then silence as the car soared over the embankment, the starry sky spinning through the jagged holes in the windshield.

*Present Day*

Winter ran down the street, around the far side of the Union. Peter jogged beside her. They didn't slow down until they reached Winter's car where she had left it in the parking lot of Carmichael Hall. Winter had her keys out and the doors unlocked before she touched the handle. She jumped in and smashed the seatbelt into place.

Peter slammed the passenger door shut. "Let's do it."

Winter squeezed the steering wheel with one hand twisted the ignition. Her BMW roared to life.

She closed her eyes and forced the last vestiges of buzzing confusion from her mind. The guiding premonition revved like her engine, filling her body. A tingling trickled down from the top of her head to her toes. Thunder rumbled in her ears. Her skin pulled taut.

Winter knew exactly where Ayden and Summer were. If she had to, she could drive there with her eyes closed.

She opened her eyes. The world shone in piercing clarity, down to the minuscule details of every leaf on every tree. Winter turned to

Peter. "Let's go."

Peter's face paled and he leaned away. "Winter, your eyes…"

She looked back at the road and smiled. "I know."

The acceleration of the Beamer pinned them to the seats. Winter held the pedal firmly against the floor and allowed the needle to climb. She didn't think about driving. She allowed the premonition to guide each movement and adjustment moments before needed.

They turned onto the highway and Winter deftly maneuvered through the traffic. The needle continued to climb.

Eighty-five.

Ninety.

Peter's knuckles turned white from gripping the armrest. He pushed back into the seat. "Don't you think you're going too…"

"No," she said. She had heard it before. All of this…everything…was a part of her memories now as if it had already happened.

"Where are all the…"

"At the school." She stole a glance at his confused expression. "The police are at the school."

"Where are we…"

"There's a national forest about twenty miles outside of town. He's going there."

Peter took a deep breath. "I wish you would…"

"Sorry, I can't help it. I hear what you're going to say before you say it."

"Well, it's a little unnerving."

Winter smiled. The needle crept toward one hundred.

"As is your driving."

"Don't worry. I'm not driving."

"Right…At this rate, we'll be there before them."

"He's already there," she said.

"How do you…"

"I just know."

Peter sat in silence for a couple of minutes, clenching the armrest and watching the road. "Can you tell if they're…"

"They're still alive."

Peter nodded. "What are we going to do when we get there?"

Winter turned to look at him, as if he'd asked a stupid question.

"Please watch the road."

"Sorry," she said, turning to face forward. "When we get there…we're going to bring them back."

"Just like that?"

Winter pursed her lips. The premonition had not told her that. In fact, the premonition was not telling her anything beyond reaching the national forest and finding them.

Winter slowed to take the exit ramp, maintaining as much speed as possible. "Hold on, Ryan."

"Who's Ryan?"

Fire stabbed through Winter's heart. The premonition vanished. The thunder in her ears squeezed silent. She slammed on the brakes and brought the car to a screeching stop.

*Four Years Ago*

The boom of rending metal against wood and the sudden whiplash sucked the air out of Winter's lungs. The car rocked and squealed. It dropped, slamming to the earth and sending a shockwave through her spine. Her lungs spasmed as fast as her heart raced.

Silence.

She pried open her clenched eyes. The headlights illuminated the trees beyond, reflecting light back into the car. Crumbled glass covered the dash and her lap. She looked down at her hands and found them covered with blood. Her face twitched from the stickiness, and she slowly reached up to feel blood running down her cheek. Through the crumpled remains of her door window she could see the road at the top of the embankment, about fifty feet away. She turned to the passenger side.

There was no passenger side.

The interior of the car had twisted and contorted beyond recognition. The trunk of a tree filled the space where the window should be, bulging into the car as far as the middle console.

"Ryan?" Winter croaked. She tried to twist in her seat, but the seatbelt was locked. She could barely move. "Ryan?"

"Winter," whispered Alison.

Winter looked back at the passenger side. A mass of blonde hair and blood turned to look at her, attached to what used to be a body, but now wrapped in twisted metal and squeezed between the tree and the crumpled dash. She looked like a demon crawling out of hell.

"I can't feel my legs."

Winter screamed, and it dissolved into sobs. "Ryan!"

She pulled against her seatbelt and fumbled with the latch. The broken glass dug deeper into her flesh. She craned to look over her shoulder, but the back seat was too dark and the roof too crumpled to see anything.

"RYAN!"

She reached over with one hand and felt around. She found his hand lying on the seat motionless. She grabbed it and tugged. "RYAN!"

"Winter, help me," whispered Alison.

"RYAN!" Winter shoved her hand back to the seatbelt latch and it finally came free. She turned and jammed her knees into the shards of glass falling from her lap onto the seat. She squeezed her head and one shoulder as far into the back as she could manage between the crumpled roof and the splintered surface of the tree.

Ryan lay slumped to one side. One arm bent unnaturally. Blood covered his face.

Winter grabbed for his head, but it wouldn't move. His skull was fused with the tree trunk.

"RYAN!" Winter pushed against his shoulder. But there was no movement. "NO! NO!"

A sudden rushing sound, like the flapping of a parachute, made her turn. Flames leaped out from under the hood of the car.

"Ryan! Wake up! We have to get out! Ryan!"

"Winter…" whispered Alison.

"Wake up!" She pulled his arm to her and tugged. "Ryan! Come on! You have to wake up! We have to get out!"

The flames roared higher.

"Winter, get me out," said Alison.

"Get up, Ryan! You can't leave me! Please! God please! NO! Ryan." She leaned back, yanking at his arm. His head pulled free and his body slumped over. She screamed. "RYAN! NO! NO! Don't leave me! Ryan!"

Heat burned at Winter's back. She turned and squinted through her tears against the raging light.

"Winter, help…" said Alison.

Winter stared at her. The twisted metal was now clearly visible as it wrapped and pierced Alison's broken body. Her hip was torqued almost perpendicular to the rest of her. A piece of metal covered in dark blood jutted from her displaced abdomen.

Every muscle in Winter's body quivered. She looked back over the seat at Ryan's body and then back to the looming flames. Winter grabbed her door handle and tried to open the door.

It wouldn't budge.

Winter leaned her face to the small opening in the crushed window. "HELP!" She turned and tried to put her feet against the door, but she could only manage one foot. She leaned her back against the tree and pushed.

Nothing.

"Winter…" Alison whispered right next to Winter's ear.

The flames flickered out of the air vents. The floorboard lit up with firelight. Black smoke simmered along the ceiling.

Winter coughed and hit the jagged window with her elbow, knocking out a little more crumbling glass. "HELP! HELP!" She slammed her shoulder into the door and it creaked a little.

Alison began to scream. Flames licked at her face where her head was pinned to the dash.

Winter's screams joined Alison's. She beat at the door and

window, slicing her hands and arms further. "HELP! Somebody, please! Help!" She slammed her full body weight into the door.

Acrid fumes and the stench of burning flesh stung Winter's eyes and throat. Alison's screeches pierced Winter's ears. Flames peeked out through the floorboard. Winter pulled up her feet and jammed them against the tree. She pressed her back into the door.

"HELP ME!"

The door creaked a little…but still would not open.

*Present Day*

*It's happening again.*

Fire flashed through Winter's mind. Smoke filled her nostrils. She squeezed the steering wheel and pumped shallow air in and out.

*Ryan's image slumped over in the back seat.*

"I…I can't do this!"

Peter touched her shoulder. "What's wrong? Why'd you stop?"

"I CAN'T DRIVE!"

"Look at me."

Winter shook her head.

"Look at me!"

She turned her head but didn't relinquish the wheel. Beads of sweat trickled down her forehead.

Peter leaned forward. "Listen. I don't know who Ryan is or what happened. But you need to get it together. You're the only one who can find Summer and Ayden. And if we don't get there, they'll die. Do you understand that?"

Winter flittered her head. "I…can't…"

"You have to." Peter reached over and grabbed both her hands. He pulled them close to his chest. "Whatever happened, happened for a reason and you can't change it. But you can save Ayden and Summer. You can do that *now*. You can help them."

"I…"

"Whatever it is you do…let it take over. This fear can't control you. Your past can't control you. You are bigger than both. And God is bigger than you."

She nodded and closed her eyes.

"Now take a deep breath and go back to doing whatever it is that you do, and let's go."

She opened her mouth and drew in air slowly. The smell of smoke disappeared. Her heart thumped a little harder at the slowing of her pulse. Winter took the haunting images and pushed them back where she had locked them before. As her mind cleared, the premonition crept back in…nudging her back to action, pouring adrenaline back into her system.

"Are you ready now?" asked Peter.

Winter nodded and opened her eyes. "I think so."

"Good. Then let's get going."

She released the wheel and wiped the cold sweat from her face. A slight rumble returned to her ears and she faced the road again. "Okay. Summer and Ayden. Let's go." Winter slammed her foot down on the accelerator, fishtailing onto the county road.

*Four Years Ago*

Alison's screams mutated into a garbled roar.

Winter spun away to shake at the door, daring not to look back. A man with gleaming blue eyes peered back at her through the jagged opening.

"Help me! Please!"

The man's eyes widened and he grabbed the edge of the door. "Together," he said.

As he leaned back on the door, she shoved her shoulder into it. It budged a few inches.

"Again!" he shouted.

Winter shoved and the door gave way about six inches, before recoiling back to its starting point.

"AGAIN! HARDER!"

She closed her eyes and put her feet back against the tree. The door opened about a foot and the man slipped his leg and shoulder through.

He pressed his back against the car and muscled the opening wider. “Come on! It’s not your time yet!”

Winter leaned out the door and planted her hands on the dirt by the man’s feet. She pulled herself out, falling to the ground.

Alison’s roars died away to a moan barely discernible from the rush of the fire.

“Help him,” Winter cried. “Help Ryan.”

“I can’t. It was his time,” said the man.

Winter let her face sink into the dirt. Unable to move. Unable to breathe. Maybe she should have stayed in the car…with him.

*Present Day*

Winter kept the car slower on the winding road into the national forest. The premonition laid out each curve and guided her perfectly to a gravel road hidden in the trees. She turned. Rain began to fall, pelting the windshield and sending small plumes of dust into the air where the heavy drops landed on the parched road.

The road led them deep into the forest. The gentle shower changed into a heavy downpour. Out of the watery haze an old beat-up sedan materialized. Winter stopped the car.

"Now what?" Peter asked.

"Come on." Winter flung open her door and plunged into the rain.

"Winter!" Peter climbed out and stood by the car, shielding the rain from his eyes with one hand. "What do you plan to do?"

The drone of the rain filled the forest like constant static. "Trust me!" she shouted. "Are you coming?"

Peter nodded and jogged to her side.

Winter led the way beneath the trees, dodging limbs, crashing through underbrush, and jumping the rapidly swelling streambeds. She didn't hesitate…she knew exactly where to go, as if an internal compass pointed the way. She set her face in the right direction and ran faster. The sunlight faded beneath the thickening thunderclouds and a deep twilight crept across the forest floor.

The premonition throbbed, telling her they were going too fast…making too much noise. She ignored it, but it continued to pulse harder and faster.

It screamed for her to stop. But it was too late. The man in the silver and black mask stepped out from behind a tree.

Winter slid in the mud and fell to her knees. The shotgun swung forward into Winter's face. She held her breath.

"Good," he growled. "Now come with me."

Peter grabbed her arm and helped her back up.

The killer circled behind them. "Walk."

The man herded them deeper into the forest, in the same direction Winter had been heading.

Finally, they rounded an embankment and came to a low mound of fresh dirt. On the other side, muddy water dripped over the sides of a hole big enough for a car, as a lull in the storm passed over.

Summer and Ayden knelt on the ground several feet from the hole's edge, hands behind their backs and duct tape over their mouths.

Xaphan stood over them, a pistol casually pointing at Ayden's head. He looked up at their approach and smiled when Winter made eye contact. "If you would please join your friends," he said.

Winter knelt beside Ayden and Peter knelt on Winter's other side.

"Hands," growled the man in the mask.

Winter grunted and shoved her hands behind her back.

The killer jerked at her wrists, sending fire through her injured arm. Duct tape squeezed her wrists together, and he released her. He leaned between Winter and Ayden turning his head to Ayden. "Did you miss me?"

Ayden squealed and whimpered. She looked at Winter with wide, terrified eyes. Bruises and blood covered her face.

Xaphan stepped before them, looking at each in turn. He nodded approval and then looked up to the man in the mask. "Where is our other friend?"

The killer stalked into the growing darkness. A moment later he returned dragging a body. Gerald Bevaldi, half unconscious, was tossed in line with the rest of them. The killer hoisted Bevaldi to his knees, and Bevaldi looked up with a sagging, defeated face.

The man in the mask stepped back behind Xaphan and held his shotgun at the captives.

Xaphan paced before them and pointed at Bevaldi. "The one who lived…"

At Summer. "The one in the wrong place at the wrong time…"

At Ayden. "The one who got away…"

At Winter. "The one who won't die…"

At Peter. "And the one that wasn't supposed to survive."

He stepped to the killer's side and eyed them all at once. "I imagine the hole is big enough for all of you."

Winter closed her eyes. She prayed. Praying for strength. Praying for guidance. Praying for a way out. Praying for something to happen…for the wind, the thunder. Anything.

Where was God?

"Have you nothing to say, Prophetess?"

Winter didn't open her eyes. "You won't get away with this."

"How cliché," he said.

Winter clenched her jaw. The premonition flickered…just enough light to tell her one word. *Patience.*

Ayden mumbled something.

"What's that?" Xaphan asked. "I can't hear you." He stepped closer and ripped the tape from her face.

"What do you want!" she screamed. "I haven't done anything!"

Xaphan leaned in. Ayden recoiled. "I want you to die."

Ayden sobbed and shook her head. "W…why?"

Xaphan sneered. "To stop you from causing great harm to my Master's future. Of course, I'm sure that pitiful excuse for a prophet never told your family that. Am I right, Gerald?"

Bevaldi stared at the muddy ground.

"I don't know wh…what you're talking about. Please, just let me go…"

"I can't do that," he said. "Sandy."

Ayden's breaths quickened, squeaking like wet rubber. "I'm…I'm…not…not…S…Sandy!"

Xaphan smiled. "Of course not. You probably don't remember any of it, do you? It was so long ago, and you were so young."

Winter squirmed closer to Ayden. "Leave her alone! Can't you see? She's no threat to you!"

"Of course she is. I'm not stupid enough to think you haven't heard the prophecy. She must die."

"I won't let her!"

"And what are you going to do? You're all equally helpless."

"It doesn't matter. You can't have her."

"It's over! I have her now!" He turned to the man in the mask. "Kill the two prophets first. I don't want anything to go wrong. Start with her." He pointed at Winter.

Winter leaned back, trying to get her feet beneath her. She slipped in the mud and fell backward.

The man in the silver and black mask towered over her. He spread his feet and tilted his head.

She watched him, heart drumming, recognizing the motions and steps. Time seemed to slow and mesh. Events future and past marched away from each other in an overlapping line, like two projectors playing different movies on the same screen.

She saw her dad. Her mom.

The killer cocked the shotgun and leveled it at her face, mere inches away.

She saw Ryan and the flaming Mustang. Her mind paused over a single moment…a single sentence uttered as she crawled out of the wreckage. She grabbed it, and her premonition erupted to full blossom.

Winter closed her eyes and yielded to the surge of power. It swelled through her fragile body, bloating her muscle and tissue. Sounds became louder and more distinct. When she opened her eyes, the colors were more brilliant, and the shadows were as bright as day.

The man hesitated, pulling the gun halfway down.

"Do it!" shouted Xaphan. "Quickly!"

He leveled the gun again.

Winter held tight to that one spoken line from her past…the one line that fueled her faith. She took a deep breath and spoke it aloud. "It's not my time yet."

"KILL HER!"

# 70

*Four Years Ago*

The heat seared Winter's legs. She didn't have the strength to stand. Her whole body was numb, and she shivered against the ground.

Winter reached up with a trembling hand to the stranger. "Help me." But nothing happened. She twisted her head and looked up. The man was gone.

The fire rumbled like a furnace, sending flickering shadows into Winter's line of vision and drowning out the last vestiges of Alison.

Winter knew she had to move. She stretched forward with clawed fingers and struck them into the ground. She pulled and the dirt gave way, leaving long finger tracks. She reached with the other hand and pressed her fingers in deeper. Her body inched up the embankment.

She mumbled, "It's not my time yet." Her body quivered. Her hair covered her face. Her dress raked across the ground. She kicked off her shoes and dug her toes into the earth.

She stretched forth her first hand and found another hold. Winter pulled herself away from the car a little more. "It's not my time yet," she mumbled through the sobs. "It's not my time."

Another hand. Another push with her feet. Another pull for more inches. With each reach, she crawled closer to the road. "It's not my time."

The sound of the roaring fire intensified the trembling in Winter's body. Each exhale came with ragged throbs. Each inhale struggled to break through her constricting throat. She couldn't see anymore through the deluge streaming from her eyes. "Help!" She clawed forward. "H…h…help…" She pushed her feet.

*Ryan.* She clawed forward. *It's not my time.* She pushed. A tire exploded. Winter screamed and clawed. *Ryan…*push. *It's not my time…*claw. *Ryan…*push.

Her hand went forward again and found level ground and hardened gravel. When she pulled up, her face emerged over the embankment to the road.

Prismed light came around the bend. She stared, not fully recognizing what she saw, and wiped the water from her eyes with her dirty hand. Tires squealed and the lights stopped.

Someone ran to her. Someone else scrambled toward the burning car. Winter pushed herself up to sit with the aid of the woman at her side. She looked back at the twisted, flaming wreckage. Another tire exploded and the man near the car backed away. He scrambled back up the embankment.

Winter could just see Ryan's slumped body through a gap in the mangled car. She pulled her knees tight as the angry flames consumed him and the rippling smoke hid his body.

Only the crackling sound of the fire and Winter's muffled sobs filled the air.

# 71

*Present Day*

"It's not my time yet," Winter said again.

The duct tape disintegrated from around her wrists. The killer's finger began to flex. Winter reached around and grabbed the side of the barrel.

The gun exploded in his face.

He stumbled backward, clawing at his mask, and crumpled to the ground.

Xaphan roared and swung his handgun to her.

"GO!" Bevaldi shouted. His legs moved. He planted his feet.

And stood.

When he opened his eyes, light streamed out. He rushed forward with clenched fists and tackled Xaphan.

Winter grabbed Ayden beneath the shoulders and pulled. Peter and Summer found their feet without help. Winter pointed into the darkening forest. "Run!"

Peter stumbled forward, leading the way. Winter followed Summer, struggling with the medical tape around Summer's wrists as they jogged.

Shouts and scuffling behind them. Winter dared not look back…wondering if God would give the old man enough power to buy them time to escape.

As they entered the deeper shadows, Winter managed to free Summer's hands. Summer reached up and yanked the tape from her mouth.

"Go! Help Peter," Winter said.

Summer ran ahead, easily outpacing the hobbling Ayden.

Winter moved to free Ayden's hands in the same way. As she started pulling at the tape, there was a shot from behind them and the struggling sounds stopped.

A pang stung Winter's chest. Dr. Cook…Bevaldi…everyone at the school…Winter clenched her teeth. It had to stop. But not here. Not yet. Just a little further away…

"Hurry, Summer!" Winter shouted. Winter tugged harder, finally slipping Ayden's hands through the stretched-out medical tape. "Faster, Ayden! Run!"

Winter surged ahead and Ayden hobbled by her side. By the time they caught up to Peter and Summer, Peter was free.

Thunder rolled. The rain picked up.

Winter relinquished Ayden to Peter and sprinted to the front of the group. "Stay close to me!"

A ledge of rocks and mud appeared before she realized it, and she slipped over the edge. Thunder rolled again. The others slid down behind her. They trudged through the mud to the other side of the gully and ran again once they were free.

Thunder rolled. Lighter, quicker thunder. Unnatural…with no lightning. A tree branch exploded near Winter's head. She glanced over her shoulder and saw a man with dark sunken eyes standing at the top of the ledge fifty feet away. His mask was gone and he held Xaphan's handgun.

"Faster!" Winter pushed forward, allowing the premonition to guide her through the dark forest. The others stayed close behind, following in her footsteps.

More gunfire, bullets sent small sprays of dirt and mud into the air. Ayden squealed.

"Come on!" Winter grabbed Ayden's other arm and pulled.

Limbs clawed at them as they passed. The rain whooshed in torrents as the wind swirled misty sheets around them. Winter could barely hear the others behind her.

Lightning flashed and thunder boomed. Winter caught a glimpse of the land sloping downward. Higher thunder. Bark erupted from a tree just in front of Winter.

Winter looked back into the watery darkness behind her, but saw nothing. When she turned forward again, she ran straight into a thick shrub. She held her arms up and crashed through.

On the other side, she stopped. The others burst through the shrub, crashing into Winter.

"Oh, no!" said Summer.

Ayden gasped and covered her mouth with both hands.

"What now?" asked Peter.

Winter wiped the rainwater from her face and stared at the solid rock cliff facing them. She looked in both directions, but the cliff extended as far as she could see through the gloom.

Peter stepped to her side. "Winter?"

Winter's mind raced. She looked around for something...anything, that might help. The only thing she saw was...glowing butterflies fluttering around an old half-dead oak beneath the shadow of the cliff.

"The tree!" She sloshed toward it, through the rivulets trickling away from the cliff. *Now what?*

A faint cracking of brush. Winter slowly turned.

The killer emerged from the forest. He stood still and watched them.

Winter planted her feet. "Behind the tree!" The others scrambled to the other side of the trunk.

The man stepped toward them, slowly and deliberately. He smiled a thin, sinister smile.

Winter took slow, steady breaths, watching him and allowing the power to seep through her body. She knew he would not shoot...yet.

"We need to get up!" cried Ayden. "We need to get off the ground!"

Ayden's words clicked in Winter's mind. That was it. That was the answer. She smiled and began to pray.

"God, lift us up...lift us high. Lord, we need you to lift us up..." Over and over, she repeated the request. And as she did, tingling trickled through every muscle, bone, and pore. The rumble grew in her ears, louder than the torrential rain, but gentle enough that Winter could hear the heartbeats of everyone around her.

Even the killer's.

"God, lift us up…" Winter's skin stretched, pulling taut against her muscles. She clenched her fists. Opened her eyes.

The rain paused. For one brief half second…there was silence.

Then the wind blasted sideways, swirling around the tree and catching the rain. The rain bands tightened and wrapped them in a spinning vortex of wind and water.

The man calmly walked into the vortex. Closer...closer…

"God, lift us up..."

The tree shook. The swirling wind closed in, spinning faster and roaring like a tornado.

Winter looked over her shoulder to the others huddled together. "Hold on!"

The ground trembled and careened. Winter held out her arms for balance.

The man was close now, braving the violent vortex. He lifted the gun.

A rending lurch that snapped wood and earth plunged Winter to the ground. The trembling stopped, but the vortex spun even faster…now swirling in all directions like a constantly adapting wave. A sheer ledge of dirt had materialized just a few feet away and the vortex swirled beyond it, beneath the tree. Through the haze of the vortex the tree line of the forest fell away as the oak lifted into the air.

Two hands appeared at the ledge. Winter backed away. The fingers bent and clawed into the ground like the talons of a vulture. The sinews flexed and the tendons bulged. A moment later a face emerged, bent with hatred and murder.

A flicker of panic quickened Winter's heart, but the power coursing through her body stamped it out. She rushed forward and grabbed one of the hands, trying to wrest it from the ground.

The killer flung his other hand up and grabbed her. His grip felt like iron as he squeezed her injured arm. With nails digging into her flesh, he pulled her toward the ledge.

Winter howled as fire coursed through her arm and shoulder. She pried at his fingers, but he jerked her forward. Winter hit the edge, careening forward and catching herself just before tumbling over.

Through the haze of the vortex she could just make out a muddy crater far below where the oak had been. Run-off water streamed into it like a whirlpool. The tree-line of the forest continued to fall as the oak lifted higher into the air.

Winter dug her fingers into the moist earth and flung herself backward. She twisted out of the killer's grasp, backing away just beyond his reach.

The killer pulled, inching his shoulders above the ledge. Placing his elbows on the dirt.

Winter kicked at his arms.

He grabbed her ankle and roared.

Winter smashed her other foot into his face. The man pitched backward. His head and the one hand that had been holding her ankle teetered away from the ledge, swinging beneath the edge and leaving only one hand clamped in the dirt.

In that moment the tree dropped, crashing back to the earth.

Winter's stomach jumped into her chest, and for a heartbeat she floated above the ground. Summer and Ayden both screamed. The tree slammed back into the muddy crater, groaning and swaying, sending rain-soaked leaves fluttering all around.

Winter collided with the ground, knocking the air from her lungs. She rolled over in time to see the swirling sphere of water dissipate and shower back to the ground as if it were nothing but ordinary rain.

Winter jerked her head back, expecting to see the killer standing over her.

A limp hand jutted out of a barely discernible crack in the ground.

# 72

Winter backed up to the tree and sat against it. She watched the forest's edge beyond the hand…waiting for Xaphan. Knowing he was coming next. The rain continued to pour in sheets, and the water fell in pregnant drops from the limbs above.

Peter slid around and pressed his shoulder against hers. "I'll help you watch." He eyed the hand and then looked to the trees.

Winter glanced around the tree at Ayden and Summer. Ayden sat with her knees to her head, hands covering her face and trembling all over. Summer leaned against her, arms wrapped around Ayden's shoulders. She lifted her wide eyes to Winter for a moment and then laid her head on top of Ayden's.

The drone of the rain seemed to last for hours. As the darkness deepened, the rain began to thin. The thunder still rolled, but distantly and more resonant. Runoff water trickled all around, created new paths in the soft earth. Forest creatures slowly came alive. Crickets chirped. Cicadas buzzed. Frogs sang. Somewhere in the distance floated the hoot of an owl.

And something big crashing through the underbrush. He was

here.

Every muscle in Winter's body tensed. She stilled herself and stood, eyeing the direction of the sound. Peter rose beside her and grabbed her hand.

A dog yelped. Multiple voices cried out. Lights flashed through the trees and emerged beyond the tree line. A spotlight panned the cliff, sweeping toward them. It settled on her and Peter.

Winter bit her lip and shielded her eyes.

A radio crackled. "Bravo Two to Alpha Echo. We've found Butterfly. Ten-zero, code three. Northeast, quadrant four."

Voices yelled. More flashlights emerged and bobbed toward them as their owners ran. They spread out to surround the tree, some illuminating Winter and the others, some flickering into the surrounding shadows. One light came straight for Winter. At ten feet away, it panned to the ground.

Agent Erickson.

The breath Winter had been holding burst out in a loud sob. Her strength drained away as gravity pulled at her shoulders. She collapsed to the ground, shaking, and put her face in her hands.

Erickson knelt beside her. "Is anyone hurt?"

Winter nodded. "Ayden and I both were shot. Summer's hurt, too, I think." Her voice trembled. She coughed and another sob escaped.

Erickson rubbed her back. "We'll have paramedics here soon."

Winter looked at the others and saw agents kneeling beside each one.

"Winter," Erickson said. "Where's the shooter?"

With a shaking arm, she lifted and pointed to the hand.

Erickson swore and flinched away. "How in..."

Several flashlights trained on the hand, and everyone started talking very fast.

Erickson looked at her, face pinched. "You can tell me later. We should get you out of here first and secure the area."

"You mean you didn't catch him?"

"Who?"

"Xaphan. He was here."

"Xaphan?" Erickson turned and gave a couple of hand signals. Several agents broke away and disappeared into the darkness. He turned back. "Don't worry. You're safe."

Winter nodded. "How did you find us?"

"Your friend Davis. You can thank him. He called me while you were still on campus. I'm sorry we didn't get there in time."

"Davis is alive?" Summer crawled toward them on hands and knees with the first sign of life returning to her face.

"Yeah. He's fine. He has a nice black eye, but that's about it. He told us about the GPS tracking system in your car. That, plus the dogs...brought us straight to you."

Summer's face split into a wide grin. She covered her mouth and started crying. Winter leaned over and pulled her in tight. Erickson helped them to stand and Winter stretched the muscles in her legs.

Winter looked over her shoulder at Ayden. "She was hit in the leg at the school. I don't know how badly they hurt her when she was taken. I think she's in shock. But at least she's safe."

Erickson nodded. "Don't worry about her. We'll make sure she's taken care of."

Winter narrowed her eyes. "I thought you'd be a little more concerned, considering all of this is because of her."

Erickson narrowed his eyes and tilted his head. "You think she's Sandy?"

Winter's stomach lurched. Her mind buzzed as her limbs numbed like ice. "What? B…but I heard him. The one who found us. He said he found Butterfly! That's why you're here…to rescue her!" She pointed back to Ayden.

He shook his head. "Winter…*You* are Butterfly. We came for you. Sandy's safe."

Winter held her breath and her heart hammered against her chest. "No. You're lying. I can't be. I saw the file."

Erickson stared at her. "That was your file. You've always been

Butterfly."

"You have a file on me?" Winter took a step back. "If…if I'm Butterfly, then what is Sandy?"

Erickson pursed his lips.

"Tell me!"

"Tulip."

Winter opened and closed her lips, trying to find the words. More scales, like the ones hiding Ayden, fell from her mind. Her numb arms and legs filled with warm blood. "Oh, no. No...no...no..."

The whole puzzle crashed into place, exposing the answer. The only answer. It could never have been anyone else.

Erickson leaned close and lowered his voice. "It all makes sense now, doesn't it? I see it in your eyes. You've finally figured it out."

"Winter? What's wrong?" asked Peter.

Winter slowly turned. "Ayden's not her."

"But...but...who is?"

"I…I…" Winter took a deep breath and turned back to Erickson. "I have to get back. We have to go back right now."

"You need to go to the hospital first. She's safe."

Winter shook her head. "No. I have to go back now. I have to talk to her."

"I don't think…"

"Now!"

Erickson grunted and ran his hand through his hair. "Fine. We'll go together."

Winter squeezed Summer's hand. "Don't worry. It's okay."

Winter followed Erickson through the forest back to the cars. She jumped into the backseat of Erickson's car and he spun the tires on the loose gravel.

As she stared out of the window, watching the blue lights flash on the passing trees and chewing the inside of her cheek, only one question consumed her thoughts.

*How could I not have known?*

# 73

*Four Years Ago*

Winter lay curled on her bed.

Days passed. She wouldn't move. She *couldn't* move. Only a shell remained…a hollow void. She had nothing. Was nothing. Every vestige of love and happiness had burned away inside the car.

With him. She couldn't bring herself to say his name. Not even in her mind.

A day passed…maybe two. She refused to go to school. She refused to talk. She refused to see Stacy…Claire…her dad.

The door opened. Footsteps. It was him again. She heard him pick up the old plate of food on her desk and set down a new one.

"You need to eat."

What was the point in eating? Winter closed her eyes and pretended to be asleep.

Her dad sighed. "You should know that the driver of the other car is out of intensive care." He closed the door and left.

Another day passed…maybe more. She drifted around her room. Staring out the window. Staring at the wall. She ate a little. Only a little. Out of habit. Then she crawled back into bed.

Footsteps outside her door. Lighter ones. Not her dad. The door opened and Winter stole a glance at the visitor. It was Daniel.

*His* dad.

Winter rolled away and closed her eyes.

He sat. Winter watched her alarm clock as the silent minutes ticked by one by one. After half an hour, he stood and walked to the side of the bed.

He reached over her shoulder and placed a white rectangle by her hand. He leaned over, rested his cheek on her head, and squeezed her shoulders.

His tears soaked through her hair, cooling her scalp.

As he left, Winter flipped over the rectangle. She took one look at it and clutched it to her chest, moaning and crying harder than she had done all week.

A few minutes later, her dad came in. She clamped her jaw and tried to still her moans.

"Will you come to the memorial?"

Winter clenched her eyes shut.

"You should come. It may do you good to say goodbye."

Her body trembled, ready to erupt. She choked the tears back and waited for him to leave.

"I'm going with Daniel in about an hour. If you want to come, you should clean up and get ready."

She opened her mouth to speak, but a soft whimper slipped out.

Her dad sighed and left.

Winter unclenched her hand from the picture…the picture Daniel had left. She wiped tears away enough to stare at the bent and crumpled photograph again.

He wore a gleaming tux. His hair was smoothed back perfectly. His smile was soft and gentle and his eyes twinkled. She stood beside him, beneath an arch of blue balloons and flowers. Her rose corsage matched the rose boutonnière on his tux. Her face glowed, and her smile radiated joy. She held his hand and leaned close. His arm draped around her body, resting on her waist.

For one night...one moment...she had found happiness again. For one night everything was perfect. She had felt beautiful and wanted. She had felt…loved.

But God hated her.

Winter clenched the picture in her hand and pulled it back to her chest, letting the hollow, empty sobs take control again.

# 74

*Present Day*

Winter couldn't believe the chaos on campus. Red and blue lights danced everywhere like a light show.

Erickson drove slowly through the disaster area as tape lines and barricades were moved before him. He turned down the road that passed most of the student housing. A Cherithville police car sat near the entrance of every dorm, keeping the residents in lock-down.

He pulled into the parking lot, right behind the patrol car.

Erickson's partner went to the officer guarding the door. They spoke in whispers. Erickson put a hand on Winter's back and guided her into the lobby.

Once inside, Winter took long strides to the interior door. She jogged up the steps and went down the hall. She stared at the door, wondering what she would find inside, and took a deep breath.

"Are you ready?" Erickson asked.

Winter nodded. "Let me go in alone first, please."

"Take all the time you need."

Winter took out her ID card and inserted it into the lock. It flashed green and she pushed the door open.

A figure sat on the far bed looking out the window, silhouetted by the red and blue lights from the patrol car below and the army of emergency vehicles all over campus.

Winter stepped into the darkness and pulled the door closed.

"They changed my age, you know. Did you know they could do that?"

Winter eased to the desk and reached for the lamp. "Why didn't you tell me?" She clicked it on.

Kaci turned to look at her, her face red and puffy from recent crying. "I couldn't. They wouldn't let me. I wanted to so many times. Guess I thought maybe you'd figure it out eventually."

Winter walked slowly to the bed.

Kaci stared at the floor, wringing her hands in her lap. "My name was Cassandra. They used to call me Sandy. When...when we *moved*, my parents wanted me to keep some form of my real name."

"Good for them," Winter whispered. "I can't imagine what it was like." Winter crept closer.

"I had to be homeschooled until I was two grades ahead. Then they let me go to school again...pretending to be older, of course."

"Kaci, I'm so sorry."

Kaci reached up to rub the flower pendant around her neck…the tulip pendant. "Don't be. My parents have done everything they could to make me forget what happened and to give me a normal life. They're not even my real parents. They're my aunt and uncle…my mom and my real mom were sisters."

Winter knelt in front of Kaci and grabbed her hands.

Kaci still wouldn't look up. "When I was older, they didn't want me to be scared of getting involved. They didn't want me to be afraid of anything. They wanted me to be able to face whatever it was out there looking for me. But after last year...I got too close. I got too involved. He could have found out. The FBI almost made us move again."

"Why did you come back?"

"You. Mom and Dad convinced me that being with you was the safest place to be. Agent Gains thought so too." Kaci's eyes darted to Winter's bandaged arm and then back to the floor.

"Kaci, look at me." Winter leaned forward until Kaci met her eyes.

The world swirled away, twisting and falling into grains of color. The color fell and collected…rearranged.

It became a classroom, with overlarge desks. Winter looked up, through the eyes of a child…through the eyes of Sandy. Of Kaci. A young woman leaned over her, pointing at something on Kaci's desk. The woman smiled and brushed back her blonde hair.

The door opened. The woman looked up.

Gunfire.

Kids screaming. The woman grabbed Kaci and yanked her out of the desk.

Gunfire.

The woman fell, pinning Kaci to the ground.

Gunfire.

Kaci held her breath. The teacher's blood soaked through her dress.

Gunfire.

Only one small voice remained, crying for her mommy.

Gunfire.

Silence.

The world swirled back to the dorm room. The nightmare rushed away, plunging back into memory and back into the past.

Winter felt tears rolling down her cheeks. She trembled and shuddered.

Kaci smiled. "I'm sorry."

*Hold her up, so she can grow again*, said the voice of God.

*Prophesy to them,* said the little girl. *Teach them to live again.*

Winter felt a warmth fall upon her, like a gentle blanket. Thunder rose in her ears, but smaller and more passionate. A tunnel formed in Winter's mind, stretching beyond knowledge and time, into infinite fullness. As the tunnel opened, the thunder transformed. It lifted and fell, quickened and slowed, organizing the chaotic frequencies and pulses into words.

Winter opened her mouth and let the tunnel flow through to her tongue. The words poured down.

And she spoke.

"Kaci, listen. This is what God says:

"Twice now the enemy has tried to crush you, and twice I have delivered you from his hand. Twice again must he come, but do not fear for I will be with you always. I have sent my prophetess to oversee you, and through her you will be saved.

"The child which you will bring forth will be a beacon to the nations. This child will defeat the enemy with love, drawing millions to the light. This child is the last hope of humanity. For when this child's work is done, so shall mine be. The end of days draws near and the remaining days of my grace have been numbered. Through this child all who have not already heard, will hear. And they all will make their choice. Then the time of my return will be upon the world.

"Many trials await you. There will be heartache and pain. But be steadfast and I, yes I the Lord, will defeat the enemy."

The tunnel closed and the thunder vanished.

Winter gasped. She reached up and grabbed Kaci by both hands. "Nothing is going to happen to you. I'm here to protect you. Okay? I'll do whatever it takes."

Kaci's chin quivered. "Winter...I'm scared."

Winter stood and wrapped her trembling arms around Kaci. "Me too."

*Then the LORD stretched out His hand and touched my mouth, and the LORD said to me, "Behold, I have put My words in your mouth."*

Jeremiah 1:9 (NAS)

Winter's story continues in

# Acolyte

**Winter Book 3**

**ISBN: 978-0-9989596-3-4**

**By Keven Newsome**

The FBI have never been this close to trapping Xaphan and they need Winter's help to set their dangerous plan in motion. But Xaphan is weaving a trap of his own.

The Acolyte is unleashed…a demon, slaughtering its way to Sandy and haunting Winter with memories she would rather forget.

As her past threatens to tear apart the present, driving those she loves to turn against her, she must now face a far worse enemy alone…

Herself.

## ABOUT THE AUTHOR

Keven Newsome began his writing career at the young age of ten by creating fanfiction of his favorite video game. He only wrote four pages, though, painstakingly in King James English since that's how they spoke in the game. It was horrible and he promptly abandoned his writing career forever. Thankfully, some years later, fourteen-year-old Keven disagreed with that hasty decision and discovered writing could actually be fun. Since then he has authored five novels, published four of those, and written and published several short stories. He has also recently returned to his favorite video game and become an award-winning fanfiction author on Wattpad. The four books of his Winter series, *Winter, Prophetess, Acolyte,* and *Mantle,* together have been finalists for seven awards and winners of three of those. Originally from south Mississippi, he and his wife live a nomadic ministry life, followed relentlessly by the collective cries of his fans to finish writing his next book already.

http://kevennewsome.com
https://linktr.ee/knewsome.author

www.ingramcontent.com/pod-product-compliance
Lightning Source LLC
Chambersburg PA
CBHW051211120726
47905CB00004B/1070

* 9 7 8 0 9 9 8 9 5 9 6 2 7 *